D0339108

Books by Robert Bidinotto

Fiction

Hunter (Dylan Hunter #1)
Bad Deeds (Dylan Hunter #2)

Nonfiction

Criminal Justice? The Legal System vs. Individual Responsibility
Freed to Kill

BAD DEEDS

A DYLAN HUNTER THRILLER

ROBERT BIDINOTTO

AVENGER

BOOKS

Chester, Maryland

BAD DEEDS: A Dylan Hunter Thriller
ROBERT BIDINOTTO

Published by
Avenger Books
P.O. Box 555
Chester, Maryland 21619

Trade paperback edition: June 2014

Published in the United States of America

Cover design by **Allen Chiu**
http://www.allenchiu.com

Formatting and layout by **Polgarus Studio**
http://www.polgarusstudio.com/

To Cynthia,
who encouraged and endured me
throughout the writing—

and to the heroes
who develop and transform nature's bounty
for the good of us all

"There exists a law, not written down anywhere but inborn in our hearts; a law which comes to us, not by training or custom or reading, but by derivation and absorption and adoption from nature itself; a law which has come to us not from theory but from practice, not by instruction but by natural intuition. I refer to the law which lays it down that, if our lives are endangered by plots or violence or armed robbers or enemies, any and every method of protecting ourselves is morally right."

— *Marcus Tullius Cicero*

PROLOGUE

CIA SAFE HOUSE, LINDEN, VIRGINIA
Eleven Months Earlier—Tuesday, March 18, 10:15 a.m.

Today he would nail the bastard.

From his hidden position, lying prone behind a fallen log atop the hill, the sniper watched the trio of CIA vehicles pull into the driveway of the safe house. This high ridge was the only vantage point that allowed him to see who arrived. And these cars were his first confirmation that they *had* brought his target here. He had needed to confirm the target's presence in the house before he started his slow, risky crawl down the slope, into his final firing position. Now he felt a wave of relief and anticipation.

He had been lying on the ridge for over five hours. The ground beneath his stomach and legs was dry, hard, and frigid, covered with sharp brown pine cones and brittle, prickly needles. But he was used to lying motionless in uncomfortable places.

He lowered his eye back to the rifle's scope. He didn't really worry that the Agency's own protective sniper team, sited on the opposite hill about a mile to his northwest, would notice. He had the morning sun at his back, so there would be no flashes off his scope's glass. In fact, that's how he had spotted *them*, at sunrise.

He felt a professional's disappointment. He had expected better opposition.

The sniper took pride in approaching missions with cool, professional detachment. He was having trouble doing that this time. In the field, trust means everything. You depend on your team for your survival. But his target had sold out his own people and gotten them killed. His type was the lowest of the low. The sniper had first-hand experience with such betrayals. Taking out this bastard would be a pleasure.

He tracked the scope's reticle crosshairs slowly across the landscape spread below him. Though the last traces of snow had vanished a few weeks earlier, it still looked cold and somber, even under the glaring sun. Except for the pines, the trees stood bare and skeletal. He had an unobstructed view of the rear porch. There, a security man in jeans, leather jacket, and sunglasses enjoyed a rocking chair next to the back door, the sun on his face. His jacket swung open as he stretched, revealing the straps of a shoulder rig.

The sniper stifled the urge to yawn. He'd caught only a short nap this morning in the dreary room of a nearby motel before his watch alarm beeped him awake at 0330. He had checked out ten minutes later, so that he could arrive here before first light.

Just after 0400, in the pre-dawn gloom, he'd taken a little-traveled road running south off Route 55. It followed a small stream back into the hills. After about a mile, his GPS told him that he was due east of the safe house. He pulled his Chevy SUV into a paved turnoff next to the creek, under a sign that posted rules for fishermen, then parked facing outward.

There, shrouded in darkness, he'd gotten out and raised the rear hatch. Then opened the flat case that held his sniper weapon system, broken down. He expertly snapped the pieces together by feel. Slipped into his camo coveralls, cap, gloves, and boots. Strapped on the web belt that held much of his kit, including the Glock 17—a "just in case" weapon. Then the boot knife—a backup "just in case" weapon. Shoved a canteen, candy bars, and loaded magazines into various pockets and pouches. Smeared olive-colored camo paint over his face.

Finally, he'd slung the weapon across his back and begun the tedious quarter-mile climb to the ridge line above the safe house…

Lying here now, he mentally rehearsed his next moves. At this point, those inside would be interrogating his target. He knew from the man's profile that he was a chain smoker. Eventually, they might allow him out onto the porch for a cigarette break. The sniper hoped that would happen within the next few hours, while the bright sun was still at his back. By early afternoon, it would no longer be in the security team's eyes, and he'd be too exposed.

The mil-dots on his Unertl day scope pegged the porch at nearly 1300 meters from his current position. He would need over an hour to crawl and creep down the hillside and set up a new hide, no more than 800 meters out. No way that he could make a shot reliably from farther than that.

He'd already plotted his path through the trees, clumps of vegetation, and shallow depressions, down to a cluster of small boulders 600 meters from the house. That would be his final firing position, where he would dope the scope for the range. Then wait. If his target didn't show today, he'd have to stay in the hide till tomorrow, maybe longer. Not a happy prospect.

He pocketed the data book that held his scribbled notes. Then slid the forearm stock of the rifle back from the rotting log on which it rested. Positioned it cross-body, on his forearms. Prepared for the slow belly crawl to his first stop, a patch of bushes ten meters away.

Then heard a distant voice...

He peered down through the overhanging pine branches. The guard was standing now, alert, and two more had emerged from the back door, fanning out toward either end of the porch.

He gently repositioned the rifle back onto the log and moved his eye to its ten-power scope. Three more figures stepped out onto the porch.

A young, dark-haired woman in slacks and sunglasses, on the left.

An older man in a gray suit, on the right.

And standing between them, centered in the crosshairs...

Muller.

He suppressed the urge to curse aloud. This might be his only chance for a shot, and his target wasn't in range. Not even close.

They moved to the porch railing. The man in gray pulled something out of his suit jacket. Muller reached over and took it, raised it. Seemed to laugh. The older guy then fished something else out of his pocket that glinted in the sun. He raised it to his face, then to Muller's, who leaned in, cupping his hands around it.

Cigarettes. The sniper felt a twinge of hope. They'd probably bring him out here again.

Muller turned, leaned forward, and braced his hands atop the porch railing. He raised his face toward the sun.

Toward *him.*

He ground his teeth. *Damn!* If only he'd had time to fetch a longer-range weapon. Like the Sako TRG, chambered for the .338 Lapua Magnum. Or maybe—

—a loud, sharp *crack…*

For a second, he was too stunned to move. A second later, in the jiggling circle of the scope, Muller's head exploded in a scarlet spray.

He snapped his own head to the right, in the direction of the shot. Spotted movement two hundred meters distant, behind another fallen log. A figure in camo rolled away, the long black barrel of a rifle clearly visible. The figure scuttled behind a massive rhododendron, rose into a low crouch, then moved rapidly back into the pines.

He stared blankly at the fleeing figure.

They sent another shooter?

Distant shouts from below. He stole another glance through his scope.

The trio on the porch were down, in a heap; the security team, weapons drawn, were scattering all over the yard, their eyes scanning this hill. This ridge line…

You have to get out of here.

He lifted his M40 sniper rifle from the log and slid behind the thick branches of the sheltering pine tree. Then scrambled to his feet, turned, and ran. After a few yards, the ground dropped away into a steep slope. Half-skidding, half-hopping, he descended fast, back toward where he had parked the Chevy.

He realized that his course was taking him parallel to that of the shooter. He had no time to figure things out, but knew instinctively that the man might be a threat to *him*, too. Transferring the M40 to his left hand, he drew the Glock with his right.

The descent seemed to take forever, although it couldn't have been more than three minutes. Nearing the bottom of the hill, he noticed a blur of motion in a clearing well ahead and to his left.

The shooter, cradling a very large rifle. Hurdling a bush with the grace of a gazelle, darting among rocks and trees like a soccer star. The guy reached the roadway first, veered left, and ran.

Heart pounding, thighs burning, he reached the pavement himself about fifteen seconds later. He glanced left. Then stopped in his tracks.

The shooter stood perhaps seventy-five meters away, at the rear of a midnight blue SUV. It was parked on the paved berm of the road, facing back toward Route 55. The shooter yanked open the cargo door, slid his rifle inside, then began to tear off his camo. His hat went in first, revealing dark curly hair and olive paint on his face. Then his boots, then the rest of his coveralls; he wore street clothes underneath. The shooter reached inside, grabbed a pair of dark shoes, slipped them on. Slammed the door, turned…

…and spotted him.

They stood motionless, staring at each other.

He realized that he still held his M40 and the Glock. Realized, too, that the shooter was wondering if he was about to use them.

Due to the distance, he couldn't be sure, but after a few seconds he thought he saw the man nod slightly—then, preposterously, raise a hand to give what looked like a half-wave, half-salute. The guy spun, and with a dance-like skip launched himself around the driver's side. Within three seconds the SUV was in motion, accelerating toward the highway and escape.

Escape...

Looking back in the other direction, he saw the turnoff where he'd left his own car. He holstered the Glock as he ran and fumbled in a Velcro-sealed pocket for the keys. Reaching the Chevy, he dumped the M40 onto the back seat, threw a blanket over it, slammed the rear door, then slid in behind the wheel.

A minute later he was back on 55, heading east. No pursuers in the rearview mirror, but they wouldn't be far behind. He tore open a packet of pre-moistened towelettes with his teeth and wiped his face. It came away covered with muddy green camo paint. He'd have to clean up and change into the street clothes he'd brought along, and soon.

In another half-minute he turned onto Route 66, the major east-west highway, then gunned it, heading toward Washington. He would get off this road in a few miles and travel the rest of the way into D.C. using a roundabout route to evade roadblocks. As he did what he could to wipe off the paint, he tried to puzzle it out.

Why would they send a second shooter, and not tell him?

Last night on the sat phone, his employer sounded desperate. The sniper had done plenty of contract work for this client in the past, and had long ago deduced that he worked for, or with, the Russians. So when the man mentioned the name of this target, James Harold Muller, the sniper connected the dots. He'd seen news reports yesterday about Muller being arrested as a Russian mole in the CIA. When his employer said Muller had to be taken out, *fast*, the sniper knew that meant: *before he talks.*

Because Muller would know about the *other* mole in the Agency—the mole who, a year ago, temporarily hid a tracker on a CIA security vehicle. Back then, it had been the sniper's job to follow that tracker…and it led him here, to discover the safe house.

For the Russians, that second mole's existence had to be kept secret, at all costs.

He tossed another used wipe on the passenger-side floor. Something nagged at him.

Last night he had asked his employer for a spotter or backup. The man said nobody else was available, not for several days. Well, assuming he wasn't lying—

Suddenly it hit him:

Maybe his employer and the Russians didn't know about this other shooter.

But if so, who was he? Who sent him? Why would anyone except the Kremlin want Muller dead?

Another thought struck him:

Then his employer wouldn't know who really shot Muller.

He stared at the highway unrolling before him as he considered further implications.

He was a man accustomed to taking calculated risks. He would take one now.

He retrieved the encrypted Motorola satellite phone from the glove compartment. Thumbed a series of numbers, waited for a tone, then clicked in another series. After about ten seconds, he heard the familiar voice.

"Yes? You have something to report?"

The voice sounded anxious.

So he really *doesn't* know about the other sniper. He smiled to himself as he answered:

"The target is down. Repeat: Target down."

He heard a long sigh that turned into a chuckle, then a hearty laugh. The client's next words confirmed that his guess was right—and that his gamble had worked. *He* would be credited for this kill. And nobody except himself and the real shooter would ever know.

"Very good!" the client said. "My associates will be most relieved. And most pleased about your exceptional work."

The man paused, then added:

"This will be your biggest payday ever, Mr. Lasher."

PART I

"Justice is truth in action."

—Benjamin Disraeli
Speech, February 11, 1851

ONE

The cries and movements awakened him.

He rolled to face her. In the skylight's illumination, he could see her head jerking from side to side, facial features contorted, inarticulate sounds coming from between clenched teeth.

Not again…

"Annie," he said gently, not wishing to frighten her further. "Honey…wake up."

Her eyes flared open, glinting wide and wild in the moonlight. Her hands stopped thrashing. She blinked, getting her bearings. Then turned, finding him. Staring at him— disbelieving.

Then understanding…

"Oh, Dylan!" she gasped, reaching to touch his shoulder. To make him real, he realized. "Oh, God!"

He pulled her close to him. Her naked body, damp with sweat, trembled against his. He didn't have to ask about the nightmare.

"I'm so sorry," she whispered, her voice weak.

He squeezed her. Put a smile in his voice and said, "Don't be silly. I'm the one who's sorry. For putting you through that."

"It's always so real," she continued, her face pressed into his neck. "The blood…you on the floor…all that blood…"

"I know," he said, stroking her hair. Feeling like hell.

"I'm afraid to go to sleep anymore…I want it to stop. But I can't seem to get past it." Her voice caught, a half-sob. "Dylan…I just can't get past it…"

"I know, love." He didn't know what else to say.

He continued to stroke her hair. After a long time her trembling stopped.

She began to stroke his back. Gently, at first. Then more insistently.

He felt it, too.

He pulled back, tilted her chin up with his forefinger, searched her face.

"Are you sure?" he asked.

The cat-shaped eyes, barely visible in the pre-dawn light, held something urgent. Then fierce. Unblinking, they held his as she lowered her mouth and wrapped her lips around his forefinger. Then began to suck on it. Using her tongue. Slowly. Deliberately.

He understood. He resisted his sudden rage to possess her.

Instead, he rolled onto his back, smoothly lifting her atop him.

Then he placed his hands flat at his sides, pressed against the cool silk sheet.

He let her mount him.

Let her regain control…

"Mrrr-eh-eh-eh…"

The cat crouched on the tattered seat of the old stuffed chair next to the cabin window. The noise from her throat sounded like a faint, fiendish cackle. Outside, balanced on a pine branch just a few feet away, a gray squirrel stared back at her, flicking its tail in insolent challenge.

Annie laughed. She finished buttoning her jacket, then smoothed it down over her jeans. "Dylan, your vicious jungle beast is having breakfast fantasies."

He came down the creaking pine stairs from the cabin's loft wearing a black pullover sweater, jeans, and low-cut boots. Even after a month, she hadn't adjusted to the sight of his scruffy red beard and hair; it fit the rustic setting, but not him.

He moved to the window and stood there in silhouette, hands on hips, looking down upon the hunched lump of black-and-white fur. The cat didn't move or acknowledge his presence.

"Eh-eh-eh-eh…"

He smiled. "Dream on, Luna. Without claws, you wouldn't last ten minutes out there."

"Why did you have her de-clawed?" she asked.

"I didn't. They had already done that at the pet store where I rescued her."

The word choice made her smile. "You seem to be in the habit of rescuing maidens in distress."

He shuffled toward her, affecting an exaggerated limp. "And look at the terrible price I paid for my chivalry," he said, drawing her into his arms.

She laughed as he rubbed his beard against her neck, tickling her. "You fake. We hiked five miles yesterday, and I could barely keep up with you. And you were certainly rambunctious enough in bed this morning. I'd say your battle wounds have pretty much healed."

"True. Now the brave knight collects his reward." His lips moved lightly against her throat.

"Cut that out. Luna isn't the only lady here with breakfast fantasies. Grab your coat."

He sighed and straightened. "You fail to appreciate male priorities."

"I appreciated your priorities just a few hours ago, mister. Now let's go, before they stop serving."

"*My* priorities?" He flashed that crooked little grin she adored.

They emerged from the fire-warmed cabin into the still, frigid air of the February morning. She drew the soft fur of her jacket collar up around her cheeks. Weak light from the morning sun filtered through the surrounding stands of pines and hemlocks.

She stood aside while he double-locked the door. He wore his long dark leather coat, but was hatless and gloveless. His eyes narrowed against the cold and little clouds of breath escaped through his lips as he bent to set his "tell-tales"—two unobtrusive twigs that would indicate if anyone entered the cabin during their absence.

He turned away and let the spring-pulled outer screen door bang shut. Startled, a cardinal chirped and streaked across the clearing, like a scarlet flare. They stepped down from the porch. She caught the faint scent of wood smoke. She took his arm and pressed against him, matching his stride.

In the quiet of the forest, the crunch of their boots was the only sound.

Ice crystals had formed overnight on the windows and dark-blue hood of his Honda CR-V. It was half-crammed with household items they packed the evening before, so they took her Camry instead. He helped her into the passenger seat, then went around and got behind the wheel. They sat a moment while the car idled and the defroster cleared the windshield.

The Camry bounced over the frozen ruts of the long dirt drive and Dylan turned south onto East Hickory Road. After a short distance, the car crossed the little bridge over the ice-covered Hickory Creek. A couple of minutes later, they reached Route 666 and rolled west, past the wood-framed houses of the northwestern Pennsylvania village of Endeavor.

"Annie, I know you're tired of the diner. Are you sure you don't want to head down to Oil City? A lot more choices, and we can be there in half an hour."

"No. I'll pass out if I don't get something into me in the next ten minutes."

He flashed that little smile again. "Seems you worked up an appetite this morning, Annie Woods."

She laughed in spite of herself. "If it weren't for *that*, Dylan Hunter, I swear I would've gained twenty pounds this past month."

"Sex and hikes in the Allegheny National Forest. Could there be a more satisfying weight-control regimen? But remember, Annie dear, up here it's not Dylan Hunter; it's 'Brad Flynn.' You slipped up yesterday in that country store."

"Yes, Brad dear. And *you* remember that up here it's 'Annie *Forrest*.' And nice as this past month has been, Mr.

Flynn, my body must get back to D.C. and some real food. It's endured all the burgers and fries it can tolerate."

"Believe me, Miss Forrest, saving your exquisite body is my highest priority."

"So, it's only my body you care about."

"Pretty much."

"I figured…As for me, it will be a relief when you finally get rid of that steel-wool beard and ketchup-colored hair. I want my tall, dark, and handsome guy back."

"Just as I want my hot, slinky brunette." He glanced over and brushed her wig with the back of his big hand. "Although, to be frank, I think this blonde is better in bed."

She had to laugh. She marveled at how he could always make her laugh. She could barely remember the nightmare now.

They turned south onto Route 62, where it hugged the Allegheny River. In less than half a mile, past some archery and wilderness outfitter shops, the diner came into view on the right, just a couple hundred feet from the riverbank.

The exterior reminded her of the Alamo, but in gray vertical planks instead of adobe. The front wall rose in several squared-off steps toward a peak in the middle. A long narrow porch with a wooden railing ran the length of the building. The sign above it said "Whitetail Diner" in carved letters; a painted image of a buck bounded over the name.

A few cars were in the gravel lot. He pulled into an open slot in front of the entrance. Annie waited while he got out and came around to open her door for her. She loved his little romantic gestures. They had fallen into these customs automatically, from their first days together. She took his arm again and he led her up the steps.

Warmth and the smell of pine smoke greeted them. So did Sherry Byczek, the stocky, middle-aged blonde behind the counter, who was pouring coffee for a male customer.

"Hey there, Brad 'n' Annie," she called out in her husky smoker's voice. "I thought you'd already left for Jersey."

"Hi, Sherry," Annie answered. "No, not yet. Thursday, or perhaps Friday."

"Jersey?" the man at the counter chimed in, smiling broadly. "I was born there!" He was in his forties, sandy-haired and unshaven. He wore a green-and-orange plaid shirt and a black baseball cap with a gold letter "P" on the front.

Dylan headed over toward the counter; she noticed how he put on the slight limp again. "Oh? Where abouts?"

"Trenton," the guy said. "But we moved here when I was still a kid. How 'bout you?"

"Just outside of Princeton." He stuck out his hand. "Brad Flynn."

"Denny Beck," the guy replied, shaking hands.

Dylan turned and motioned her over. "And this is my fiancée, Ann Forrest." She saw the twinkle in his eyes.

She approached Denny, extending her hand and a smile. "Call me Annie."

He eyed her up and down. "Fiancée, huh? You're one lucky guy, Brad."

"Don't I know it." He winked at the man.

Sherry gestured with the coffee pot. "You two grab a table, I'll be right over."

Dylan led the way toward the welcoming heat of the big stone fireplace, steering them past a table where a white-haired elderly couple smiled up at them. On the varnished knotty pine walls above the mantelpiece hung the mounted trophies of Sherry's late husband, George: four antlered deer heads surrounding that of a large black bear, its teeth bared in eternal menace. To add to the atmosphere, a variety of antique farm tools and hunting-and-fishing items hung on the walls to either side of the fireplace.

He selected an empty table that would seat four. Like the others, it was covered with a red-checkered vinyl tablecloth. He dragged out a chair with his boot, shrugged off his leather coat, and dumped it onto the seat. Then, ignoring her, he slid into another chair and immediately began to browse the menu.

Astonished, she remained standing beside her own chair for a few awkward seconds. Then she got it. Amused, she unbuttoned her jacket, folded it neatly atop his coat, then pulled out her own chair and sat.

"I gather Brad Flynn isn't the chivalrous type," she whispered.

"Brad is way too *macho*. Like Denny. See him watching us? He expects Brad to show his little lady who's the boss in this relationship."

"'Little lady,' huh? Have I told Brad lately just how much I want to dump him and get back to my charming, well-mannered boyfriend in Washington?"

"About ten minutes ago, I recall."

"So, what'd you finally do with that bear you shot?" Sherry asked Denny while she scooped up some silverware and napkins for them.

"Had the head mounted on the wall in our living room. Tucker's Taxidermy up in Warren, they did a real nice job.

The skin—it's a nice, thick fur blanket in our bedroom, now." He rotated his stool to face their table. "Hey Brad—you do any huntin'?"

Dylan looked up from the menu. "Used to. Deer, mostly. Did I just hear Sherry say you bagged a bear?"

Denny beamed. "I sure did. You know where Yellow Hammer Road goes off 666?

"Sure."

"You go all the way up Yellow Hammer to 209, then keep going to where it turns into Forest Service Road. You park there and hike on in, and down near Otter Creek you'll find lots of bear. I nailed a five-hundred pounder a few months back."

"That must have been a thrill."

"You better believe. Hell of a thing for us to haul it outta there, though, let me tell you. I had to borrow my brother's F-350, and bring along—"

He was interrupted by a sudden commotion. At the entrance, a man stood holding the door open for two women, who hurried inside. None wore coats or gloves.

They all looked scared.

TWO

Annie noticed that Dylan had already pushed back from the table and was poised to leap to his feet.

The man, in dress shirt and tie over slacks and wing-tip shoes, moved quickly toward the counter. "Sherry, I need you to call the state police."

She dumped the silverware on the counter with a clatter. "What? You okay?"

Denny slid off his stool and intercepted him. "What the hell happened, Ed?"

"WildJustice," the man said. "A bunch of them just stormed into our office and started smashing things with clubs. Lucky for us we were in the back on coffee break when they came in. We didn't have time to grab our cell phones or do anything except run out the back to my car. Lucky I had my keys in my pants pocket. We got out of there fast. But in the mirror I saw one of them run out to the road and watch us drive off." He glanced back at the door. "I'm afraid they may come after us."

One of the women, a young redhead in her twenties, hugged her bare arms around her body and stood at the front window. "I don't see them. Maybe they decided not to follow."

Annie watched as Dylan got up and approached the man.

"Excuse me. What's 'WildJustice'?"

"You know—that environmental gang," the other woman interjected. A thin brunette in her fifties, she stood trembling, one hand on the back of a chair to steady herself. "The paper calls them 'ecoterrorists.'"

"Sons of bitches," Denny said. "They spike our trees, wreck construction equipment. Set fire to sawmills—the one up in Kane last fall. Cost my brother-in-law his job. Tree-hugger bastards are tryin' to put us all outta work."

"And now they're after fracking companies. Like ours," Ed said. "They cornered a couple of our workers out on a drilling pad a couple of days ago and roughed them up. One of them needed stitches…Helen, please get away from the window! You don't want them to see you."

Annie stood and walked over to the older brunette. She put a hand on the woman's quivering arm. "Why don't you sit down and tell us what's going on."

The trio looked at each other and moved to a table. Dylan, Annie, and Denny pulled up extra chairs; Dylan's faced the door. As they were settling in, Sherry emerged from the kitchen and came over. Annie saw the worry on her face.

"Cops are all tied up with a big truck accident in Tidioute. Say they'll be down here soon as they can. It may be half an hour, though."

"Great," Ed said. "I hope they don't spot my car. I parked around the far end of the building."

"Why don't we start with some introductions," Dylan suggested.

They went through the formalities quickly. Ed Gerardi was manager of an Adair Energy clerical office, three miles south. The younger woman, Helen Stutts, and the older one, Corrine Ringwald, were staff. Adair, Ed explained, was a natural gas exploration-and-development company.

"It's bad enough with the EPA threatening to shut us down with a fracking moratorium," Ed said. "Now we have to deal with these nutcases, too. Over a hundred of them arrived here last week. From all over the country. A lot of them came in on a chartered bus. They're camping out in the forest somewhere."

Sherry frowned. "How can those hippies afford to charter a bus?"

"Buddy of mine manages the doughnut shop up in Warren," Denny said. "A few days ago, a bunch of 'em wandered in. Says he overheard one of 'em say, 'Don't worry, chow down—our sponsor in Washington is picking up the tab.'"

"What? Are you serious?"

"What the man told me, Ed." Denny rested a gnarly fist on the table. "I figure it's CarboNot. They're in Washington, right? They probably paid for them buses, too. I bet they're all in this together—CarboNot, EPA, WildJustice—all of 'em.

"I'm sorry," Dylan said. "I haven't been following the news for a while. What is 'CarboNot'?" Annie could tell from Dylan's eyes that his interest was intensifying.

"It's that big 'green energy' outfit that's working with the EPA to target us and stop fracking. They've been—" Ed's voice trailed off. His eyes widened. "Oh God..."

They followed his gaze to the window. An old, garishly painted VW minibus was slowing on the highway. It lurched into a tight turn and rumbled into the lot, swinging broadside behind the parked cars. Blocking them in.

She heard the chair beside her scrape the floor.

Dylan stood.

Hunter cursed himself silently for leaving his Sig Sauer and boot knife locked up in the cabin. But just for a second. Regret was a distraction.

Distractions got you killed.

The first time he ate here he had inventoried the decorative implements hanging on the wall. Trout net. Fishing rod. Two-man crosscut saw. Broken wagon wheel. Ancient Winchester. Horse bridle. Canoe oar. Kid's sled. Sledgehammer, but with a visibly cracked handle. Except for the oar, nothing handy in a fight. And all bolted securely to the wall.

The useful items would be in the kitchen.

The side panel of the van bore a big white peace sign against a swirling backdrop of psychedelic flowers. Now it slid open and the occupants began to jump out.

"Okay, everyone, listen up."

They all looked up at him, fear on their faces. Except for Annie: She rose to her feet, eyes wide and riveted on the front door. She could take care of herself physically—but emotionally? Ed looked like he wouldn't be worth a damn in a fight, but Denny might be okay. He recalled the beefy young ex-Marine who sometimes served as part-time cook.

"Sherry, is Fred working today?"

"No. Just Amy's in the kitchen."

The first two guys out of the van looked to be in their twenties. They separated and moved toward the opposite ends of the building. He knew they'd circle around to block the rear exit.

"All right. Everyone into the kitchen. Sherry, run ahead and lock the back door." As they all got to their feet, he turned to assist the terrified elderly pair at the next table while he continued to call out instructions. "Corrine, call the cops again; tell them it's an emergency and to hurry."

He looked back at the window. A huge bald guy was squeezing out of the van, and the whole thing rocked when he stepped down.

Annie turned to him. He saw what was in her eyes.

"Annie, Denny, Ed—grab the biggest carving knives back there, one in each hand. If they come in, you wave them around"—he held her eyes—"and use them if you have to."

Hunter turned and gently directed the frail old couple toward the kitchen. Then he strode toward the front door.

He heard steps behind him and glanced over his shoulder.

She was following.

"Annie, get back in the kitchen."

"Like hell I will," she said. Her face was pale, but her expression resolute. "I'm not letting you go out there alone."

He didn't have time to argue. As he approached the front window he saw that seven more people, five of them males, had piled out of the minibus to join the big guy. Ten in all, counting the two heading behind the building. Three brandished ax handles, though not the bald giant. They gathered around a skinny, dark-bearded man who was talking and gesturing.

So he was their leader. Organizing the assault.

Hunter reached the door. Then paused, hand on the knob.

She stepped beside him. "So, how do we play this?"

He looked down at her. She looked small and vulnerable. But from their workouts in the Bethesda *dojo*, he knew better. He saw steely determination in her gray cat's eyes.

"Rule number one: Never let your enemy attack first. Especially if you're outnumbered."

She nodded. "Element of surprise."

"I'll take out the big guy and the ones with the ax handles. Can you keep a few of them busy?"

"Got your six, Dylan Hunter." She hesitated, then added: "Please be careful."

He smiled, leaned over, and kissed her forehead. "Don't worry about me. They're amateurs. Ready?"

She released a breath. "Let's go."

In one motion he flung open the door and shot through it, leaping from the porch. He had darted halfway past their own parked Camry before the gang could react to the noise.

His first target of opportunity was a kid in a hooded parka with his back turned to him. The kid held an ax handle resting casually over his shoulder. He just started to turn when Hunter reached him, yanked the handle from his grasp, and kicked the back of the kid's right knee. Not pausing to watch him fall, he continued to rush right at Baldy.

The man stood at least six-six and had to be close to three hundred pounds. His chest and belly looked like a beer keg; it was covered by a gray sweatshirt the size of a tent that bore the faded image of John Lennon. Above his right eye, an actual *dent* depressed his forehead—souvenir of some past battle. Surprised, he took a step back as Hunter closed on him, and began to raise fists the size of dinner plates.

Hunter shifted the ax handle into a double-handed grip. But instead of swinging it like a club, he pivoted right, lunged forward with his left foot, and rammed the end of the handle forward like a bayonet.

Right into John Lennon's chin.

Which rested on Baldy's solar plexus.

The wheeze of his escaping breath sounded like a blacksmith's bellows. The giant's mouth gaped open and his eyes popped wide. As his hands fell to grab his belly and his body bent in the middle, Hunter stepped forward with his right foot, twisted his hips to add torque, and swept around the trailing end of the ax handle, smashing it into Baldy's left temple.

The hollow *crack* sounded like a Major League home run. Baldy's massive head snapped to the side. For a split second he tried to keep his feet as the stunning blow registered. Then his eyes rolled up, his knees buckled, and he toppled to the gravel driveway like a falling tree.

Hunter spun to face the rest of the gang. He saw that another man was down at Annie's feet, holding his head in his hands and moaning. One of the two women lurched to grab at her; but Annie spun easily, using the woman's forward momentum to flip her over her hip. The woman landed on her back. Hard.

"*Michael! Jeff!*"

The guy in the beard—backing toward the van, looking off toward the side of the building where the first two had gone.

"*Get back here! We need help!*" he yelled.

Hunter went for the other two guys holding ax handles. The first—attired like a ninja in black watch cap, sweater, and gloves—swung his like a bat at Hunter's head. He stepped inside the swing, parrying it easily, then jabbed the opposite end of his own into the guy's mouth. He heard and felt the crunch of teeth. The ninja staggered backward and fell on his butt, shrieking.

He turned to the other one. Just a long-haired teenaged kid, and he looked terrified. The kid dropped his weapon to clatter on the ground and raised his hands in front of him, palms outward.

"Hey man! Don't! I give up!" he pleaded, backing away.

Six out of play.

Four to go.

Hunter turned from the kid and headed for the bearded leader. The second woman stood close beside him. The pair backed toward the minibus while Annie snatched up a dropped ax handle and came at them from the other side, hemming them in.

"You're the leader of these losers, right?" Hunter said as he slowly advanced on them. He dropped one end of his handle to let it trail on the gravel, scraping menacingly.

The guy stopped retreating. He stood there, glaring at him, holding his eyes. Looking wary, but not intimidated. He appeared to be in his late thirties, thin and homely, with an unusually narrow, oblong face. Its apparent length was exaggerated by cold, close-set dark eyes, a pile of thick brown hair at the top, a full brown beard at the bottom.

"We're *not* losers," he snapped. "We're fighting those who rape the Earth."

"Well, so far, I haven't seen *you* do any fighting." He swung the piece of wood in an arc, indicating those scattered on the ground, groaning and wailing. "But I guess that's what *they* are for. You're the *intellectual*—right?"

The man's eyes blazed with fanatical intensity. "I'm not afraid of you." He stepped forward, balled his small hands into fists, raised them awkwardly.

"Zak! Don't!" the woman cried out.

Hunter sighed. *Martyr complex. Looks like he's never been in a fight in his life…* He dropped the handle, walked over to the guy. Lowered his hands and stuck out his chin, presenting an easy target. Let the man flail a wild, looping right at him, which he ducked easily. Then an even more awkward left, which he blocked with his right forearm.

And answered with a left hook that tagged the guy solidly on his right cheekbone. The man staggered sideways, then wobbled on his feet, eyes unfocused. He was starting to sag when Hunter followed with a big right uppercut into the man's beard that lifted him right onto his tiptoes. He crumpled like a marionette whose strings had been cut.

"Zak!" the woman screamed and rushed to his side.

Hunter heard applause behind him. He turned. On the porch, Denny and Sherry stood at the railing, clapping. Behind them, the others were emerging through the doorway.

"I thought I told you all to stay in the kitchen," he said.

Denny clambered down the steps first, a big carving knife in his hand. "No way we was going to let you two fight our battles for us, Brad."

At that instant the other two—*Jeff and Michael*—came running from around the side of the building. They skidded to a halt as they took in the scene. They exchanged looks, then backed off.

"Come and join the party, fellas," said Annie, smiling sweetly as she tapped the ax handle against the side of the van.

The woman huddled over the unconscious man on the ground, sobbing, her long tangle of curly red hair hanging down like a shroud into his face. "Zak!" she cried. "Zak!" She glared up at Annie, revealing a thin, malnourished face. Hatred burned through her tears, and she pointed a bony finger at Hunter. "He killed Zak!"

Annie rolled her eyes. "No he didn't." She dropped the handle and went over to check out the prostrate man. Unexpectedly, the woman launched herself at Annie, howling unintelligibly, trying to claw at her face. Annie dodged, batted her hands aside, then responded with a swift, sweeping backhand that rocked the woman onto her heels. She stumbled back, her hands covering her mouth. When they came away, her lips were bleeding.

Denny and Ed came down from the porch and trotted over. Denny's broad grin revealed a gap between his yellowed front teeth.

"Holy shit! Where the hell you two learn to fight like that?"

Before Hunter could respond, Sherry walked over with Corrine and Helen in tow. "Amy just got the cops on the line. They'll be here in about ten minutes."

He and Annie exchanged a look. Things were going sideways. They had to get out of there.

"Look, folks—we're finishing our vacation. We can't afford to get stuck here filing police reports and going to court." He lowered his voice. "Besides, these nutjobs might wind up suing *us* for assault. So we'll be on our way. Please do us a big favor and keep our names out of this?"

"Hey, we owe ya," Sherry said. She looked around at the others. "Far as we're concerned, you 'n' Annie were never here, Brad."

He winced at the mention of their names, while the others smiled and nodded.

Hunter turned to Ed. "You, Helen, and Corrine are the only witnesses to any actual crimes they committed. You can press charges for what they did to your office."

Ed rubbed his chin. "To tell the truth, I didn't get a good look at them there. Did either of you?" The two women shook their heads. "See, we were too busy getting away." He nodded at Zak, still lying unconscious near the van. "That man—he's the only one I know I saw for sure. He was the first one who came in the door."

Hunter nodded. "Okay. You might be able to prosecute this 'Zak' guy, and he seems to be their leader. That should keep them out of your hair for a while."

"He doesn't look like he's going anywhere till the cops show up," Ed said. "Neither does that big one you laid out. Okay, let's move that hippie van, and you two can be on your way."

"I'll go get our coats," Annie said, trotting toward the restaurant.

"You think you can manage these people when we leave?" Hunter asked.

"Ha," said Denny. He picked up an ax handle and handed it to Ed. "You didn't leave many for us to manage." He brandished his carving knife at the stragglers hanging back in the distance. "Ain't that right, fellas?"

They buckled into the Camry and he backed out carefully to avoid those still lying on the ground. Then he paused the car at the edge of the parking lot.

He noticed that she was trembling, just a little, now that it was over.

"You were great, Miss Forrest."

"You too, Mr. Flynn." Her hand was balled into a fist on her lap.

He put his hand on hers. "See? I told you not to worry."

She nodded. "That big guy…he…"

"…made you think of Wulfe. I know. But Wulfe knew what he was doing. This guy was a moron. No threat at all…Are you all right, now?"

She sighed and nodded again.

He moved his hand to her thigh. "Want to head back to the cabin?"

She stared at him, then burst out laughing. It broke her tension, as he knew it would.

"You're incorrigible! But I'm still hungry. Remember?"

"Oh. That."

"Yes. *That.* And if you expect to get laid again this month, you'd better get me to a decent restaurant in Oil City in the next half-hour."

"In that case, you'll be eating in twenty minutes."

THREE

The music was pleasant…familiar.

Rhapsody on a Theme of Paganini…

She blinked, waking up. Found herself snuggled against his warmth under the down comforter, her bare left leg draped over his, fingers on the curve of his chest, cheek resting on his solid upper arm.

His face lay on the pillow next to hers. Clean-shaven now. Hair back to dark brown. The skylight above their bed revealed the hazel glint of his eyes, watching her.

A smile played at his lips. "Nice to wake up to Rachmaninoff," he said softly.

Then it registered. *Cell phone…*

She rolled off him and groped the nightstand for her phone. Found it.

"Hello?"

"Good morning, Annie." The familiar gravelly voice of her boss, the Deputy Director of the CIA's Directorate of Clandestine Services. "Hope I'm not waking you."

She met Dylan's inquiring look and said, "No, Grant, it's quite all right." She pushed the button to put their conversation on speakerphone. "We were up late…packing." Dylan raised a brow at her. She nudged him with her foot.

"Sorry to bother you, but I only had a minute this morning to try to catch you," he went on. "I wanted to see if you could get back to the office on Saturday instead of Monday. Some situations have come up that can't wait through the weekend."

"That won't be a problem. We're driving back early on Friday."

"Good. I look forward to seeing you again. We've missed you around here, Annie. Have you enjoyed your month of R&R in the woods?"

"It's been great. We both love it out here. Very relaxing— until yesterday. I'll have to tell you all about it."

"So, how's our boy? That knife wound healing?"

"Almost completely. He's right here. We're on speaker."

"Hi, Matt. How are you feeling?"

"Matt Malone can't come to the phone right now; but if you'd like to leave a message—"

"Sorry. *Dylan.*" He coughed.

"Dylan Hunter is doing just fine, thank you. But it sounds as if Grant Garrett is at death's door."

"Ha. I wouldn't give my enemies the satisfaction. Glad to hear the leg is better. That knife wound was nasty. But you always were a quick healer."

"I owe it all to clean living."

Garrett grunted, his shorthand for laughter. "Well, I'm eager to see both of you when you get back. Maybe we can have dinner in a few days. You have any plans?"

"Only today and tomorrow, before we head back," Dylan replied, sitting up and stretching. The comforter fell away, revealing the taut muscles of his chest and stomach. And more than a few scars. "I've owed the editor of the *Inquirer* a fresh story for weeks. So I'm going to poke a bit into something nasty that's going on up here. It could be nothing, but the locals think there may be some kind of Washington connection."

"Be careful, okay?"

"It's not like that, Grant. It's just a newspaper story."

"I seem to recall that your latest hospital stay started out as 'just a newspaper story.' You remember—the one that almost got you and Annie killed on Christmas Day."

Dylan laughed, keeping his eyes on hers. "Fear not. The only danger this story poses is that it may bore me to death."

"Things never stay boring around a sheepdog like you."

"A what?"

Garrett coughed again. "I'll explain the reference another time. Gotta go."

And just like that, he was gone.

She sat up next to him, hugging the comforter around her. "He's right, you know."

"Right about what?"

She raised her eyes to the cabin's exposed ceiling rafters. Near the overhead skylight of the loft she noticed the faint, glistening tracery of a spider web.

"Every situation you get involved in starts out looking simple and safe. But you just keep poking and probing and pushing. And suddenly, you're tangled up in something complicated and violent and dangerous."

He smiled. Reached a big hand and gently ruffled her hair.

"Come on, Annie. You saw them. Burnt-out derelicts of the Sixties. All of them together couldn't even take the two of us."

"It's not only them. You think there may be a Washington connection."

"I'm just speculating, because that guy Denny was speculating. And anyway, what are we talking about? Just some legal feud over natural-gas drilling—"

"—that already turned violent yesterday." Before he could reply, she continued. "Dylan, the things you get mixed up in—they *always* seem to escalate into violence. Grant told me it happened all the time when you were with the Agency. He said he always worried about you when he sent you off on clandestine missions."

"That was years ago."

"It wasn't even a year ago that you shot James Muller at the safe house."

He looked away. "That was personal."

"And then you went after Wulfe and his pals for attacking Arthur and Susie. That was personal, too—right?"

He turned back to face her. "They were three vicious sociopaths on the loose. Somebody had to stop them."

"But you didn't end it with just them. You expanded that into a one-man vigilante crusade. And—as Grant said—it damn near got us both killed."

He sighed. "Come on, that's not quite fair. Wulfe planned to come after you and Susie, regardless. My actions didn't provoke him. Besides, this situation is completely different, Annie. What do we have here? A pathetic band of anemic vegans. Maybe a few fat Washington lawyers and bureaucrats.

How could investigating them possibly escalate into anything dangerous?"

"It's not them, Dylan. It's you. *You* escalate things."

She stopped, resting a hand on his arm. When she spoke again, she tried to keep her voice soft.

"Darling…It's not just your history at the Agency. I've lived around you for a few months, now. And I've seen the things—the scary things—you do. I saw it again yesterday. At the diner. I watched how you reacted when those three terrified people rushed in. It was like a switch flipped on inside you. Your eyes went cold and narrow. And when the gang showed up, you sent everyone else back into the kitchen. But you seemed *eager* for a confrontation. You were going to go out, unarmed, and attack all of them—*alone*. You instantly, automatically escalated to violence."

He remained silent, watching her.

"I'm not like you, Dylan. Okay, sure, I've had training. I can defend myself if I have to—like at the diner. I do what I *have* to do. But it scared me to death. I'm just not used to that sort of thing."

She paused; he didn't respond, so she went on.

"When I joined the Agency, just out of college, it all seemed so romantic and exciting. *The CIA!* I was going to be a spy and run off around the world, on daring missions for my country. But after I finished my training at the Farm, I knew that wasn't for me. I'd just married Frank, and I wanted to stay near him. So I decided that I didn't want to be in Operations. Instead, I put in for a posting at Langley. I applied to the Office of Security. And I've stayed here, stateside, ever since…Dylan, I haven't been on ops out in the field, like you. I haven't experienced all the nasty things that you have. Or done the nasty things that I know you've done. I've never had to kill anyone. I haven't had violence and bloodshed as part of my daily life...So, when I saw—"

She shuddered.

"Dylan...I can't stop seeing you fighting Adrian Wulfe in my kitchen. Stabbing each other with those knives...and you bleeding, so much, all over the floor, and crawling to me..."

She stopped, realizing that she was digging her nails into his forearm.

She watched him take a deep breath. Let it out slowly. Then he slid closer and drew her into his strong arms, blanket and all. He held her close, resting his chin on her head. She felt his breath stir her hair.

"Love," he said quietly, "all I'm planning to do is interview a few people. That's all. No confrontations. No fights. No violence. No blood on the floor." He gave her a little squeeze. "I promise."

She leaned back. Looked up into his eyes and ran her hand along his pale, smooth-shaven cheek. Along the thin plastic-surgery scar at his jawline.

"I almost lost you," she whispered. "I couldn't bear that."

He gave her that lopsided grin. Stroked her hair. "You're never going to lose me."

Boggs emerged from the back entrance of the Warren County Prison into the bitter breeze coming out of the gray northwestern sky. He shivered and turned up the collar of his thick flannel coat. But the chill couldn't distract his attention from the throbbing ache in his head and jaw that had kept him awake all night.

He spotted at once the minibus idling in a parking spot nearby, a plume of exhaust behind it lifting and flaring like a colt's tail. The sight of the pollution made him feel even worse. He saw Jeff behind the wheel, Dawn in the passenger seat. She noticed him at the same time, got out and came running toward him.

"Oh honey!" she exclaimed, opening her arms to him. "You look awful!"

"Don't touch me!" he growled between his teeth, not daring to open his swollen jaw. She winced and jerked back. He saw the hurt look form on her face. Noticed her own swollen lips. "Sorry," he grunted, making a beeline for the vehicle. "I feel like I must look."

He walked slowly, but each step sent a jarring spike through his skull. She paced him warily, searching his face with a concerned look. "Zak, I understand…I brought the ibuprofen you asked for."

He nodded. Immediately wished he hadn't. Reaching the van, he opened the passenger-side door and climbed up gingerly into the seat she had just vacated. He noticed a couple of vague shapes in the back; he didn't bother to look and see who. He settled into the seat, feeling Dawn's residual warmth through his jeans. He eased his head back against the headrest, released a long breath, and closed his eyes.

Nobody said anything. He heard the side panel door slide open behind him. Dawn getting in. She slid it shut with a thump that made him cringe.

"Here, Zak. The ibuprofen and some water."

He opened his eyes a slit. Saw her hands floating beside his face. One held a mustard-colored canteen. The other, palm flat, offered three brownish pills. He picked the pills from her hand one at a time, opening his mouth just enough to shove them past his teeth. Then he tilted the canteen to his lips and sipped as best he could. Cold water dribbled down his beard and neck. *Damn.*

"Give me two more," he croaked. She did.

"So you wanna head back to the camp, Dr. Boggs?" Jeff's obsequious voice.

"Mmm...First, though, I have to make a call. And I don't want to stand around freezing outside...Head back to that doughnut shop where we were the other day."

It took ten minutes to find the place on the other side of town. By that time the ibuprofen was starting to kick in and the throbbing had slightly receded. He got out and went inside alone. They all understood he needed privacy for his many mysterious calls.

The smell of coffee and pastries greeted him. He navigated around the line of customers waiting at the counter and made for what he knew was a single-occupancy men's room. Fortunately, it was empty. He went in and locked the door behind him.

When he turned, he caught his image in the mirror—and sucked in a breath. It was the first time he had seen his face since yesterday. Above the beard, his right cheek was visibly swollen and a dark purple bruise spread upward and around his eye.

Great.

He pulled out his cell. Like the minibus, it represented another despised, but necessary, concession to modern technology. This one wasn't his smartphone, though—just a cheap store-bought model, what they call a "burner phone," which he replaced frequently, courtesy the cash supplied regularly by the man he was dialing now. A man who used similar phones for calls like these—calls that had to remain untraceable.

His old friend answered on the second *chirp*.

"Are you out yet?" the man asked. No greetings or preliminaries. And, of course, they never used names.

"Yes. Thanks for posting bail," he mumbled between his teeth. "I appreciate—"

"You are damned lucky I didn't leave you in there! And of course I could not post bail personally. I had to have...our associate arrange it, through intermediaries. So, tell me: What in hell did you think you were accomplishing?"

He didn't need this, not on top of the headache.

"You know what we do. We're a direct-action group. That was an *action*."

"And I have always supported your past 'actions.' Generously, as you well know. But just what kind of action was *that* supposed to be—and in broad daylight, no less?"

His teeth hurt, and he realized he was clenching them.

"People who work for companies that despoil the planet can't claim moral immunity, just because they're low-level employees. If they learn that *they* will be held personally accountable for the harm their companies do, then perhaps–"

"For God's sake, a lot more is at stake than whatever a few paper-pushing clerks are doing! There are moral priorities here. We are after an entire industry that is doing tremendous environmental damage. We have to pick and choose our battles carefully. You are supposed to be a genius. Well, why didn't you use that brain of yours?"

He closed his eyes and leaned against the door. "My people were going stir-crazy, sitting on their hands. Besides, you agreed long ago that I should have operational autonomy."

"But *you* agreed long ago to keep me in the loop, so that we can coordinate our efforts. You seem to forget that. And you seem to forget that without my assistance years ago, you might well be rotting in a cell today."

He hadn't forgotten. A flood of images from a decade before, during his campaign of corporate bombings, washed through his mind:

How he'd used his physics and chemistry background and access to university labs to construct the bombs...The crazy risks he'd taken in transporting them to his targets...The composite eyewitness sketches of "the Technobomber," as the FBI dubbed him, disguised with a hat and sunglasses, shown everywhere on TV and in the newspapers...The FBI news conferences hinting at solid leads and physical evidence...The many nerve-wracking nights lying awake, waiting for the sound of the footsteps outside his door from those coming to arrest him...And then the evening when the insane pressure finally got to him—when, in desperation, he broke down and went to the home of his old ally, to seek the help of a man whom he knew to be as ideologically driven as he...How, over bracing glasses of Jack Daniels, the man nodded sympathetically after listening to his long and rambling confession, and then rested his hand on Boggs's shoulder and promised that he would see what he could do...

In the weeks that followed, the man worked his magic, calling in favors from well-placed friends to concoct alibis for Boggs and divert police suspicion. Next, he helped Boggs devise a plan to plant explosives and other incriminating items in the Boston apartment of an MIT chemistry grad student—an anarchist notorious for violent rhetoric, and arrested repeatedly for fomenting anti-corporate riots. It was that kid who had been arrested, indicted, tried, and convicted, despite his tearful protestations of innocence.

It was that kid who later hanged himself in his jail cell.

As Boggs remembered it all, the man on the phone maintained a pointed silence. A silence meant to underscore just how much Boggs owed him. For his help had come at a price. That price was perpetual dependency. And so, over the years, Boggs did a number of favors for him, in return. Acts that the man had to have done, but was too fastidious to do himself.

Boggs loathed being in anyone's debt, let alone being under anyone's control. But there was nothing he could do about it. At least, not for the time being…

The man on the phone finally spoke again, this time his tone conciliatory.

"Look, we have made a lot of progress over the years, you and I, by coordinating our activities. Right now, the media is on our side and the polls are trending our way. But this sort of juvenile, quixotic stunt could backfire and build sympathy for the other side."

Juvenile…quixotic. Boggs stared at his battered face in the mirror—a literal reflection of his commitment, of how much he was willing to sacrifice for his convictions. He wondered just how much his friend was willing to sacrifice. But this was not the time and place for that discussion.

He took in a slow breath. "All right. I'm sorry. I do owe you a lot. I should have warned you."

He heard a matching sigh. "Then let's see if we can put this behind us. Right now, I am preparing for a meeting that is relevant to the issue that mutually concerns us. You will be hearing from me."

The man clicked off without saying goodbye.

Back in the vehicle, the rest knew better than to ask about the call. This time when he entered, he glanced in the back and noticed a few members of the core cell were missing.

"Did the others stay behind at the camp?"

Jeff flicked a nervous glance his way. "Well, as for Cobra—maybe you saw. He got bashed really hard in the mouth by that guy. Lost some teeth and stuff. It really messed him up. He's seeing an oral surgeon today. Says he doesn't know if and when he'll be able to rejoin us."

If and when. He then recalled the giant who had been felled by the attacking man. "How about Bear?"

Uncomfortable silence for a few seconds. Then Dawn piped up.

"Bear came to only a minute before the cops arrived. You know he's got a serious rap sheet. So he didn't hang around. Before they started taking statements, I saw him slip away behind the building. We haven't seen him since."

"Okay," he said, trying to keep his voice steady. "What about Michael? Rabbit?"

"Michael told me he never expected anything like *that* to happen. And Rabbit...well, you saw how scared he was when that guy came after him. They both left, too...I'm sorry, Zak."

"Scared Rabbit!" Jeff said, chuckling. One look at Boggs and his laughter trailed off.

They all fell silent again. Jeff followed the street signs back to Route 6, crossed the Allegheny River, then headed south, back toward the forest.

"I've been wondering who those two were," Boggs said at last. "The man and woman."

"I heard somebody call him 'Brad,'" Dawn said. "And I think someone else called the woman 'Emmy.'"

"Naw, it was 'Annie,'" Jeff interjected. "The lady who owns the diner said 'Annie.'"

Boggs watched the fields and trees roll by. The pain had dulled a bit more. But his anger had not. It had been building all night.

He thought of the man and woman. Unreal how they were attacked like that, by only *two people*. So fast, too. Like a martial arts movie. And that cocky little smile on the man's face as he stuck out his chin, taunting him.

And now, the phone call.

Juvenile, quixotic actions.

He clenched his fists in his lap.

Then another image arose in his mind. The image of the satchel he had transported here secretly and hid in the woods near the camp. He thought about the satchel...and its contents.

Right then, he knew exactly what he was going to do.

"'Brad' and 'Annie,'" Dr. Zachariah Boggs murmured through his teeth.

Who are they? *Where* are they?

He would find out. And he would make them pay.

FOUR

The first thing he saw as they crested a hill was the bright red top of a metal derrick poking above the trees.

"That must be the place," Annie said, spotting it, too. "Well, this should be interesting. Thanks for inviting me along. I'm curious to see for myself what this 'fracking' business is all about."

"Me, too," Dylan said, peering ahead for the access road. "I've read about it. But there's nothing like seeing things for yourself."

"Do you think anyone from the diner will recognize us?"

"Unlikely. Those people were from their clerical office. They have no reason to come out here to the drilling site." He spotted the entrance, put on his turn signal, then stole a quick look at her. She had ditched the longish blonde wig and returned to her short natural brunette. Her smoky gray eyes were well-hidden behind large, bronze-tinted sunglasses. "Besides, I think we're both unrecognizable now."

"You are—thank God. I hated that hideous beard. At least you don't look like Erik the Red anymore. You even walked and talked differently. I don't know how you remember to do all that, Dylan. It's like you really become another person."

"A skill that's proved to be useful over the years," he said. "So Grant tells me."

He turned down a hard-packed dirt access road that cut a path through the trees. They emerged into a flat, open area of several acres. It was crammed with trucks, vans, box-like containers, and pipes, all surrounding the derrick mast. It towered above the site, held upright by guy wires.

Hunter pulled the CR-V next to a group of pickup trucks and cars. Several workers in yellow hard hats and beige coveralls stood at the edge of the site watching them. One approached. He carried two hard hats under one arm, and two sets of protective goggles dangled from his other hand. They got out of the car to meet him.

"You must be the reporters," he said. He was a slim, pale-haired guy in his early twenties.

Hunter smiled. "Dylan Hunter. I'm the reporter. This is Annie Woods. She's just along for the tour."

The guy didn't smile in response. He leveled a cool glance at Annie and then back at Dylan. "I'm Will Whelan. Dan is expecting you…Oh, and you have to wear these while you're on the pad."

They each took a hard hat and goggles from him. Whelan turned without a further word and headed toward the site. Annie looked at Hunter, an eyebrow raised; he shrugged. They donned the gear as they followed him.

Not much seemed to be going on at the moment. About twenty workers stood around the site in small groups, chatting, smoking, and looking at them with obvious curiosity.

"They find you perversely attractive in that male get-up," he whispered.

"That's just psychological projection," she replied. "*You're* the pervert."

They crossed the pad to what looked like a long white motor home. Whelan went to a door on its side, climbed a couple of steps and entered. They followed.

Hunter expected a rough, messy office, the kind his father used to occupy on construction sites. He was surprised to find a tidy, high-tech workspace, whose electronics compared favorably to some foreign CIA stations he'd been in. Along the length of one wall was a continuous counter, covered with laptop computers, calculators, and notepads. Four men in the company's coveralls sat in swivel chairs along the counter, working the laptop keyboards and consulting papers. Above them, flat-screen monitors hung along the walls, displaying complicated full-color graphs and charts tracking the drilling operations. Spaced windows gave the occupants a clear view of the site.

The men all stopped what they were doing and stared at them when they entered.

A man seated at a separate counter at the far end of the van stood and approached. He wore blue jeans and a brown flannel shirt. Hunter recognized the craggy-handsome face from a news photo he had seen on his laptop last night.

"Dan Adair," the man said in a stern baritone, nodding and extending his hand. He stood tall and erect. His sandy, gray-flecked hair and beard were trimmed short; his eyes and mouth were pressed narrow.

"Dylan Hunter," he replied, gripping a hand that was strong and calloused. "And this is my fiancée, Annie Woods. Thanks for allowing her to accompany me."

Adair turned to her. A smile spread. "Pleasure," he said.

Annie turned on her own smile, one that would melt ice. "I'm delighted to meet you, Mr. Adair."

"Dan. Call me Dan...both of you."

"Then please make it Dylan and Annie," Hunter said. "I know that many in the media have been tough on you, Dan. So I appreciate your willingness to give us a tour and answer questions."

"Tell you the truth, before I returned the call to your secretary in Washington to schedule this meeting, I did a bit of homework about you. I read a few of your pieces online, and what people say about you. You don't seem afraid to be politically incorrect or make waves."

Annie directed a glance Dylan's way. "As I know, only too well."

"Most important to me, though, is you have a Washington media platform. Our industry can't get its story out in that town. All the other papers there are in bed with our enemies. Yours seems to be the exception. And if I haven't misjudged you, maybe you are, too. At least I hope you'll give us a fair shake."

"Dan, I promise only to take this story wherever the facts lead."

Adair chuckled. "Well. If that's the case, then I don't have a goddamned thing to worry about. Let me show you around...Will, I'm expecting a call. Could you hold the fort?"

Whelan didn't look at him or answer, but slid into the swivel chair Adair had vacated. Adair grabbed a worn buckskin jacket from a hook on the wall and led them back outside.

Hunter offered Annie his arm as she stepped down from the van.

"'*Fiancée*,' huh?" she whispered, looking mischievous.

He shrugged. "Just maintaining our cover."

She poked him in the ribs with her elbow.

The dismal morning overcast had broken up, leaving tattered gray streamers in the ice-blue sky. Shafts of sunlight stabbed here and there through the trees, glittering off the crusty ice and patches of open water on Queen Creek.

The WildJustice campsite spread out along the bank of the stream, which meandered through the remote center of the Allegheny Forest. Dozens of tents of various sizes, shapes, and colors dotted the landscape. From the dirt access road on the hillside above, they looked like bright, ungainly flowers scattered under the dark hemlocks and pines. A community tent, big, rectangular, and bright yellow, stood in an open area; it served as the central gathering place for meetings and nightly entertainment. Nearby, a broad fire pit still smoldered from last night's bonfire.

One side of the large tent was tied open. For several minutes nearly a hundred people wandered in, ready to hear what their leader had to say. Most remained standing, shifting on their feet and rubbing their cold hands. Some, not knowing how long the meeting might last, sprawled on cloth folding chairs or nylon sleeping bags that they brought from their own tents.

Zachariah Boggs stood with Dawn Ferine at the opposite wall, waiting patiently while the stragglers entered and the murmur of conversations died down. His eyes roamed from face to face, passing instant judgments born of long experience.

Most were young, in their twenties and thirties, though some were gray and old enough to have attended Woodstock. Their appearances and dress ran from L.L. Bean to organic farm to urban grunge. Many, he knew, had come here for little more than the adventure of role-playing—to become "green revolutionaries" for a week or two. They would carry home tales to impress their timid, more conventional friends, stories to prove their environmental commitment and moral superiority. He was glad that he wouldn't see most of them again.

Others, though, were sincere in their love of nature, righteous in their indignation about environmental degradation. The thought caused his eyes to move instinctively to Dawn's. She looked up at him just as she had the first time, seven years ago: with the unconditional, irresistible adoration of a devoted acolyte, a woman willing to follow him anywhere. Yes, those others were like Dawn: peaceful, passionate followers.

But not true soldiers. Vital to the cause, of course. But lacking the philosophic rigor, the unswerving focus, the sheer emotional *toughness* to do everything necessary. His eyes swept once more over their expectant faces. All watching him. He felt the faint, familiar pangs of sad loneliness. No, they were not like him. So few were like him.

Which was why only those few, though not Dawn— *especially* not Dawn—could ever know certain things about him.

Things he had done.

Things he was about to do.

He took a step forward, then began to speak…

Adair led them out a short distance onto the pad and stopped.

"Normally, it's so noisy here with the pumpers going that you wouldn't even hear me. So I told the guys to knock off for a few minutes." He tapped his boot on the pad surface. "We're standing above the Marcellus Shale Formation. It's a layer of sedimentary rock over a mile down, and it runs all the way from the southern half of New York, down through much of Pennsylvania, eastern Ohio, West Virginia, and into far western Maryland and Virginia."

He reached into his jacket pocket, drew out a piece of dark rock and tossed it to Hunter, who caught it and turned it over in his hand.

"That's a chunk of Marcellus shale from this site. It came from sediment deposited 400 million years ago. Under time and pressure, the sediment compressed into black shale, trapping the organic matter that later became petroleum and natural gas. The Marcellus is the second-largest natural gas play on earth. It's—"

"'Play'?" Annie asked.

"Sorry. A 'play' is a natural gas reservoir that we're working. The Marcellus is located here in the East—the country's biggest natural-gas market. And it's the most important source of energy since 1859, when Edwin Drake drilled the first commercial oil well just west of here in Titusville."

Adair pointed to the derrick in the center of the pad. "We have to drill down over a mile to reach the shale. The hole is called the 'wellbore.'"

He turned to them. "Lots of folks worry that our drilling will pollute their water. The first thing you need to know is that we drill down *way* past the groundwater that people use for drinking water. The deepest groundwater lies only about three hundred feet deep. Well, *thousands* of feet of solid rock separate the shale layer from the aquifer at the surface. It's physically impossible for what we're doing over a mile below the surface to pollute the aquifer."

"But can't your pipes break or leak?" Hunter asked.

Adair shook his head. "You see, after we do the first drilling phase, we insert what we call a 'conductor casing'—that's a steel pipe, almost fourteen inches in diameter—down the hole about sixty feet. We then pump cement down through the pipe and out of it, filling the entire hole around it. The cement fixes the casing in place, and it also creates a second barrier to protect the groundwater. And we pressure-test the casing to make sure there are no leaks."

Adair began to cross the pad, heading toward the derrick.

"But that's just the beginning. Next, we insert the drill back inside that casing and continue drilling three-to-six-hundred feet, down past the aquifer. Then we insert a *second* pipe inside the first one, and fix that casing into place with a new layer of cement. We repeat this process again, with a *third* casing and cement layer inside the first two, which goes down two-to-three-thousand feet. When we reach the shale layer, we use special equipment to change the path of the wellbore and start drilling horizontally through the shale. And we finish with a *fourth* pipe. It goes all the way to the end of the well, also surrounded by a layer of cement. That's the pipe that ultimately carries the natural gas back to the surface."

He paused to let his words sink in. "All those concentric rings of steel and cement," he said, making circular gestures, "create multiple barriers to protect the groundwater. And as I said, the fracking process itself takes place thousands of feet below the aquifer, separated from it by millions of tons of impermeable rock. So you see, leaks of natural gas or any of our chemicals into the groundwater are simply impossible."

"All those precautions," Annie said. "It's certainly not the impression I've gotten from what I've seen and heard in the media."

"Tell me about it," Adair said, scowling.

"But what about chemical leaks up here at the surface?" Hunter asked.

"When we first arrive and clear the area, we build this protective, leak-proof pad of multiple layers of felt and plastic." Adair's hand swept around the site. "And as you can see, the whole pad is surrounded by a berm, to further contain any spills. Same goes for that wastewater holding pit over there"—he pointed to what looked like a rectangular pond—"where we temporarily store the water we pump from the wells. That's completely lined, too. Eventually, we pump out that water and truck it away…You should know that my company has *never* been cited for a single health, environmental, or safety infraction."

"Until now," Hunter said.

"Yeah," he said, looking grim. "Until now."

FIVE

"You and I stand in one of the most magical and majestic places that remain on earth," Zachariah Boggs began. "Each day, I look up at the giant trees towering over us; each night, I look up at the most star-filled sky in the Northeast; and each time, I stand humbled with a sense of awe."

The crowd listened, captivated by his voice, as they always were.

"We have come here because this sacred place is now threatened. What is happening here, with swarms of drillers and loggers and killers of animals, has been allowed to happen everywhere on earth. At some place, at some moment, those of us who revere the earth must make our stand."

He looked down, stomped his boot on the ground.

"This is that place. This is that moment. We have come here to do *whatever is necessary* to stop those who are raping the earth."

Boggs could gauge the effect of his words by the complete stillness in the tent, by the subtle changes in expressions on the faces before him. He began to pace slowly back and forth before them, mesmerizing them with both sound and motion. *Like a snake charmer*, Dawn had once described it.

"Our enemies say that we put nature over humans. And our enemies are *right*. I make no apologies. For what has man wrought? From hunting to agriculture, from mining to logging, from building to drilling, what we absurdly call 'human civilization' has collided violently with our planet's fragile ecosystem. We have driven countless species and indigenous cultures to extinction. And now the heavy-heeled carbon footprints we leave behind threaten the very future of all life on earth!"

He paused after the angry crescendo, then dropped his voice to evoke sad concern.

"Removing just a single strand from the web of life threatens to unravel its entire fabric. The seminal thinker of ecology, George Perkins Marsh, understood this. He wrote that 'Man is everywhere a disturbing agent. Wherever he plants his foot, the harmonies of nature are turned to discord.' And the spiritual prophet of preservationism, John Muir, understood it, too. 'How narrow we selfish, conceited creatures are in our sympathies!' he said. 'How blind to the rights of all the rest of creation! If a war of races should occur between the wild beasts and Lord Man, I would be tempted to sympathize with the bears.'"

Boggs paused as a burst of laughter and applause filled the tent. As he knew it would. He loved that quotation and used it a lot. It never failed to generate that reaction.

"Once our final casing is in place, we're ready to start hydraulic fracturing of the shale—what everyone now calls 'fracking,'" Adair continued. "Follow me over here, and I'll show you what's involved.

They threaded their way through a bewildering maze of pipes, valves, trucks, tanks, and hoses. Adair pointed to an area where four large pipes rose vertically from the ground in jointed segments, like metallic totem poles. Each stood about ten feet tall, linked to a spider web of smaller pipes and valves.

"Those are our wellheads. After we finish drilling, we insert a perforating tool into them. Starting way down at the very end of the wells, the tool blows holes through the casing and into the shale. We then pump a mixture composed almost entirely of water and sand into the pipe. That slurry pushes out of the pipe holes at high pressure, and into the shale, forcing open small cracks that extend a few hundred feet. When we pump the water back out of the pipe, the sand remains behind in the cracks, holding them open. The natural gas then flows out of those fractures, right through the porous sand, and back up the pipe. We repeat this perforation process all along the horizontal casing, and we seal off each section when we're done."

Adair pointed out and explained the various pieces of equipment: tanker trucks that hauled several million gallons of water to and from the site; big rectangular containers that held the sand and "frac fluid"; boxy white trucks containing chemicals; blender trucks to mix them; and flatbed trucks bearing large yellow engines—the "pumpers" that forced the slurry down the pipes.

"Drilling horizontally from this one site," he said, "our wells radiate outward for thousands of feet. We pay local landowners handsomely for their underground mineral rights, too. Most are thrilled because until we came along, the economy was tough around here. Our monthly royalty payments have been a godsend to them. Companies like mine also employ lots of locals. And the out-of-state truckers and drilling teams fill the area motels and restaurants."

"I've seen the changes," Hunter said. "When I was a kid, my dad used to take me here to go hunting. The whole area has really boomed since then."

"And for all these economic benefits, here and across the country, each drilling operation takes up just a few acres. Even then, what you see here is only temporary. When we first arrive, we remove the topsoil and store it nearby. When we're done, we replace that soil, then plant local grasses, flowers, and shrubs, creating meadows. The only things we leave behind are a few short wellheads in the middle of the grass, and a little access road."

He stopped and smiled again. "And that, in a nutshell, is fracking."

"All this equipment and expertise must cost a fortune," Annie said.

Adair nodded. "About five million bucks for a single well. And sometimes you get a dry one, too. They don't all pay off for us. Although with the latest seismic and electronic testing techniques, our geologists have gotten really good at finding the right spots to drill."

As Adair spoke, he stood hands on hips, muddy boots rooted wide. Stood surveying his domain with what Hunter knew was an owner's pride.

He turned to Hunter. Studied him a moment. "That's a funny look. What's on your mind?"

"You remind me of somebody."

"Anybody I might know?"

Hunter shook his head slowly. "Somebody you would have liked."

When the laughter died down, Boggs stopped pacing and faced them. He lowered his voice, speaking with quiet, simple urgency.

"I founded WildJustice on a simple moral principle: *We do not accept a human-centered worldview.* We do not view nature as here for *us,* for *our* sake. We believe that all life exists for its *own* sake. All life has *intrinsic value* of its own. And by that moral principle, our entire human-centered civilization—and the ideas that support it—are *anti-nature,* and our industrial and technological activities are *unnatural.*

"In fact, humans—hard-wired to alter nature for our own greedy profit and selfish benefit—are really the only *unnatural* life form. Perhaps one day some virus will come along and set things right again. But for now, if what is left of nature is to be spared, then what we call 'civilization' must be stopped—by any means necessary!"

He saw the shock registering in many of the eyes. Even though he had said and written similar things many times before, he knew that a lot of them just didn't get it. This time, though, it seemed to be sinking in...and it was making some of them uncomfortable.

Some, but not all. He saw the dawning realization, the eager intensity blazing in other eyes. And he took note of who they were.

They would be his soldiers.

"Any questions, Dylan?" Adair asked.

"Plenty. But let's cut to the chase and start with that proposed EPA moratorium. You've described all the precautions you take against leaks of chemicals into the groundwater. But the EPA says radioactive and toxic chemicals from this site were found in wells around here, contaminating the drinking water."

"That's what they say, all right."

"But you say…?"

Adair held his eyes. "That it's a fraud."

Hunter had an intuition for detecting liars, honed by special training from the Agency. He caught no sign of deception in this man.

"So how do you explain their claims?"

"Simple. Those contaminated samples were planted."

He wasn't expecting that. "Planted?"

"At this site, and in all those water wells. And we can prove it. Or, rather, a toxicologist I hired—a damned good one—can prove it."

Hunter exchanged glances with Annie; her eyes reflected his own surprise.

"Planted by whom?"

Adair shrugged. "Wish I knew. We've had some turnover of employees. And many people truck in materials, coming and going all the time. Lots of possibilities. But that's not all of it. Other funny stuff has been going on around here, for a long time…Here's what I'd like to do: Are you two free into the evening? I want to introduce you to our toxicologist, Dr. Adam Silva. And some other folks who have stories to tell. At my place, over an early dinner. You like steak?"

Hunter looked at Annie again; she shrugged, leaving it up to him.

"Sounds great."

Boggs began to pace again.

"As you know, yesterday a group of us began an action against a local fracking company, Adair Energy. We targeted it because it was caught polluting the pristine, natural waters of this forest with toxic and radioactive chemicals. The EPA is dragging its feet, so we took the first step to shut them down *now*. But as you know"—he stopped, gestured at his bruised face, and smiled sheepishly—"as you can *see*, we were met with violence."

It generated the expected chuckles.

"Well, my friends, that won't stop us. Not by a long shot. Our action yesterday was only the beginning, the first skirmish in a war against this deadly industry and its ruthless profiteers."

Applause and shouts of "Right on!"

"In the past, the cops have tried to infiltrate and disrupt our organization. So for operational security, we are organizing future actions in small 'cells.' Only cell members will have advance information about their own actions. That will legally protect all of you not specifically involved in those actions. And, as always, your participation in any action is completely voluntary. Are you all cool with that?…Great. All right, then, I think we're done here. Thanks for coming."

Another ripple of applause went through the crowd and they began to leave.

Dawn moved to him, beaming, stood on tiptoes, and kissed him. "Oh Zak, that was wonderful!"

He smiled at her. "Hey, be careful with your beautiful injured lips…Oh, could you give me a minute? I have to grab Rusty before he leaves."

He pressed his way through the milling crowd to an older, red-haired man. A man he had known, worked with, and trusted for years. He tapped him on the shoulder.

"Could I have a word, Rusty?"

He led the man away from the others, to a quiet corner of the tent. He spoke to him for a couple of minutes, then squeezed his shoulder and returned to Dawn while Rusty left.

"I just sent him on an errand," he explained in answer to her inquiring look. "I told him to go to that diner and see if he could learn about that man and woman."

"And if he learns something, then what?"

Boggs saw the worry in her soft blue eyes and smiled reassuringly. He knew her limits. She was fine about actions against *property*, like the Adair office. But she had hesitated to go after the *people* there. It wasn't fear; it was just her gushy sentimentality. He had learned long ago that there were things he couldn't trust her to do. Things she had to be shielded from knowing.

"Why, we *sue* them, of course!" he lied easily. "We hadn't done a thing to those two. But they came outside without provocation and attacked us." He brushed a loose strand of her hair away from her face. "I'm guessing they're friends of the Adair people. So maybe if we file charges for physical assault, Adair will drop charges against *us* for our action at their office."

She bought it; her answering smile held relief.

"Now, I have to run an errand of my own. I'll be back at our tent in fifteen, okay?"

He kissed her cheek and left. Then headed off into the woods and over to the creek. He followed it downstream for about two hundred yards, to a rock outcropping about five feet high.

He looked around, made sure nobody was in sight. Then knelt and dragged away the brush he had piled beneath it. He leaned in, groping inside a wide fissure in the base of the rock.

Found the ice-cold handle of the satchel. Lifted it out— carefully. Set it on the ground.

He thought of the man and woman and smiled as he unzipped the bag and looked inside.

The pipe bombs were stacked exactly as he had left them.

SIX

Dan Adair led them back inside the site's mobile headquarters, what he called the "data van." He spoke to a man at one of the desks, getting a progress update. He spent a few minutes on the phone making dinner arrangements. Then he walked over to Will Whelan, still occupying Adair's seat at the end of the van and working at a laptop keyboard.

"Will, since we're short-handed here tonight, I'll need for you to stick around till about eight and take those phone reports from Texas when their crews knock off."

Whelan spun his chair to face Adair, frowning. "Hey, I had things I wanted to do tonight."

The snippy tone surprised Hunter.

"Look, I'm sorry about that. But I'm heading home now with these folks to continue our conversation. They'll be staying for dinner."

"Well, that's just great. What about *me?*"

Hunter stared at Adair, astonished to see that he looked apologetic rather than angry.

"There's plenty here in the fridge. And you'll get the O.T. rate for the extra hours."

"Yeah," the young man snapped, turning his chair and his back on Adair. "Whatever."

"You can have tomorrow off. Okay?" It sounded almost like pleading.

Whelan didn't respond. Hunter caught Annie's glance, eyes wide in disbelief.

"Anyway, it'll be steak when you get home, Will. I'll make sure your mom keeps a hot plate for you." Adair turned back to them and smiled sheepishly. "Let's go."

They dropped their hard hats and goggles on a shelf and left. After the door closed behind them, Adair led them a distance from the van before speaking.

"Sorry about that. I should explain—"

"No need," Hunter interrupted. "Not our business."

"No, really. You'll probably run into Will again while you're up here doing research. You see, he's my stepson."

"Ah," Annie said.

"Hell, you don't think I'd let anyone but family talk to me like that."

"Dan," Hunter said, "I didn't think you were the type to let anybody talk to you like that."

Adair didn't respond or look at them. He kept walking, leading them to the parking area. Hunter already pegged him as unpretentious and practical, so didn't expect that he'd be driving pricey show-off wheels. Adair confirmed it when he stopped at the door of a cherry Nissan Titan SE pickup. The man knew his trucks; this one was best in its class for off-road work.

"It's still early," Adair said. "I'll introduce you to the family over drinks and snacks before dinner. I just arranged for a couple of others to join us. You'll find their stories interesting. Follow me."

It was just after four p.m. when Rusty Nash ambled up to the counter of the Whitetail Diner and planted himself on a stool amid three of the regulars. He knew they were regulars because they were chatting up the busty blonde behind the counter like they were old friends. He smiled and nodded at them all, then asked her for coffee. As he sipped quietly from the steaming mug bearing the restaurant's jumping-deer logo, he listened and sized them up.

All three customers and the woman behind the counter were fiftyish, like him, though he wouldn't see that birthday for a few more months. One guy, sitting apart from the other pair, wore a tidy uniform that matched him up with the phone company truck parked outside. The other two, dressed rougher, obviously belonged to the building-contractor pickup beside it. One man was chubby, the other skin-and-bones.

He had already prepared his line of bullshit on the drive over. He was proud of how good he was at bullshitting people. He also was proud that Zak relied on *him* for this sort of thing. Zak liked that he didn't look like the rest of the group. Partly, Zak said, it was because Rusty was a lot older than most of them. And partly because he dressed and talked just like a regular guy. And partly because he was so easy-going. Zak admitted that he himself and most of the others came across as "pretty intense." His words. "I like the fact that you are so laid-back and friendly, Rusty," he said. "You have the knack for fitting in anywhere—for blending right into the background, like…" What the hell was that lizard he mentioned?

Anyway, it turned out that he didn't have to use his line of bullshit on these people at all, because they made it easy for him. They were already talking about what happened yesterday when he sat down.

"I had to check with my insurance agent," the blonde was saying to Skin-and-Bones, "to see if the policy would cover me if they tried to sue me for the injuries."

"How could they sue you, Sherry?" Phone Guy cut in. "They started the trouble."

"You never know these days. Laws ain't what they used to be. And the injury lawyers, they're all sharks. Still, I'm just glad Brad and Annie were here to kick the crap out of them. No telling what that gang would've done to us or to my place if they got in here."

His opening. "Sounds like you had some excitement here." He grinned.

The woman, Sherry, turned to him and chuckled. "Did we ever! You know 'bout that environmental gang, WildJustice?"

"Not sure. They local? I'm just visiting a cousin up here for a few days."

Sherry then unloaded her description and opinion of his group, in language so salty he was surprised to hear it coming out of a woman's mouth in public. The three guys roared, so he had to force himself to laugh, too.

"Well anyway," she continued, "they come here yesterday chasing three poor scared clerks from a fracking office down the road." Sherry then delivered her version of what happened. Which further pissed him off. He wanted to throw his coffee in her face, but he held it together and made sure to look amazed and say "No shit!" and "You're kidding!" at all the right places. When she ran out of steam, Chubby said, "Boy, I wish I was here to see all that go down."

"Me too," Rusty chimed in, keeping the grin plastered in place. "Man, I'd a loved to see them punks get their sorry asses whipped. And you say it was just *one guy* and *a girl?*"

"Unbelievable, huh?" Sherry laughed and wiped her hands on her apron. "Brad, he's tall and tough-looking; I think he fought in Iraq. You can see how he could take care of himself. Annie, on the other hand, she's just a little thing. But boy, can she ever fight!"

"So you know them. They locals, then?"

Sherry shook her head. "From New Jersey. But they've been staying here on vacation this month."

"Yeah? My cousin, he told me all the rentals around here was shut down for the winter."

"They don't rent. Brad has his own cabin out past Endeavor. You know where that is?"

"I think I been through there. Out on 666, right?"

"Just past there. Up East Hickory Road."

This is too easy. "I didn't know there was any cabins up there. Just woods."

"Well, that's what you think when you look around from the road. But if you drive up past the little bridge over Hickory Creek…" She then described exactly where the driveway was.

Rusty grinned again. This time he didn't have to force it. "Well, I sure am glad there's still some people who stand up to the creeps trashing this country. I'd love to shake their hands while I'm here visiting. They come in here a lot?"

Sherry said, "Yeah, but you probably won't run into them anymore. They'll be heading home tomorrow or Friday."

Not good. "That's too bad." He took a last swallow from the mug, then dumped a couple of bucks on the counter. "Well, my cousin oughta be home from work by now, so I better push off." He rose, stretched casually, nodded his goodbyes.

He kept the grin till he reached the door.

Dan Adair's house on Higgins Hill Road commanded a bluff overlooking the Allegheny River. Like its owner, the dwelling was a combination of rural unpretentiousness and modern attitude. Its natural-wood exterior seemed of a piece with the surrounding trees, but rose in angular, contemporary lines. The western side of the home ended in a sharp triangular outcropping, a glassed-in porch that jutted over the embankment. It afforded a panoramic view of the river valley.

Hunter stood beside Adair at the window of that porch, sipping a superb Lagavulin single malt. Across the river, the setting sun rim-lit the deep green rolling waves of mountains. Standing here, where the panes of glass intersected, he felt as if he were at the prow of a ship. Adair, his lean legs planted apart, blue eyes trained on the horizon, looked like its captain.

He recalled what he'd read about the man in a magazine profile. Born and raised near Cincinnati, Adair studied petroleum engineering at the University of Texas in Austin. He then took a job in oil-and-gas exploration with a nearby start-up company. Adair had a knack for figuring out inventive solutions to difficult drilling problems and was promoted fast. But his dream wasn't to work for somebody else. With savings from almost every paycheck, he scooped up company stock during its growth years. Eventually, he cashed out and used the proceeds as seed money to hire a first-rate geologist and open his own exploration and drilling outfit.

Adair borrowed heavily to lease mineral rights on promising land. But like most wildcatters, he struggled during the oil glut of the Eighties. Prices collapsed, wells tapped out, companies closed, and many petroleum engineers left the industry. Scrounging for cash, he sometimes contracted out his engineering and drilling services to larger companies. But with a young wife and baby daughter to support, he barely managed to meet the mortgage on their cramped, 900-square-foot ranch house.

Hunter watched Adair savor a slow sip of the Scotch. Traces of the battles he had endured were etched in the lines around his eyes and mouth.

In desperation, Adair tried out ideas that he read and heard about. He drilled one of his wells at a slant and hit a "payback" reservoir in a bed of naturally fractured limestone. That strike got his creditors off his back. And when he experimented with new horizontal drilling techniques on other wells, their impressive output attracted new investors.

Adair became a pioneer at combining horizontal drilling with fracking. This proved so lucrative that, had he been able to focus fully on emerging opportunities, he might now be a billionaire. But his momentum stalled for several years while he cared for his wife, who finally succumbed to ovarian cancer. The brutal loss also left him the single parent of a little girl. With his responsibilities and attention divided, Adair lost ground while his competitors forged ahead.

Now this man found himself in a new battle, this time with foes of a different kind. He hadn't yet spoken of it, but

Adair Energy's future—and much more—rested on the precarious foothold that he had established here in the Allegheny National Forest.

From inside the kitchen behind them, Hunter could hear Annie and Adair's second wife, Nan, laughing and chatting like old friends. In the darkening valley below them, scattered lights appeared in the homes along the river. Its surface had become a flaming ribbon, reflecting clouds ignited by the now-hidden sun.

"I can see why you love it here," Hunter said quietly.

Adair held his gaze on the unfolding spectacle. "Did I say that?"

"Your eyes betray you."

The man chuckled and faced him. "Well, it's true. I've always loved being out in nature. The wilder, the better."

"Your environmentalist enemies would be surprised to hear you say that."

He took another sip. "That's what I don't get. You know, Dylan, until lately—since they've been trying to shut me down—I called *myself* an environmentalist. Hell, I even used to donate to environmental groups. Drillers like me, we love the environment. We do our damnedest to take care of it. Look"—he gestured with his glass at the world beyond the window—"and tell me why I'd want to ruin all that. I hate pollution as much as anybody."

"But your critics say you're, quote, 'vandalizing natural vistas.' That you're 'plundering the world's precious resources.'"

"Which is total bullshit. We don't ruin the natural landscape. As I told you, we restore it when we're finished. And we don't waste resources. Why would we? We can't afford to. We even purify and reuse our waste water. We use nature responsibly."

"I know, Dan," Hunter said. "But to them, that's the problem."

Adair frowned. "That we use nature responsibly?"

"That you use nature at all."

Adair was about to respond when they heard the sound of the doorbell.

Dawn Ferine stood atop the hill overlooking Queen Creek, where the path down to the camp joined the access road. Her gaze was fixed on the dazzling, shifting color patterns in the sunset sky above the Forest.

She always experienced her most intense sense of spirituality at the beginning and end of day—with the sun's first kiss upon the sky in the morning, and with its parting kiss upon Gaea's lips in the evening. Each day she stopped whatever she was doing at these two sacred moments. She paused to remind herself of the timeless enormity of the Cycles of Life, of the grand Ecosystem in which she and everyone and everything were just insignificant parts. This was her form of prayer: a daily ritual in which she always felt this overwhelming surge of *belonging,* experiencing her oneness with the Cosmos. Her prayer, at sunset and at dawn…

Dawn.

She recalled the day that she chose that name, not long after she met him. She shed the ugly, meaningless name of her birth—*Judith Hernstein.* It annoyed her that she even remembered it. How she hated the crude, harsh commonness of the name that her parents had hung upon the shy, lost child that she had been. But she was no longer adrift, and no longer that person, not anymore—not since she met her soul mate.

She shuddered, partly from the icy breeze, partly from the ecstasy of the moment, partly from her memory of the time when she held his hand and chose her new Self: one name to remind her of the start of day, the other to remind her of the beauty of Life, untouched and wild and free:

Dawn Ferine.

Her vision began to blur with tears. She knew she had to share this with him.

"Zak…"

She turned away from the luminous sky to look for him.

He stood about twenty feet away, his back to her, staring up the road into the distance. The mysterious black bag was on the ground at his feet.

"Zak…"

He raised his hand to his face to look at his watch, then said something under his breath; she could hear only the name "Rusty."

She glanced back at the sun for an instant; its colors already were slightly muted.

"Zak!"

He spun and looked at her. "What?" he snapped.

It rattled her. She tried to hold onto the feeling.

"Zak…please come here for a moment. Share the sunset with me."

He stared at her blankly.

She felt the familiar pang of anxiety rising once again. She walked toward him, but he had already turned his back and was looking up the road again.

"What in hell could be keeping him?" he muttered. She reached out a gloved hand to touch his arm—then hesitated and drew it back. Fearful to intrude on his thoughts.

"Zak. I just…"

He turned to her. "What? What's the problem?"

"It's just so…*spiritual.* I want us to share it."

"Share what?" His voice cold and impatient.

"The sunset."

He glanced up at the sky for a few seconds. Nodded.

"That *is* very pretty." He smiled at her, his lips twisted from the swelling on his face. "It's lovely, honey. Thanks for pointing it out."

She didn't know why she suddenly felt so hollow. Why she felt that touch of fear again.

He turned to look once again up the road. "I hope he didn't get a flat."

She licked her lips; her tongue ran over the sore puffy part that had split. "It's what you said, Zak. Earlier today."

"What did I say? What are you talking about?"

"That…that when you look at Nature, you stand humbled, with a sense of awe."

"Oh that…I wondered what you meant." He reached out his gloved hand to wipe away the tear on her cheek. She felt the coarse cloth crawl across her skin. "I'm sorry, sweetheart. But you can see I'm preoccupied. It's really hard to enjoy nature when humans are screwing it up."

"Well, can't we stop once in a while, for a few minutes—and just appreciate it?"

His features tightened; so did his voice. "I suppose it's a matter of priorities." Then his expression softened. He shook his head slowly and squeezed her shoulder. "Sometimes, I wonder if you are tough enough for this war."

A flash of light caught their attention. Headlights emerged from the west, around a bend in the tree-lined road.

"Finally!" Zak leaned over her and kissed her cheek. "I'll be back in a few hours. Meanwhile, you go get yourself warm. And have something to eat, okay? You haven't been eating enough."

She nodded, saying nothing.

Rusty stopped his battered pickup where they stood. Zak hefted the satchel over and got in on the passenger side. Slammed the door. She stood aside as Rusty turned around in the intersection of the road and the path, grinding through the worn gears. Zak gave her a little smile, and a little wave.

Then she watched the truck accelerate away, back in the direction from which it had come. Watched until its tail lights vanished in the dark tangle of trees.

She walked slowly back down the path that led into the campsite.

She had asked him earlier where he was going. And what was in the bag. He laughed and ruffled her hair and said he and Rusty had to drive over to Tidioute and deliver something to some people. He reminded her of what he said this morning, about cells. "This is 'need-to-know,' Dawn. And you really don't need to know about this stuff."

She shivered as she walked, but only partly from the cold. The other part was the unsettling, nagging doubt that she still was not fully part of his world. And maybe never would be.

SEVEN

From the campsite, a dog-eared map steered them through the narrow, winding dirt roads—first west, then south to an intersection where they picked up East Hickory Road. The dying light of the sky clothed the surrounding trees in shrouds of deep shadows. After a few minutes, Rusty hit the brakes, and the old truck shimmied as it slowed.

"That must have been it. That little dirt path back there."

Boggs peered ahead and pointed. "Okay, turn around at that wide spot near the little bridge."

They saw no traffic on the isolated road, so Rusty took his time executing a K-turn. They came back north slowly, and Boggs told Rusty to kill the headlights and hug the narrow berm at the side of the road. They continued rolling past the break in the trees that marked the rutted driveway. After about twenty more yards, he had Rusty pull off onto a patch of scrubby grass and dead leaves.

"All right, let me go over it a last time." Boggs said. "You stay here with your lights off and your walkie-talkie on. I'll go in on foot and check out the place. If no one is home, I'll signal you, get inside, and rig the bomb. If you see them coming home, warn me and I'll get out of there, then circle back here through the woods."

"Got it," Rusty answered. "Just like what we did at that animal research lab in Michigan."

Boggs remembered. When was that—five years ago? He had to smile. "You're only bringing that up to remind me again how I almost got caught by that rent-a-cop."

"And you would've—except for me." Rusty's grin flashed faintly in the shadows. "I sure did save your skinny ass that night."

"You won't ever let me forget that, will you?" In truth, Rusty Nash had earned his trust years ago. Only one other ally had worked with him longer—or knew as many of his secrets.

Boggs hoisted the heavy black-canvas satchel from the floor to his lap. It contained the necessary tools and accessories, along with the pipe bombs and detonators. He turned up the collar of his Army field jacket, whose pockets were useful for actions like this one. Tugged his gloves tight. Pulled the black ski mask down over his face.

"Don't go blow yourself up, now," Rusty said, rapping him lightly on the shoulder.

"You know better than that."

He opened the door and slid out. Closed it quietly behind him. He paused a moment, staring down the dark path that led back into the trees. Aware of the weight of the bag in his hand. Aware of the wool scratching the tender flesh of his bruised cheek.

Aware of the familiar rush of energy and excitement.

It never got old.

The crystal chandelier reflected off the dining room window like a spray of fireworks. A wood fire blazed and crackled in the large, pass-through fireplace, sharing its heat with the living room.

Dylan and Annie sat across the table from Adair and his wife. Nan Adair was a petite brunette in her mid-forties. She explained that, like her husband, she had been widowed for several years when "Danny" stopped by the Tionesta real estate office where she worked, trying to learn who owned the mineral rights to some local land.

"That was four years ago," she said, looking at him. Their eyes told the rest of the story.

"Good thing she was a realtor," Adair said, winking at her. "She got us one hell of a deal on this place."

"Yes, I can see that you only married her for mercenary reasons," Annie said, and they all laughed.

At the end of the table near the fireplace their other guest attacked a thick slab of rare steak. For someone with such a prominent reputation in his profession, Dr. Adam Silva was surprisingly young. A graduate of the University of Maryland program in toxicology, he looked to be barely in his early forties.

"A few other people, including my daughter and her family, will be stopping by in about half an hour for dessert," Adair said. "But I wanted you to have a little time with Adam first. He does contract work all over the country, so we're lucky that he lives so close by, in Warren."

Hunter said, "Dan tells me you've reached some surprising conclusions about that Nature Legal Advocacy report."

Silva's eyes twinkled behind his squarish glasses as he finished chewing and swallowing a piece of steak. "'Surprising.' Well, I suppose that's one word you might use."

"What word would you use?"

Silva set down his fork. "How about 'criminal'?"

Hunter leaned forward. "Tell me."

For a moment, Boggs got nervous when he saw the Honda SUV parked near the cabin. He moved slowly up to the vehicle and looked inside. It was packed with household items. Which confirmed what Rusty heard at the diner: They were moving out.

He also remembered what Dawn said: that while he was unconscious at the diner, they had driven off in a red Toyota Camry. A different car—which wasn't here, now. And he could see no lights on inside the cabin through the front window.

Maybe he was in luck.

Shivering in the sub-freezing cold, he crept toward the front door, stepping gingerly over twigs and dry leaves that might make noise. Then paused at the bottom of the old wooden porch steps, realizing that they were likely to creak. He stood in shadow, pressed against the rough log wall under the window, thinking it through.

The Honda was locked. He didn't know how to break into a car without leaving evidence. And the particular pipe bombs he brought with him weren't powerful enough to do much damage to those inside if he rigged them to explode underneath.

He considered the porch area. To enter, they would come up the steps to the front door. But the porch was bare and exposed. Hard to hide a bomb out here.

Next, they would open the screen door. Then the inner front door. He could easily rig one to go off when they opened the screen door…

He shivered again. His fingertips felt numb from the cold, even through the gloves. And he'd have to take them off in this freezing air in order to work. Not good—not when you are rigging explosives.

He stared at the screen door, then back along the driveway. No, if they arrived home within the next few minutes he would be seen out here. Besides, it was too damned cold. Better to rig the bomb inside…set it to go off when they opened the front door.

He tip-toed around the side of the cabin, hugging the heavy bag to his chest. Ducked low as he reached a window. Stood slowly to peek inside.

No one visible within the big, dark, single-room interior; it looked empty, except for a few cardboard boxes and paper bags scattered on the floor. He relaxed. They were probably out having dinner. He looked back toward the front of the house and realized that this spot could be seen from where they parked their cars, though. No good.

He continued around to the rear of the cabin and found another window. He took a flashlight from a big pocket in his field jacket and examined the frame and glass. No alarms, as he figured, but the window's inner latch was locked. Stowing the flashlight, he unzipped the bag, pulled out a small crowbar, and used it to smash one of the panes. Reaching in carefully around the jagged shards, he flipped the latch, then used the crowbar to lever the window up.

He reached inside and lowered the bag and crowbar to the floor, hearing the soft crackle of glass fragments under them. The next bit was harder. Boggs was no athlete, and climbing in through the window wearing the bulky jacket proved to be an ordeal. But he managed, though awkwardly, almost falling onto the broken glass.

Once again he fished out his flashlight and clicked it on to look around.

Out of the darkness, two yellow-green eyes flashed back at him.

For the next ten minutes, Silva summarized the results of tests he'd conducted on samples collected from the site and area water wells. The low-level radioactivity, he said, came not from naturally occurring underground radium, but from medical wastes—probably material stolen from a hospital— which someone had then mixed into the waste water taken from the fracking site's retaining pond. The fracking chemicals were then added in proportions completely unrelated to the mixtures used in fracking.

"Another dead giveaway of a hoax," Silva concluded, "is that whoever did this added in a chemical that they found on the site, but which had nothing to do with the fracking process. It was a cleaning solvent."

"So, it was planted, then. Are you absolutely sure?"

Silva gave him a wry look. "Is the Pope a Catholic? Whoever did this was an idiot. He or she knows nothing about chemistry."

"Or hydraulic fracturing," Adair added.

"What's your next step, then, Dan?"

"Two weeks ago, I filed a letter with the EPA requesting the opportunity to submit our own report to their Science Advisory Board's hydraulic fracturing panel. Those scientists advise the Agency about pending regulations. I didn't give them many specifics, only that a toxicologist I hired—I didn't say who—had scientific proof that the evidence in the NLA report about our fracking operations had been faked. I just heard back from them yesterday. They agreed to let us present our case at a hearing scheduled for the end of the month."

"That sounds encouraging," Hunter said. He turned back to Silva. "Will you be submitting just the report, or your physical samples, too? I assume those are critical to make your case."

"Which is why they are under lock-and-key in my home lab. Yes, the samples along with the report. I haven't even begun to write it yet; I'll get to that next week. But I did draft an executive summary." He reached into the inside pocket of his corduroy sports jacket and came out with an envelope. "Here. I figured you might like a copy."

"Thanks," Hunter said, reaching across the table for it. He paused a moment, tapping the edge of the envelope on the table top. "Dan, you've been getting hammered in the media. Wouldn't it be helpful to go on the offensive?"

"What do you mean? How?"

"Well, my editor at the *Inquirer* has been sending me daily text messages, begging for a story." He gestured with the envelope. "This really looks big. Based on what is going on up here, I could file a preliminary piece, perhaps quoting from this executive summary. But I might have to identify Dr. Silva by name, in the article and to people I interview. Would that be all right? And Dr. Silva, could you also give me a sneak peek when your full report is ready?"

The two men exchanged glances. "Fine by me," Adair said.

"I have no problem with any of that," Silva added.

"Since all that is settled now, let me get the dessert ready," Nan said, rising. "The others will be arriving any minute."

Boggs gasped and nearly dropped the flashlight before he saw that it was only a cat.

"Goddamn!" he muttered, training the beam on the animal, which half-closed its eyes in the glare. "You scared the hell out of me." He saw that it was a mottled black-and-white, with a dark patch of fur around one eye. It hunched on the floor, looking nervous at his intrusion.

A complication.

Boggs peeled off his ski mask and jammed it in a pocket of the field jacket. He stood near the open window, wondering what to do.

For all his rhetoric, he actually felt little personal attachment to animals. He accepted and advocated animal rights, but as a philosophical position rather than a sentimental one—one he had derived from the works of the great German idealist philosophers. Even though this particular animal meant nothing to him, as an *animal-in-itself* it possessed inherent value—and an intrinsic right to its own life. These people had no moral right to keep this creature enslaved, as their "pet."

But he had no right to harm a sentient creature, either. When his bomb went off, the shrapnel and nails packed inside would harm not only the humans, but probably this animal, too. Morally, they deserved to die; the creature did not.

However, if he turned this helpless, domesticated animal loose here in the wild, it surely would die—although at least it would die as a free creature, in harmony with the natural ecological order.

Boggs tried to analyze the competing moral claims and counter-claims, growing anxious because the clock was ticking down, and he really didn't have time for this. But the ethical dilemma here was a real one. Moral absolutes either *mattered* at times like these, or they meant nothing at all. And above all, he prided himself for being a man of principle.

In the end, he chose the only proper moral course.

He didn't approach the cat. Instead, not moving from the window, he knelt and slipped off his gloves. The cat eyed him warily.

"Here, kitty," he said, extending his hand…

He wheeled around at the sudden screeching.

Dan Adair was hauling his two small grandchildren into the dining room, one under each arm. The platinum-haired twins squealed with delight.

Hunter relaxed. His right hand came away empty from beneath the tail of his sports jacket, where he carried his Sig P228 in a small-of-the-back concealment holster. He tried to cover the abrupt movement by extending his arms into a feigned stretch.

Standing close to him, Annie noticed. She leaned in and whispered: "Think it through. If you shoot the kids, they won't let us stay for dessert."

"Good point."

Adair deposited the children on their feet and began to help them off with their winter coats.

"Grampa Dan, I wanna sit by you!" pleaded the little boy.

"No! Me!" shouted the girl.

"Well. Timmy, you sit here, on this side of me. And Kellyanne, you sit on the other side, between me and Nana Nan."

"I get to sit beside Nananan!" she taunted her brother, who scowled back at her.

Nan led in the new arrivals and performed the introductions. First, the children's mother, Kaitlin Bell—a tall, slim blonde in her mid-twenties, and Dan's daughter by his first marriage. Kaitlin's husband, Tom Bell, was an affable-looking, brown-haired man with a firm handshake and direct gaze; he owned a small construction firm in Warren. The last guest was a short, beefy man in his late forties, Don DeLuca.

Over pie and coffee, Adair explained their presence.

"Dylan, I mentioned that something funny is going on around here. It's more than just trying to shut down fracking operations. I wanted you to meet Don and Tom because they have stories to tell." He nodded first at DeLuca. "Don used to cut here in the Forest and supply logs to a sawmill out of Kane."

DeLuca explained how he used to drive a "skidder," dragging logs out of the Allegheny Forest for a small logging company, and later took over the firm when his boss retired.

"I busted my ass to stay in business," he said. "We were squeaking by, barely, till 1997. Then the goddamn greenies sued the feds over logging in the Forest. In two years, timber sales nosedived, and then I was in the red. The last straw came in '99. The feds claimed they found this 'endangered species' in the Forest—the 'Indiana bat'—and they shut down all logging here for six months. Well, like lots of the other small loggers, I couldn't keep up payments on my equipment…Can you believe? We were all unemployed because of some goddamn *bat!*"

Hunter noticed the man's fists had clenched; even after a decade, the wound was still raw.

"I had a wife and two young kids to support," DeLuca went on, "and we damned near lost our house and everything. I had to take all kinds of odd jobs, doing carpentry and stuff. My wife was working part-time in a convenience store in Tionesta. We were at a dead end. I didn't know what the hell I was going to do with the rest of my life." His gaze shifted to Adair. "Till about three years ago, when I saw this ad in the paper for entry jobs in the natural gas industry."

Adair said, "Don was one of my first local hires, and he's still one of my best."

Hunter saw gratitude in DeLuca's eyes as he looked at Adair. But also a hint of wistfulness. The look of a once-proud independent businessman, now forced to work for somebody else.

"So, environmentalists have been making trouble for you folks for a long time, then," Annie said.

Employer and employee exchanged bitter smiles. "You have no idea," said DeLuca. "Wait till you hear what's been happening over the last few months."

Boggs had seen Dawn play with cats enough times to know that if you make a sudden move, they retreat; but if you talk to them softly and arouse their curiosity, they'll come to you. He held his extended hand a few feet away from the cat.

"Come on," he coaxed quietly. "I'm not going to hurt you...That's right...All I want to do is pet you...There you are."

The animal approached cautiously, sniffed his fingertips, and now let itself be stroked. Within a few seconds, it was weaving back and forth under Boggs's hand. After another minute, it had relaxed enough that he was able to put his other hand on it.

Then grabbed it and picked it up.

The cat began to squirm ferociously in his arms. Boggs smothered it against the thick field jacket and turned. As he started to dump it through the open window, the cat twisted and bit him on the back of his bare left hand.

"Ahhhh!" he cried out and let go. The cat flipped in mid-air, landing on its feet on the ground outside, then quickly disappeared from view.

EIGHT

The two children, now thoroughly bored, began to fuss, interrupting DeLuca's narrative. Kaitlin shepherded them to the den to watch TV while Nan began to clear the table.

"Our house is on Grange Hall Road," DeLuca continued. "You know where that is?"

"I know where that is," Hunter replied.

"We're up on an area where Dan plans to do some exploratory drilling. He already talked to me and other property owners there about leasing our drilling rights. So, three months ago, I get this call from a guy who says he's with something called 'Capital Resources Development.' I wrote it down when he said the name. He asks: Would I be willing to consider selling my property. I say: No way, I'm happy where I am. He gives me a figure that they'll be willing to pay. I tell him: That's way too low, even if I wanted to sell, which I don't.

"Anyway, the next Saturday I get a visit from this guy who shows me his credentials. He's from the Army Corps of Engineers. He points to the field behind my house, where I've been moving some fill dirt around to level it out. And he says I'm violating a federal 'wetlands' regulation. I say: Are you kidding me? There's nothing wet out there—not even a mud puddle. It's all bone dry, except during a heavy rain, of course. So he hands me this letter."

DeLuca passed it across the table to Hunter; it obviously had once been crumpled up, then smoothed out. The message was short.

Hunter looked up. "It accuses you of 'discharging a pollutant into navigable waters of the United States, under provisions of the 1972 Clean Water Act.'"

"Dylan, we live two miles from the nearest *creek,* let alone any 'navigable water.'"

Adair broke in. "I have to deal with that 'wetlands' stuff all the time. My lawyer told me that a federal court back in 1975 expanded the definition of 'navigable waterways' to include swamps and bogs. Later on, a government manual expanded the definition of 'wetlands' to even include land that's waterlogged by rain as little as seven days per year."

"So what's this 'pollutant' they say you were 'discharging'?"

"The fill dirt I was moving around," DeLuca said.

"Just a minute," Annie said. "You're telling us that the feds regard *natural soil* as a 'pollutant'—and treat a mostly dry field as a 'navigable waterway'?"

"Oh wait, it gets even better," DeLuca said, bitter creases showing at the corners of his mouth. "One week after that, I get a second phone call from the guy at this Capital Resources outfit. He asks me—get this—he asks me 'if anything may have happened in the past week' to change my mind about selling my property. Then he makes me another offer. Only this time it's ten thousand bucks *lower* than the first offer."

The room fell silent. In the fireplace, glowing embers hissed and popped.

Adair finally spoke. "When Don told me that, I started asking around. I found out that other property owners up there who might lease their mineral rights to us have been experiencing similar things. Capital Resources has been quietly buying up land around here for the better part of a year. But whenever a property owner says no, within a short period he's contacted by some government agency. Sometimes it's EPA, claiming some kind of pollution violation. Other times, it's the Interior Department, saying they're not in compliance with some National Forest regulation. A couple of homeowners were told their properties were under consideration to be declared 'endangered species habitats.' Then, each time, the same thing happens: They get a second call from Capital Resources, with a lower-ball offer for their property."

DeLuca looked at Hunter, his eyes blazing. "So, you tell me that this is all just coincidence."

Hunter leaned back in his chair. He shook his head slowly.

"I don't believe in coincidences."

"Damn it!" Boggs gasped, sucking on the bleeding wound. He found the bathroom, rinsed off the blood, patted it dry with a towel that he dropped onto the floor, then wound toilet paper around his stinging hand. He pulled out his walkie-talkie and keyed it.

"I'm inside the cabin. It's empty. Any sign of those two?"

"No, nothing...I was getting worried," Rusty said. "You've been gone, like, ten minutes."

"I was held up. They held an animal in here that I had to liberate."

"Well, okay. But you better get moving."

"I'm on it."

He fetched the bag and studied the area around the front door. Then he unpacked the various items and placed them in a tidy order on the floor.

Pipe bomb, sealed against moisture in a plastic bag.

Detonator, wrapped in cloth.

Wiring.

Battery, its terminals covered by tape.

Electrical switch.

Electrical tape and duct tape.

Ball of twine…

He started the assembly, working with a speed and confidence born of long experience.

"So, what's your story, Tom?" Hunter asked.

"We live just outside of Warren, so we aren't in the middle of the stuff Don and Dan are talking about." Bell settled his coffee cup back onto its saucer. "Or so I thought. Since Kaitlin and I were married, my company's done some building work for Dan over the past few years. A couple of his area offices, the big garage over in Tionesta for all his trucks and vehicles—even a lot of the work on this house."

"Nice job," Silva said, looking around appreciatively.

"Thanks," Bell said, smiling. The smile faded. "Then, six weeks ago, I received notice from the IRS that I'm being audited. Business *and* personal. It came in the mail two days after Christmas."

"Funny thing," said Adair, "my audit notice arrived the same day."

"And I got mine a week later," DeLuca said. "Happy New Year."

"Speaking of coincidences," Adair continued, "chew on this. Two more of my employees, besides Don and me, have been approached by that Capital Resources company to buy our property. All four of us refused. Now, all of us have been notified that the IRS is going to audit us."

He paused, shifting his eyes between Hunter's and Annie's. "Oh yes, and one other thing: All four of us who got IRS audit letters also started to receive anonymous hate mail and phone threats. The callers seem to have a *lot* of specific personal information about us, especially financial. And from the language they use, they sound just like those WildJustice ecoterrorists. So tell me: How would a group like WildJustice be able to get our private financial information—unless somebody at the IRS is feeding it to them?"

Hunter nodded slowly. "It wouldn't be the first time that the IRS—and the EPA, for that matter—have been caught targeting individuals and leaking their personal information to political groups, in order to gin up harassment campaigns."

"Do you think that's what is happening here?"

"Dan, you've convinced me that *something* is going on here. Stopping fracking certainly seems to be a big part of it. But maybe only one part of it. Maybe several completely unrelated things are going on."

"Maybe, maybe not," DeLuca said. "All I can tell you is, if something isn't done to stop what's going on, nobody's gonna want to live around here anymore. Or be able to. If they put people like Dan out of business, there won't be any jobs."

His fists were clenched again, and the bitter lines carved around his mouth were even deeper.

"And what good is private property, anyway, if we aren't allowed to do anything with it? The government and these greenies—they're killing our property values. Pretty soon, our deeds will be almost worthless. That's why I just don't get it. Why would anyone even *want* to buy us out, now? Who's crazy enough to buy bad deeds?"

By flashlight, Boggs finished putting the last piece of duct tape into place. Then stood back to survey his workmanship.

It was simplicity itself. He had securely duct-taped a pipe bomb to the inside wall, just above the door. Right beside it, he also had taped a battery and electric switch. Next, he fastened one end of a length of twine to the inside door knob, and tied the other end around the switch, currently set in the "off" position. Finally, he carefully wired the battery to the switch, and the switch to the detonator he inserted into the bomb casing.

When the door was opened, the drawstring would pull and flip the switch, completing a circuit from the battery to the detonator. A hail of pipe shrapnel and nails would blast down onto the first person entering. If the second person wasn't directly in the path of the blast, he or she would nonetheless witness their loved one torn to pieces. Which would be far more painful, he thought, than that person's own sudden death.

He smiled at his handiwork. It was foolproof. At least one of the two who had humiliated him before his followers would pay tonight with his life. And the survivor would pay emotionally forever.

For a few seconds, he thought of his ally and financier. The man wouldn't like this at all, if he knew. But of course, he didn't know. Some things, it was better that he *didn't* know. "Deniability," they called it.

Boggs methodically gathered up and packed away his materials, checking to make absolutely sure that he had left none of them behind. Then he returned to the rear window, which he had left open for a fast exit, if necessary. He placed the bag on the floor and signaled Rusty with the walkie-talkie key switch, three fast clicks, to let him know he was finished and leaving. He donned his ski mask and gloves again and climbed out of the window, this time feet first. Then reached in to retrieve the bag. Finally, closed the window.

He didn't risk leaving by the driveway, in case the couple returned. Instead, he circled through the woods and back to the truck, as quickly as the heavy bag allowed.

The pickup was still idling as he approached. When he entered, its interior was deliciously warm and the heater had kept the windshield clear of frost. Rusty put the vehicle in gear and moved off.

"So how did it go?"

Boggs could barely keep his teeth from chattering when he answered.

"The first person to enter will have his head blown right off and turned into shredded wheat." He paused to yank off the ski mask, wincing as the cloth dragged across his cheek. His hand throbbed where the cat had bitten it.

"Personally, I hope it's the bitch. I want the guy to survive and suffer."

NINE

"He reminds you of your father, doesn't he?"

She saw his hands tighten on the steering wheel. He kept his eyes on the road. After a few beats, he answered: "A little, I guess."

"I'd guess more than a little."

She remained quiet a moment, studying his face as he drove through Endeavor, then took East Hickory Road when it branched off to the left.

"You miss him a lot, don't you, Dylan." A statement.

He nodded almost imperceptibly.

"A lot."

She put her hand on his thigh. "I'm sorry. I don't mean to pry."

A smile flickered on his face. "Sure you do. But it's okay…They don't really look at all alike. Their styles are different, too…Were. I mean…"

She gave his thigh a squeeze. "I know what you mean."

"Both entrepreneurs," he continued. "Both self-contained and independent. Both proud and confident. They would have liked each other. In fact, I told him that—sort of." He paused, then added: "I was watching him looking at his daughter. And how he was with his wife and grandchildren. Big Mike was a lot like that, too. A great husband." He paused again—longer. "And a great father."

She smiled. She adored him for his own strength and confidence and independence. But she found herself loving him more deeply at moments like these, when she sensed his deepest passions and private vulnerabilities.

"I'm sure he was enormously proud of you, Dylan," she said softly.

His face appeared to tighten again, as did his hands on the wheel. He didn't say anything.

After a moment, he slowed the car and turned up their driveway. The headlights bounced and flashed off patches of ice, then off the windows of the Honda and the cabin.

As always, he pulled up near the structure, then backed around parallel to the Honda, facing outward.

"We don't have much left in there," he said, shutting off the ignition. "If I pack it in here now, we can head out first thing in the morning."

She ran her hand along his thigh. "I don't know. Maybe we can, um, sleep in tomorrow morning, and leave for D.C. around noon."

He grinned at her. "Maybe we can do that."

He got out, came around as always to open her door for her and help her out. She tilted her face up to meet his kiss. His lips felt hot in the cold air.

He handed her the keys. "You go on ahead. I'll root around in the back here and bring in a bottle of wine and an opener."

She found herself smiling and humming to herself as she crunched over the frozen soil to the porch. The stairs creaked underfoot, and she stopped outside the screen door to fumble for the keys. She turned and held them up in the weak light, flipping through them to find the right ones—one for each lock. Finally did.

She turned and was about to open the screen door when he called out to her.

"Oh, and don't forget to check the tell-tales."

"I *did* almost forget." She opened the screen door and bent to look for the twigs. Found them undisturbed.

"They're fine," she shouted back. She turned and put the bottom key in the lock. Turned it open. Fumbled around for the other key.

He said something else, and she didn't quite hear it. She stopped and turned. "What?"

He stood up from behind the open rear door. "I said: Do you think our cat will need me to bring in some extra food tonight?"

"No," she answered. "*We* might starve in the morning, but we have more than enough food for Luna!"

She turned and bent to put the key in the deadbolt lock.

"Mrrroww."

She stopped, frowning. For an instant, it seemed that the sound had come from *this* side of the door.

"I'm coming, Luna!" She scraped around for the keyhole. "Just a minute!"

"Maaowwww!"

It startled her. It was *definitely* from somewhere behind her. She straightened and turned.

Luna was huddled on the bottom step, face turned up to her. *"Meooowww!"*

She was stunned.

"*Luna!* What are you doing out here?" She walked over to the steps and crouched down to her.

"What did you say?" Dylan called out.

"Dylan, you won't believe this!" she said, picking up the cat. "Luna is *outside!*"

"What?" He set down the wine bottle in his hand on the seat and came trotting over. Then stopped and stared in disbelief. "What the hell?"

"She's *shivering*, the poor little thing! She must be half frozen!"

Dylan continued to stare. Then looked past her, toward the cabin.

"God knows how long she's been out here, Dylan," she said. "Luna, how in the world did you get outside? We've got to get you inside and warmed up."

She turned back toward the stairs.

His big hand on her shoulder stopped her.

"How *did* she get outside?" he said quietly.

She turned to him. His eyes were still staring past her, at the dark front window of the cabin.

"This makes no sense," he said softly. "The cabin is completely air tight. No openings anywhere. I make sure of that, to keep animals out. And I checked all the windows before we left. As I always do. There's no way she could have gotten out."

He paused, and she saw something change in his eyes.

"Not without help," he added.

The sudden chill in his voice matched the night air. It sent a small tremor through her.

"Move back to the car," he commanded, smoothly opening his overcoat and jacket with his left hand. In an instant the Sig appeared in his right.

They retreated quickly toward the Camry. He walked backward, left hand on her shoulder, the pistol in his right, his cold eyes never leaving the cabin door. When they reached the car, he guided her around to the driver's side and opened the door.

"Get in, put Luna on the back seat, and get the car running. Then lower the window so we can continue to talk," he said, still watching the cabin. She did. "Now reach into the glove compartment and hand me the flashlight…Okay, fetch the Beretta from under the driver's seat. That one's for you."

"Dylan, what are we doing?"

"I have to check out the cabin. I think the odds of anyone still being in there are small. But just in case, you keep the pistol and your cell phone in your lap. Don't call me; that's a distraction. I'll call *you* once I'm inside and have cleared the place. But if things go sideways—"

"Dylan!"

"—you get the hell out of here, fast. You do *not* wait for me, and you do *not* come inside. No matter what. Remember, we've discussed these kinds of scenarios before. I have to focus, and the last thing I need is the distraction of worrying about where you are. Which could get us both killed. Got that? *No matter what.*"

She knew that switch had flipped on inside of him again. His eyes gazed hard and unblinking into the distance. She swallowed. "I understand."

"Okay. Good. This could take a few minutes." He sent the briefest smile her way, then continued to watch the dwelling.

"Don't worry, Annie Woods. I'm good at this sort of thing, you know." He reached inside with his left hand and touched her cheek. Before she could seize his hand, he withdrew it and moved away.

Old training and long-time experience kicked in. Hunter knew that the first thing he had to do was check the exterior perimeter. He was pretty sure that if anyone were armed in the woods, they probably would have been attacked already. Still...

He moved forward in a slight crouch, the left side of his body angled forward. He held the flashlight in his left hand, underneath and parallel to the barrel of the Sig, that forearm supporting and steadying his gun hand. He started around the building counterclockwise, scanning the ground ahead and the trees above and beside him with the beam of the light. He suddenly realized that he was automatically, absurdly looking for trip wires for IEDs. *Old habits die hard, but they let you die old.*

He reached the window on the right side of the cabin, ducked beneath it without looking inside, then continued around to the back—

—and found the smashed window pane.

Well, then. You're *not* crazy.

Rather than stop, he made his way around the rest of the structure, checking out the surrounding trees. Nothing.

He returned to the broken window. What was he up against? Odds were high that it was a burglar—probably some druggie looking for cash or valuables. Though that didn't square with the fact that the packed Honda sat unmolested. Who else, then? The odds that he could have been tracked down by some old enemy were vanishingly small. He'd covered his tracks far too well.

He gave it up. He would know soon enough. Anyone inside surely was aware of their presence now, so the element of surprise was gone. If he tried to make entry through the front door, he'd be a sitting duck for any armed intruder waiting up in the loft or in the bathroom. Same thing if he tried to go in by the side window, where he'd have to do what was done here: break a pane of glass to unlock it, then be completely exposed while he climbed in.

This window was the least-bad option. It was directly beneath the loft and tucked back in a broad corner alcove, formed by the interior wall of the cabin on one side, and a closet housing the water heater on the other. He'd have some protection from three sides and above as he entered; any assailant would have to confront him directly from the front.

He decided to use the flashlight first to try to draw the fire of anyone inside. Standing to the right side of the window, his body protected behind the thick log wall, he reached out and aimed the beam through the window, flashing it around the interior of the cabin, listening hard for any sounds of movement.

After a full minute, he drew no fire and heard no sound.

Okay. Moment of truth.

Aiming the flashlight through the broken pane, he took a quick peek at the interior before ducking back. The quick glance revealed only the boxes and bags on the middle of the cabin floor. He did this a couple more times, aiming the beam at different positions around the room. He could only see part of the bathroom.

He risked a longer look. Crouching beneath the window, he raised his head just high enough to see inside while he directed the beam methodically around the room. He could see most of it, and it looked just as he had left it. The circle of light tracked across the floor and walls and ceiling, across the front door, then across the far wall to…

He jerked the bright circle back to the front door. To something silvery just above the door. It was hard to make out at this distance…Then the beam caught a bright vertical streak extending from the shiny object down to…

"Oh Jesus," he whispered aloud.

…He stood in the alley in Kandahar, pressed tight against the wall next to the warehouse door, and his hand reached out to the cold metal knob, then slowly turned it and pulled the creaking door open, ever so gingerly, and then there was the flash of a thousand suns…

His hand began to shake, making the circle of light wobble.

Annie…Annie almost walked through that door…

A blinding, murderous rage roiled up in him.

Just as suddenly, as inexplicably, the rage died. The shaking stopped. Everything turned cold again. Icy cold. He felt his return to his home in the cold, high place. Where he looked down at himself, detached. Aware of little things…

The faint aroma of wood smoke.

The rustling of nearby leaves in the frigid breeze.

The rough, brittle bark of the log wall scraping against his knees.

And from his cold, high home, he looked down at himself and knew what he had to do.

TEN

Ten endless, agonizing minutes while she stared at the cabin door...stared, barely blinking or daring to breathe, worried sick about what was going on inside, waiting for something to happen, dreading that something would happen, hoping this was all some silly mistake or paranoia...stared, willing him to emerge from that door unharmed and to trot over to her and lean down and flash that crooked smile and say, "Everything's fine, Annie Woods."

Luna had come to sit in her lap, seeking and giving a small measure of warmth and comfort. She was purring now, looking up at her, her eyes glittering faintly in the near-dark.

"Oh Luna," she murmured, stroking the cat. "Oh Luna...Please let there be some simple, stupid explanation for this...I'm just glad you didn't wander off. You wouldn't have stood—"

Lights came on inside the cabin.

She caught her breath.

Five seconds later, her cell chirped. She snatched it up from the passenger seat.

Saw that it was him.

"Dylan!"

"It's okay, sweetheart. I'm fine, I'm fine. Relax. There's no one here…But there was. I have to be in here for a few more minutes to do…some tidying up."

"I was so worried! I'll be right in to help—"

"*No!*"

She flinched, shocked.

"I'm sorry," he said immediately, his voice normal. "I didn't mean to yell. It's just that whoever was here left something behind. I have to attend to it before I come outside. No, don't ask me to explain right now. Just give me a few moments, love. Okay?"

She was bewildered. But she trusted him. "Okay. I'll wait here."

"Good. Stay alert, all right? Keep an eye out, in case our visitors return."

"I will…I love you, Dylan."

"Love you too."

Ten minutes later he emerged from the house. He was carrying a paper shopping bag.

Heart racing, she jumped out of the car and ran to him. He held the bag away from her and gathered her in with one arm and hugged her tight.

"Oh, Dylan, I was so scared!"

"Me too," he said, his voice unnaturally calm.

She looked up at his face. "What happened? What's wrong?"

He looked at her without expression. "Let's sit in the car. I'll explain there."

Inside, she picked up Luna from the passenger seat and held her. Dylan got in behind the wheel. He held the bag closed in his lap and turned to her. His face looked just as it had at the diner, when he stood to confront the gang. He reached out and took her hand. He stroked the back of it gently with his thumb.

"Annie, I want you to try to remain calm, okay?" he began.

"Okay."

"Somebody tried to kill us tonight."

"*What?*"

"I'm afraid so." He looked down at the bag. "They left a bomb in the cabin."

"That's a *bomb* you're holding?"

"Don't worry, it's harmless. I disarmed it. A simple pipe bomb. No transmitter or fancy detonator—just an electrical switch and battery. I learned about these things during my training at Harvey Point, and when I traveled with EOD guys over in Sand Land. They showed me how to disarm far more complicated IEDs."

"But *why?*"

"I don't know why. Not yet."

"How did they—?"

"As for the how…" He paused. "They rigged this to go off when we opened the door."

She felt numb. Her brain couldn't process it. Or the calm manner of his saying it.

"I see that this thing is making you nervous. Here, let me put it on the floor behind us…There. All right. We can only speculate about the 'why.' But if I had to bet, I—"

"Dylan…I was about one second from opening that door."

A pause.

"I know."

"I'd already opened the lower lock, and—"

"I know," he repeated, his voice tight.

"—and I was just *one second* from turning the dead bolt when I heard Luna meow behind me."

"Yes." It was a whisper. "I know. I know." He was holding her hand too tightly; the other hand rubbed the cat's head. "Annie. I know…God, Annie—I almost lost you again!"

She placed the cat gently down on the floor. He fell into her and she pulled him close.

He held her so tightly that she could barely breathe.

She stood at the open door of the cabin, scanning the area outside, Beretta in hand. Behind her, he packed the last of their items.

"So you think it's probably that gang from the diner, then," she said. "But how could they find us?"

"They're the most likely suspects. As for how they found us, who knows?" He straightened from a box on the floor. "Sorry we can't stay another night, love. But whether it's those people or somebody else, obviously it's no longer safe here." He looked around. "I'm going to miss the place. But until I figure out who's responsible and take care of it, we'll have to stay away from here."

"What do you mean, 'take care of it'?"

He bent to continue packing.

She approached and stood over him.

"What do you mean?"

He didn't look up. "I mean I'm going to find out who did this, and take care of it."

"No! Dylan—you can't go there again."

She knew that he understood. He got up and went over to the deer antlers hanging on the wall beside the door. She marched after him, her boots thumping across the bare planks.

"Dylan, you listen to me. You can't do that."

He lifted the mounted antlers off their hook on the wall. "I can't do what?" He turned and placed the antlers gently atop a cardboard box, then headed for their bathroom.

"You can't run around killing people!"

He wheeled to face her. His eyes were blazing.

"Tell that to the people who nearly blew you to pieces tonight!" he thundered. "Has it sunk in to you yet what almost happened here? Do you get the fact that our lives were spared tonight only by a *cat?* I unscrewed the cap on that pipe bomb, Annie. It was filled with nails. You said it: You were one second away from being torn to bits."

She stared at him, not knowing what to say.

"And if I had gone in first, it would have been *me.* Decapitated and ripped to pieces, right before your eyes—if the blast didn't get you, too."

"I know! I know. I get that. But this is attempted murder. That's a felony, so we can report it and let—" She stopped.

He nodded. "That's right. You see why that's impossible. 'Brad Flynn' reporting a bomb planted in 'his' cabin? My whole cover here would unravel. And from there, probably the rest of my life as Dylan Hunter. My life with *you.*"

His expression softened, as did his voice.

"You see why we can't go to the cops. Which is why I have to deal with this myself."

"I can see why we can't go to the cops," she said slowly. "But that doesn't mean you have to go after them."

"What are you talking about? Are you suggesting that I just let these sons of bitches get away with this?"

She knew she had to be careful now. She reached out and took his hands. Entwined her fingers through his.

"Darling. Listen to me. You know how I've been since…since Christmas." She hesitated, then pushed on. "You know the trouble I'm having, dealing with that. With what we went through. You know how hard it's been. I can't have any more of that in my life. The thought of you involved in that kind of violence. I just can't. I can't be waiting at home, knowing that you're out somewhere risking your life, dealing with—" She shook her head. "With the kind of people that would do things like this."

"But that's exactly my point! You're asking me to allow animals like these to remain on the loose?"

"Listen to me. Listen to me, Dylan. Yes, we came close to dying tonight. But we didn't. We're alive, and we're lucky that we're alive. Because we still have a future. I want a future for us. A future for us, Dylan. So yes, I'm asking—I'm *pleading* with you: Please let this go. For *us*. Because…because if you don't, I know I won't be able to handle it. And…and I know I won't be able to stay with you."

She saw in his eyes the battle being waged between the combatants of indignation, pain, and love. She felt his fingers squeezing hers, so hard that they hurt her. But she didn't dare say anything, didn't dare take her eyes away from his. She knew that their future rested in the outcome of the battle in his eyes. And she knew that he knew it, too.

She felt his fingers slowly relax. Watched the storm of conflict in his eyes slowly clear. Watched the indignation slowly fade—and the love remain. The love, touched only by a residual hint of the pain.

"I'll never forgive myself if whoever did this ever harms another soul," he said, his voice low. Then he raised her hand to his lips and kissed it. "But I'll never forgive myself if I do anything to hurt you. Or to lose you, Annie Woods."

She felt her chin trembling. She tried and failed to stop the flow of tears as he took her into his arms.

After a while he kissed her.

"You'd better get back over there and keep an eye on the perimeter," he said. "I think there are just a few things left in the bathroom. And I have to cover that broken window to keep the critters and snow out. After that, we'll be on our way and find a motel somewhere down the road."

"Okay, but hurry up. Luna must be freezing again in the car."

She returned to her station at the door.

"Hell-o," he said almost immediately.

She turned. He was standing at the entrance to the bathroom with a white towel in his hands. He opened and spread it. She saw red stains on it.

"This was on the floor," he explained. "I think one of our visitors cut himself. Probably on the window glass when he came in." He looked at the towel for a moment, then back at her. A slow smile grew on his lips. "Now we have the perp's DNA sample. I seem to recall that you're familiar with DNA samples—aren't you, Annie Woods?"

She laughed. "Yes, I guess I do know a little about those. So maybe that will help the cops—" She caught herself again. "Right, we can't go to the police. But I bet Grant can use his law enforcement contacts to do that for us."

"That's exactly what I'm thinking. It's a long shot that they'd have any record of this guy—I'm assuming it's a man, not a woman. But still, this might come in handy someday." He considered it for a moment. "You know, I've had a funny feeling about the leader of that gang. He's a very strange dude. But now because he was arrested, we'll be able to find out his last name. Wouldn't it be interesting if this DNA sample matched up with his?"

"You mean that 'Zak' guy."

"Yes," Dylan said. "That 'Zak' guy."

PART II

"The dead cannot cry out for justice. It is a duty of the living to do so for them."

— Lois McMaster Bujold

ELEVEN

Avery Trammel stood at the curving gray-tinted window and looked down upon the city of Washington.

Jaded as he was, it still reaffirmed his sense of personal power to see the city from a commanding height. And here—from the thirty-first floor of this glass-walled office tower on the bank of the Potomac in Arlington—one sweeping glance could take in, simultaneously, all the iconic structures that symbolized American government.

They were laid out in the approximate shape of the Christians' cross. At its head, nearest him on the opposite river bank, the stately Lincoln Memorial. The Jefferson Memorial at the right; the White House at the left; the Capitol dome gleaming in the far distance, representing the foot of the cross. And at the center, at its heart, the Washington Monument, a defiant spear against the gray winter sky.

Even in his sixties, Trammel's eyes were sharp as those of a bird of prey: They could discern mid-week tourists moving like tiny colored bugs at the base of the obelisk that this country had erected to honor its founder and father.

Turning slightly to his right, those sharp eyes settled on the Pentagon.

The sight of it transported him back to that night in the fall of 1971, when he sat in grim silence with two others in a dark, roach-infested apartment in Takoma Park, just a few miles northeast of here…sat there, waiting for the phone call that never came. The phone call was to signal them that they were cleared to begin their phase of yet another assault on the Pentagon. Out in their driveway sat the VW Beetle that would transport the bombs, soon to be delivered to them by the cell in New York.

But hours earlier, a paid FBI informant betrayed the cell. And when the call didn't come at the prearranged hour, the trio was forced to scatter back into the underground.

Trammel still felt a tiny pang of anger, rising across the span of almost forty years…

His reverie was interrupted by voices behind him. He turned to see a group entering the sleek, modern conference room. At the center of the pack, turning to his companions like the hub of a wheel, strode Ashton Conn.

Their eyes met, and they both nodded. But as a symbol of their respective power in this city, he remained at the window, waiting for the United States senator to come to him.

"Avery!" the man sang out, angling past the conference table, his right hand outthrust. "It's been so long!"

He endured the politician's pumping handshake and too-familiar grip on his shoulder. Conn's smile was broad, like his face and his waist. Though he was in his mid-forties, not a single strand of gray intruded upon the bronze sweep of his thick, straight hair—a tribute to the meticulous craftsmanship of the Capitol's stylists. But drink and worse had transformed his face, once lean and tanned and handsome, into something fleshy and ruddy and dissolute. Folds of puffy flesh hid the color of his eyes behind narrow slits; only memory informed Trammel that they were an intense blue.

Still, he thought, Conn looks like he belongs in this town of power and prestige—standing here flashing the perfect teeth, the impressive Cartier Santos watch, the obligatory oval Harvard Law School ring, and the well-tailored Armani suit at least half as expensive as his own. He wondered: Does Conn belong *in* this town or *to* it?

"Ashton, how is Emmalee?" he asked.

"Great, just great. And Julia?"

"Still fielding the occasional screenplay, looking for the right role. Sadly, good ones seldom come along anymore for women over fifty."

"Fifty? Good God, Avery! She looks a decade younger...Oh, I see Damon over there looking impatient to get underway. We had better grab seats." He lowered his voice. "Let's chat a moment after the meeting, shall we?"

They joined the others taking positions in the black, soft-leather swivel chairs surrounding the cherry conference table. A slick green folder embossed in gold with the company logo was centered on the table before each of them. Trammel recognized most of the others, but before they could launch into their own greetings, the man at the head of the table spoke.

"I wish to thank all of you for attending this special meeting at our request," he began. "For those of you who don't know, I'm your host, Damon Sloan, CEO of CarboNot Industries." Sloan was very tall and bony, with a long, horse-like face. His suit, hair, and eyes were all the color of cold steel.

"I know some of you have come from distances, and I appreciate the courtesy of your presence on such short notice. Let's begin by going around the table and introducing ourselves." He took his own seat and nodded to the portly, balding man seated on his left.

"Hal Judd, president, Zephyr Energy."

"Robin Manes, vice-president, GreenSmart Investments." She was a too-thin, too-tanned woman who dressed too young.

"Gavin Lockwood, executive director, Nature Legal Advocacy," said a tall, boyish-looking man in his fifties with premature white hair and wire-rimmed glasses.

A burly, beetle-browed man was next. "Chip Crane, deputy administrator, EPA."

"Lucas Carver, executive director, Vox Populi Communications." The fiftyish, gray-haired man turned to Trammel and smiled. The smile didn't reach his pale blue eyes, but then again, his smiles never did. Trammel nodded slightly in acknowledgment. They had worked together before, many times, and of all the people at this table, they understood each other best and had the most in common. They even had friendly nicknames for each other: Carver called him "Geppetto," while he referred to Carver as "Maestro."

"Avery Trammel, private investor."

"Ashton Conn, United States senator from Pennyslvania."

"Thank you so much for attending, Senator," Sloan interjected, then nodded at the bald, bespectacled man seated beside Conn.

"Stu Kaplan. I'm the senator's chief of staff." Behind rimless glasses Kaplan had eyes that reminded Trammel of a barracuda he'd once caught in Florida.

"Thank you, all. I know you are busy people, so I aim to keep this meeting brief. Let me get right to the point. Before each of you is a copy of the material I sent you last Thursday. I am sure that by now you are familiar with the contents. The report outlines the difficult situation in which CarboNot now finds itself. For those among you who are investors"—his eyes moved around the room, discreetly failing to pause on anyone in particular—"it delivers unsettling financial news. For those of you in the environmental community or on the Hill, this same news may cause political problems. Our purpose today is to brainstorm informally about how we move forward in the light of these circumstances. Would anyone wish to offer preliminary comments?"

Hal Judd leaned forward. "As I understand it, CarboNot has blown through the entire capital put up by the investors *and* the loan guarantees from the Energy Department—is that correct?"

Sloan's chilly expression became even frostier. "'Blown through' suggests irresponsibility. I can assure all of you that such is *not* the case. The situation is simple: European governments have canceled almost all their contracts for CarboNot's wind-farm construction projects. They claim that their existing green energy programs are failing to prove cost-effective. Because of the recession, they have cut back on subsidies to alternative energy projects and are reverting to importing cheaper fossil fuels. And that, in turn, has left CarboNot in an unexpected cash-flow crisis."

"Which means that *my* company, which produces your wind turbines, hasn't gotten paid lately," Judd continued. "I wonder if you understand what kind of position this puts me in, Damon."

Before Sloan could respond, Robin Manes jumped in.

"Damon, I appreciate your company's circumstances, but this has put GreenSmart in a difficult position, too. We've been bullish on CarboNot from the outset, and we've steered tens of millions in private investment your way." She paused; her tongue darted across her lips. "In fact, some of our firm's partners, myself included, have substantial positions in CarboNot. We pride ourselves on putting our money where our principles are. But under these circumstances, how can we continue to recommend CarboNot to our investors? And if *our* firm pulls back, the bottom could fall out of your stock price. That would leave a lot of our clients, including some seated at this table, losing substantial sums. Very substantial sums." She licked her lips again, tapping the folder. "But now that we have *this* information, my partners and I can't exactly pull back from our *own* portfolio positions without risking an 'insider trading' investigation down the road. So we're stuck."

As she spoke, Trammel watched the faces of the others. Few were public about their investments; in this town, it was best to keep such information close to the vest. But he noticed that Gavin Lockwood looked at his hands and fidgeted, while Ashton Conn maintained a stiff, blank expression. He wondered how much they had sunk personally into CarboNot. He had put in plenty himself—though with his billions, he could afford to lose mere millions without great worry. The potential failure of CarboNot troubled him for other reasons, however.

Sloan said, "In fairness, Robin, this problem is not unique to our company. Most domestic alternative-energy companies are in trouble, too—mainly because of the fracking boom."

"That is the main problem, right there," Conn interjected, slapping his hand down on the table top. "All that cheap natural gas is sucking the wind right out of those turbines of yours, Damon." He turned to the man from the EPA. "Chip, what are your people doing about that? Could you give us an update?"

"Sure," he replied, rocking back in his chair. "We've been doing a lot—much of it behind the scenes. As you know, we've been concentrating our efforts in your state, up in the Allegheny National Forest. It sits right atop the Marcellus Shale Formation, which crosses several states and contains some of the biggest natural gas reserves in the nation. So, we figure that if we can win some big test cases up there, we have the potential to shut down the entire goddamned fracking industry." He looked around, saw their expressions. "No, I mean it." He leaned forward again, lowering his voice. "I'm going to assume that what I'm about to say stays off-the-record, right?" He paused. "Okay, good."

He began ticking off the points on his fingers.

"*One:* We got in touch with people over at the Interior Department to go around the area looking for Endangered Species issues. That worked some years back, at least for a while, against the lumber industry up there. We found this endangered species, the Indiana bat, and that completely shut down logging for six months. But logging a large expanse of forest is one thing. It's harder to argue that they're endangering a species when they're drilling on small pads of just a few acres. So we don't think that's going to get us very far.

"*Two*—and *this* stays inside the room, okay? How should I put this? Let me just say we've found out that some of the fracking firms up there—one in particular, Adair Energy—have been scheduled for IRS audits."

Conn stirred in his seat. "Wait—should I be hearing this? I assume that must have happened only in the course of routine IRS audit practices. Right, Chip?" He stared pointedly at Crane.

Crane got it. "Oh, sure! You may certainly assume that, Senator. The IRS contacted us only to see if we had information about Adair that might help their investigation."

For a moment, nobody spoke. Then Crane continued.

"Okay, *three:* EPA has been responsive to lawsuits from the environmental community on pollution concerns in the Forest. Gavin, maybe you want to elaborate."

"Certainly," Lockwood responded. "Nature Legal Advocacy is preeminent among nonprofits that mount aggressive legal challenges over environmental threats. One of our biggest litigation efforts has been to stop all fracking in the...to stop all fracking *abuses* throughout the natural gas industry."

He leaned in, lowering his voice a bit, almost conspiratorially.

"A few months ago, an anonymous whistleblower working inside Adair Energy approached us, claiming that he had proof that their fracking practices were causing leaks of dangerous toxic chemicals and cancer-causing radon into area water supplies. He supplied NLA with samples, which we analyzed, and which confirmed his claims. Two weeks ago—

as everybody with a TV or newspaper knows—we issued a report to the national media with our findings. Our study concluded that Adair's practices were standard throughout the natural gas industry—and therefore that fracking *per se* constitutes an intolerable risk to public health...I want to thank Lucas Carver here, whom we hired to run our big media effort. Once again, Vox Populi Communications did a fantastic job in getting the word out for us."

Carver's lips pressed into another empty smile. "It's what we do—engaging our hundreds of sympathetic media contacts to coordinate publicity on behalf of important social issues. In this case, we got news of the NLA fracking study carried simultaneously on all the major networks, the front pages of the ten top-circulation newspapers, and in two women's magazines."

He turned to Trammel. "A lot of the credit must go to Avery's wife, actress Julia Haight. We enlisted Julia early on as our national spokesperson against fracking. She opened a lot of doors for us in the media and on Capitol Hill. Thanks for arranging that for us, Avery."

Murmurs of appreciation arose around the table; Trammel acknowledged them with a slight smile and nod.

Carver went on. "Our carefully orchestrated media campaign ignited a public uproar against fracking that generated tens of thousands of protest calls and letters to Congress, and also—correct me if I'm wrong, Gavin—over $750,000 in new contributions to your organization, right?"

"That's true. And, timed to follow on the heels of our report, we then sued EPA to issue an emergency moratorium to halt all fracking, pending a new, extended investigation into the safety of the process. From there, we hope—"

Crane interrupted. "Gavin and Lucas contacted EPA about three months ago, explaining to us exactly what they were planning to do. Of course, we welcomed their lawsuit."

Judd blinked. "Why would you want that?"

Crane smiled. "Hal, we cooperate all the time with NLA and other environmental groups in their lawsuits against the Agency. Responding to lawsuits speeds things along for us. Instead of having to go through the tedious regulatory process, with hearings and waiting periods before we can impose orders and rules, we just go ahead and issue injunctions against companies and industries in response to the suits." He winked at Gavin. "And of course, NLA also sues us to recover all their court costs, too, so they aren't out a nickel for their litigation. It all winds up being funded by the taxpayers. In fact, you guys actually *make* a lot of money off Uncle Sam, don't you, Gavin?"

Lockwood looked uncomfortable. "That's not really the point, Chip. Our aim is to halt anti-environmental activity as expeditiously as possible."

Sloan broke in. "Your anti-fracking publicity campaign is all well and good, and we deeply appreciate it. But what's the status of that lawsuit, Chip? Why hasn't EPA gotten an anti-fracking moratorium from a judge yet?"

"We tried," Crane answered, "but Adair went to court and got a stay of the moratorium, till NLA's study could be checked out at an upcoming meeting of an EPA Science Advisory Board panel."

Lockwood jumped in to explain. "Damon, the EPA is compelled by law to take into consideration the findings of SAB panels. The problem is that those panels are often stacked with outside scientists who consult for *industries*, and have an ax to grind."

Judd raised a hand. "Wait a minute, Gavin. Scientists have to make a living, too, right? Not all of them can work for the government. I've hired and relied on my share of them, and they seem like straight shooters. So what makes *their* research dishonest and tainted if it's funded by an industry, but *your* group's research valid if it's funded by political activists? Don't *your* researchers also have axes to grind?"

Lockwood's face grew red, but Sloan raised a hand.

"Look, let's not get into a pissing match over whose research is good, and whose isn't. Frankly, I don't care. I just want to know where the moratorium stands. How do our prospects look before that EPA panel?"

Crane sighed. "Well, we just hit a new snag." He rooted through the briefcase at his feet. "Adair hired his own toxicologist. That guy just reviewed the chemical samples that Gavin's group provided to EPA—the samples they used as the basis of their report." He straightened, scanning a sheet of paper. Then looked at Lockwood. "Gavin, according to this letter from Adair, their toxicologist claims your chemical samples are totally bogus. Fake."

"*What?*"

Crane waved the letter. "Adair says his guy has geological and chemical-signature proof that your samples could not possibly have come from any Adair fracking site. In fact, he speculates that somebody—maybe your whistleblower—deliberately planted them. And now Adair plans to submit his own toxicologist's report to the SAB."

In the stunned silence, Crane went on, his voice low. "Look, I don't know who is correct about those samples,

Gavin. I just hope that your researchers got it right. Because if they didn't..." His voice trailed off.

"If they didn't," Trammel said slowly, looking from Lockwood to Carver, "then your big scare campaign against fracking is going to backfire. There even may be a criminal investigation." He saw Lockwood's eyes widen, then turned to Sloan. "If fracking is exonerated as a safe form of cheap energy, then all our efforts to stop it will fail—"

"—and so will our efforts to save CarboNot," said Ashton Conn. He was staring off into space, out past the floor-to-ceiling expanse of glass, toward Washington and its monuments. "Wind power can't compete with natural gas. Not at current prices."

They fell silent for an awkward moment.

"I've poured all I have into my business," said Judd, "If CarboNot goes under, I don't get paid. And I lose everything."

"A lot of people will lose everything," Trammel said, scanning their faces.

"So, what can we do?" Robin Manes asked, her voice on the edge of shrill.

"The first thing," said Stu Kaplan, who had remained silent until this moment, "is that we have to find out who their toxicologist is, then go after him." He saw their looks. "I mean, we have to discredit him, in advance. Point out that he's a hired tool of industry, just another paid mouthpiece."

"'Poison the well'—so to speak," Judd said, a cynical look on his face.

Kaplan stared at him coldly. "To your point: Okay, so maybe every scientist has an ax to grind—Adair's guy, Gavin's people. But if that's the case, then it's all subjective, anyway.

Then it comes down to a matter of public credibility. Who are people going to believe? It's one industry guy's opinion against all the other environmental experts. *Our* experts."

Kaplan removed his glasses, held them up to look at the lenses.

"Look, I've been a Hill rat for all of my adult life. Since I was a congressional intern. And I've learned that there's only one way you win these things. You win by being preemptive. You have to strike first." He began to polish his glasses with his tie. "We have to create a *narrative* about Adair's guy—a toxic one, so that by the time he submits his findings, the public won't believe a word he says."

"But what if the SAB scientists agree with him?" Trammel asked.

"Whatever we do," said Sloan, "we'd better do it before he submits that report."

Before adjourning, Sloan proposed that they schedule a follow-up conference call among select members of the group, to settle on an action plan.

Trammel rose and joined the others as they filed from the conference room. They were quiet; their steps echoed off the polished gray marble floor as they passed the broad-leafed potted plants and abstract wall hangings. They reached the private elevator, reserved for tenants on the top floors.

He felt a hand on his arm.

"Do you have a minute?" Ashton Conn's earlier bravado was gone. He looked deflated and worried.

"Why don't we ride down together?"

They let the others take the first elevator. When its doors closed, Trammel pressed the button and they waited.

"Do you have some idea about how to handle this situation, Ash?"

"Not really. Not yet…Actually, the reason I wanted to talk to you was about—you know. My candidacy."

Trammel smiled. "Ah. So you've decided to go for the big one, have you?"

Conn shrugged. "A lot of people have been encouraging me. And I was wondering…about your own commitments at this point."

"You mean, do I intend to back Carl Spencer."

Conn grinned sheepishly. "Something like that. If not, I hope I might count on you to add your name to my exploratory committee."

Trammel paused, savoring his power to make the senator wait.

"Carl Spencer is popular in establishment circles," he said slowly. "Yet I always wonder about his true commitments. His convictions. He's never struck me as one to let his nominal principles get in the way of crude self-aggrandizement."

The elevator door opened and they stepped in. It was a small glass cage that clung to the outside southern wall of the building. In the far distance, he once again spotted the Pentagon.

He turned to search Conn's face, peered into the thin slits that hid his eyes, sought some reassuring reference point deep within the man.

"You began your political career in the nonprofit world, Ash. You started out as a crusader for environmental issues. And you wrote the best book on environmentalism since that of your mentor, Al Gore—in many respects, a better book."

"Why, thank you, Avery. That means a great deal, coming from you."

Trammel waved his hand dismissively. "As you know, that kind of intellectual pedigree means a great deal to me. I am a man of ideas. Of principles, if you will. Ash, you have never given me cause to doubt yours…So, yes—at this point, you may count on my support. I shall be happy to add my name to your exploratory committee. And I'll also send off a check to your political action committee."

Ashton Conn flashed his white teeth and extended his hand again. "I cannot tell you how grateful I am for that, Avery. I promise you that I won't betray your trust."

"I am not concerned about any personal betrayal, Ash," he said, releasing the politician's grip and turning to face the city again.

As the elevator descended, he was amused to watch the Pentagon appear to sink into the Potomac. *There are ways other than bombs.*

"Just don't betray our *cause*, Ash," he added.

TWELVE

The doors of their train car slid open at the Dupont Circle Metro stop. He gripped Annie's arm, holding her back, letting all the other passengers depart first. Then they darted out just as the doors closed. He paused with her on the platform as the silver-gray train pulled away and accelerated into the tunnel, drawing a cool column of air in its wake.

Hunter pretended to inspect the list of subway stops posted on a nearby directional post while he surreptitiously watched the departing passengers move on toward the escalator and the exit. When the platform cleared, he said, "Okay. Let's go."

They headed toward the escalators that led to the Metro's south exit onto Dupont Circle, at Connecticut Avenue and 19th Street. The click of her boot heels on the reddish brown tiles echoed off concrete walls that arched overhead, in a honeycomb pattern.

"A bit paranoid, don't you think?" she said.

"You're not paranoid if they really are out to get you."

They took the short escalator to the upper platform, exited through the turnstiles, and stepped onto the longer escalator that would transport them to the street. He kept his eyes on the growing blue oval of light above him and scanned the people descending on the parallel escalator to his left. His long leather coat was unzipped, and he stood so that his right hand rested casually inside it, on his hip—just inches from the concealed holster at the small of his back.

"After everything you've said about this 'Wonk' guy," she said, "you've aroused my curiosity. I can't wait to meet him."

"You may change your mind in a few minutes."

"Seriously, I'm glad he agreed to let me accompany you."

"It took some persuading. He didn't even like the idea of *me* visiting him in his apartment. This will be a first for me, too."

"So, he's a reclusive genius."

"Genius—definitely. Reclusive? I don't think so. Only hyper-secretive."

"Just like you, then. But he could have met us at your office. It's just a short walk down Connecticut."

"For Wonk, there's no such thing as a 'short walk.' You'll understand when you see him. But he told me he has a cold and didn't want to come outside into the chill. That's the only reason he relented and is letting us visit him here."

They emerged from the escalator next to a massive, block-long office building, a twelve-story high-rise in red brick. The aroma of pastries wafted in the air; its source was the building's doughnut shop, right next to the Metro entrance.

"Wonk's favorite cuisine," Hunter said. "Probably why he chose to live here."

Annie laughed. "As the realtors say, 'Location, location, location.' To make a good first impression, let me run in and buy him a couple."

"A couple? You don't know Wonk."

They went in and he ordered a box of a dozen assorted doughnuts. Then they walked a short way down 19th and into the building's entrance.

The floor, walls, decorative planters, and guard desk of the Art Deco lobby gleamed in complementary, tasteful tones of brown and beige marble. While the security guard announced them, Hunter looked at the building directory. The offices were filled with media outlets, healthcare consulting firms, and—ironically, he thought—environmental nonprofits.

During the elevator ride to the eighth floor, he tried a last time to prepare her. "Remember, his personal hygiene is a disaster. You may not even have a place to sit down in there—or want to."

"I consider myself warned."

They left the elevator and walked down the hallway past a number of doors bearing company logos. They found his number and Hunter knocked.

When the door opened, what stood before them was someone the approximate size and shape of a small mountain.

Annie thought the man looked to be in his late thirties. He had tea-colored, curly, unkempt hair, and ruddy cheeks the size of baseballs. In place of a neck, a bag of flesh hung from the stub of his chin and tucked into the open collar of his gray plaid pajama top. The huge pajamas were covered—barely—by a vast gray terrycloth bathrobe, the largest she had ever scene. A large red stain—spaghetti sauce? pizza?—splotched its lapel; it was held shut—almost—by two mismatched cloth bathrobe belts, knotted end-to-end and tied in a small bow that rested on his enormous belly.

The man's dark eyes glinted at her suspiciously from behind black-framed eyeglasses; one temple clung to the rest by white adhesive tape; they balanced on a nose that looked red and irritated.

"Hi, Wonk," Dylan said, smiling. "I want you to meet Annie. Annie Woods, this is Freddie Diffendorfer."

It was the first time she had heard his real name. She could barely tame a laugh into a mere smile. "So very nice to meet you," she said, balancing the doughnut box in one hand and extending the other.

He looked at her palm with horror. "No! I am ill," he said, retreating a few steps back into the room.

"Oh, I forgot," she said, remembering. *Well, at least he's considerate.* "Dylan told me that you were sick."

"Yes I am," he said. "And obviously, I do not wish for anyone to make my condition even *worse.*"

She had to stifle another laugh.

"Obviously," Dylan repeated. She caught his eyes; he was having trouble suppressing his own mirth. "May we come in?"

"You may. However, please forgive the appearance of the apartment." His voice was high-pitched and a touch whiny. "My cleaning lady has been out of town, and I thus have been unable to maintain it properly, due to my illness."

She entered, followed by Dylan. Then stopped in the foyer and gaped.

Small replica Greek sculptures adorned end tables in the living room and niches on bookcases. Several framed Dutch master reproductions hung on the walls. Well-tended broadleaf plants sprouted from large, colorful ceramic planters sited strategically around the room. She couldn't spot a single speck of dirt or errant thread on the thick, dark-burgundy expanse of carpeting beneath their feet.

Their host shuffled like an ungainly walrus into the living room, stopped beside a massive stuffed chair, then turned to them. "Please be seated on the sofa," he said, puffing slightly from the exertion.

Dylan looked at her and spread his hands.

"We got something for you from downstairs," she said, gesturing with the box. "Shall I bring it to the coffee table?"

"Oh, no! Thank you very much, Miss Woods. But I permit absolutely no food in any area of my residence except for the kitchen. Would you please leave it in there, on the table?"

"Certainly. But please call me Annie."

The apartment had an open floor plan and she walked into the kitchen area. The metal fixtures sparkled. Lights reflected from the polished black surfaces of the refrigerator and stove. Not one dish or cup, clean or dirty, marred the granite countertops, kitchen table, or sink. She couldn't see a single crumb, smudge, or fingerprint anywhere. The faint fragrance of lemon was in the air. It was as if this were a model apartment, uninhabited and meant only for show.

She left the doughnut box on the table and returned to the living room. "And what name do you prefer that I call you?"

He looked at Dylan uncertainly, then back to her.

"Dylan has a nickname for me, which is fine, as we are friends. But if you do not mind—until we know each other well—would you please refer to me as 'Frederick'?"

Frederick?

"Of course. Your home is lovely, Frederick. How do you manage to keep it so spotless?"

He frowned. "Spotless?" He gestured toward a box of tissues on the lamp table beside his chair, and then at a small copper wastepaper basket beneath it, half-filled with used tissues. "Look at that. It is a complete *mess*. I hope you do not mind."

She stared at the morbidly obese, disheveled man in the soiled bathrobe, then at his impeccably neat surroundings. "No, I don't mind at all, Frederick."

Hunter waited for Annie to take a place on the sofa, then seated himself before the neat stack of files that Wonk had waiting for him on the coffee table.

"Before we begin, Dylan, allow me to take a precaution first." Wonk picked up what looked like a complicated remote from the lamp table beside him, raised it, and pressed a button. "There. We can speak freely, now."

"Jammer?"

Wonk nodded. "Though I have already conducted my daily sweep for electronic bugs, you cannot be too careful when you are dealing with the federal government."

"Tell me about it," Hunter said, looking Annie's way. She answered with a mock scowl.

Wonk plopped himself down into his oversized club chair, which groaned under its burden. "I keep the jammer down the hall in my office. It is short range—only a fifty-foot effective radius, but sufficient to block nearby electronic surveillance devices. I do not use it for extended periods, however. Interrupting cell communications in adjacent rooms might draw the attention of two 'Other Government Agencies' that maintain front-company offices in this building."

"Really." Annie sat forward. "How would you know about such agencies and their surveillance capabilities?"

Wonk laced his pudgy fingers across the massive arc of his belly. "Internet and communications surveillance happen to be my chief areas of expertise, Annie. In fact, those two entities engage my services regularly, as an outside contractor. Several years ago, for our mutual convenience, one of them— located only an elevator ride away—made a special arrangement with the building management so that I could maintain my private residence here, in what otherwise is a strictly commercial office building."

"Good for you, Wonk," Hunter said. *Maybe those affiliations will prove useful to us in the future.* "I gather you were able to find out some things for me about WildJustice and CarboNot?"

"Indeed. In addition to the usual newspaper and magazine articles, I discovered some investigatory material in federal law enforcement files. The top folder in the stack is about WildJustice. The thick one beneath it contains material relevant to its founder and leader, Zachariah Boggs. The rest are about CarboNot."

"Let's talk about him first," Hunter said, opening the second file. "Can you give me a summary?"

A slight, cherubic smile formed. He closed his eyes and began to recite from memory.

"Zachariah Joseph Boggs, Ph.D. Age 40. Born May 1, 1968, near Asheville, North Carolina. The only child of devout fundamentalist Baptist parents." Wonk opened his eyes. "I assume that may explain his somewhat 'biblical' name. Hence, his antipathy to it. Today, he prefers to be called Zachary, and to a few intimates, Zak." He closed his eyes again. "His parents were not highly educated. But Boggs universally was regarded as intellectually gifted. He also was described, even at an early age, as arrogant, brash, narcissistic, and cruelly indifferent to the feelings of others. During his youth, he surpassed his parents in religious zealotry. One source from that period said, 'He wielded the Bible like a billy club.'"

"Well," Annie interrupted, "I guess he had the fanatical personality of a 'true believer' even then."

Wonk opened his eyes and nodded. "So it would seem. During his teen years, however, he experienced some sort of disenchantment and rebelled against his parents and their religion. Due to his academic achievements, Boggs received several full scholarship offers. He studied physics at Carnegie Mellon University in Pittsburgh, then did graduate and post-graduate work at MIT, where he received his Ph.D."

He paused to reach for a tissue, then blew his nose loudly. He used two fingers to hold the tissue by its corner, leaned to the side, and deposited it carefully into the wastebasket. Then he reached for a tiny bottle of hand disinfectant on the lamp table.

"How did he get involved in radical environmentalism?" Hunter asked.

"It apparently began during his undergraduate years." He squeezed the bottle into his palms, returned it to the table, then rubbed his chubby hands together vigorously. "Those were the early days of alarm about global warming. Government scientists had extrapolated doomsday prophecies and worst-case scenarios from their mathematical computer models. According to a magazine profile, Boggs seized upon the theory like a convert to a new dogma. He became as fanatically outspoken about global warming as he had been about his earlier religious beliefs."

He watched, amused, as Wonk dried his clean hands on the dirty bathrobe.

"Soon he began to read more broadly about environmentalist philosophy. When he transferred to MIT, he began to associate in Cambridge with proponents of what is known as 'Deep Ecology.'"

Hunter nodded. "I've read about it. The 'John Muir wing' of the environmentalist movement. They believe humans are no more significant than bugs. And considerably more malignant."

"After college," Wonk went on, "Boggs began to work as a scientific consultant for Nature Legal Advocacy and other green groups. Even though his physics specialty had little to do with the subject matter of their various studies—which dealt mainly with toxic chemicals or endangered species— NLA would add his name as a 'peer reviewer.' His Ph.D. from MIT helped lend their reports a scientific cachet with the media."

"That sounds extremely cynical," Annie said.

"And extremely interesting," Hunter added. "NLA is the group behind the current fracking scare. So there's a direct connection to Boggs."

"Cynical, yes," Wonk said. "However, I do not believe there is a connection any longer between Boggs and NLA. In fact, it was the group's cynicism and hypocrisy—rampant among mainstream environmental groups—that eventually disillusioned him. NLA resisted his calls for greater militancy. Eventually, he had a nasty public break with them. In a movement publication, he accused them of selling out. He complained about their plush Washington headquarters and high salaries, as well as their lobbying machinations and political compromises."

Hunter riffled the documents in the file folder with his thumb. "You mentioned federal law enforcement reports. What are those about?"

Wonk raised his forefinger. "That is where matters took an ominous turn." He tried to lean forward, but gave it up and fell back into the chair. "Do you recall the 'Technobomber' case of about ten years ago? When someone was sending bombs to various corporate headquarters?"

"I do. He killed several people and maimed a lot of others. They finally got that guy—some activist in Boston, right?"

"Martin Malleck. An MIT chemistry student working on his Ph.D. Based on an anonymous tip, the FBI searched his apartment and found physical evidence, including chemicals that they linked directly to several of the bombings. Malleck was arrested and eventually convicted. Later, he committed suicide in prison." Wonk nodded at the file folder in Hunter's hand. "However, Dylan, you may be interested to know that he was not the FBI's initial suspect. For several months prior to that, as you will see in the reports, they were investigating Zachariah Boggs."

He felt a little jolt. "Really."

"It is a fact. Even after his conviction and imprisonment, Malleck continued to profess his innocence. He insisted that the explosives in his apartment had been planted by someone. He claimed the same thing in the suicide note that he left in his cell. As you will see in the investigative file, some people who knew him—and at least two FBI investigators—believed him. Meanwhile, Boggs had airtight alibis, and the physical evidence proved sufficient for the federal prosecutors and the jury to establish Malleck's culpability."

He was no longer seeing Wonk; he was envisioning the bomb rigged to the cabin door. After a few seconds, he caught himself. He dropped the file atop the stack and sat back. Glanced over at Annie. She was staring at him, eyes wide.

"What else?" he asked.

"Soon after, Boggs established WildJustice—in his words, 'to reclaim the ideals of the corrupt environmental movement.' To date, it has attracted only a few hundred followers, and its core group is even smaller, perhaps a dozen. For the most part, the latter live—what is the term?—'off the grid': simply, ascetically, and naturally, eschewing most technology, practicing veganism, while engaging in acts of 'monkeywrenching.'"

Hunter saw Annie's puzzled expression. "It comes from the phrase, 'tossing a monkey wrench into the works.' It refers to sabotage directed against corporations, scientific research labs, and advanced technology."

"As the reports I have compiled indicate, Dylan, a host of such incidents have been attributed to WildJustice over the years. Yet, though they publicly endorse such criminality, they have been extremely careful not to leave behind incriminating evidence. Until this past month, that is. In recent weeks, they have overtly attacked hydraulic fracturing enterprises in Pennsylvania. It appears that Boggs and his associates are trying to foment and lead a wider rebellion among environmentalists."

"Which brings us to CarboNot," Hunter said. "What have you learned about any possible links between that company and WildJustice?"

"The connections are attenuated. The folder contains background on CarboNot's principals, staff, and some of its investors. I have run a database query. One possibility is the CarboNot CEO, Damon Sloan. Also, Avery Trammel is known to have invested significantly in CarboNot and also is a donor to and trustee of Nature Legal Advocacy. Both men lived and worked in Boston during periods that overlap with the known presence of Zachariah Boggs. And both men have reputations for ruthlessness."

"Trammel," Annie said. "He's the billionaire who supports all those left-wing causes, right?"

"That's the guy," Hunter said. He turned back to Wonk. "Anything more?"

"I shall continue to work on it."

"Just follow the money."

Wonk looked around his upscale apartment and smiled. "I always do."

He bent forward. Pressed puffy hands that looked like small catcher's mitts against thighs that looked like fallen tree trunks. Then rocked several times and pushed up to his feet. He stood wobbling for a few seconds before gaining his balance.

"If that is all for now," he said, panting, "I believe I shall have a look at the present you brought me."

They were back in the elevator before they spoke.

"Dylan…" she began, then stopped.

He looked down at her. Involuntarily visualized what had almost happened to her. He placed his hands on her arms.

"If only I had known his history, the other day at the diner—" He stopped, seeing her stricken look.

"Dylan—let it go."

"I'm trying, Annie."

THIRTEEN

The aroma of vegetable soup wafted into his face from the steaming kettle suspended from a tripod over the campfire. Strands of smoke curled around him and rose aloft, dissipating into a sky the same color.

Rusty was enjoying both the aroma and the fire's warmth when he noticed Zak emerge from a distant tent, spot him, then head his way. He paused his stirring; he could tell from Zak's stride and the look on his face that something was wrong.

"Marcy, take over for a minute, okay?" he said to one of three women who sat at a nearby camp table, peeling potatoes. He handed her the big wooden spoon and walked off to intercept Zak away from the others.

As his friend approached him, the strain on his face was even more obvious.

"Hey, Zak. What's up?"

"I asked one of the kids with a radio to tune in to the local news and let me hear if anything interesting was going on."

"And?"

"Nothing."

A chill breeze cut across the clearing. Zak jammed his bare hands deep into the pockets of his field jacket. He continued.

"I had Jimmy and Sarah visit a few stores this morning and chat up the clerks for local gossip. Our action at the diner was mentioned several times. But nothing about..." He looked around, as if wary that his voice might carry. "You know."

Rusty nodded slowly. "Yeah, it's been, what? Three days?"

"I rigged it in the cabin Wednesday night. Today is Saturday. If it had worked, we should have heard something about it by now."

"Maybe it did, but nobody knows yet. That place is isolated."

"With what I used, there should have been a fire," Zak said. "That was part of the plan. But if the cabin went up, it would have been all over the news."

"Well, maybe they never came back there...Do you want me to go take a look?"

Zak stared at him, those dark eyes of his not blinking. Like—what do they call them?—like black holes.

"We'll both go, Rusty," Zak said. "I may need to check things out. But after dark. I'll meet you at your truck at six-fifteen."

She finally pulled back from him, laughing. "You're the third man who's kissed me like that this week."

"What?" Hunter said, surprised.

"First Brad Flynn, then Dylan Hunter, and now...what did you say your name was, sailor?"

He laughed, too. "Yes. Now you get to sample Vic Rostand—you promiscuous hussy." He took her coat and hung it on the rack near the front door. "So how were your morning meetings?"

Her smile died. "Meeting, singular. With Grant. He's worried." She hesitated, then sighed. "He thinks we may have another mole."

It shocked him. "*Two* moles in the CIA, in one year?"

"That's why he needed to see me so soon. Next week he and I have to hit the ground running and launch another investigation, all over again." Her face brightened. "But for the rest of the weekend, I don't want to think about any of that. Why don't you show me around?"

The house on Connor's Point stood midway along a narrow, mile-long peninsula that poked out into a tributary of the Chesapeake Bay. Located east of Annapolis, across the Bay Bridge on Maryland's Eastern Shore, it still was only an hour's drive from Washington. The Bay Bridge Airport, where he kept his private plane, was fewer than ten minutes away.

Hunter explained how he had purchased the brick Colonial home four years earlier, under the Victor Rostand alias, as part of his secret plan to leave the Agency and drop off the grid. He led her through the front parlor, dining room, den, small kitchen and breakfast nook, then out onto the enclosed back porch that faced the marsh. Upstairs, he showed her the four bedrooms—one of them transformed into his office, another his library. In the master bedroom they found Luna sprawled on the bed's comforter.

"So there you are, you lazy girl!" Annie said. The cat sniffed her extended hand and closed her eyes while she scratched her head. Then Annie went over to gaze at the marsh through a sliding glass door that led out to a miniature balcony.

"It's charming here, Dylan."

"The rooms are much smaller than what you're used to in Falls Church."

She turned to him. "But this is so cozy…You know, I was cooped up in the car for an hour and a half on the way over here. I could use a walk now."

"Sure," he said. "Okay, Luna, you stay here and protect the house."

He meant it as a joke. But Annie looked serious as she said: "I'm sure she will."

It was much warmer here than it had been in Pennsylvania, even this late in the day. The sun hung low over the marsh as they walked down the quiet street, hand in hand, toward the northern end of the peninsula. He pointed out that the homes on his side of the street abutted the marshland, while those on the eastern side enjoyed open water.

"Why didn't you choose the water view?"

"I like the marsh. We have every kind of bird and critter out there. Blue herons, geese, red-winged blackbirds, mockingbirds, ospreys diving for fish. The occasional bald eagle. I've had rabbits, deer, and foxes in the backyard. The foxes even dug a den there last year, at the edge of the water."

He felt her squeeze his hand. "I've seen you in the forest, and now here. You're a real nature-lover, Dylan Hunter."

He heard puzzlement in her tone. "That surprises you?"

"All things considered—yes," she said. "I wouldn't have expected you to be an environmentalist."

He paused at a break between two homes to view the sunset. The sun was a big red disk now, almost touching the tops of the waving grasses in the distance.

"Loving nature isn't the same thing as being an environmentalist."

"No?"

"No." He pointed at the flaming sky. "Environmentalists think there's beauty out there. And meaning."

He waited while she took in the sight. Watched her brow wrinkle. "You don't think that's beautiful or meaningful?"

"You didn't quite hear what I said, Annie. I said: Environmentalists think beauty and meaning is *out there.* But it isn't 'out there.'" He pointed at her eyes. "It's *in there.*"

She still looked unsure, so he went on.

"The beauty and the meaning are in your eyes, love. In our eyes. Without us here to watch that, it's nothing but solar rays and weeds. Without us, the entire universe is just clusters of meaningless stuff. It's our *awareness* of the world, our interpretation of it, that gives it beauty and meaning."

"'Beauty is in the eye of the beholder,' then."

"More than that. Without an intelligent beholder, there *is* no beauty in nature. And no meaning."

"That's what Vic Rostand, Nature-Lover, says. But environmentalists say…?"

"That beauty can somehow exist without our eyes to see it. That meaning can somehow exist without our intelligence to make sense of things. That nature is somehow 'valuable in itself'—without anyone to *value* it."

He draped his arm around her shoulder and they watched the red disk sink slowly into the dark grasses. A blue heron rose suddenly into the air, a sharp angular silhouette against the russet sky that skimmed gracefully across the shimmering water.

"I never thought of it like that," she said, her voice soft, her hand tight on his arm. "But then again, I didn't major in political science at Princeton."

"I didn't learn that at Princeton," he said. He thought about it. "I guess I learned it from my dad." He watched the earth swallow the last fiery curve of the disk, and added: "I learned most of the important things in my life from Big Mike."

They remained quiet on the way back to the house. No traffic interrupted their walk down the lightly traveled street. Around them, warm yellow light poured from the rectangles of neighboring windows; overhead, a few cold white stars winked in the dark blue field.

"I wanted you to see this place. While I still have it."

She stopped. "You're planning to sell it?"

He nodded.

"But why, Dylan? Why would you want to get rid of it? You told me you love it out here."

"You want me to cut the strings to my past, don't you?"

"Hey, Vic!"

They looked down the street in the direction of the female voice. Hunter saw his next-door neighbors, Jim and Billie Rutherford, in their front yard. Jim gripped one end of a leash; on the other end a puppy strained to run in their direction.

"Remember," he whispered, "It's 'Vic Rostand' and 'Annie Forrest.'"

They walked over to the middle-aged couple. Hunter performed the introductions while trying futilely to fend off the golden retriever pup, a fuzzy blond ball that bounced and rolled around his feet. He gave it up and bent to tussle with it. Jim explained that they'd just bought the pet a week earlier and that her name was Happy.

"No kidding," Hunter said, letting the little dog chew his fingers enthusiastically.

"It's so nice to meet you," Billie said to Annie. "Vic has told us nice things about you—and your cat."

"What? Oh. Yes. My cat," she said, shooting a look at Hunter. "Luna has taken quite a fancy to Vic. In fact," she added, dead-pan, "I honestly don't know how we'd live without her."

"So how did you two meet?" Jim asked.

Hunter jumped in. "We were both standing in a check-out line." He smiled at Annie. "I couldn't pass up the opportunity to ask for her phone number."

"He was very persistent," Annie said. "I'm still not quite sure what I've gotten myself into."

"Well, I can tell you're well suited for each other," Jim said. "If you're going to be around for a few days, we'll have to invite you over for dinner."

After another moment of pleasantries, Hunter and Annie left them with their puppy and returned to his house. As they hung up their coats, he spoke first.

"You see? I can't be myself here. To all these neighbors, I'm a traveling marketing consultant named Vic Rostand. Just as to everyone in Pennsylvania, I'm a reclusive Iraq vet named Brad Flynn. And now, whenever you are around either of those guys, you can't be Annie Woods, either."

"I have to admit, I don't like the prospect of hiding forever behind aliases. Pretending to be people we're not."

"Which is why I have to sell this place. And the cabin. Leave it all behind. Jettison all the aliases and cover stories, and become only Dylan Hunter."

"Is that what's going to happen?"

He understood what she was really asking. "You mean, am I retiring from the vigilante business? I never meant it to be a career, you know."

Her expression remained solemn. "But as I said the other day: You are easily provoked."

He moved close. Felt her warm curves press against his body.

"Then I guess I'll just have to learn to control myself."

She looked smug. "You don't feel as if you're doing a good job of that right now."

"Oh. Well, *that's* different," he said. "Which gives me an idea. What do you say we go kick Luna off the bed?"

He bent to greet her lips with his.

Rusty parked the truck in the same place as he had on Wednesday night. Boggs got out and moved through the trees, rather than up the driveway. As he approached the cabin, he saw no parked cars. And the cabin door looked intact and closed.

Maybe Rusty was right. Maybe they came back here that night, and one of them just got into the other car, and they both drove off without ever entering the cabin.

Then he remembered the cat.

No, that didn't make sense. They wouldn't leave without the cat.

The place was dark. He didn't think anyone was inside—how could they be?—but he approached and circled it cautiously, just in case. He reached the window on the right side and peeked in. Seeing nothing, he risked flicking on the flashlight.

The boxes and bags he'd seen on the floor three nights ago were gone. He played the beam across the floor and walls. The place was completely empty.

But how?

The angle made it impossible to see the cabin door from the side window, so he continued around to the back. Then stopped and stared, disbelieving, at the sight of a rectangle of plywood nailed in place across the lower broken half of the window.

He stood on tiptoes, barely managing to peer over the plywood. He aimed the flashlight beam into the room through the upper unbroken panes, toward the spot above the door.

"Holy shit, Zak!" Rusty exclaimed when he entered the truck. "You looked totally spooked."

He sagged in the car seat. His head, jaw, and hand were throbbing again. He closed his eyes.

"The cabin," he muttered. "It's completely cleaned out. Like nobody had ever been in there."

"But…what about—"

A flash of fury tore through him. His eyes snapped open and he whipped around to face him.

"The bomb is gone, Rusty! *Gone.* Don't ask me how—I don't know! I don't know how they possibly could have avoided setting it off. But it's *gone*—and so are they."

He flopped back against the seat, closing his eyes again. Rusty fell silent, leaving him alone with the dull rumble of the idling engine, the steady rushing noise of the heater's blower, and an image floating in his mind: the cold, savage face of a red-bearded guy named Brad.

The man had looked and fought like a demon. Now, impossibly, he had survived and vanished, like a ghost…

As if reading his thoughts, Rusty said, "No wonder you look spooked."

FOURTEEN

"Thanks for agreeing to see me on such short notice," Hunter said to the three people facing him across the conference table.

"We're used to dealing with newspaper deadlines," Gavin Lockwood said. "And we're delighted that the *Inquirer* is interested in the results of our new study. By the way, I hope you enjoyed the tour of our offices by our receptionist."

"It certainly was interesting," Hunter said, his eyes wandering around the glassed-in conference room to the space outside. "Sunlight pouring in through all these windows and skylights. Plants in every cubicle. And your lobby display— I've never seen a work of art consisting of ivy growing up an interior office wall."

Lockwood's easy grin made him look even more boyish, despite his white hair. "We at Nature Legal Advocacy like to be reminded constantly about our mission—about what is most important to us. That's why bringing in a lot of green from the outside has been a priority."

"Well, you've certainly been successful at doing *that*," Hunter replied. He saw Lockwood's grin waver, so he offered his own and continued. "Nature Legal Advocacy is widely regarded to be the single most effective environmental organization in Washington."

Lockwood smiled again, relaxing. "Environmental litigation, lobbying, media outreach, congressional testimony, publishing research reports and scientific studies—yes, we do it all."

Hunter glanced down at his notepad. "Let me see if I have the basic facts right. I understand that you have an annual budget of over one hundred million dollars, about forty percent of which is devoted to energy issues."

"That's right. We're actively fighting the infrastructure that supports production and use of fossil fuels. That's why we litigate and lobby against such things as environmentally intrusive pipelines, refineries, coal mining, and shale drilling for oil and natural gas."

"To do all that, you maintain a staff of—what?—three hundred lawyers, scientists, media people, and other specialists, in offices all around the country."

"Also true. And our staff is the best." Lockwood nodded at the two people flanking him at the table. "Lars and Wendy are stellar examples of the kind of talent we attract."

As the man began to summarize their backgrounds, Hunter studied each of them more closely.

No one would mistake Gavin Lockwood for anything other than a slick denizen of Capitol Hill. His impeccably tailored charcoal designer suit, expensive red repp tie, and silky manner, just faintly condescending, presented the perfect portrait of the Beltway patrician.

The man slouching beside him was a visual cliché, too, but of the asocial think-tank researcher. Dr. Lars Sunstrom wore round wire-rim glasses, a baggy navy sweater over wrinkled brown cords, and scuffed, thick-soled black shoes. Almost completely bald, his scalp's gray-brown fringe merged into matching beard stubble. Despite the dressed-down appearance, with his arms folded, chin lifted, and eyes half-shut, he managed to project an aura of bored arrogance. Lockwood touted Sunstrom as a national authority on radiation and toxic chemicals. He also was the lead scientific author of the NLA's report, *On Shaky Grounds: Fracking's Risks to Our Children's Health.*

The other participant—a pretty, blue-eyed blonde lawyer, introduced as Wendy Hathaway—wore a cool blue suit and hot red lipstick. She appeared to be in her late twenties, barely out of law school. She also looked eager and guileless. Lockwood explained, to everyone's amusement, that her main contribution to the report had been to transform Sunstrom's excruciatingly arcane technical language "into something that human beings would want to read."

"Obviously she succeeded," Dylan said, looking at her. Her face went slightly pink, and dimples showed as she lit up a dazzling smile. "I downloaded the report from your website and read it. I can see why it has caused such a nationwide commotion. It certainly presents a disturbing picture of hydraulic fracturing."

Sunstrom tried not to look smug, and failed. Lockwood leaned forward; he clearly anticipated another media score for the organization.

Hunter reached down into the battered old briefcase he'd brought with him, retrieving a couple of file folders. "Here it is. I scribbled some notes in the margins." He offered them a sheepish look. "I hope you'll be kind enough to clarify a few things for a non-scientist. And if Dr. Sunstrom starts to go over my head, perhaps Miss Hathaway will be kind enough to translate for me."

They laughed. Good. All nice and relaxed, now.

"But before I get into those specifics, let me begin with this." Hunter slipped the executive summary of Adam Silva's report from a file folder and slid it across the table to Lockwood. "I wondered if you all might share with me your opinion of this document."

Still smiling, Lockwood held it so that the others could lean in and read it, too.

Hunter settled back in his chair. Crossed his legs and folded his hands. Watched their expressions as they began to read.

Sunstrom was the first to react, apparently at the sight of Silva's name atop the document. His sleepy eyes widened comically, and he leaned in closer, his eyes scanning down the page. Lockwood's placid features changed more slowly. First, the ever-present hint of his smile evaporated; then his lips tightened; then he shot a look at Hunter and blinked; then his eyes dashed back to the page. Wendy Hathaway's faintly puzzled look morphed into utter bewilderment.

Sunstrom remained hunched as his dark eyes found Hunter's. "Just what the hell *is* this?" he snapped.

Lockwood's own expression had lost its warmth, too; but as a Hill veteran, he was practiced enough to maintain his composure.

"Easy, Lars," he said, laying a neatly manicured hand on Sunstrom's wrist. "Mr. Hunter, you have caught us at a bit of a loss. None of us has seen this before. May I ask how you obtained it?"

Hunter shrugged. "Why, certainly. From its author."

He shut up and counted the seconds to see who would respond next, and how.

"I don't understand." Wendy was blinking rapidly, as if that might clear her brain of its confusion.

"*I* do," Sunstrom stated loudly. "This is an ambush interview."

Hunter shook his head. "Not at all. I heard that Dr. Silva was going to challenge your report at an EPA hearing. So, after I spoke with him, I thought I would share it—with his permission, of course—and then invite you to respond."

"But…he's claiming that the water samples we tested were *planted* by somebody," Wendy said, astonished. "And what's all this about an EPA hearing?"

"Gee. You don't know?" Hunter asked.

"No! *What* hearing?" Her glance flitted from Lockwood to Sunstrom.

Lockwood placed his other steadying hand on her wrist. "It's all right, Wendy. We thought Adair might withdraw his challenge to our report; so we didn't want to alarm you needlessly until we were sure there would actually *be* a hearing. But it's scheduled for the 27th."

Hunter saw shock, incredulity, and anxiety in the girl's expression. He felt sorry for her. Just another naïve idealist, head crammed with years of propaganda and pseudo-science, heart inflated with the thrill of doing important things with Washington big shots to save the planet.

Big shots, he thought, studying the men. He'd encountered plenty of their type in Princeton's Woodrow Wilson School: brimming with sanctimonious intellectual arrogance, lusting to manage and manipulate others—including kids like

Wendy. He wanted to lean across the table and slap their faces. Instead, he put on his most cheerful grin.

"So, would you care to respond for the piece I'm preparing about this controversy?"

"It's garbage!" Sunstrom shouted, raising his back and chin. "Those samples were *not* faked. I'm a scientific expert in this field, and believe me, I would know."

"Actually"—Hunter kept his tone even and his grin in place—"I've read some challenges of your credentials to do this particular research, Dr. Sunstrom. Your field of expertise is physics—not radiation or chemistry, isn't that correct?"

"That's not—"

"And I gather that a decade ago, while you were an independent consultant to other groups, at least two scientific bodies publicly criticized a couple of previous laboratory studies you did—for, quote, 'cherry-picking data and the absence of proper procedural controls.'"

Sunstrom was about to explode, so Lockwood intervened. "It's not fair to expect Dr. Sunstrom to defend himself like this, unprepared. What I can assure you is that the methodology he used to produce *On Shaky Grounds* passed a stringent peer-review process."

Hunter was ready for that. "Was it submitted to an independent scientific journal before you released it to the media?"

"Well, no. What we did was submit it to a committee of scientific experts in the related disciplines. And they—"

"Weren't those 'experts' all hand-picked from among your organization's own scientific advisers?"

"Are you saying they weren't *objective?*" Sunstrom demanded.

"You sent your report only to NLA's official list of scientific sympathizers. To people already predisposed to agree with your point of view, and who have a vested interest in promoting NLA. Do you call *that* 'objective'?"

It shut up Sunstrom, but now Lockwood looked angry.

"Mr. Hunter, you asked for our response. But this"—he shook Silva's document—"just makes a bunch of wild, unsupported claims. By contrast, Dr. Sunstrom's study offers plenty of facts and data. So, until this Silva fellow, whoever he is, does the same, then I think we are justified in dismissing his contentions as a pack of arbitrary assertions by a hired gun for the fracking industry."

"Actually, I agree with you," Hunter said. "As you see, that's just the executive summary to his forthcoming report. He told me he's still in the process of writing the actual report itself. If he doesn't offer any proof of these claims, then of course you are in the clear." Hunter paused. Spread his hands. "On the other hand, if he *does*…"

He let the sentence fragment hang in the silence.

"That will be for the EPA to decide," Lockwood said, his voice chilly.

"Which reminds me," Hunter said, looking at his watch, "I have an appointment scheduled with Jonathan Weaver, the EPA administrator, at two this afternoon. I thought he might wish to see Dr. Silva's executive summary, too. So, if you don't mind…" He extended his open palm toward Lockwood.

"I'm done here!" Sunstrom launched himself from his chair and stormed out of the room, his heavy shoes drumming across the tiles.

Lockwood pushed the document back across the table to Hunter. "I believe all of us are done here," he said, rising. He stared at Hunter, unblinking. "I do hope that you will exercise prudence and caution in reporting on this controversy, Mr. Hunter."

"Prudence? Always." Hunter rose, again grinning. "As for caution…" He stared back, also refusing to blink. "Why, Mr. Lockwood. What could I possibly have to fear?"

Lockwood blinked first.

"I'll let Wendy show you out." He nodded and left.

Hunter turned to the girl. She looked stricken.

She walked beside him toward the elevator bay, not saying a word.

"Wendy," he began, keeping his voice down. "I want you to know that I'll keep your name out of the paper. This isn't about you. It's about them."

She wouldn't look at him.

"I know you think that by working here, you're doing the right thing," he continued. "It's always hard to challenge your basic assumptions. But facts—no matter how uncomfortable—are never your enemy." He considered, then added: "I've learned, the hard way, that it's always best to face reality without lies and deception."

They reached the elevators. A moment passed; she seemed to want to say something. But she couldn't find the words— or perhaps the courage to utter them.

He watched her walk away.

Avery Trammel felt the beginning of a headache coming on. Its cause was the brief phone chat he'd had moments ago, as his limo arrived at Dulles International.

"Lockwood just called me," Sloan had said. "A reporter is poking around. He sounds like trouble."

"I am not able to talk freely right now. I shall be airborne and alone in thirty minutes. Call me back on my sat phone."

"All right. And I think the senator will want to be in on the call, too," Sloan replied.

"Set it up, then."

He was the sole passenger in his Gulfstream G-200 for this short flight from IAD to JFK. The occasion would be a board meeting of one of the many nonprofits he supported—a quick turnaround flight that would have him back in D.C. this same evening. He needed to go over his talking points. But he had trouble putting his mind to it.

He did not like the news about the reporter.

For privacy, he chose to sit in the rear, in the lone seat farthest from the cockpit. He sank his head and neck back into the soft suede and tried to relax. He raised the glass of Ardbeg Uigedail single malt that they had waiting for him in the galley; studied its color; savored the lingering taste of the previous sip. The aircraft's vibration caused the lone ice cube to rattle against the crystal.

His phone rested on the polished mahogany side table; the plane's Iridium satellite phone system allowed him to use it while airborne. Transmissions were encrypted and highly secure. But not completely secure. He knew the capabilities and inclinations of various governments, including the American one. These days, no electronic communications were completely secure.

When the call came through, he let it ring three times before picking up.

"Yes?" He spoke softly and rotated his swivel seat to face away from the cockpit.

"It's me again." Sloan. "We're conferencing with the other party's representative. He is the gentleman that you met at my office."

"How do you do, sir," Stuart Kaplan's voice cut in. "I hope you don't mind if I stand in for my boss."

"No. I quite understand." Trammel knew that Conn had to be hyper-cautious. "I assume that you have been granted the authority to speak on his behalf."

"Of course."

"Good. Now, if you would please tell me what happened."

Speaking elliptically and not mentioning any names, Sloan described the meeting between Lockwood and the reporter, and conveyed Lockwood's alarm over how much the man already knew.

"And I should mention that he has scheduled an appointment this afternoon with the administrator of...of the agency central to our concerns," Sloan concluded. "That individual has been alerted, of course."

Trammel knew who that was. "I see. What can you tell me about this reporter?"

"We're trying to learn more about his background," Kaplan said. "In our preliminary search online, we found very little information that goes back more than a couple of years. But I can tell you that he's the guy who's been at the center of the recent vigilante controversy."

Trammel paused in the middle of another sip and put down his glass carefully.

"That one. I remember reading about him. From what I gathered, he is a real troublemaker."

"Which is not good for us," Sloan said.

"No. Not good at all."

Kaplan cut to the chase. "Is there something we can do about him?"

Trammel noticed that he said "can" and not "should." It was clear that the "should" already, tacitly, had been settled.

"What does your boss think?" Trammel asked.

"He's worried."

He has every reason to be. "That is not quite what I was referring to. I meant: What does he think…tactically?"

"He tasked the staff to begin by finding out everything we can about this guy."

"A prudent first step. Know thine enemy. But after that, then what?"

"If it should become necessary," Sloan said, lowering his voice, "I might ask some of my contacts to…meet him. Perhaps dissuade him from pursuing this inquiry."

Several seconds passed, during which Trammel recalled what he had read about the reporter.

"That may indeed become necessary."

FIFTEEN

The tingling sensation on his scalp started immediately when he got off the rising escalator.

The familiar feeling that he was being watched.

The escalator at the Federal Triangle Metro entrance fed Hunter out into a vaulted arcade area beneath the Ariel Rios Building, the home of the Environmental Protection Agency. Overhead, pendant lanterns, the kind found in churches, hung by chains from the ceiling. A series of archways opened to the west onto the pedestrian mall known as Woodrow Wilson Plaza, while those to the east revealed a bit of the Old Post Office Building across 12th Street.

People bustled by him, passing through the arches or to and from the building's entrances. He paused to make a show of turning around, getting his bearings, looking at his watch, stalling to spot anyone with eyes on him. Anyone hanging about, inexplicably idle in the cold air. But he saw no one like that.

He made his way toward the entrance into the building's south wing. Probably just a touch of paranoia, he thought, because of the incident at the cabin.

The guards and body scanners he faced today had forced him to leave his weapons home. He relaxed only when he entered the building. After passing through the security checkpoint, he moved into a circular lobby. The floor and walls were executed in brown and beige marble that reminded him of the entrance to Wonk's building. But this one was far more spectacular. Burnished bronze gleamed everywhere: from the frames surrounding an interior entranceway and the building directory; from the chandelier and the clock suspended above the entrance to the stairwell; from the golden surface of the imposing elevator door.

Hunter showed his ID to the guard behind the marble security station and waited to be announced.

"Mind if I take a look at those stairs?" Hunter asked him.

"Go right ahead. Your escort will be down shortly."

Rising through the seven floors of the building, the marble spiral staircase was another spectacle. Its bannister gleamed with more bronze. A chrome-and-brass globe chandelier hung by a chain from the top of the stairwell; along its length, starburst fixtures of exposed bulbs illuminated each floor.

"This *is* the EPA's headquarters, right?" he said to the guard.

The guy got it and chuckled. "Sir, you haven't seen anything yet."

The elevator door opened and a young man with black spiked hair emerged. He introduced himself as Jared Bale, an aide to Deputy Administrator Chip Crane.

"Mr. Crane and Mr. Weaver will both meet with you, but they're in a meeting that's running late. They asked me to bring you up and make you comfortable."

"No rush. I was just admiring your lobby."

"Well, since we have a few minutes, maybe I can show you a few things. I often give tours to their guests."

Bale explained that the structure had been built during the Great Depression as the New Post Office Building. For the next fifteen minutes Hunter got a look at some of its majestic corridors, rooms, and murals. Most impressive was an enormous two-story room stretching the length of a corridor on the third floor. Originally called the Postmaster General's Reception Room, it boasted a stunning green marble floor, paneled walls and doors surrounded by ornate columns, pilasters, pediments, cornices, and friezes, plus an elaborately carved ceiling—all in rich butternut wood. The expanse was lit by huge chandeliers made of glass tubing and polished chrome, decorated with gold eagles.

"Jared, did you know that when the EPA started out during the Nixon years, Spiro Agnew sequestered it in run-down offices above a dumpy strip mall near the Southwest Waterfront?"

"Really? Wow. That's hard to believe."

He gestured at the chandeliers. "So is this. These rooms are worthy of a European palace."

"Well, that's no surprise," Bale said proudly. "Its architects were inspired by the Place Vendôme in Paris." He glanced at his watch. "Okay, their meeting should be breaking up now. I'll take you over to the office."

"Sorry you had to wait," Jonathan Weaver said, shaking his hand. Though in his early fifties, he retained youthful good looks, enhanced by sweeping waves of dark hair that he kept fashionably long and casually combed. The touch of gray at his temples matched the color of his eyes; but the touch of a nervous smile on his lips never reached those eyes. "And this is Chip Crane, our deputy administrator."

Crane looked wary during the handshake. He didn't speak. And didn't smile.

When he'd told Lockwood about this meeting, it had been a test to find out if they were all working in collusion.

Now I know. Lockwood tipped them off.

And no one from the Agency's media relations staff was present. Clearly, this pair wanted no witnesses to anything that was said.

"No trouble at all," he said, keeping his manner amiable. "Mr. Bale gave me an informative tour. The architectural detail here is magnificent." He let his gaze drift like that of a typical tourist, taking in the rich dark paneling, the gleaming parquet floor, the antique mahogany sideboard, the marble fireplace, the glittering chandelier. "He informed me that this building was modeled after the Place Vendôme in Paris. If I remember my European history, that was designed as a monument to the armies of Louis XIV. He called it the *Place des Conquêtes.*" He looked from one man to the other. "The Place of Conquests. It must be inspiring for you to work here."

Weaver lost even his forced smile. Crane's eyes narrowed further.

"I won't take up much of your time," he added quickly. "I just wanted your input on a few questions."

"Why don't we sit here," Weaver said, gesturing to a nearby conference table.

They took chairs near one end. Hunter sat facing them, dumping his overcoat onto the seat next to him. He took out his small notepad and a pen.

"I suppose you know why I'm here," he said, watching closely.

It startled both of them.

"Why…no," Weaver began, looking even more uncomfortable. "How could we? Your secretary didn't say, when she called to make the appointment."

"Suppose you tell us." Crane's voice and manner both were gruff.

"Of course. I just figured that since the hydraulic fracturing controversy was on everyone's mind these days, you'd guess it had to be about that."

"Well, what about it?" Crane leaned back and crossed his beefy arms over his broad chest.

Hunter flipped open his notepad. Pretended to consult a page. Looked up at them.

"I have been told that Adair Energy has hired an expert toxicologist who is challenging the NLA report."

Weaver nodded. "We received word of that from our Science Advisory Board."

"I understand that the toxicologist Dan Adair hired is prepared to demonstrate that the toxic samples NLA acquired and studied actually were concocted by someone and planted in the local water wells."

"That seems to be the claim. Whether he can demonstrate that remains to be seen."

Hunter put down the pad. "But, for the sake of argument, let's say that he *can*. I assume that would eliminate the rationale for your proposed national moratorium on hydraulic fracturing."

"It would be only one factor that we would have to consider," Weaver said. "There are others."

"Really. Such as?"

Crane broke in. "The agency is obligated to weigh all potential risks and hazards to human health and the environment. Just because one study fails to demonstrate that fracking is dangerous, doesn't mean it is safe."

"Do you have any hard evidence, from any other study, that it's unsafe either to human health or to the environment?"

"No," Weaver said. "Nothing yet. But that's not the point."

"It isn't?"

"It's not our policy to prove that something is *unsafe.* Rather, it's up to those who invent or use a product, chemical, or technology to prove that it is *safe.*"

"Are you saying that you *presume* an action or product to be harmful, unless it is somehow proved otherwise? That, in effect, it is guilty until proved innocent?"

Crane glowered, shifting in his chair. "We're saying that we'd rather be safe than sorry. Look: In the past, we acted to ban products or prevent activities only on the basis of hard evidence of danger. But today, in a lot of areas, the risks of doing nothing preventive are too great. Now, we're forced to act on theory alone. On prediction alone. We've made clear to our Science Advisory Board that they should stop insisting on certainty and precision in ambiguous situations. This is known as 'the precautionary principle.' Uncertainty alone is enough to compel the agency to take preventive measures."

"We compare it to buying insurance," Weaver added. "Insurance in the face of uncertainty."

"Let me see if I've got this straight," Hunter said, also leaning forward. "You admit that you have no evidence, just a theory—really, just *speculation*—that hydraulic fracturing may be harmful. But you insist that Adair and his toxicologist are somehow supposed to *refute* a mere speculation for which you've offered no evidence. In other words, you're demanding a logical impossibility: that they 'prove a negative.'"

"Now, wait a minute." Weaver's cheeks had turned pink. "Would you rather risk the lives and health of millions over a technology whose potential risks are filled with uncertainty?"

"I am only trying to understand your position, so that I can report it accurately. Let me summarize what you seem to be saying. First you label your lack of evidence as 'uncertainty.' Then you ban things, based on that very lack of evidence. So the agency's position seems to be: 'Precisely because we have no case, you'd better do what we say.'"

"That's insulting," Crane said, his voice rising. "And you also sound like an advocate. I thought you were supposed to be an objective journalist. You're supposed to be neutral."

Hunter sat back and folded his own arms across his chest. "An objective journalist is not supposed to be neutral about facts or logic. And speaking of lack of objectivity, it sounds as if you've already made up your minds to ban fracking, even in the absence of facts or logic."

"That's not true!" Weaver said. "We are not prejudiced about any scientific matter. Before we decide anything, we'll wait until we hear what Dr. Silva presents to the Science Advisory Board."

Hunter smiled slowly.

"Dr. Silva? Gee, I didn't mention any Dr. Silva. I wonder who might have told you about him."

Both men flicked a look at each other, then back to him. Weaver licked his lips before he spoke.

"I'm sure that the Science Advisory Board mentioned his name to me."

Hunter held his smile and their eyes. "Impossible. I've seen Adair's correspondence to the SAB. And his letter to you. He never mentioned the toxicologist's name." He paused, watching them grow more uneasy by the second. "But I knew his name; and I've mentioned it only one other time. This very morning." Hunter picked up his notepad and pen and put them inside his suit jacket. "In fact, an individual I met called you to reveal the man's name, as soon as I left his office."

Before they could protest, he pushed back his chair, picked up his overcoat, and stood. Looked down at them.

"Lockwood also tipped you off about my investigation." The shock on their faces at the mention of his name was so transparent that he couldn't help laughing. "That investigation is just getting started. I'll leave you now to make all your frantic phone calls…No, don't bother getting up to see me out. I can find my own way."

At the door Hunter paused with his hand on the brass knob and his back to them.

"You know," he said, "with all your blather about saving energy, you guys really need to cut back a bit on the chandeliers."

He turned the knob and left.

He exited the building the same way he entered.

And felt it again.

He had to be sure. Instead of descending the nearby escalator into the Metro, he stepped out into Woodrow Wilson Plaza, then turned to glance back at the massive building. The great granite and limestone wall curved out around him, embracing him in a semicircle. A score of Doric columns towered above him, between the rows of windows. It reminded him vaguely of the Coliseum in Rome. Appropriate digs for modern bureaucrats who acted like ancient emperors, throwing people to the lions.

In his peripheral vision, extending out from behind a nearby archway wall, someone's shadow wavered on the pavement.

He set out across the plaza at a brisk pace, heading toward the Ronald Reagan Building.

The tail had picked up his target around 1400 hours, when the man arrived for his appointment. He had just received a cell call alerting him that the target was leaving the building. His job now was to follow him back to his office or residence, then provide the address to the man who had hired him.

He expected the target to re-enter the Metro. But he did the unexpected and, seemingly at whim, darted out into the plaza and toward the Reagan Building. This posed a dilemma. If he hung back, he risked losing the guy in the vastness of the building. If he followed him out into the open plaza, however, he risked being spotted if the guy glanced behind him.

He had no choice, really. He gave the target a forty-meter lead, then emerged from the archway and headed out in pursuit across the brick expanse. He tried to gain on the target, but the guy seemed in a hurry and at times even trotted for a few steps.

The target reached the building entrance still about forty meters ahead of him. At that point the tail accelerated into a run to catch up. He reached the entrance himself less than eight seconds later.

But inside, the target was nowhere to be seen. He couldn't believe it. He hurried through the crowded building as unobtrusively as possible, checking the Atrium Hall, the various exhibits, the lower level food court, the restrooms.

Nothing. The man had vanished without a trace. Like a ghost.

Miserably, he phoned the man who had hired him to conduct the surveillance, knowing that he would not be happy at the news.

And he wasn't. The man was too classy to chew him out with profanity. Instead, he questioned his professional competence.

"The fellow is a *reporter,* for God's sake. How could you lose him? I thought you were better than that."

"The Reagan Building is a big place. And surveillance is normally done by a team, not a single individual."

"Are you making excuses?"

He sighed. "No. I'm stating simple facts. Look, you know I'm good. In fact, you know just *how g*ood."

The man on the other end of the call remained silent a while. Then:

"I shall inform you the next time he surfaces. That should be quite soon. When it occurs, I expect you to do better."

"I will," he said. Then realized that the bastard had already hung up on him.

SIXTEEN

He told her to "dress up" and be ready at six-thirty. She knew that he planned to take her somewhere nice for Valentine's Day, so she spent two hours putting herself together. Not knowing where, she strove for elegance, selecting a turquoise, cap-shouldered satin dress, knee-length. It fit her perfectly, and she loved the ruching in its bodice, sleeves, and waist sash. After trying on some coral accessories, she decided instead to keep it simple and go with silver heels, purse, bracelet, and earrings. She knew the color of her fox fur coat was a good complement.

She was ready, but only barely, when the doorbell rang. She opened the door to find him standing under the sconce light in a black tux and overcoat, bearing a stunning bouquet and a dazzling smile.

"Damn, you're beautiful," he said, looking her up and down.

"So are you," she answered, meaning it. "And those flowers! Thank you, love."

He stepped inside, wrapped his free arm around her. As he pressed his lips softly into hers, she fell back against his arm, feeling its muscles even through his overcoat. She felt the stir in her body, knew that he felt it, too.

After a moment she pushed him back, gently.

"I knew you'd do that, so I didn't even bother with my lipstick yet. Let me put these in water and touch myself up in the powder room. I'll be right back."

When he led her outside, she saw a black BMW sedan gleaming in her driveway.

"Wow. Where did you get *this?*" she said as he opened the passenger door for her.

"I've had it for over a year. 'Wayne Grayson' bought it, slightly used, through a Saudi security officer stationed in their embassy here."

"Wayne Grayson?"

"Have you forgotten? My rich-guy alias—the one who lives downstairs in the Bethesda apartment building. Wayne keeps this heap in the garage there."

"Ah yes. Wayne." She ran her fingers over the sedan's exquisite suede interior as he went around to his side and got in. "Wayne certainly lives very well," she continued. "And he's been holding out on me. Why haven't I enjoyed this vehicle sooner?"

"I drove it here once before." A slight hesitation. "You know…on Christmas." She felt a twinge and he went on quickly. "I left it a block away that night. Later, while I was in the hospital, I asked Grant to have his people deliver it back to the apartment building."

She noticed the array of interior buttons light up as he started the car. "What is all this stuff?"

"Oh, just a few toys," he said, activating a rear-view monitor that allowed him to back safely out of the driveway.

"Everything a security team might need to protect their diplomats. You know: Floor and wall armor against mines and high-powered weapons. Bullet-proof windows. Alarms and auto-locks in case of assaults. Poison gas sensors that close the windows and turn on the internal fresh-air supply—"

"You're joking!"

"—police strobes in the grille and back windows. Side-vision cameras, night-vision cameras, self-sealing fuel tank, run-flat tires. Interior and exterior fire sensors and extinguishing system…"

"I don't believe this."

He accelerated smoothly down the street, the car's powerful engine whisper-soft.

"Mmmm, what else? Did I mention the intercom system? This baby has concealed microphones and speakers that allow me to communicate with people outside without opening the doors or windows." He tapped the center console. "Oh, and here's the gun case. It's built to house two machine guns. Which is ridiculous, of course. Why would I ever need *two*?…Now, don't look at me like that, I left my machine guns home. After all, this is *Valentine's Day*…Although, hey, come to think of it, isn't this the anniversary of a famous massacre?"

She burst out laughing. "You're incorrigible."

"You say that a lot."

"Because it's true…So, where are you taking me, mister?"

"Someplace appropriately historic."

"Oh, Dylan!" she whispered as he pulled up in front of the 1789 Restaurant in Georgetown. "I've never been here, and I've always wanted to."

"I know." He got out to meet the valet, leaving her to wonder just *how* he could know that. Then he came around and opened her door.

She got out into the wintry air and snuggled her fur around her. Pausing outside the historic two-story inn, she took in the American flag hanging over the brick sidewalk; the gilt eagle above the door's half-moon transom window; the glowing antique lanterns on either side of the entrance, reflecting off the shiny brass door fittings and the restaurant's nameplate.

Inside, the manager greeted them with a little bow. He pulled Dylan aside and she heard him say softly, "Everything in the John Carroll Room is as you arranged, Mr. Hunter." A staff member took their coats and the manager guided them inside.

She heard voices and the clinking of crystal and silverware from nearby. Then the sound of string music, which grew louder as they approached their dining room.

She stopped in the entranceway.

The large room was entirely empty of tables or guests— except for a lone candlelit table on the far side, set before a blazing fireplace. Three members of the wait staff stood next to it. And at this end of the room a string quartet played Vivaldi's "Four Seasons."

"Dylan…" She couldn't think of what else to say.

"Happy Valentine's Day, love." He raised her hand to his lips.

He took her arm and the manager led them to the table. Dylan seated her, then said, "I have to check on something. I'll be right back."

She watched his dark, elegant figure follow the manager from the room.

A young member of the wait staff poured her water while their waiter, an older man with a white mustache, introduced himself.

"The gentlemen must love you very much to do this for you." He gestured around the room. "I've been here for nearly three decades, and this is the first time we've consented to close this room for a single couple, let alone to do so on Valentine's Day."

"Really? How could that happen?"

"You don't know, then?" He looked around with a mock-conspiratorial air, then leaned in and spoke softly.

"Please don't tell Mr. Hunter that I shared this with you. But I think you should know *how* much he cares for you. He contacted us about a month ago. Of course, by then we already were booked full for this room. He said that he understood. But then he made a remarkable proposal.

"Mr. Hunter asked our manager to contact all the guests holding reservations in this room for tonight, and to convey an offer to them. If they would be willing to forgo dinner here, he would arrange instead for all of them to stay at any hotels of their choosing tonight; he would pay, not just for their lodging, but for any restaurant meal anywhere in the city, at a lavish price per person; he also would transport them to and from each location in hired limos; and, finally, he would give each individual an additional generous sum, in cash, as compensation for their inconvenience." He peered at her, then paused to laugh gently. "My dear, you should see the look on your face."

"It's...unbelievable."

"Yet that isn't the end of it. Before the manager could even open his mouth, Mr. Hunter raised the obvious matter of all the sales and gratuities that we would lose from those many displaced customers. So, to compensate us for that, he offered to pay the restaurant a sum *double* our average per-customer price for dinner and drinks. And he pledged to reward every member of the restaurant staff with gratuities in amounts that none of us could hope to earn during a busy week." He nodded toward the entrance to the room. "I imagine that he is taking care of all of this right now with the manager."

"So you accepted his offer."

He shrugged. "How could we refuse such a grand gesture in the name of love—let alone his generosity to all concerned? I understand that one party scheduled to be in here resisted his offer at first. The manager told me that Mr. Hunter then 'sweetened the deal' substantially—he didn't say exactly by how much. Anyway, they changed their minds. All of us have been buzzing about this for weeks, trying to estimate just how much he has spent for this evening." He smiled. "For you."

He straightened. "As I said, I just thought you ought to know. Let it be our little secret, all right?" He winked at her.

She could only nod, numb and mute, before he walked away.

By the time Dylan returned to the table, she was trying to hold back tears.

"What's wrong?" he said, alarmed.

She shook her head, looking at him in awe, laughing. "Nothing is wrong." She raised her hand to touch his smooth cheek. "Everything is just perfect, darling."

His expression softened. "Not yet. But the night is young."

They began with the duck confit strudel baked with mascarpone cheese, cran-apple compote, and foie gras cream. At the waiter's recommendation, he ordered a bottle of Pinot Noir Belle Glos.

"You're going to have everyone wondering how a lowly newspaper reporter has such extravagant wealth," she said as they touched glasses.

"I told the manager that I recently inherited a lot of money from a rich uncle, and decided to splurge on my lady love. He thought that was exquisitely romantic."

"So do I, she said," saluting him with her glass.

Warmed by the cheery fire, they laughed and chatted quietly, hands often touching, eyes rarely leaving each other's faces. After a while, she thought to ask him about his progress on the first article.

"The research is coming along, but slowly. These people hide their tracks pretty well."

"I'm sure." But once the topic was broached, the feeling that she had harbored for days percolated to the surface again. "I hope everything will settle down. Now that we're back home."

He was watching her. She knew those gorgeous hazel eyes saw right through her.

"Don't worry about them, Annie. They don't know who or where we are. We left them, and any threat they pose, back there in the woods."

"I try to tell myself that. But I'm still having the bad dreams."

"I know." He squeezed her hand.

"Violence just seems to follow you everywhere, Dylan."

"Not anymore. From now on, my battles will be strictly journalistic."

She tried to make light of it. "Oh...the pen is mightier than the sword."

"Something like that."

She studied his face. Saw that he was keeping it blank—on purpose. That bothered her.

"You *say* you want to walk away from all that."

"Of course I do."

"I don't doubt you mean it. But the question remains: Can you?"

"I *need* to. It's no way to live."

He looked irritated. Then he seemed to push it aside and recapture the mood. He took her hand in both of his.

"I want to build a normal life. For you, Annie."

She swallowed. "For both of us."

The entrees arrived. She had chosen the pork, he the rack of lamb. Their presentations and accompaniments were spectacular, and the wine pairing continued to work. Afterward, they ordered dessert—she a white chocolate pistachio specialty, he the carrot cake. The wait staff drifted away, giving them time and space alone. They relaxed in the warmth of the room and the meal, finishing off the bottle, watching the fire die down. The string quartet continued to work their way through a Baroque repertoire.

"They're superb," she said. "I don't recall ever hearing better musicians."

"Well, they'd *better* be good. They're from the National Symphony."

"*What?*"

"When I hired them, I promised that they couldn't possibly have a more appreciative listener tonight than you. Nor one more beautiful."

He motioned their server over and asked for a bottle of Dom Perignon.

"Dylan!" she protested. "I'm stuffed. I can't possibly handle a bottle of champagne now."

"Oh, let's just have a sip to cap off the evening. Besides, whatever we don't finish I'll have them cork, and we'll take it home." He grinned. "I'm sure we'll find uses for it before we pass out."

They laughed. Imagining.

The waiter materialized again, placed glittering cut crystal flutes before them, and uncorked the bottle with practiced flair. Dylan reached across the table for her glass. Slid it near him.

"Why don't you fill hers first?" he told the waiter.

The two men's eyes met. The waiter gave a slight nod. He bent to fill the flute, then poured Dylan his serving.

"I'll leave the bottle here for you, sir."

The waiter left. Abruptly, the string quartet swung into a modern standard: "It Had to Be You."

She remained silent, unable to find words equal to the occasion. Or to him. She found herself transfixed by the rugged contours of his face. The reflected glint of candlelight in the brown-green eyes. The cocky grin.

After a moment she said, "Dylan, we've known each other only a few months. I don't know how I deserve all of this yet."

"*Yet?*"

She felt her face grow warm.

"I mean, we've managed just fine—for these past few weeks. But what about…"

She stopped.

"What about longer?" he finished. "Much longer?"

She dropped her eyes. Studied the polish on her nails. "I don't know. I'm not sure of anything."

"I am. As for you, maybe the champagne will help."

He extended the flute to her.

She reached for it, then her hand froze in mid-air.

She saw what was in the bottom of the glass.

Her heart began to pound.

Never losing his cocky grin or his eye contact with her, he tilted the flute slightly, reached in with his forefinger, and lifted out the ring.

And then Dylan was down on one knee before her and holding her trembling hand in her lap and she tried, tried very hard, to focus on every word he was saying as he stared up at her, his beautiful face serious now, his voice strong and steady. She was vaguely aware that somewhere lights were flashing and somewhere there was music but all she could see, really see, was that face staring up at her, and all that she could hear, really hear, were the words pouring from his heart.

"Annie Woods, I have adored you since the first moment I saw you. You are everything I have ever wanted from a lover. From a companion. From life. We both know that what we have together is so rare, so special, that it seems almost impossible. We both knew it on our first date. We both knew it even at the times when we were hurting each other. And we both know it now.

"It had to be you, Annie Woods. And it has to be us. We belong together. For the rest of our lives."

She was shaking all over now and the tears were flowing freely and she knew that of all the men that ever were, she would never find one better, or better for her.

She watched him draw a breath. Let it out. Felt his hand, so big and strong and steady, tremble a little, too, as he said:

"Annie Woods, would you do me the honor of becoming my wife?"

She gripped his hand tightly. Looked around to anchor the reality of this moment forever in her memory. Noticed only now that the wait staff had assembled near the entrance, along with some smiling guests from other dining areas, and that the flashing came from their cameras. Noticed now that the strings were playing her personal Sinatra favorite, "Night and Day."

She tried to absorb it all—overwhelmed by the firelight and candles, by the flowers and music, by the antique furniture and relics, by the silver and crystal, by the beamed ceiling and the framed Currier and Ives prints on the walls.

But most of all, by him.

She rested her other hand on his head, ran her fingers through the softness of his dark curls, and whispered:

"Yes, Dylan."

He closed his eyes. When he opened them again, she saw her future in them.

Again, he raised her hand and kissed it.

Then slipped the dazzling diamond on the third finger.

SEVENTEEN

Hunter finished moving the soiled dishes from the sink into the dishwasher. He looked around the counter, fetched a stray wine glass hiding behind the paper towel rack. Noticed the lipstick smudge on it.

He smiled, remembering…

He found himself whistling "Night and Day" as he went about the tasks of putting the apartment back together after her weekend stay. Luna, curled on the rumpled bed, opened her eyes and frowned.

"Sorry, girl. You're going to have to move." He shooed her off the comforter. She thumped to the floor and scurried under a chair in the corner, where she turned and glared at him.

"Plotting revenge, I see," he said as he stripped the sheets. "Well, spare me your hairballs, and I'll let you come back up here after I'm done."

He glanced at his watch. Just after nine. She'd be at work now. Probably in Garrett's office planning their new mole-hunt. He'd call her in about an hour. He liked that she could connect with him by cell phone from inside the walls of the CIA, through a special coded relay—and by a special dispensation from the D/CIA. Garrett had made that unprecedented arrangement for her when he hand-picked her from the Office of Security to become his special assistant for counterintelligence. Rank had its privileges for the boss's golden girl.

He was just smoothing the comforter when he heard the cell in his office chirp. Only two people had the number for his latest burner phone. He hoped it was her.

He saw on its screen that it was Wonk instead.

"Hey, Wonk."

"Hello, Dylan. I thought that I would update you with the results of my weekend research. I have left material for you to peruse in our Option Two location."

He meant their private, encrypted cloud storage site. Their Option One location was a local dead drop, for physical items.

"Thanks. I'll check it out."

"Because of the sheer volume, I felt that I first should 'give you the headlines,' as you so often request."

Hunter slid into his desk chair. "Thanks. Go ahead."

"First, you asked me to learn more about the old 'Technobomber' cases and their *modus operandi*. I did find an intriguing discontinuity."

Discontinuity? Hunter wondered, not for the first time, what kind of home life Wonk must have had while growing up.

"Further examination of the FBI files clarified the reason for their initial skepticism concerning Malleck, the student activist who was convicted for those bombings. Though he was a Marxist who belonged to violent groups that promoted 'revolution' against business interests, he was not known for an environmental focus. However, the construction of the bombs, and some of the messages left by the perpetrator, suggested that environmentalism was his or her central obsession."

"What do you mean, the bomb construction?"

"As in the equally infamous 'Unabomber' incidents, this individual often included barium nitrate in his explosive devices. That compound serves no practical purpose; however, when ignited, it releases green-colored smoke. Also like the Unabomber, the bomber sent communiques to the media written in green-colored ink. Finally—once again in the manner of the Unabomber—the perpetrator mixed natural elements, such as stone chips and bits of wood, into the bomb shrapnel."

It set him back in his chair. So *that* explained the mysterious pebbles and wood splinters he'd found inside the pipe bomb...

"Dylan, all of that suggests to me that Malleck may well have spoken the truth when he claimed that he had been framed by someone else. And if so, it also suggests that the FBI may have been premature in ruling out Boggs as a suspect."

"I think you could be right," Hunter said carefully. It was hard—both practically and morally—to keep his friend completely in the dark about his past life and current activities. But it had to remain that way, to protect them both. "What else did you find out?"

"I was able to determine that Boggs paid in cash for that bus charter. Because he does not maintain a bank account or credit card, his cash deposit was substantial—thousands of dollars. Nor was this the first such instance. Boggs as an individual and WildJustice as an organization often pay in cash for their transportation, equipment, accommodations, and provisions. Indeed, they never seem to be without considerable financial resources."

"Which confirms our hypothesis that somebody *is* funding him surreptitiously, just as the locals suspected," Hunter said. "Probably out of pocket, too, to avoid being traced. And those pockets have to be deep."

He shuffled through a small stack of papers on his desk. Found the one with the large "mind map" he'd scribbled: a chart containing random circles, each bearing a name, and each of those interconnected with others. It looked like a giant spider web. The larger "hubs" of circled connections included Boggs/WildJustice; NLA; EPA; CarboNot; and Avery Trammel.

"All right," he continued, "let's summarize what we know so far. We know that CarboNot's Damon Sloan was working in Boston during the period when the Technobomber was active."

"Yes, Dylan. But of course, so were countless other individuals. And, except for the political alliances that have enriched his business career, Sloan is not known to be ideologically motivated."

"He does seem an unlikely ally for somebody like Boggs. Just another crony corporatist, cashing in on the 'green energy' fad. So let's assume for the moment that his presence in Boston back then was a mere coincidence. We also know that Avery Trammel was there, too. And we know he's been funding left-wing causes, including environmental ones, for decades. That included Nature Legal Advocacy while Boggs worked there."

"True. However, once again, a host of other individuals passed through the doors of NLA while Boggs was an employee. It serves as conduit for environmental activists into government agencies and departments, such as EPA, DOE, Interior, and Fish and Wildlife. Its donors, corporate sponsors, and political cronies are legion."

"Incestuous, isn't it."

"That is my point. The overlap of Boggs and Trammel at that organization during that period does not constitute anything unique or unusual."

"Still, as I think about 'deep pockets,' I keep coming back to Trammel." Hunter tapped the man's circled name with his forefinger, pondering all the spokes connecting it to others. "That bastard has his fingers into everything. Leftist activism and media advocacy. Crony corporatism—masquerading as 'socially responsible investing.' He's getting more directly involved in electoral politics, too. Did you hear that he's announced his support for Ashton Conn's presidential bid?"

"Do you mean 'Senator Sustainability'?" Wonk offered. A rare stab at humor.

"That's the guy…So far, we have only indirect links between Trammel and Boggs. But Trammel could fund WildJustice out of his pocket change."

"Given his staggering wealth, it is indeed possible. Nor would he necessarily be unsympathetic to a direct-action organization. He has openly acknowledged his membership in revolutionary fringe groups back in the Sixties. However, Trammel long ago repudiated the violence of that period, stating that it had been counterproductive."

"So he says. But that could simply be an attempt to rehabilitate his past and build a new cover. Construct a new identity for himself."

Wonk laughed; his high-pitched voice made it sound like a giggle. "Dylan, you sound as if you have been reading spy novels."

"I suppose," he said, keeping his tone matter-of-fact.

"Incidentally, it is serendipitous that we should be discussing all of these individuals. Over breakfast, I scanned the *Post*. Are you aware that Damon Sloan and CarboNot are receiving an award from the EPA at noon today, outside of the agency's headquarters? Senator Conn and Avery Trammel are both scheduled to speak."

When he stepped off the escalator of the Federal Triangle Metro this time, he sensed no one watching him. He paused to make sure. And to wonder, once again, who had been waiting to tail him the last time he was here. The guy had been a pro; he kept his distance so that Hunter never got a good look at him.

But who sent him? He thought of the mind map on his desk. Too many possibilities to continue the useless speculation. At least he could relax today; this time they wouldn't be expecting him.

He headed toward the archway leading out into Woodrow Wilson Plaza—then stopped and hung back inside the arcade to take in the spectacle.

A long, blockish van sat parked on the bricks. It reminded him of Adair's data van, but this one was bigger and pale green. Full-color outdoor scenes of dark trees, blue waterfalls, sunlit skies, and furry animals decorated its polished length.

Above these, large white letters announced the CarboNot company name and logo, as well as its tagline: *For a Clean Green Energy Future.* On its top, the van sported an array of tilted solar panels. From their midst, a small wind turbine rose on a telescoping post, like a sprouting daisy, its three white blades motionless in the still air.

A speakers' platform, about three feet high, had been erected in front of the van. It bore a standing row of what this town called *dignitaries*, but which reminded him of a police lineup of rich suspects. He spotted Weaver near the middle, flanked on one side by his flunky, Crane, and on the other by Senator Conn. Some of the rest he recognized from photos or TV.

On Conn's left loomed Damon Sloan, an austere, horse-faced giant. Beside him stood Trammel, who cut a dapper, imposing figure. Attired in a long black overcoat and dashing red neck scarf, he stood unmoving, arms clasped behind his back at parade rest. Dark brows hovered over his deep-set eyes, crowned by a high forehead and a thatch of white hair.

Hanging on his arm—and clearly the target of most of the attention from the crowd and photographers—was his wife, the famous actress Julia Haight. A portrait of long-limbed elegance, she looked half Trammel's sixty-four years, even though Hunter knew she wasn't. She was wrapped in a hooded coat made of what he knew had to be *faux* leopard. The furry hood framed her face and revealed a little of her hair, which was of the same auburn color; the coat's hem ended at mid-thigh, baring legs worthy of a young showgirl. From everything he'd heard or read about the woman, he despised her as much as he did her husband; but he had to admit to himself that she looked smashing.

Before the platform milled several hundred people, at least a score of them familiar faces from the local press. He figured that most were here solely to see Haight. Half a dozen Capitol Police officers stood between her and the crowd, while others roamed the periphery.

Weaver stepped up to the microphone and tapped it. As the crowd noise trailed off, Hunter slipped out into the plaza and moved toward where the media were assembled.

"...And so, Mr. Weaver—on behalf of the entire CarboNot family of employees—I am honored and humbled to accept this *Innovative Green Power Program of the Year Award* from the Environmental Protection Agency. Thank you."

Hundreds of pairs of gloved hands began muffled clapping. Trammel watched Weaver shake Sloan's hand once again, then maintain the pose for the cameras, holding the award plaque between them.

"A recognition well-deserved," Weaver concluded as Sloan stepped back into line with the others on the platform. Weaver half-turned and swept his hand toward the van. "CarboNot's 'Sustainability School on Wheels' has already visited some thirty states to spread the green energy message. It's exactly the kind of innovative social responsibility that we at EPA hope to encourage throughout the business community.

"We have heard today from a host of distinguished environmental leaders—including our very special guest, Julia Haight..."

Trammel gave his wife's arm a supportive squeeze as the applause rippled again. She smiled radiantly at him, then at the eager faces raised to hers. Incredible, he thought, how she could stir affection and loyalty in everyone she encountered, even complete strangers. *You chose wisely, Avery.*

"After this ceremony," Weaver continued, "we invite you to stay and take a tour inside the van. There's hot chocolate waiting, which is just what we need on a day like this. But before we do that, I would like to invite our foremost champion on Capitol Hill to share some brief closing remarks. Ladies and gentlemen...Senator Ashton Conn."

Conn strode forward, shook Weaver's hand, and basked visibly in the applause before beginning.

"My friends: We know that for too long we've been consuming the earth's finite resources. We're eating up our seed corn, leaving less and less for future generations. And the pace of our consumption is increasing recklessly. Logically, this is unsustainable."

Trammel watched his gestures, listened to his studied phrasing and inflections. He certainly looked and sounded presidential enough...

"And that is why I am here today—to commend CarboNot, a visionary company that is leading the way toward a sustainable energy future. A future not reliant upon nature's dwindling stock of fossil fuels, but upon renewable energy sources—sources that are constantly replenished, such as sunlight and wind..."

Trammel listened closely, not merely for the words, but for the emotional nuance. He could find no fault with the former: They were pitch-perfect in philosophy and eloquence. As for the latter...Something seemed to be missing, leaving him unmoved. He struggled to find the word to describe what was absent...

"…as we fight to break our foolish dependency on dirty energy sources that only pollute our sky and water. Now is the time for revolutionary thinking. Now is also the time for revolutionary champions of the cause of sustainability, both in Washington and on Wall Street. Some of us in the political world are trying to do our part…"

It hit him: *authenticity…*

"…while in the business world, companies like CarboNot are taking the initiative. They are proving that we can break our mindless addiction to fossil fuels. They are proving that we can turn away from the most dangerous energy fad of our time: fracking."

Trammel scanned the faces in the crowd. They were eating it up. But to him, Conn sounded as if he were going down a checklist of talking points. His words seemed more calculated and self-serving than heartfelt.

Have I misjudged you, Ash?

Conn wrapped up with a brief quotation from his political hero, Al Gore. Once more the audience applauded enthusiastically.

At least you still know how to work a crowd.

The politician turned to shake hands with the others onstage when a man's voice rose from the press area.

"Senator, do you and Mr. Sloan have a moment for just a couple of questions?"

Conn looked at Sloan, who shrugged. They both returned to the microphone.

"*Only* a couple. We all need that hot chocolate," Conn said, arousing laughter.

Trammel's line of sight to the questioner was blocked by a couple of other reporters. But the unseen man's voice cut through, deep and clear.

"Mr. Sloan, you and others here have said that wind and solar are more 'eco-friendly' than natural gas. But according to my research, it takes eight of CarboNot's giant wind turbines, covering acres of windy hilltops, to generate the equivalent energy output of a single Pennsylvania shale gas well—which takes up less space than a garage. In addition, your turbines require miles of above-ground transmission lines and pylons to get the electricity into cities, while that gas well sends its energy through buried underground pipes. Finally, those big turbine blades slaughter thousands of eagles and other birds on the EPA's Endangered Species List. How is any of that more environmentally friendly than natural gas?"

Trammel had felt Julia's hand tightening on his arm as the man went on. Now, in the dead silence that followed, Sloan stood mute at the microphone. Behind him, Weaver was craning his neck, trying to catch sight of the questioner.

"I...I have no idea where you get such information," Sloan finally sputtered.

Weaver suddenly seemed agitated. He started to approach the microphone, but Conn stepped in first.

"Your comments are completely out of place at a ceremonial event," he snapped. "I don't know which media outlet you represent, but—"

"*The Inquirer.*"

A dark-haired man stepped into view from behind the other reporters. He stood there, hands jammed in the pockets of a knee-length leather coat.

Avery Trammel suddenly knew who he was.

"Oh!" Conn said, involuntarily. "You must be—"

"That's me," the man cut in. "And now my question to you, Senator. You preach energy 'sustainability.' Geologists have confirmed natural gas reserves that will last us hundreds of years. By contrast, out here under a cloudy sky, with no wind"—he pointed toward the van—"those solar panels and that little windmill are useless. So why do you think the output of CarboNot Industries is more 'sustainable' than, say, that of Adair Energy?"

Weaver maneuvered past Conn to the mic. "That's quite *enough*, Mr. Hunter. I'll be contacting your editor about this outrageous conduct."

The man shrugged. "While you're at it, be sure to provide him answers to the questions I just asked."

"Stop showboating!" a male reporter called out to Hunter. Others nearby nodded.

Hunter faced them and grinned. "I'm done. Now all you ladies in the secretarial pool can go up there, sit on their laps, and take dictation."

He turned his back on them and walked away.

That evening they gathered in the paneled den of Sloan's Georgetown home, seated in a rough semi-circle of leather club chairs. Muted amber light filtered through the bronze-colored silk shade of the overhead lamp and reflected off the casement windows.

Trammel studied his two companions. He wondered which of them would prove to be the more decisive.

"So now we have *two* problems," Sloan concluded, gesturing with his cigar. "Not only do we have to worry about whatever Silva will tell the Science Advisory Board; we also have to worry about what this Hunter character is going to say about us in print."

Conn took a slow sip of whiskey before speaking. "Silva is the greater problem."

"But Hunter is the more immediate one," Sloan cut in. "He could publish something any day now. And we have no idea how much he already knows."

Conn nodded slowly, swirling the whiskey in his glass. "Fair point. Stu, my C.O.S., brought me up to speed about your conversation. I had him put the staff on this. So far, they can't find out anything about this man's background."

"Neither have my people, and that makes no sense," Trammel said. "Anyone in his profession would have compiled a significant work and personal history. Which causes me to wonder if Mr. Hunter is writing under a pen name."

"Who knows?" Sloan said, tapping his cigar into the gray marble ashtray balanced on the arm of his chair. "But is that the most important thing right now, Avery?"

"It depends. If he is hiding something, it may prove useful to us to find out exactly what that might be."

For a time the only sound was the ticking of the silver antique clock on Sloan's bookcase. Sloan finally broke the silence, voicing the thought that Trammel knew was on all their minds.

"We do agree that we have to do something about this guy. And Adair's toxicologist. Right?" He looked from Trammel to Conn.

Conn's mouth was set in a hard line. "I had hoped it wouldn't come to this."

"Well, Senator, it has," Trammel said, watching him closely. "As you know, Damon and I already had a preliminary chat about this with your man, Kaplan. He stressed your lifelong reputation for idealism. But now it is time for some hard decisions."

Conn sighed. "I agree that we must do something. But we will be running a big risk."

"However, you also realize that the threat to all that we are trying to accomplish will become even greater if Silva issues his report, and Mr. Hunter continues to nose around."

"I am well aware of that."

"Damon has already said that he would enlist some people to confront Mr. Hunter."

"But what about you two?" Sloan demanded. "I refuse to go out on a limb by myself."

"I shall be out there with you, Damon. I have my own plans." Trammel turned to the politician. "Ash?"

Conn's gaze was fixed on his nearly empty glass.

"All right," he said. "Count me in."

"Did you receive your money?" the man on the phone asked.

Boggs stepped farther away from the gas pump where Rusty was fueling his truck.

"I did," he replied, his voice low. "Thanks. It'll keep us up here for at least another month, if need be."

"Good. It probably will be necessary. We need to keep the pressure on. We are running out of regulatory options…You recall that the last time we spoke, I mentioned that the EPA's Science Advisory Board is going to review NLA's toxicology report in a few weeks."

"Yes. What about it?"

"Rumor has it that Adair's hired toxicologist—his name is Dr. Adam Silva—could very well refute the NLA study. Apparently, he has figured out that the samples your people planted in the wells could not have come from the drilling site."

"Damn it, I *warned* you that those samples would never stand up to scientific examination!"

Rusty glanced over at him; Boggs moved farther away.

"I know you did," the man replied. "I anticipated that the EPA would not look at those samples very closely."

"But you didn't anticipate that Adair would insist on a review by the SAB, did you? They'll take one look at Silva's data and conclude that the NLA study is a hoax. The EPA will have no scientific grounds to impose the fracking moratorium. There will be nothing to stop it."

"I realize that now. This whole scheme was a bad idea on my part. I take full responsibility. But we had no better options. Your preference for 'direct action' would have backfired, too."

Boggs didn't answer.

"Look. I know you are upset. Everyone is—you, me, the EPA, CarboNot…"

"I don't give a damn about CarboNot!" Boggs said. "As you well know. That company is only a slower form of the cancer that's metastasizing over the entire earth. Its wind turbines are perpetrating a holocaust among the raptors. Its solar panels are a blight on the land that will—"

"I know. I know all that. But remember: CarboNot is only our temporary ally of convenience. A tactical means to an end. Our overriding goal right now must be to stop fracking. It represents a far greater planetary danger than their windmills and solar panels. First things first. We can worry about CarboNot later."

Boggs kicked a small stone, sending it clattering across the pavement of the gas station. He knew the man was right.

"You know how I hate compromises on matters of principle," he said. "Still, I agree that fracking is the greater and more immediate threat...But why did you call me *now* about all this?"

"Because I need your help."

"Doing what? Do you want us to picket this Silva guy's house?"

"No, of course not."

A pause. When the man spoke again, his voice sounded firm. Decisive.

"I need you to get rid of his research data and samples. And anything else in his lab or on his computer. A fire, perhaps. I leave the particulars to you. You know how to do that sort of thing."

The man's cold determination surprised him. "Yes, I know exactly how to do that sort of thing. But I don't see how that helps us, long-term."

"What do you mean?"

"I mean, it will only delay things for a little while. He'll still be able to get new samples and eventually reproduce his work."

Almost half a minute went by before the man spoke again.

"Then you will have to make sure that will never happen."

It caught him off-guard. "Exactly what are you saying?"

"Just that."

Boggs felt his anger rising again.

"Listen, my friend: To me, this Silva is just one of billions of leeches sucking life from the earth. Why should I stick my neck out to target one man?"

"Because the damage he is about to do will affect *all* of us."

"That may be. But if you expect me to do what you're only hinting at, then you're going to have to man up and at least *say* precisely what you want from me."

Silence. Then:

"You are right, of course. I am merely being careful."

"Well then?"

"Get rid of his lab, his research—everything."

The man paused once more, but not long. This time his voice was even colder.

"And get rid of Silva, too."

EIGHTEEN

"This is great, Annie." Grant Garrett raised his fork, displaying a piece of lamb roast.

Annie smiled at him from her seat at the head of her dining room table. "Why, thank you, Grant."

"Lucky you, Dylan. The lady has brains, beauty, *and* she cooks up a storm."

"'Lucky me' is right," Hunter said. "I'm hopeless as a cook."

"I know," Garrett said. "It was in your file."

"What wasn't? I'm glad I persuaded you to delete it."

"I don't need it. I have a great memory." Garrett poked at the last bit of lamb on his plate. "So Annie…when you invited me here to your lovely home, you mysteriously intimated that you had a surprise for me."

She looked at Hunter, her eyes bright, waiting for him to say it.

"We do," he said. "Grant, we wanted you to be the first to know…Annie and I are going to be married."

The CIA man put down his knife and fork. His dour features were inscrutable except for a flicker of amusement in his eyes.

"I thought you said you were going to surprise me."

They laughed while he remained deadpan.

"So you guessed," she said.

"I've never known two people better suited for each other." He raised his wine glass and when he spoke, his gravelly voice sounded softer, gentler. "To my favorite people in the world: May you find and enjoy every happiness together—today, tomorrow, and always."

Hunter had never heard anything like that from him.

"Thank you, Grant," Annie said, her voice barely above a whisper.

They all tapped glasses and sipped the Malbec.

Hunter said quietly, "One more thing. Would you do me—would you do *us*—the great honor of being my best man at our wedding?"

Garrett remained silent for a moment, his expression empty, unrevealing. Only his jaw muscle stood out, pulsing, as if he were rhythmically clenching his teeth. Then he coughed, though it didn't sound like his normal smoker's cough.

"*Now* you have surprised me," he said at last, the gravel back in his voice. Then his flinty features softened and Grant Garrett smiled—actually *smiled*. "Thank you. But the honor will be entirely mine."

"That's it," Zak said, pointing.

Rusty slowed the truck and rolled up parallel to the home. Perched well back from the road on a small hill in the wooded, residential area east of Warren, Pennsylvania, its lights shone through the trees. He strained to see the dimly lit mailbox; it bore the name *Silva* in white, hand-painted letters. "Yeah. That's it, all right."

"We're far too early. From what we learned online, Silva has a wife and kids. They will all be up for a while, so we have time to kill. Now that we know where he lives, let's go back into town and have something to eat before we return here. Then I'll check the layout and figure out how to proceed."

"Sure," Rusty said, trying to tamp down his excitement.

Garrett lowered his coffee cup. "Oh. I meant to tell you. I heard back from the FBI about the bloodstain on that towel. You guessed right."

"Boggs," Annie said, an edge in her voice.

He nodded.

Hunter picked up his napkin from his lap. He folded the white cloth precisely, along its original fold marks. Placed it on the table next to his plate. Lined it up carefully with the edge of the table. Smoothed it slowly.

When he looked up, Garrett was watching him.

"What?"

Garrett ignored him and dug into his slice of apple pie. "Annie, this is just unbelievable. *Brava.*"

"Thank you, for the hundredth time."

"Come on, Grant. You have that look."

The spymaster remained bent over his plate. "I don't know what you mean."

Hunter decided to let it go and changed the subject.

"Annie tells me you think you have another mole."

Garrett straightened. "That's right. I thought it had ended on the day you iced Muller. But more has happened since. Things that just don't add up. Things involving Ivan."

"The Russians? I thought you dismissed that line of speculation when you figured out that I was the shooter, not them."

"We did. But lately the Kremlin has been acting in ways that suggest they know, in advance, what we are up to. Things involving our C.I. ops."

Hunter caught himself absently running his forefinger along his jawline. Along the scar. He lowered his hand to his lap. "So, you have a leak in counterintel? Or how exactly do you read it?"

Garrett was working on a mouthful of pie, so Annie answered.

"Working in the Office of Security, Muller had access all over Langley. We think he had a contact on the inside—somebody giving him assistance, protection, and serving as a conduit to Moscow for his information."

With sudden clarity, Hunter grasped something that neither Annie nor Garrett had ever brought up to him before.

"But I blew your investigation, didn't I?" he said slowly. "I killed Muller before you could interrogate him. Before you could get him to flip—perhaps rat out his contact...the second mole."

Garrett and Annie exchanged a sober look, but didn't answer.

"So it's true," Hunter continued, his voice low. "When I heard that you had him, all I could think of was revenge. So I went off half-cocked and shot him. Before he could open his mouth to you." He felt like hell. "I may as well have been working for the Kremlin myself."

"Don't be hard on yourself," Garrett said. "You couldn't have known. And there is no certainty that Muller would have spilled his guts about an inside contact, anyway. He was a congenital liar and manipulator. He *loved* jerking us around. He could very well have continued to play us."

Hunter shook his head. "Look, I appreciate that you're trying to make me feel better. But let's face it: I blew it, big time." He sighed. "In retrospect, it's too damned bad that your sniper didn't spot me sooner than he did, and just take me out."

"Dylan!" Annie looked horrified. "Don't say that!"

Garrett frowned. "What do you mean, 'sooner'? My sniper team never saw you. And from where they were positioned, a mile away on the opposite hillside, they couldn't have hit you, anyway."

It was Hunter's turn to be puzzled. "No, I mean the guy you had positioned on *my* hill."

Garrett stared at him. "*What* guy?"

It took them the next half-hour to sort it out. Garrett paced around Annie's living room, looking jittery. Hunter knew he was having a nicotine fit but didn't want to break this off and go outside for a smoke. Abruptly, the spy chief halted at the fireplace and turned to face them.

"So. The long and short of it is that a second shooter *was* present. Since hunting season was long gone, that eliminates the possibility he was out there for deer or bears. You didn't recognize him, perhaps because of his camo. But he carried a sniper weapon that you think may have been a Dragunov, plus a sidearm. You even waved at the guy before escaping— but he just stood there and did nothing to stop you. Do I have it all right?"

"That about sums it up. I never could figure out why he didn't take a shot at me, if he was part of your team. He had me cold, if he'd wanted to."

"Because he was *not* on our team...Look, nobody else had a motive or means to take out Muller, except you and the Russians. I figured that Muller's shooter had to be you, because I didn't think the Russians could possibly know where the safe house was. But if there is a second mole at Langley, that could explain how they knew. Ergo, that other guy you saw had to have been dispatched by Moscow. To do exactly what you did."

"You simply beat him to it," Annie interjected. "Do you see, Dylan? Muller would have been shot and silenced, anyway."

"Maybe. Maybe not," Hunter replied. "You're still just trying to make me feel better."

"Speculating about whether their man could have made a shot is pointless," Garrett said. "But you've just done us a huge favor by revealing the existence of this second sniper." To Hunter's questioning look, Garrett answered: "You've explained *why* the Kremlin had to have Muller silenced. Not just for the secrets he had stolen and passed along to them, but—"

"—to keep secret the existence of a second mole," Hunter finished.

"Exactly." He coughed a bit, then eyed the front door. "Look, I want to continue, but I need a smoke break. And I want to check in with HQ. Would you excuse me for about five?"

Annie said, "Sure. Just watch out for snipers."

Garrett gave her a mock-scowl, grabbed his overcoat from a rack near the door, and left.

Rusty pulled up past Silva's driveway and slowed to a stop. A few lights still glowed through the trees from the house.

"All right," Zak said, checking his watch. "I'll wander around in there and try to determine where his office and lab are. I hope it's in a detached structure."

"Yeah." Rusty recalled the internet profiles of Silva and the photos of his wife and two kids. "No point in doing the whole family if you don't have to."

Zak looked at him. "That's not the issue. My concern is that it will be impossible to break into an occupied house and plant the bombs without being heard. And for all we know, they may have a dog. But if his lab and office are separate from the house, I can enter, rig the bombs, then draw him out there and set them off when he goes inside."

"Oh."

"Just make sure to be back here in exactly forty-five minutes. I should have it all worked out by then. And don't do anything suspicious. With what you're carrying in the back, the last thing we need is for a cop to stop you and search the truck."

Rusty licked his lips. "Gotcha. I'll be careful."

He watched Zak get out, close the door quietly, and move into the darkness of the trees.

"I was watching you watching him," Annie said after the door closed. "You miss working for him, don't you?"

Hunter shifted around toward her on the sofa. Took her hand. "A little. But I couldn't tolerate it anymore. He understands why."

"You hated the Langley office politics. And the betrayals."

"Those things were a big part of it." He looked around her living room. At the tasteful furniture. At the expensive Oriental rug spanning most of the polished hardwood floor. At the large Impressionist print hanging above the fireplace. All of it from her previous marriage to a rich guy named Frank Woods who had cheated on her.

His gaze moved to those large gray cat's eyes. To the full wide lips. To the curves of her breasts beneath the soft pale blue sweater. To the long bare legs stretching from her pleated skirt to a foot rest. It returned to those incredible eyes, and to what he saw revealed in them: intelligence, spirit, wit, courage, character…

How could any man betray a woman like her? He ran his thumb over the diamond of her engagement ring. She felt it and smiled, closing her other hand over his.

"So, that's part of it. What's the rest of it, then?" she asked.

"I went into the Agency expecting to be able to fulfill a specific motive. But I found that I couldn't do it there."

"Let me guess: Matt Malone expected to be able to mete out *justice.*"

He shrugged.

"But you couldn't," she added. "Because of—what, Dylan? You say office politics and betrayals were only part of it. What else?"

He thought of the night when his Princeton professor of Politics and International Studies—on contract for the CIA—first approached him with the pitch.

"When Don Kessler recruited me, he already knew I was pretty much a loner."

"'Pretty much'?"

"Okay, a loner—period. I'm sure Grant told you that they never wanted me to be stuck under official cover in some embassy, making the rounds of diplomatic cocktail parties. They specifically recruited me to be a NOC. No official cover, out in the field, cut off from regular contact with station chiefs and ambassadors and—above all—the bureaucracies at Langley and at State."

"He told me. Grant was to shield you from all that."

"Exactly." Through the diamond-shaped, leaded panes of the Tudor living room's casement window, he watched Garrett's silhouette in the front yard, hands in his coat pockets. A red dot glowed at his lips, then faded. "And for the most part, he did a fantastic job. I ruffled a lot of feathers. He was always there to smooth them for me. So I got away with plenty...But still, I couldn't accomplish what I set out to do there."

"They weren't interested in justice."

"It's not that they weren't interested. As you know, the Agency has a lot of good people. A lot of *great* people. It's just that they were—are—captives of politics. The seventh floor—what Grant refers to, collectively, as 'the Corner Office'—answers ultimately to politicians. And justice is the last thing on the minds of politicians." He saw her weak smile, realizing that it must mirror the one he felt on his own lips. "I tried to do the right things, Annie, the things the Agency is supposed to do: You know—make sure our friends were rewarded, our enemies punished. But I was thwarted at every turn. Again and again, simple justice was sacrificed for political expediency and bureaucratic convenience. It took me a long time to realize that I didn't belong there. That bureaucracy and justice just don't mix."

"God. You make *me* *w*ant to resign."

"Don't even joke about that. Look, it's just me. I'm temperamentally unsuited for work inside an organization. Any organization, really. But you and Grant—you've learned to navigate the bureaucracy. To turn it to your own purposes and be effective. I can't tell you how much I admire you for that. It's a skill I lack. Annie, I'm glad you're both there, doing what you do. You and he are keeping the wheels from falling off."

She ran her warm palm over the back of his hand. "But you—you need to be autonomous."

"As Kipling said: 'He travels the fastest who travels alone.'"

She pouted. "*Alone*, huh? And *how* autonomous?"

He raised both her hands to his heart. "Not *that* autonomous, Annie Woods."

They heard the door. Garrett entered, coughing, and saw them.

"Oops. Am I interrupting something?"

"Just a discussion about the boundaries of Dylan's autonomy," she said.

"Ah." He looked straight at Hunter. "Something I wanted to chat about with him myself."

"Well, let me give you that opportunity," she said, rising. "I need to freshen up, then put on some going-home coffee for you and the gentlemen you left freezing outside."

Rusty parked the truck behind a large pine off the opposite side of the road from the Silva place. He made sure it was invisible to the rare passing cars.

A few minutes later, Zak was back inside with him, explaining what he had found. Then they sat quietly for a while. Through a gap in the overhanging branches Rusty could make out a single glowing rectangle across the road.

"It won't be much longer," Zak said, giving voice to his own thoughts. "When that bedroom light goes out, I'll wait ten more minutes, then go in and set the charges."

"I'm sure glad he does have a separate lab," Rusty said. "But how are you going to get him to go out there?"

"I'll set off a small incendiary device in the back of his office, away from its entrance. Then I'll phone him, posing as a passing neighbor, and tell him about the fire. I know his type: He'll order his wife to call the fire department while he rushes out there to save his work." Rusty watched a slow smile form on his friend's lips. "But unlike what happened at the Flynn cabin, I'll be hiding in the trees, watching it all happen."

Zak picked up the cell phone resting on his lap and tossed it lightly in his hand. His smile broadened.

"And this time, I won't depend on the bombs going off all by themselves. All I'll have to do is place a call."

NINETEEN

Garrett took a seat in a recliner beside the sofa. He nodded toward where Annie had just left the room.

"You've got yourself a great future there, fella."

"Don't I know it. She's the best thing that ever happened to me, Grant."

"Then don't blow it."

The harsh tone startled him even more than the words.

"What in hell makes you think I'd ever want to do that?"

"I didn't say you'd *want* to." Garrett eased back the recliner and settled his hands onto the armrests. "But if you aren't careful, you might do that anyway."

Hunter fought down a jolt of anger. He was about to speak, but Garrett raised a hand.

"Hear me out. I speak from experience…In all the years you've known me, you must have noticed that I don't talk about my personal life. Ever. Want to know why? Because I don't *have* one."

He looked past Hunter, into the distance.

"But I did, once. A long time ago. When I was in my thirties…A wife and a daughter. A really cute little girl…"

He paused. The jaw muscle was working again.

"I had it all, Dylan. Beautiful wife. Adorable daughter. The proverbial house in the 'burbs with the proverbial picket fence and the proverbial dog. A loving little mutt named Taffy...But I blew it. She put up with me for about seven years before she had enough. Because I was never around. Never on the important days. Never on the unimportant ones, either—which are just as important, if you think about it. No, Grant Garrett was always off somewhere in Africa or Asia or Europe, on some grand adventure, some holy mission for God and country. You know—those sacred missions of lying to people, stealing their secrets, corrupting them so that they will betray their countries. And sometimes killing them."

He coughed a few times.

"I was like you, then, Dylan. An idealist. I always did all those things, those nasty and terrible things, for the noble cause. Or so I told myself...But do you want to know the truth? The truth was that normal life *bored* me. I was an adrenaline junkie. Danger was my drug of choice. The rest— the noble cause with its high-minded oaths, its codes of conduct, its mission statements—that was all just bullshit rationalizing. The pathetic fact was that I loved living on the edge. I became addicted to it. And you can't make a normal life with a wife and a kid and a dog, and expect them to live out there on the edge with you. Or to wait forever until you come back from it. *If* you come back."

He cleared his throat again.

"You're not quite like that, though, are you, Dylan? No, I don't think you're in love with danger for its own sake. But that doesn't mean you don't have your own addiction."

Hunter thought about it.

"It doesn't feel that way to me, inside," he said. "But I'll bite: What do you think I'm addicted to?"

Garrett moved the recliner upright; rested his forearm on his knee. "Not a feeling. But an abstraction. An ideal. What you call 'justice.'"

Hunter looked at him while he searched his feelings some more. Then shook his head.

"What I call 'justice,'" he said, "isn't an abstraction. Not to me."

Garrett said, "So when you take action, it's mostly personal."

"When I take action, it's *always* personal."

"All right," Garrett said after a while. "Good. That means you aren't a fanatic. You only respond to personal provocations. When someone you care about is involved. Victimized."

"That's right."

"Well then. I guess it's only a matter of establishing some priorities." Garrett's eyes tracked down the hallway where Annie had disappeared. "Just make sure you keep your priorities straight, Dylan."

"I'll try to do that."

"I'm worried about that word 'try.'"

Hunter nodded slowly. "I hear you." He heard Annie moving in the kitchen. "Sometimes—" He stopped.

"Sometimes what?"

"Sometimes it's hard to know where your highest loyalty should lie."

"You mean, whether it should be to the person you love— or to your own sense of personal honor."

It startled him.

"Dylan, I get that. You sometimes wonder if you'd be able to love her as much as you do—or if she'd love you as much as she does—if you were the kind of man who could just 'walk away' from things, as you like to put it. You wonder if she could possibly understand why you sometimes feel compelled to do things that you know she would hate. Things that could threaten your relationship. Like all that vigilante stuff last year."

Hunter didn't respond.

"And sometimes, you hate the fact that you *can't* just 'walk away.' Life for you would be so much easier if you could. But you can't, can you? And that bothers you, doesn't it? So, you worry about your future with her. You know yourself well enough to realize that sometime, somewhere, somehow, push will come to shove again. And then you'll be forced to choose between her and your sense of honor…And you know what? That's exactly why I picked you out of all our CSTs, son. Because such things matter to you. Because you're that kind of man." A smile grazed his lips. "Yeah, I had all that in your file, too."

Hunter remained silent for a moment. Then:

"Are you talking about me, Grant…or about yourself?"

It was Garrett's turn to be startled; the only evidence was that he blinked a few times.

Hunter said, "What you just told me about your family— about losing them because you were an adrenaline junkie— that wasn't true, was it? You loved them. You hated to be torn from them. You weren't off chasing cheap thrills. You were off doing the work you had to do, because you knew it had to be done. And *you* couldn't 'walk away,' either—could you, Grant?"

Garrett didn't reply. Only his jaw muscle moved.

"Thank you for caring enough to tell me...what you just told me," Hunter said.

Garrett coughed. Then glanced toward the kitchen. "I wonder if that coffee's ready?"

The dash clock said ten-fifty.

"You want to give it more time?" Rusty asked.

"No. I've allowed them twenty minutes after the lights went out. They should be asleep." Zak stretched in the cramped front seat; rolled his neck. "I figured out how to lay out the charges. His lab is not big at all. I'd bet that he just does basic screening and preliminary work here, then farms out more complicated stuff to outside labs. But from what we surmise, he did all the work on the NLA report here, by himself."

Rusty didn't ask Zak who he meant by "we."

He recalled the photos on Silva's professional website. The guy looked youngish and pleasant: brown hair, squarish glasses covering soft brown eyes, gentle smile. His wife and kids, appearing with him in a family portrait, looked white-bread wholesome, too. She was a pretty blonde; the two teen kids, a boy and a girl, looked cheerful and intelligent. He thought of them losing their husband and father. It bothered him, a little.

"So...you can't just burn down his lab and office, then."

Zak rolled his eyes. "*No*, Rusty, I can't just burn down his lab and office. As I explained, he would simply redo his tests with new samples. And that would undermine the whole rationale for the EPA fracking moratorium. So he needs to be taken out of the picture, too."

"I suppose so…But this action—it'll be so obvious that it's no accident, Zak. Won't the cops figure out that somebody targeted this guy because of his work on fracking?"

"Which is precisely why I'm sending out a statement to the media tomorrow." Zak sounded impatient now. "It will say that Silva was targeted because of his *past* work doing toxicology testing on animals. That should throw them off the scent—at least long enough for the EPA's hydraulic fracturing panel to meet in another ten days and recommend the moratorium." Zak sat motionless, peering at him in the near-darkness. "Getting cold feet, Rusty?"

"No! Hell, no, Zak. You know you can count on me. I'm just wanting us to be, you know, careful."

"You realize how important this is, right?"

"Yeah. Of course I do."

He reached behind Rusty's seat for the black satchel, grunted as he lifted it and plopped it into his lap.

"This job will be more complicated because of the number of charges," he said, unzipping the bag. "And because of what I'm using. I'll need about forty-five minutes in there. But we'll do it the same way as last time, with the walkie-talkies."

Zak went through his familiar rituals: checking the bag's contents and his field jacket pockets, pulling down his black ski mask, donning his gloves…

Then he faced Rusty. In the pale light of the dash, through the holes in the ski mask, his dark eyes gleamed and his teeth looked sharp and yellow. It took a few seconds for Rusty to realize that Zak was grinning at him. The man reached out and gripped Rusty's shoulder.

"You know I couldn't undertake these actions without you."

Rusty felt a rush of pride. He swallowed.

But before he could think of what to say, Zak turned away and got out. He watched him cross the road, then once again vanish into the trees.

She laid aside the book she was reading and checked her bedside clock again.

11:15 p.m.

What is keeping him?

Grant had left a couple of hours earlier. Dylan told her he would be up "in a bit," and she left him sitting on the sofa, a glass of wine in hand, staring into the glowing embers of the fire.

Something had seemed a bit off in his mood. She first felt it when she returned to the living room after she'd left the two of them to chat without her. Something in the way Dylan looked at her, then…

The thin curtains of her canopy bed hung around her, stirring slightly in the breeze from the slowly rotating overhead fan. She had expected him here an hour ago…perhaps to play their little game.

It was a ritual that they had somehow fallen into, wordlessly, in their first weeks together. Once in a while, he would approach her bedroom entrance and pause, leaning against the doorframe, arms crossed, silent. He would watch her through the gauzy white fabric, lying atop the dark brown comforter, nude or nearly so. Tonight she was nearly so—just a few wisps of translucent, cream-colored lace lingerie that he had bought her. "Gift wrapping," he called it. Eyes closed, pretending to be unaware of his presence, she would move slowly, languorously, provocatively, sliding her long legs over the satin surface of the comforter, rubbing them together, running her hands up her body—then, sitting up, she would arch her back and stretch, displaying her breasts. Eventually, she would open her eyes, turn slowly to face him…and wait, motionless.

He would wait, too—for as long as he could stand it…

After ten more minutes of waiting, she decided to go find him. She slid out of bed through the veil of cloth and slipped into her sheer chiffon peignoir. Barefoot, she went to the stairs.

Descending, she paused on the landing. The living room below lay in complete darkness.

"Dylan?" she called out.

"Here," came his voice.

She continued her descent.

"Stop there," he said.

She halted, three steps from the bottom. She felt uneasy.

A new game?

She heard a soft clink—recognized it as a glass being set down on the marble top of her coffee table. From the light of the upstairs hallway above her, she saw shadowy movement on the sofa. Then the shadow rose, approached—and stopped.

"Damn…you are beautiful, Annie."

She was then aware that the light behind her was pouring through her sheer lingerie, that she was practically naked before him. He stepped forward into the light, weaving slightly. His dark curly hair was disheveled. His eyes glowed like the embers he had stared at hours earlier.

"Dylan…are you all right?"

"So beautiful," he said, moving to her.

For an instant something in his eyes caused her to flinch. She was about to retreat up the stairs, but he lunged forward and wrapped his arms around her waist. She gasped as he lifted her from the stairs and spun, in one motion. Then, crushed against him, she felt herself rush through space, backward. She gasped again as he tossed her roughly onto her back on the sofa...then she felt his hands on her, harshly ripping away the thin fabric that barely covered her.

"Dylan!" she cried out.

But then the weight of him was on her, and his mouth, tasting and smelling of wine, pressed hard on hers, and she could only hold him tight until whatever torment had driven him to this had passed...

Voices and noise woke Marty Silva. It took him a few seconds to get his bearings. Then he heard the voices more clearly.

Mom and Dad...Are they arguing? They never *fight...*

He lay still, listening for a few seconds more, until he heard the stomp of footsteps and his parents' door open down the hall.

"No, Shari—you stay right here! Get on the phone with the fire department and tell them how to get out here!"

Dad...

Fire department?

He threw off his covers and groped for the switch of his bedside lamp. Then rolled out of bed and ran to grab his bathrobe from the door hook. He slid into it as he yanked open the door.

His father's receding footsteps pounded down the stairs.

"Dad! What's happening?"

He heard the front door open and slam.

"What's going on?" Naomi, poking her head out of her own room. Her eyes large and frightened.

"I don't know!" he said as he ran past his younger sister, toward the lit rectangle of their parents' room. "Something about a fire!"

"A fire?"

He stopped just inside their bedroom. Mom, clutching her own bathrobe around herself, had a cell phone to her ear.

"—and please hurry!" she was saying. "...That's right, he's gone out there with a fire extinguisher...I know!...Yes, there *are* dangerous chemicals, so please hurry, okay? I'm worried and—"

Damn!

He spun around, pushed past Naomi and raced for the stairs.

"Marty! Don't you go out there, too!...Marty!"

He ignored his mother's shouts and stumbled down the darkened stairs in his bare feet. He was just reaching for the front door knob when an electric blue flash lit all the windows and the entire downstairs as if it were morning—followed by a deafening *bang* that shattered all their glass and shook the floorboards beneath his feet.

Ears ringing, he could barely hear screams behind him, upstairs...his mind, dazed for a second, trying to function...then remembering...

"Dad!" he screamed. His voice sounded muffled by the ringing in his ears.

He fumbled at the door knob, tore it open, lurched outside. To his right, twenty yards away, Dad's lab, a converted guest house—ablaze...coils of smoke and shards of flame billowing from gaping windows…the surrounding trees shimmering an eerie red-orange…

Horrified, he rushed down the porch steps into the yard.

"Daaaaad!" he screamed again.

He had managed only a few strides when a second blinding blue-white flash lit the building's interior before him, and another shockwave, far more violent, knocked him to his hands and knees…then he was being pummeled with hot stinging debris…then something heavy smashed down on his back…

Face-down on the cold ground, numb and deaf, he saw-felt a third searing flash-concussion…a fourth…then nothing more…

TWENTY

"I'm sorry."

She heard his soft voice, not much above a whisper, and opened her eyes.

Light from the pre-dawn sky outside the bedroom window filtered through the gauzy canopy curtains, lending pale illumination to the room around her. He stood next to the bed in his bathrobe, holding a tray bearing her favorite coffee cup, an apple Danish, and a lone red rose in a tiny crystal vase.

"How sweet of you!" She sat up, hugging the warm comforter around her. She reached out and parted the hanging curtain for him. He extended the short legs of the tray and positioned it across her lap.

"I owe you an apology for last night," he said. "I was a bastard."

"Something was bothering you—that's all." She watched him while she took a sip of the hot coffee. His eyes looked red and tired, as if he hadn't slept much. Whatever had been troubling him was still there. She lowered the cup and hoped her smile would encourage him. "Care to talk about it?"

"All right," he said. He sat on the edge of the bed beside her. "I know you haven't much time before you have to get ready for work. We can talk about it more tonight."

"That's fine. What is it?"

He drew in a breath. "I'm afraid of losing you."

It shocked her. "What? How could…But Dylan, *why?*"

He looked off, toward the dull gray rectangle of the window.

"Something Grant said. About himself, but just as applicable to me. About personal priorities." He looked back at her. "Annie, I am thirty-eight years old. Have you ever wondered why I haven't been married before?"

She forced a smile, placed her free hand on his arm.

"Well, I know you're not gay. So I guessed you just hadn't met the right lady."

He didn't return the smile. "Of course there's that. But there's something else…I think that, deep down, without ever admitting it to myself, I've always been afraid that whoever I loved might not be my highest priority. Might not command my first loyalty."

Something fell inside her. Before she answered, she sipped some coffee to collect herself; the cup shook a little in her hand. "What do you mean?"

"My little chat with Grant forced me to face the fact that I've always placed one thing above everything else. Above any person." He put his big hand on hers; it pressed down on her engagement ring. "Grant called it my sense of personal honor."

"But I don't understand. I *love* that about you. Dylan, I wouldn't want you to be any other way! How could there ever be a conflict?"

"I'm not exactly sure. But something in my gut, something elusive—like an omen—tells me it's so. When I was talking with Grant, he said his devotion to his work eventually cost him his family. I knew instantly what he meant. Not devotion to some *job*—hell, jobs are a dime a dozen. I mean something much greater than any job."

"You don't take on jobs," she said. "You only take on missions."

"Which, to me, is a commitment of honor. Of soul. Of *self*. Last night I finally asked myself: If I feel that way, can I make a higher commitment than that? Can I make a full commitment to *you*—a commitment that you have every right to expect, Annie?

Something froze within her. She became aware of the pulsing in her throat, in her fingertips beneath the weight of his palm.

"That's when I suddenly felt afraid. Afraid that someday I might have to do something, out of honor, that will hurt you…Love, the last thing I would ever want to do is hurt you."

She said quietly, "Then it's not the last thing."

She saw that he understood.

"We should talk about this some more," she said. "But I need to get ready for work now."

"And I should get ready to head back to the apartment."

She stood under the needle-spray of the shower, the temperature turned up high. But still found herself shivering.

She got out and wrapped the towel around herself. She had thought of something that she wanted to tell him before he left. He wasn't in the bedroom. Had he gone already?

"Dylan?" she called from the doorway.

"Down here." A harsh rasp from the living room.

She went down there. Dylan was on the sofa again, now fully dressed.

He was bent forward, elbows on knees, head down. His cell phone was in his hand.

"What's wrong?" she whispered.

He raised his head. His eyes no longer held pain. They held something else—something she had seen before, and didn't want to. He gestured with the phone.

"Adair just called. Adam Silva has been murdered."

He followed her back up to the bedroom, sharing the details as she dressed. It was an effort to keep her fingers steady enough to do up her blouse buttons. She recalled what Adam Silva had looked like over dinner. Now sickening images arose in her mind, unbidden.

"Nail bombs. Incendiary bombs." She zipped up her skirt. "That means—"

"—that Boggs is behind this, yes. But I don't think it stops with him."

"What do you mean?"

He began to pace the floor. "*Qui bono?*"

"A sociopath with a martyr complex may not be thinking in terms of who benefits."

"Normally, I'd agree," he said. "But something has been bugging me about all this. For one thing, I don't believe in coincidences."

"What coincidences?"

"Just how conveniently his ecoterrorism against Adair happens to align with unified government and environmentalist efforts to put the entire industry out of business. And with CarboNot's interests, too. It's the targeting. Boggs could have chosen to strike anywhere in the country. So why would he and his gang come all the way to this isolated spot in Pennsylvania to target *this* scientist, and *this* fracking project, right now?"

She rummaged through a rack of necklaces on her vanity. None appealed. "You said that was 'one thing.' What else?"

"All of a sudden, right before a pivotal event in this entire controversy, they show up. On a chartered bus. Who paid for that bus? Wonk said it: Boggs and his gang always seem flush with cash. Where do they get their money? We've been looking into it, and we have our suspicions, but nothing definite yet. Just lots of links in a tangled chain."

"And you're going to follow those links."

"Right back to the end of the chain. To the person or persons yanking that chain."

"If you're right—if any of these other people are involved with Boggs—then they may have been in on Silva's murder last night."

"I think that's a virtual certainty."

Then it hit her.

She went to him. She tried to keep her voice steady.

"But if they're desperate enough to do *that*—and you are investigating them—then you would logically become their next target."

"Don't worry about that. They wouldn't dare. I'm too high-profile."

"Dylan…"

He wrapped his arms around her. "It's all right, I tell you."

She rested her head against his chest. Felt-heard the beating there.

"I didn't tell you last night," she said. "I didn't want to ruin our evening. But when I was in the kitchen during the afternoon making dinner…I reached for one of the knives on the island." She felt his hands stop moving on her back. "And all of a sudden, it was just like…I forced myself to grab it, anyway, but my hand was trembling and I dropped it. And I looked at the knife on the floor and that was even worse. But I told myself to stop being stupid, so I reached down to get it from where it slid under the island…Dylan, there was *dried blood* down there! The cleaners must have missed it. I couldn't tell whether it was yours or…or *his*, but"—she was shaking, now—"*Damn it!* It all came back into my head again—you down there covered in blood and crawling toward me and the trail of blood behind you and—"

"It's okay." He held her tight, his hand rubbing her back slowly. "It's okay," he kept repeating. Her legs felt weak, but his strong arms kept her standing. After a moment he guided her to the bed and sat her in his lap; held her and rocked her gently in his arms.

"Sweetheart, when you get to work today, I want you to schedule some time with their counselors. You need to deal with this, and they are experienced with PTSD. Will you do that?"

"All right."

"Promise?"

"I promise," she whispered. "Dylan…they already tried already to kill you once, at the cabin. And if you keep after them…" She looked up at him. "I think about what they just did to Adam…and his family. You need to make a promise to me, too. Let the police go after them, now. Promise me that you will back off and—"

He stopped rocking. Held her still.

"I got him killed, Annie. It's my fault. I revealed his name to these people."

Now she understood. She slid off his lap.

"You can't blame yourself for that! He *said* it was okay to mention his name. You couldn't possibly have imagined that it would lead to this! Besides, his identity would have come out eventually, anyway."

He shook his head. "No. The whole point of killing him was to silence him *before* he finished and submitted his report. Afterward, it wouldn't have mattered to them anymore. He would have been safe. But they didn't know who he was—not until I told them." He flexed his big hands slowly, studying his fingers. "I was looking for an exposé, a big journalistic coup. But I only got him killed because of it."

She realized that they were both thinking of his earlier words.

"It will be okay, Annie Woods. Please trust me." He leaned in to kiss her forehead. "Are you all right now? I need to get to my apartment. I promised Dan I'd call him back and talk some more. And you need to get off to work, too…Are we still on for Friday night, out at the house?"

She tried to force a smile. "I guess."

"Great," he said. "And we'll talk by phone, every night, till then." He stood. "You're sure you're all right?"

She looked away. "I'm managing."

"Love, if it's too hard for you to stay here at night by yourself, I—"

"No. It's okay. Really. It's better if I…face things."

In the eloquent silence that followed she felt the weight of his glance. After a moment he bent, tilted up her chin, and kissed her softly.

Then she watched him go.

"I don't know what the hell I'm supposed to do, now."

Dan Adair's voice, previously so upbeat and confident, was subdued and dispirited.

From the window of his apartment office, Dylan watched the dark shapes of birds fluttering in the claws of a bare tree in a distant yard. For the past few minutes he had let Adair vent emotions that he didn't want to entrust to his own words.

"Look, it's not just about me. You understand that, don't you?"

"I get that, Dan."

"It's about all of us. Since we can't prove these bastards faked that goddamned 'study,' the EPA will not only shut *me* down; they'll shut down every fracking operation in the country. We're all screwed now."

Hunter heard him sigh. When the man spoke again, his voice was cracking.

"Jesus, Dylan! They *murdered* him! I never would've hired Adam if I ever imagined—"

"I know, Dan. I know." Then he heard himself add: "You can't blame yourself for that."

"Really? How can I *not*? If I didn't get him involved in this, he'd still be alive. And his wife and kids…Shari—that's his wife…his *widow*—she's under sedation in the hospital. Their son, Marty, he's in there, too, all banged up. And the daughter, Naomi—I hear she's a basket case over this…Dylan—did I tell you that at first he said he was too busy to get involved in this? But I kept after him. I insisted–"

"It's still not your fault," Hunter interrupted. "It's no one's fault but theirs." He watched the distant birds take wing, disrupted by something unseen. "It's all on them, now."

"You think so? You really think they'll pay any price for doing this? I don't! My God, Dylan! This is supposed to be *America*. What in hell has this country come to, that people can get away with shit like this?"

"Dan, listen to me. I don't want you to throw in the towel. This is not over."

"Oh, really."

"Really. I'm not going to let go of this."

"Look, I appreciate that. I really do. But you're one reporter. What can one man do against these people?"

Hunter closed his eyes.

"I can do more than you think."

"I'm grateful for you saying that. But I won't hold you to it. This is way too big. These people are all connected to each other, and they're way too powerful. Nobody can stop them now."

The image of Adam Silva's youthful, cheerful face invaded his consciousness. He opened his eyes.

"Don't be too sure. Don't give up on justice. I won't."

He thought of Garrett.

Of Annie…

Outside, the tree stood alone, bare and bleak in the distance.

"I promise you that, Dan. On my word of honor."

He leaned back from his computer screen and rubbed his eyes. They felt gritty and dry from the lack of sleep. And from the after-effects of the wine.

He glanced at his watch. Ten-twenty. He got up to make more coffee.

Luna was standing sentry again at the entryway to the kitchen, looking impatient.

"Bowl empty, huh? Want some treats?"

"Mrrrowww."

"Okay. Move aside."

She trotted after him as he pried off the lid of the large storage tin and ladled out some dry food into her bowl. Then gave her a few reassuring strokes as she hunched down and began to crunch.

"You should hold out for something better than fast food," he said.

He washed his hands in the kitchen sink, then brewed another cup in his coffeemaker. When he returned to the office, he noticed the message light of his new burner phone was flashing on his desk. He checked; it was a text message from Danika.

Danika Cheyenne Brown was the secretary-receptionist for the "virtual office" company on Connecticut Avenue downtown, where he rented space by the month. She intercepted his incoming messages, then either waited for him to call in for them, or—if they seemed urgent—texted him. Her texts were routed through a tangled network of spoof websites and call-forwarding from other burner phones.

He read her message and whistled softly.

Luna ambled in, sat next to the desk, raised her front paw and began licking it, then washing her face.

He punched in the number Danika had left him and waited. The burner's outgoing calls were similarly routed through a convoluted maze of websites and forwarding phones. It took nearly a minute for his calls to go through, but the odds of them being traced was almost nil—especially since he removed batteries after each call and swapped out new phones daily.

A secretary answered. Hunter identified himself, then waited another half-minute.

"Mr. Hunter!" Damon Sloan's voice was far more jovial than Hunter had any reason to expect, given their confrontation outside the EPA the day before. "I hope I'm not interrupting anything important."

How about the life of Adam Silva, you son of a bitch?

"I confess that I'm a bit surprised to hear from you, Mr. Sloan. You didn't seem eager to answer my questions yesterday."

"Oh, well, you just caught me off-guard, that's all." He forced a laugh. "It wasn't quite what I expected, given the occasion."

"No doubt about that." Hunter glanced at the copy of the *Post* on his desk, folded open to their article about the confrontation. "So, I gather you'll chat with me now? It'll have to be very soon; I'm putting the finishing touches on my first article."

"Please, before you publish your—did you say your 'first' article? Well, I do hope you'll hear me out before you do that. I'm sure that I can clear up a lot of misunderstandings. Believe me, that's all I think this is about, really."

Perhaps I understand too much. "Well, I appreciate your cooperative attitude, Mr. Sloan. If it works for you, I can drop by this afternoon, and we—"

"I'm sorry, but I'm all jammed during the workday. Why not come by our offices over in Arlington right after work— say six-thirty tonight?"

Hunter felt a little smile tug at his lips. He had a suspicion what this meant. He decided to test it.

"Maybe we could grab a bite at a local restaurant, instead."

"Oh no! I mean, I have access to all of the background material that you might want right here in my office. But I'll be happy to treat you to dinner afterward."

Hunter felt a full smile form.

"Why, that's awfully nice of you, Mr. Sloan. As a member of the working press, I'll have to decline your generous offer to pick up the tab, of course. But let me come by your office, and then we'll play things by ear."

"That's great! Will you be walking over from the Metro stop?"

"No, I figure that I'll drive."

"Fine. You can park right in our underground garage. It should be virtually deserted by then. The attendant will be off-duty, too, so let me give you the gate code…Oh, by the way, what car will you be driving?"

He was trying not to laugh. "Is that important?"

"It's for our building's guest registry. They want us to keep records."

"I'm sure." Hunter told him, and Sloan gave him the code.

"Just proceed down the ramp to the lower basement level, labeled double-L. You can take the elevator there right up to our floor."

"You make everything so convenient, Mr. Sloan. I can't wait."

He heard the man chuckle. "Neither can I. I look forward to this evening, Mr. Hunter."

Sure you do, you prick.

Hunter ended the call and broke out laughing while he removed the phone's battery. He noticed Luna looking at him, paw paused in mid-air. She made a little noise in her throat; it sounded like a question.

"That's right, girl. I'm walking into a trap."

TWENTY-ONE

He had been circling the block in the BMW since five-fifteen. He watched the steady flow of cars from the building's garage entrance until about five-thirty. Then a slowing drain of vehicles until five-forty-five, when it became a mere trickle. Just before six he saw the guy operating the security gate packing up to head home. Another circuit of the block and the guy had gone.

On another pass five minutes later, he spotted them. They had gathered outside a couple of parked cars in an unmanned open-air lot across the street. There were four of them, dressed down and wearing hoodies, looking over at the garage entrance. He zipped the BMW around the building again, and on his return pass only two of them remained in the lot, watching a third enter the garage, head down to avoid the security cameras. They were going in one at a time, to avoid attracting attention.

On his next pass, the lot across the street was empty. He pulled his car to the curb next to it and put on his four-way flashers. Then got out and walked over to their parked cars. The bumpers and windows of both vehicles bore decals for the local branch of a building trades union. It rang a bell in his memory, but he couldn't recall the connection.

He returned to the BMW and went around the block a couple more times, giving them ample time to set up their ambush. And more time for him to think this through.

He asked himself again why he was doing this. For a while, he had rationalized that he needed to "stir the pot"—force their hand, make something happen. But he knew that was a lie. This made no sense—not practically. Only emotionally.

It had festered for days. He wanted—no, *needed* to pound the crap out of somebody connected to this, somebody who deserved it. That's why he didn't trust himself to carry weapons to this confrontation; he was afraid he'd be tempted to kill someone. But that meant going in unarmed.

Stupid. Insanely unprofessional.

No, he didn't *have* to accept the after-hours appointment with Sloan—didn't *have* to confront these goons. Even now, he could just walk away.

Just walk away.

Garrett's words. And Annie's.

"You've got a great future there, fella...don't blow it"...

"Someday I might have to do something, out of honor, that will hurt you...Love, the last thing I would ever want to do is hurt you."

"Then it's not *the last thing..."*

Then he remembered the sight of Annie up on the cabin porch, putting the key into the lock...remembered the sight of Adam Silva at the end of the dinner table, eyes twinkling behind those squarish glasses, filled with life and intelligence...

He rounded the corner and approached the entrance to the garage. He had always believed that there were moments in one's life when a single decision could set the course of one's entire future.

He knew in his gut that this was such a moment.

Hunter's mouth was dry, his hands damp on the steering wheel. He thought of Annie as he drew abreast of the entrance.

Keep going…

His foot moved from the gas pedal to stomp on the brake, and his hands jerked the wheel. He found himself stopped before the lowered gate arm, next to the protruding security keypad.

He sat still for a moment. Decision made, he felt himself once again entering that high, remote, cold place, the place where Dylan Hunter became something else…

He lowered the window, tapped in the security code, and eased forward into the gray cavern. He swept the big black BMW around a turn, then prowled toward the ramp that led down, into his future.

Smoky Scanlon heard the sound of a car engine echoing from somewhere above in the garage. His watch said 6:24. He chucked his cigarette butt onto the concrete at his feet.

"Okay, that could be him," he told the others. "Let's move into the stairwell and see."

He waited as they preceded him, shuffling into the cramped space inside the stairwell door. Once he moved in and closed the door behind them, the stink of their workday sweat and of somebody's dried piss under the stairs assaulted his nostrils.

He thought of his phone chat last night with Uncle Lou—
his wife's uncle, actually—the guy who got him his first job in
construction, and later greased the wheels to get him his
union card. Lou Russo ran the District Construction Workers
Council, the umbrella group for the area building-trade
unions. Lou had phoned him after dinner to ask the favor.
The request made Smoky nervous.

"Look, Uncle Lou. I know I owe ya, big, and I'll do
anything for you, okay? But this—beating up a reporter—it
sounds risky, you know? I'd like to know what it's all about."

"Fair enough, Walt." Uncle Lou always called him by his
given name; his voice reminded Smoky of that MGM lion at
the beginning of the movies—the low growly sound it makes
in its throat right before it roars. "I know I can trust you to
keep this between us, right? It's a favor for an old buddy of
mine. Damon Sloan. Guy runs CarboNot Industries. This
reporter, this Hunter character, is about to cause him big
problems. Damon promises to throw lots of work our way,
future construction projects, if we do this for him."

"Okay. I get that. But it's my ass that's gonna be sticking
out on a limb here. Just how far am I supposed to go?"

"Just rough him up a bit. Bang him around, but nothing
serious. You don't have to break bones or put him in the E.R.
But make it clear to him that he's stickin' his nose where it
don't belong. And if he keeps it up, next time it *will* get
serious."

"Next time?"

Uncle Lou laughed; it sounded like coughing.

"Don't worry, Walt. You put the fear of God in him, there
won't be no next time. Any unexpected complications, I'll
take care of things. Promise."

Uncle Lou gave him the guy's description, told him he'd be in a dark blue Honda CR-V and would park in the basement level, in spot M-12, near the stairwell and the elevators. What he said next changed things considerably.

"Walt, look. I can't approach Joe about this. He's not *reliable*, you know? A pain in the ass, in fact. I need somebody I can trust, you know? You do this for me, I'll see what I can do about getting him sacked as shop steward. Put in a good word for you to take his place, you know?"

"Man, Uncle Lou. That would be—"

"Hey, I know you're ambitious, you always say you wanna move up. You do this, like you done stuff for me before, and I'll have your back—okay?"

"Yeah. All right. Sure!"

"Bring along two, three guys just as hungry as you, who can handle themselves and keep their mouths shut. Scare the crap outta this guy, deliver the message—bingo, you're outta there. Nothing to it…"

Now, waiting in the stairwell, he sized up his guys a last time, to see how they were handling this.

There was the black kid, Devonn. Early twenties, new hire, no work experience. He came cheap, though, because he needed a job to satisfy his probation officer. He looked tough enough, but his eyes had a faraway look. Probably doped up before he got here.

Then there was Terry. Big guy, nearly thirty, and definitely tough. Word was that he had been an amateur middleweight about to turn pro when he was sent to prison for aggravated assault. Like Devonn, he had gotten the unskilled laborer job a few months back as a condition of his parole.

Devonn and Terry were both hard dudes. They'd give him enough backup.

Billy, the skinny dago kid, was a question mark, though. He looked either excited or nervous—hard to tell. He bounced on his toes, and he seemed to be breathing fast. But he was ambitious, and when he overheard Smoky pitching Terry, he begged to come along.

"Hey, Billy. Chill."

"I'm cool," he replied, looking anything but.

Through the security window on the metal door, Smoky saw headlights flash into view. A dark car, he couldn't make it out clearly, swept around quickly and moved toward the parking space.

"Okay, this is it. Remember: We belt him around some, but no serious damage. You hear that, Terry? Don't beat him into the pavement. And I do all the talking. Got that?"

They all nodded.

He pushed open the door and went out, followed by the others. Then stopped in his tracks, so abruptly that somebody right behind him jostled into him.

It wasn't a blue CR-V. It was a big black BMW sedan. And the guy getting out wasn't a curly-dark-haired man dressed for business; he was some guy with blond hair wearing glasses, a short leather jacket, and jeans. And he had parked right in M-12, nice as you please.

Shit. This clown is going to blow everything.

"Hey! You can't park there!"

The guy closed the door and turned to face them. "Who says?"

"I do," Smoky snapped. He began to march toward the dude, hearing the footfalls of the others behind him. "That place is reserved."

"You don't say," the guy replied, leaning back against his car door and crossing his arms. "You don't look like you work here. You have any credentials?"

"I'll show you some credentials," Smoky said, doubling his fists and stepping in toward the guy, who seemed to shrink back in sudden fear.

Then the guy moved and there was a blur and something crashed into the side of his skull...

He sized them up fast as they approached. Four normally would be tough odds; but if they weren't pros, and if he kept his back to the car so that they couldn't circle him, they'd mostly get in each other's way. The mouthy blond kid in front looked strong, but the way he moved didn't suggest any special fighting skill. Take him out fast, give the others something to think about...maybe peel off a coward or two.

The blond kid raised clenched fists and walked in wide open. Hunter went for shock value, snapping out a right front kick over the raised fists and into the left side of the guy's face. He didn't want to kill the jerk, so he made sure to take something off it, and angled it to catch him with his instep, rather than his steel-reinforced boot toe.

Even before the kid had toppled, Hunter slid into a martial arts stance—turned to the side, knees flexed, hands raised for parrying and open for grabbing.

The rest of them skidded to a halt and automatically fell back a step. The skinny kid bringing up the rear kept retreating, out of play; he clearly didn't have the stomach for this. But the other two fanned out in front of him, undeterred.

Big, beefy, dark-haired guy, jaw like an anvil—shuffling to Hunter's left, lowering his chin protectively to his chest, raising his fists and forearms just the way an experienced boxer is supposed to...

Short, lean black kid, puffy dead eyes—sliding to Hunter's right, his right hand diving into the pocket of his hoodie. It emerged with a knife that he flipped open with a flick of his wrist...

The glitter of the blade in the garage lights made Hunter suddenly aware of the still-sore tightness in his left thigh, where a blade had penetrated deep, not even two months earlier. Nothing the boxer could do with his fists posed that much of a threat. As the black kid started to brandish the knife, Hunter knew that he'd have to take him out first.

The kid held the knife in his right hand, whipping it around fast, feinting a few times. Hunter moved to his right, away from the boxer, keeping his still-healing left leg in contact with the car, so that the big guy would have to step over his fallen comrade to get in close. He kept his right leg poised forward, on tip-toe, ready to strike—and to give the knife artist something to think about.

But time was on their side, and from experience he knew what to expect. In a few more seconds, the big guy would make a move to distract him, then the black kid would dart in to carve him up. He would turn to defend himself from *that* attack, and the boxer would tag him.

He had to act first.

Pushing off from his right foot, he lunged back toward the boxer, just as the guy was raising his leg to step over his buddy's unconscious body. He shot a right front kick at the guy's left knee. It caught the big man off-balance, in mid-step, but it didn't catch him quite right—it was more a glancing blow off the top of his calf—but it was enough to cause him to grunt and stagger to the side.

As Hunter anticipated, the black kid rushed forward, knife pointed to dart into him, like the needle on a sewing machine. Still balanced on his left foot, Hunter leaned his upper body away from the oncoming kid and shot a reverse right kick to the rear. The kid's forward momentum caused him to lurch into Hunter's boot heel, which smashed the blade aside and crashed into his ribs and liver. As he buckled, the kid's arms clutched instinctively toward his midsection...and accidentally tangled around Hunter's extended foot.

Wobbling on his left foot, Hunter yanked his right leg away from the falling kid and tried to regain his balance—but not before the boxer had regained his own. Out of the corner of his eye he saw the guy stepping in, fast. He knew what was coming, so he ducked—

—not quite fast enough. The thunderous left hook only grazed the right side of his skull; but already off-balance, he knew he was going down. He held his forearms alongside his ribs, fists alongside his face, just in time to intercept the guy's crushing follow-up right. It banged into his right bicep with such force that it bounced him off the side of the car as he fell.

He landed on his left side and arm. His entire right arm went numb; he couldn't even raise it to cover his exposed ribs from what he guessed was coming next. He drew up his knees toward his chest as he watched the big man limp into position to kick the crap out of him with his right, uninjured leg.

The problem for him was, he was a boxer. He was trained to fight with his fists—not with his feet.

Hunter was.

The guy stepped forward, balanced unsteadily on his injured left leg, and started to raise his right. Still on his left side, Hunter snapped out his own legs in a scissoring motion. His left foot, moving forward along the concrete, smashed against the big guy's left ankle, while from the opposite direction his right heel swept backward, simultaneously crashing against the inside of the guy's already-damaged left knee. The scissoring motion swept the man's leg right off the floor and forced his leg to buckle outward at the knee joint. For a fraction of a second both legs were in mid-air; but then he crashed down, landing first on the now-dislocated left knee.

He screamed for a second after he hit, but only for a second. Continuing with the momentum of his own legs, Hunter rolled to a sitting position, then silenced the wailing guy with two solid elbow strikes to the guy's massive jaw.

By this time, the skinny kid who had backed out of the fight was on the run. He was struggling to open the stairwell door just as Hunter regained his feet. A quick glance told him that the three unconscious men would do him no good; he needed answers to some questions. So, ignoring his pain and his useless right arm, he took after the fleeing guy. The fellow finally got through the door, but he was in lousy shape. Hunter caught him on the stairs before he reached the door on the ground floor.

He grabbed the terrified kid with his left hand, spun him around, and shoved him into a corner. Then gripped the collar of his hoodie and pressed against him with his whole body. Put his face three inches from the kid's, close enough to smell his rancid breath.

"You want me to do to you what I did to your buddies?"

The kid, shivering, could only shake his head.

"Then you're going to talk to me, tell me who sent you here, and why. Aren't you?"

The kid could only nod.

Perched thirty-one floors above the garage, rocking in a big high-back chair behind a big cherry desk, Damon Sloan turned his gaze away from the city across the Potomac to check once again his gold desk clock. 6:46. He should be hearing from Russo any moment, as soon as he, in turn, heard from the men he'd dispatched here to deal with Hunter.

Before that happened, though, he heard something else: even through the thick windows, and from this lofty height, the sound of approaching sirens. Then they cut out abruptly.

He rose, went to the window, and looked down. He saw three police cars pulled to the curb on the street far below, at the garage entrance.

They better not have killed the bastard...Or maybe he reported the assault...

Two more minutes went by. Then he heard the famous melody from *The Ride of the Valkyries*, announcing an incoming call on his cell. He grabbed it from its case on his belt.

"Yes, Lou?"

"Is this Mr. Sloan?"

Hunter's voice! What the hell...?

"Ah…yes. Yes, this is Damon Sloan. Is that you, Mr. Hunter? I, ah, have been waiting for you, and…I wondered…"

"I am so terribly sorry, Mr. Sloan, but you won't believe what just happened."

Silence.

"I…I don't know. What happened, Mr. Hunter? I hear sirens outside. I hope you haven't had…some sort of accident, or—"

"Oh, no. It was no *accident*, Mr. Sloan."

Silence again.

His mouth felt parched. "Then…what?"

"It was a deliberate mugging."

His heart was pounding. "What? You were *mugged?*"

"Oh no, Mr. Sloan. Not me. Some other guy."

Sloan collapsed in his chair. "I don't understand."

"You see, just before six-thirty, I entered the garage, using the code—just as you instructed. But when I got down to the parking area you described—well, there was a fight going on. Three or four guys were attacking some blond-haired man, right next to what I suppose was his car—a fancy black BMW. I took one look and there was *no way* I was going to stick around. So I got out of there fast. And then I called the cops."

"*You* called them?"

"I did. I don't have to tell you, it really rattled me. I had no idea something like that could happen in your building."

"Neither…did I."

"Yes, I can tell it has you rattled, too. Obviously, you understand why I didn't make our appointment. Maybe we can reschedule sometime in the near future. But really, I was only meeting with you as a courtesy. I have enough information now to write my first article. I'll give your office a call on the day it's published, so that you can have a heads-up."

"Yes…I'll appreciate that."

"Well, I've got to get back home, now. I think I need a stiff drink or two tonight. You sound as if you could use one yourself."

"I suppose."

"Have a pleasant evening, Mr. Sloan."

He stared into space a long moment.

So who was the guy they beat up?

He closed his eyes, wondering how things could get any worse, when the Wagnerian theme sounded again.

"Yes?"

"It's Lou," came the familiar voice.

Then Damon Sloan discovered just how much worse things could get.

TWENTY-TWO

Hunter rubbed his eyes with the back of his hands. The soreness along his right cheekbone reminded him of the fading bruise there. A glance at his watch reminded him that it was Friday and that it was now after three o'clock. He realized that he had been working nonstop for five hours on his operational plan for the coming days.

He pushed back from his desk, stood on stiff legs, and moved to the office window. The marsh behind the house on Connor's Point was frozen over; fugitive weeds stuck up here and there like tufts of hair through bald patches of ice. A light snow coated the dead grass out there and in his back yard, and the gray overcast threatened more to come. Not a single bird or other living thing was in sight.

He thought of the funeral he'd have to attend tomorrow. He thought of Annie, and his need to talk to her again tonight about all of this. He didn't look forward to either prospect.

He returned to the desk. Using a fresh burner phone and a spoofing website, he keyed in the private cell number of the *Inquirer* editor. It rang a few times before he heard the familiar growl.

"Listen, whoever you are, I don't know how you got this number, but I'm not buying whatever you're selling."

"That's too bad, Bill. I guess I'll have to peddle my next article elsewhere."

"Hunter!" Bronowski barked. "You've taken your sweet time returning yesterday's call."

"Sorry. I didn't check in with my answering service till just a few minutes ago."

"Oh yeah—I forgot. Your *answering service.* I suppose it's out of the question for His Royal Majesty to use voicemail and a phone number that shows up on Caller ID, like the rest of us mere peasants."

"I told you before, Bill: I piss off the wrong people. I get lower insurance rates if they can't track me down."

"Well, plenty of the wrong people had no trouble finding *me* since I ran your piece yesterday. Gavin Lockwood of Nature Legal Advocacy called first thing this morning to say they're considering a defamation lawsuit. The EPA's press office issued a statement around noon accusing us of 'groundless and irresponsible speculation.' Then Senator Conn's chief of staff—some snotty piece of work name of Kaplan—phoned to demand a retraction and apology. And all that before Addison chewed me out for half an hour this afternoon. He told me Conn himself had just called *him* to bust his balls. "

"Oh my. Have I provoked our dear publisher again?"

"He's not the only person you provoked." Something changed in the newspaperman's rough voice. "You also got a threatening email."

Hunter watched a low cloud scudding over the marsh. "How threatening?"

"Threatening enough for me to call the FBI."

"Okay, you'd better forward a copy to me at the file storage site."

"Already did…You know, reading this message, the language sounds like it could be one of those crazies up there in the woods that you wrote about. But whoever it is sounds really pissed off at you."

"I can't imagine why."

After the call, he logged into his folder at the online cloud site, through a chain of "backdoor" computers that included a netbook that he'd stashed at a distant public wi-fi hot spot. He downloaded and printed out the message, then spent another half-hour pondering it.

Its author had to be Boggs. He'd been reading the man's past writings, and the style was too similar to be coincidental. Most of it was a long rant against fracking and the "falsehoods and half-truths" in Hunter's article. He skimmed through the turgid ideological prose—but paused when he saw the name of CarboNot:

"You insult the millions of us who cherish the Earth when you falsely align our interests with those of so-called 'green energy' corporations, such as CarboNot. We reject entirely, on moral principle, their manipulative abuse of nature and their empty claims of environmental sensitivity. To us, the horrifying holocaust of birds perpetrated by windmills erected by such rapacious companies is no moral 'alternative' to the use of fossil fuels. Neither is their desecration of miles of pristine landscape with ugly solar panels…"

It sounded sincere. So, maybe he was wrong to assume there was an alliance between WildJustice and the rest of the anti-fracking crowd.

He read on. A few paragraphs later, Boggs got personal:

"Mr. Hunter, your very name gives unapologetic voice to the arrogant human impulse that has so long defiled and disrupted our fragile ecosystem. In rationalizing that destruction, you prove yourself to be far more dangerous than the developers and drillers like Adair, whom you champion. Your perverse anthropocentric 'values' have damned you. That is why you must be—and will be—stopped."

The following paragraph, also curiously personal, caught his attention:

"I can tell from your past articles that, in a strange way, you are a lot like me. You believe in a black-and-white morality—except that yours is the inverse of mine. To you, black is white. But you and I both make binary moral choices. Things are 'either/or' for us. That makes you predictable—and that is your Achilles's heel."

He read and reread it, faintly aware of the rasp of ice crystals whipped against his window by the rising wind.

Luna sat on the kitchen mat watching him pour a glass of wine. He heard the front door open, then the sound of her footsteps approach behind him.

"Hey, you," she said. The sound of a smile in her voice.

He pulled out the cork and turned. "Hey, you."

The smile vanished. "Your face! What happened?"

"Would you believe me if I told you I fell out of bed?"

"I'd believe you if you told me the truth!"

"Oh. That. Well, the CEO of CarboNot invited me to meet him at their offices. He sent a reception committee to wait for me in the garage."

"Damn it, Dylan! You said they wouldn't go after you, because you were too famous."

"Clearly, I need to fire my publicist."

"Stop it! Look what they did to you."

"You oughta see the other guys."

She stalked off into the den.

The cat looked after her, then back at him.

"Well, *I* thought it was funny."

They rose early on Saturday morning for the flight to Adam Silva's funeral. He drove them out to the Bay Bridge Airport on Kent Island, where he kept his Cessna 400. It was the first time she had seen it or flown with him, so he could tell that she was a little nervous when she buckled in. But in a few moments, after he made the loop north, he saw her unclench her hands and relax.

"You fly well," she said. "And this is a gorgeous little plane."

"Thanks. It's the fastest single-prop on the market."

"You haven't radioed any towers yet."

"I don't have to. The airport here doesn't have one, and it's just far enough out from D.C. that I can stay on Visual Flight Rules. That means I don't have to file a flight plan or call any towers—not if I don't climb above 3500 feet for a while." He nudged the outboard side stick a little to compensate for a bit of turbulence. "But we don't have to stay down here forever. Once we get farther north, I'll be able to climb to just below 18,000 and push it to about 220 knots. That should get us to Tidioute in about an hour."

"How convenient to live near an airport so close to D.C., but where you can come and go without having to file a flight plan. I suppose you considered that when you bought the house out here?"

"Remember what you said about Wonk's apartment over the doughnut shop? 'Location, location, location.'"

Smooth engine noise filled the comfortable breaks in their conversation. Conversation had not been so comfortable the evening before. It took a long time and two large glasses of Syrah to calm her. He didn't bring up that he had anticipated, and could have avoided, the confrontation in the garage. Not only would that have infuriated her; in retrospect, his actions were too embarrassing to mention. It was grossly unprofessional to walk into a trap like that, let alone unarmed. It easily could have turned into a disaster—and almost did.

Instead, he reassured her that the failed assault had probably discouraged his enemies and scared them off. He didn't believe that, though, and vowed to himself that he would never again take such stupid, impulsive actions. He had let anger overwhelm reason, something he never did in the field. Against superior forces, a lone operator's only advantages lay in asymmetrical tactics: staying on the offensive, careful planning, using stealth, surprise, and technology as force-multipliers, and—above all—maintaining icy mental control during ops.

Fifty-five minutes later he put the plane down on a private paved landing strip just west of the small town of Tidioute. He explained to Annie that, for an annual fee, he had arranged with its owner several years earlier to use the strip for visits to his cabin, and also to leave a locally purchased Subaru Forester on the airfield lot.

"It gives me travel flexibility, especially when I don't need to transport Luna or supplies up here."

"And an emergency escape option, I suppose," she said as she unbuckled herself.

"There's that."

This time, though, he didn't have to use his car. Dan Adair, who didn't live far away, had offered to meet them and drive over to Warren. He stood waiting outside his Nissan pickup while Hunter swung around the Cessna next to the field's small hangar.

Annie was shocked at the change in Adair's appearance. In little over two weeks, he looked as if he had added five years and lost ten pounds.

"Sorry Nan couldn't join us," he said to her over his shoulder as she settled into the rear seat. "She was looking forward to seeing you again. But it's Will's twenty-second birthday today, and she has a party planned for the afternoon. He had a hissy fit when he thought Adam's funeral might interrupt it."

"I understand," she said.

"You couldn't. Not really." In the mirror his eyes looked dull. "It's complicated. Will was Nan's only child with her late husband. He was thirteen when his dad died. He took it hard. And he didn't like it much when his mother remarried. Especially to somebody like me."

"Like you?" Annie prompted.

He eased the truck out of the lot and onto the road.

"See, Will's dad was a college professor. Sociology. About as different from me as anyone can be, from what Nan tells me. And as Will loves to remind me." His voice held a tinge of bitterness.

"Then why is he willing to work for you?" Dylan asked.

"Beats me," Adair said. "It's certainly not the kind of work I would've expected he would want to do. He went to school at the same place his dad taught—University of Massachusetts in Amherst. He majored in—what the hell was it?—oh yeah, 'Social Thought and Political Economy.' I had to write it down once, just to remember. And after school last year, he just seemed…I don't know. Rootless. I offered him a job till he could sort things out. At first he just sneered at me. Which pissed me off. But then a few months later he came back to me, all apologetic, and asked if the offer was still open." Adair sighed. "So you see how it is. How could I refuse a job to my wife's kid?"

"I see how it is," Dylan said.

They exchanged few more words during the somber twenty-minute drive along the Allegheny River to Warren. It was ten-thirty when Adair pulled into the lot of a large Methodist church.

Inside, family members and friends milled at the rear of the sanctuary prior to the funeral service. Annie held Dylan's arm as they followed Adair in the queue leading to a blonde woman in black; two teenagers stood on either side. She recalled their names: *Sharon. Martin. Naomi.*

When Dan Adair reached them, she noticed that his shoulders were trembling.

"Mrs. Silva," he began. "I'm…Dan Adair…" He stopped. Swallowed. The trembling became shaking. "I…" His next words were a whispered sob. "I am *so sorry.*"

Sharon Silva's vacant, reddened eyes offered no response. Her cheeks were hollow pits, and the black dress she wore seemed a size too large. She only nodded, not releasing the hands of her two children. Annie realized that she was probably sedated. Martin, whose forehead bore a long scratch, was struggling to hold back tears, while Naomi wiped her eyes with a handkerchief.

Dylan rested his free hand on Adair's shoulder. The man took a shaky breath and moved on.

Then they were face to face with the family.

"Mrs. Silva, I'm Dylan Hunter, and this is my fiancée, Ann Woods. We met your husband a few weeks ago, for a newspaper story I'm working on. We came to express—"

She blinked. "You're the reporter he talked about."

"Yes."

"The one investigating this."

"That's right."

Something awakened in her eyes. She released her son's hand and seized Dylan's.

"Find out who did this!" she hissed between clenched teeth.

He nodded slowly. "I will."

Her eyes began to fill. She looked at each of her children, then back at him.

"They have to pay."

He raised her hand. Pressed it to his chest.

"They will."

They remained through the service, then the luncheon reception that followed in the fellowship hall. Church members brought an abundance of home-cooked comfort food and desserts, served on paper plates with plastic utensils. Everyone tried to be cheery and friendly. At most funerals, that helped.

Adair sat on Dylan's far side, away from Annie, at a long folding table, chatting with him quietly. She gave the men their space. She knew Dylan was trying to reassure him, restore his confidence. She picked at her salad, drank a few sips of lukewarm coffee with powdered creamer that floated on the top. It tasted like it looked.

After a while, Adair drove them back to the airstrip, where they said their goodbyes.

"Be strong, Dan," she said, hugging him.

He nodded. It seemed only out of courtesy.

Once airborne, she expected him to speak first. He didn't.

"Dylan?"

"Yes?"

"I don't like the way you look right now."

"How do I look?"

"Like you did in the diner. Before the fight."

He remained silent, eyes on the distant horizon.

"What do you plan to do now?"

His smile didn't reach his eyes. "Let's operate on the basis of 'Don't ask—don't tell.'"

"Please. For me. For *us*. Don't cross the line again."

"I didn't cross it. They did. They think they're untouchable. They expect everyone to obey laws—except themselves. And they're right. They're getting away with it. That's not supposed to be our system. We're supposed to be a government of laws, not of men. But these days, those kind of men *are* the law."

"I know. But—"

"No 'buts.' Tell me: What are ordinary folks supposed to do when the people who make the laws, who enforce the laws, who interpret the laws, become outright criminals—stealing from them, pushing them around, even murdering them? And when they have enough power to bury all evidence of their crimes? Just what are people like Dan Adair and Adam Silva's widow supposed to do when they're up against the likes of Sloan and Trammel and Boggs?"

"I don't know! I don't. But how is Dylan Hunter single-handedly going to stop them? *All* of them?"

He said nothing.

"Answer me: What are you going to do? Dylan, I have a right to know!"

"Yes. You do."

He set the autopilot, then shifted to face her.

"You need to know this: Boggs sent a threatening message against me to the newspaper. And Sloan was behind the attack on me in the garage. I don't know whether they're working together or not, or who else may be involved; but I think there are a lot of them, and now they've escalated to violence. What they did to Adam shows just how far they're willing to go.

"So for my own safety's sake, Dylan Hunter is going to have to lie low for a while. And for *your* sake, you'll have to stay away from me for a while—and we have to postpone any mentions or public announcements about our engagement. Until I can find out who is responsible—and stop them."

"Stop them?" The expression on his face scared her. "Dylan, please don't do what I think you're going to do. I've already warned you about how I'll react."

Through the windscreen the bright sun above the cloud bank made his eyes glitter like chips of green ice.

"I'll do what I have to do. You'll do what you have to do."

The words were like a slap in the face. It was so unlike him. They sat just two feet apart, but what was in his eyes—or perhaps absent from them—made that tiny space suddenly feel like a chasm.

"Dylan...I don't know whether I can take any more of this."

"Neither do I, Annie."

TWENTY-THREE

"So why did you insist upon seeing me *here* again, Dylan?"

Wonk settled back in his armchair. Three weeks had passed, and he had gotten over his cold. He wore a red short-sleeved shirt hanging over blue jeans. Either contained enough fabric to reupholster the sofa where Hunter sat.

"Security. You're sure your jammer is on?"

That provoked a grimace.

"Sorry I asked. As you know, Wonk, I'm after some very powerful, very dangerous people. People who have killed, and who won't hesitate to do so again to cover their tracks or to stop anyone in their way. But I can't get enough information to pursue this much farther...not legally. That's why I need to ask you a big favor."

Wonk shifted in his chair, which moaned in protest. "What favor?"

"I'm sure that their computers and cell phones contain damning communications that might break this whole thing wide open. And from what you mentioned last time, I inferred that you've either developed, or have access to, some hacking software."

"Now, Dylan, wait a minute—"

"Hear me out, Wonk. I wouldn't ask this unless it were life-and-death. Literally. I believe Dan Adair may be targeted next. I already have been. By Boggs and by others."

"Your face…"

"They wanted to send me a message. Warn me off. I don't think I'll get a second warning."

Wonk blinked several times. He heaved a heavy arm from his lap, took off his eyeglasses, then began to polish them with the bottom edge of his shirt.

"Dylan, I must tell you: I do not like this."

"I don't, either."

"I mean, I do not like where this might take us."

"Wonk," he said softly, "we're already there."

He stopped polishing his glasses. Then nodded.

"All right. What, specifically, do you need of me?"

Hunter told him.

"That poses no challenges at all. Please wait here."

Wonk put his glasses back on, and once again went through his labored ritual of rising from the chair. He stood teetering a few seconds, then shuffled around and wobbled down the hallway toward his office.

Hunter had to look at his watch to remind himself what day this was. Thursday. Where the hell did the week go?

He'd been working nonstop on planning his next moves since Annie left the house last Saturday night. She was too upset to stay through the weekend. They hadn't seen each other or even spoken by phone since.

Yesterday he had spoken to Adair. The man still sounded depressed, though he had managed to get the EPA's Science Advisory Board to grant him a two-week emergency delay in the hearing.

"Not that it's going to do any good," Adair said. "It would take at least six weeks, probably longer, for anyone else to come in and duplicate Adam's work. And under the circumstances, who would want to?"

"I'm still working on things, Dan. Just hang in there. And please watch yourself and your family—okay?"

"Yeah. Yeah, I know."

Hunter was examining a Vermeer print on the wall when Wonk reappeared ten minutes later. He waddled to his seat, collapsed into it, and held up a thumb drive.

"This," he said, panting, "contains exactly what you will need. Let me explain..."

Jonathan Weaver looked up toward the light rapping sound on his open office door.

"Come on in, Sally. What's that you have?"

His white-haired executive assistant, an EPA veteran, bore a dark box and a bright smile. "You are going to like this, sir. A gift."

She rested it carefully on his desk. It was a mailing carton, already opened and checked by building security. Paper tissue blossomed from the top.

"What's this?" He probed and parted the tissue, revealing the top of a small bronze bust. He lifted it out. "Would you look at that! That's John Muir!" He raised his eyes to her. "Who is this from? I have to thank them."

"But look at the package. It's been water-damaged. The ink on the return address label is all smeared. You can't even read it. And there wasn't a note inside, either...So you weren't expecting this? Some award from a recent talk, maybe?"

"No idea. None at all."

She shrugged and chuckled. "Well, then, you must have a secret admirer."

He laughed, too. "Well, don't tell my wife. What a shame, though, that I can't call or send a note. I hope the sender doesn't get upset with me. Maybe I'll hear from them soon, though."

"So what will you do with this? Take it home?"

"Oh, no. It belongs here, don't you think?" He lifted it in his hands. "I suppose I could stick it over there on the bookshelf. But it's so nice-looking—and only a few inches tall, even with this nice wooden base. Just the right size to be a paperweight. No, I'll keep it right here on my desk."

He slid it over beside the phone and faced it outward, toward the visitor chair.

"It'll be a great conversation piece."

Becky Hill, the receptionist at Nature Legal Advocacy, tried to interpret the bewildering sheets of paperwork that the guy had just handed her. It was on official District Department of the Environment stationery, with lots of stamps and signatures.

She looked up at him. He had dark sleepy eyes, longish blond hair, a scraggly goatee. His coveralls were smudged with dirt on the knees. He chewed gum with his mouth open. The plastic-covered contractor credentials pinned to his shirt read:

DONOVAN KANE
Environmental Mitigation Services

"You say radon inspection, Mr. Kane?"

He shook his head. "Passive monitoring. The new DDE regs. I was just down in your basement. It tested positive. So now I gotta install these digital radon detectors up here." He shook the boxes in his arms, making the contents rattle. "Make sure there's no infiltration. You don't want bad elements comin' in here."

She looked around. It was lunch hour and all the bosses were out. "I don't know…"

"Won't take me long—half hour, tops. I'll just stick these in a few spots, outta the way. Nobody will even notice where they are." He glanced at his watch. "Gotta be across town at one." He looked back at her.

"Okay…all right."

Still chewing the gum ferociously, he gave her a smile and a wink, then sauntered off into the office area, whistling.

Diane Baer looked at the clock on the wall. "But it is Friday after four, Mr."—she squinted again at the plastic badge on his overalls—"Stone. There's nobody here to help you."

"Hey, that's okay," the red-bearded man said with a grin. "I really don't need anybody's help to do what I have to do. Sorry about the time of day. I tried to get up here and see your boss last week, but my appointment was interrupted."

She scribbled down his name and "SS Energy Audits" from the paperwork he gave her. "So you are a contractor for the EPA?"

"That's right." He flipped to the second page and pointed to a line. "See, it's right here. Like I said, this is for their annual energy award programs. EPA hires us to do energy efficiency audits of nominated companies." He looked around. "And I can see why this company is a finalist."

"So what, exactly, do you have to do?"

"Just unscrew and check the thermostats in your offices, see if they're working properly." He tugged the brim of his baseball cap. "Do some ambient air-quality readings in the A/C ducts. Then check the solar panels up on the roof. Those are your company's, right?"

"Yes. We had them installed when we moved into these offices."

"I see you're watching the clock. Don't worry, I promise I'll be out of here before four-thirty."

"Oh sure, then, go ahead. Our president will be so excited when I tell him we're a finalist."

He leaned forward conspiratorially. "Well, frankly, I shouldn't have told you that much. Finalists are supposed to be confidential till the official announcement next month. But if things turn out like I expect, I think your boss will be in for a big surprise."

She laughed. "If you're right, Mr. Stone, I can't wait to see the look on Mr. Sloan's face."

He laughed, too. "Call me Shane."

Dressed in his long coat and carrying a large paper bag, Hunter took the stairs down from his ninth-floor apartment. A minute later, still carrying the paper bag, he emerged from the stairwell into the sixth-floor hallway wearing a gray trench coat, blond wig, mustache, and glasses. He nodded to a man waiting for the elevator and continued down to the end of the hall. After checking an unobtrusive telltale, which hadn't been disturbed, he entered the apartment of Wayne Grayson, investment advisor.

This second apartment fulfilled multiple roles, especially now that the police knew about Hunter's residence three floors above. It was a nearby place to bolt to, quickly and discreetly, during a police raid or other emergency. It served as a cache for items that he could not afford to be linked to Dylan Hunter. It allowed him to keep a couple more vehicles in the building's garage, including the BMW 7 Series sedan, registered to the innocuous and seldom-seen Mr. Grayson.

It also permitted him to maintain independent systems for secure communications, just in case the cops or some enemy ever tried to bug Hunter's apartment or hack his computer and phone. That was the role it was serving now.

He closed and bolted the door, left the bag containing his coat on a nearby chair, then disarmed the alarm system. He added the raincoat he was wearing to the pile on the chair and walked casually around the room closing the curtains, just as any law-abiding citizen might.

He spent the next five minutes sweeping the place for planted bugs. Finding none, he moved to the closed door of the interior bedroom, which he had set up as an office. It was the only room without a window, insuring a greater level of privacy. He checked another unmolested telltale before entering.

Next, he powered up the waiting laptop. Following Wonk's instructions, he inserted the thumb drive, and from it installed email client software that the researcher had customized. He launched the program and tweaked its settings to retrieve email from Dylan Hunter's public email account—but routed through a high-anonymity proxy server that Wonk had established for other secretive clients. This would create an additional barrier to anyone trying to track back his email correspondence.

All this took a while, but once everything was ready, Hunter let the software retrieve his waiting email. He watched as the stream of messages downloaded.

"Ah…there you are."

Both Sloan and Lockwood had replied to emails he'd sent them earlier in the day. Sloan's note was terse. He didn't know when he'd be able to reschedule an appointment, or "if it would even be worthwhile, given that you already seem to have made up your mind about the facts." Lockwood was blunter, reiterating that NLA was weighing legal action, and that any further communication should be through the firm's attorneys. He found no email replies from Weaver or Trammel.

It didn't matter; he already had what he needed.

He reopened Sloan's message. Using the "redirect" function in the customized email software, he created a new email. Then he used a second program that Wonk had provided—routing modification software—to strip out all prior header routing information, except for Sloan's. He then deleted Sloan's subject line and the text of his reply.

Now he had a blank message whose routing header—even if expanded and checked—would seem to have originated directly from Sloan himself.

He typed in on the subject line: "Re: Inquirer reporter"

In the body, he wrote:

"All:

"The attached from a quick web search re: DH. Not much, but perhaps useful if you have not seen it. Delete this after reading. No need to reply; out of office.

"Damon"

In the "BCC" field of the message, he typed in the email addresses he had compiled for Lockwood, Weaver, and Crane. He liked that touch: It made it appear that Sloan was trying to keep the recipients' names confidential by blind-copying them.

Finally, he copied a third file from Wonk's thumb drive onto his computer, then attached it to the new email message. It was a JPEG copy of a newspaper article about the role Dylan Hunter's articles had played during the recent wave of vigilante killings in Washington. However, Wonk had embedded some hidden code in the image file.

"Bombs away," he said as he clicked the "Send" button on the doctored message and watched it vanish from the screen.

He had one more task. From the office's walk-in closet he rolled out a tray table containing a military-grade, full-spectrum radio receiver. He plugged it in, got it running, and adjusted it to scan between several specific frequencies.

One frequency was set for the bug that he had hidden in the thermostat in Sloan's CarboNot office. Its signal was amplified by a relay transmitter he had attached to a solar panel on their roof.

Another frequency was set for the bug in the radon detector that he had installed unobtrusively in Gavin Lockwood's office. Its signal was amplified by a relay transmitter hidden in the basement of the building housing Nature Legal Advocacy.

The last frequency was set for the bug inside the bust of John Muir on Jonathan Weaver's desk at the EPA. Unlike the others, its signal had started up on a timer delay, so that it would pass through security undetected. That signal was amplified by a relay transmitter housed in a nondescript, locked metal container bearing the stenciled words "EPA AIR QUALITY MONITORING," along with the agency logo. He'd placed it beside some water control meters in a courtyard outside the Ariel Rios Building.

The scanner test showed that all the transmitters and bugs were functioning.

He checked the time. Almost midnight. Nothing much would happen over the weekend.

He turned off the receiver, powered down the laptop. Got up, stretched, and yawned. It would be nice to get a couple nights of uninterrupted sleep. He would need it for what lay ahead.

Now, the only thing left to do was to provoke them to communicate with each other.

He had already planned the provocations.

TWENTY-FOUR

Dick Wilson peered ahead through the smeared windshield. That, the sleet, and the weak street lights in the business park made it hard to see a damned thing.

"You spot it?"

"Not yet." Andy Elias sat next to him in the cab of the truck. "I think it must be up past that next building on the right."

Dick tapped the gas a little more, and the flatbed hauling its heavy, oversized load moved forward. They drifted past the two-story office building to a flat-topped, single-story one. It was obviously new—no grass in front, just lumpy dirt frosted with a few patches of snow. Just beyond it, a driveway curved into a parking lot.

"There he is," Andy said, pointing. Dick leaned forward and spotted him—a guy standing under a light in the lot, next to an SUV. He hit the turn signal—just habit, nobody out here on a Saturday night—and moved down through the gears, slowing the rig to make the wide turn into the lot. He pulled up beside the guy and rolled down the window.

"Where you want it?" he yelled out over the idling engine.

The guy wore a parka with the fur hood up, half-masking his face against the sleet. "Offload it right over there, near the edge of the lot." He pointed.

It took Dick a bit of back-and-forth to position the rig. Then he shut it down and set the brakes. He and Andy got out and unhooked the four tie-down chains from their anchors, followed by the tie-downs on the boom and bucket. They lowered the ramps onto the pavement. Andy climbed into the machine on the bed, powered it up, raised and curled up the bucket, then eased it down the ramps while Dick guided him.

The guy walked up, face tilted down against the sleet. "I really appreciate you delivering it all the way out here at this ungodly hour."

"Hey, you're paying for our O.T.," Dick said, laughing.

"Mind if I take a quick peek inside?" the guy asked. "We can do the paperwork in there."

"Like I said, we're on your clock."

They stepped up on the track and Andy opened the door to the operator cab for them. It was a squeeze for them all to fit.

The guy took off his glove and stuck out his hand. "I'm Rob." He kept the hood on; Dick could only make out his grin in the darkened cab. They went through the introductions.

"Why you need this delivered now?" Andy asked. "You working Sunday?"

Rob laughed. "Crazy, isn't it?" He nodded toward the building. "We just put up that place. Now they get a big new contract and decide they don't have enough space. So we gotta start on the new foundation and work 24/7 if we're gonna get the expansion wing up by late April."

"They must have money to burn," Dick said. "What do they do?"

"You know—the usual thievery."

They all chuckled.

"I got the paperwork here for you to sign," Dick said, reaching inside his jacket.

"And I gotta pen here," Rob said, reaching into his shirt pocket.

"You just initial there, and there—that's the rental liability and damage waivers. Then you sign down there at the bottom…Okay, I see you left them a big deposit. If you keep the digger out here over a week, they'll take whatever extra you owe out of your refund."

Rob paused, pen in hand. "I won't need it that long." He reached out with the pen and tapped the joystick controls. "These things handle a lot easier than when I was a kid. You shoulda seen what my dad had to work with."

"He in construction?"

"Yeah. Big Mike—that's what everyone called him—he ran his own company."

Rob leaned down again and scrawled his name on the paper.

"There you go. Thanks again. You guys did me a big favor, comin' out here this late on a Saturday night. Here—let me give you a few bucks extra. Go buy yourselves a beer and thaw out before you go home…Naw, take it—I insist."

"Well, thanks," Andy said, smiling and pocketing the twenty. "I sure hope this job is worth your while."

Dick saw Rob's teeth flash again in the dark.

"It ain't work if you enjoy what you do."

It took a few minutes for them to maneuver the big flatbed out of the lot and down the street. He watched them go. Then he turned to the excavator perched on the pavement. It was similar to an oversized backhoe that ran on tracks, like a bulldozer. From a distance in the dim, misty light, it looked like a mechanical brontosaurus.

He climbed back into the cab, settled into the seat. He hadn't been at the controls of anything like this since he was a teenager, with his dad, Big Mike, beside him to show him how and to make sure he didn't screw up. But you could learn almost anything these days from YouTube.

He closed his eyes for a few seconds, recalling the sequence in the video clip he had seen posted. He pushed forward a red handle at his left, freeing the lock. Then turned the ignition switch on the console to his right. A brief high-pitched squeal, and the engine was running.

Tentatively, he pulled back the right-hand joystick. The boom rose smoothly and obediently, lifting the basket from the pavement where Donnie had rested it.

Now to get this beast moving.

He wanted to go forward, so he put his hands on the twin sticks in front of him—one controlling each of the tracks—and pushed them forward. The excavator began to roll backward.

Damn.

He stopped, remembering the video. Counterintuitively, the controls worked in the opposite direction. He pulled the sticks back, toward himself, and the big machine began to roll forward.

So far, so good…

He released the right-hand stick, pulling the left one only, and it began a slow pivot. When it was facing the back of the parking lot he pulled back on both sticks again, and it lumbered forward. He went off the pavement and across the soil, maneuvering into position behind the building.

He stopped there. It took a few minutes to get the hang of the SAE joysticks, which maneuvered the boom and its bucket. He pulled back the right-hand joystick to raise the boom high, moved it right to open the bucket, then pushed the left-hand joystick forward, extending the boom outward.

Taking another deep breath, he pulled back on the other sticks and the excavator rumbled across the frozen earth toward the back wall of the building. When he was close, he stopped again.

He pushed the right-hand joystick forward, and the bucket came crashing down onto the roof of the offices of Capital Resources Development.

It made a lot of noise. He winced. Even though the business park was a good distance from any residential area, sound carried at night. It wouldn't be long before somebody wondered who in hell was making such a racket so late on a Saturday night. He'd have to hurry.

Fortunately, ripping a building apart took infinitely less time and expertise than putting one up.

Gavin Lockwood sprawled across his padded wicker sofa in the big glass-enclosed porch of his estate. A half-empty crystal coffee cup rested on a glass-topped table nearby, and the Sunday *Post* lay at his feet in scattered remnants on the polished oak floor. Last night's wintry mix had pushed off to the east, leaving clear skies. Though it was still frigid outside, the morning sun had warmed the porch enough that he felt quite comfortable lounging out here in his monogrammed green silk bathrobe, a recent birthday present from Selena.

From the house's perch atop the hill he watched the sun dance on the Severn River below. He loved the water. He much preferred this big Arts and Craft home, just a few miles north of downtown Annapolis, to his two-bedroom apartment at the Watergate, which, though smartly appointed, had a city view and felt claustrophobic. That place was a reluctant necessity; a daily commute into the D.C. office of Nature Legal Advocacy from out here was too inconvenient. But this was his weekend retreat.

The home had been in his family for generations. He'd inherited it along with a formidable trust fund, both fruits of his grandfather's department-store fortune. His eyes scanned the five acres that sloped down to the river, finding rest on another byproduct of that wealth: *Sundancer*, his 60-foot Bermuda Cutter, tied up at the dock. He couldn't wait for summer, when he could take her out, put up her sails, and feel the spray in his face.

His gaze moved to the lot next door. It was still undeveloped, and Lockwood was determined that it would stay that way. It had been part of a large estate whose owner had died without a proper will, letting the place fall into ruin during a decade of legal battles among the heirs. A few years ago the house had been torn down, and the land was subdivided and sold off piecemeal. Now, young oaks and maples had taken over the adjacent parcel, providing spectacular fall color against the blue of the river, and a buffer against the intrusive sight of other homes. But three months ago some Wall Street shark had bought the parcel, aiming to put up a summer home.

It incensed him that some rich bastard could just waltz in here, knock down all those trees, stick up some garish McMansion, and mar his commanding southern view of the river. Just one more incremental crime against the environment. So he'd spoken to local conservation groups, the zoning board, and the planning commission. For openers, he demanded a wildlife audit on the property and a study of potential hazards from runoff into the river during the construction. One way or the other, he was determined to raise legal obstacles and regulatory compliance costs to the point where the guy would give up and go away.

He sipped his coffee, finding it had grown cold. He was weighing the wisdom of a third cup when Selena rushed onto the porch, startling him. She wore pink exercise sweats and an alarmed expression.

"It's Senator Conn," she whispered, his own cell phone outthrust in her hand. "He sounds *really* upset."

He sat bolt upright and grabbed the phone.

"Good morning, Senator. I trust that…Well, no. I haven't watched any…"

His grip tightened on the phone.

"They did *what?*"

Ed Cronin sat on his bed tying his sneakers when his cell buzzed. He fished it from his pocket and saw that it was his partner, Erskine. He frowned. *On a Sunday morning?*

"Yeah, Paul."

"You see that new *Inquirer* article yesterday by our old pal Dylan Hunter?"

When Erskine opened a conversation this way, it was never to bring good news.

"About CarboNot—that 'green energy' company. Sure. Why?"

"You know how we both thought he might be involved with the vigilantes, until you said you got confidential information that ruled him out?"

Cronin felt a stab of guilt. *No, Paul—I didn't rule him out. But I was ordered to tell you that.* "What about it?"

"Well, I just heard some news that has me thinking maybe you were too hasty."

"Paul, I have to take my kid to a basketball game. Don't tell me another dirtbag just got whacked."

"No, nobody whacked. But last night, somebody takes a backhoe or something like that, and he, or they, use it to demolish the offices of Capital Resources Development."

The name rang a faint bell. "What's that got to do with Hunter?"

"Okay, in his article about CarboNot he also mentions this other company, Capital Resources. Remember? The one he says is involved in private land grabs up in Pennsylvania?"

"I remember now. Well, they must be making a lot of enemies. Maybe somebody wanted to get back at them. Again, what's that got to do with Hunter, or the vigilantes?"

"How's this: Remember all the news clips left behind at the vigilante crime scenes, and how a lot of them were written by Hunter?"

Cronin pulled in a slow breath. "You're about to tell me this latest Hunter article was found at the vandalism scene."

"Bingo. And not just that. They also leave a sign behind, planted right on top of the rubble. In big red letters: 'PRIVATE PROPERTY—NO TRESPASSING.'"

Oh shit...

Erskine continued. "So we have this Hunter article. Then somebody demolishes the office of this company he mentions in that article. And they leave a message at the scene, suggesting their motive. Sound familiar?"

"Unfortunately."

"I mean, if they just wanted simple revenge, they torch the place, right? But this backhoe stuff, and the clipping, and the sign—that's ritualistic. Symbolic. The same M.O. as before."

"You're right...Okay, Paul. I'll talk to him."

He snapped the phone shut. Heard the sound of a basketball bouncing in the driveway.

"Goddamn you, Hunter!"

He pawed through his desk drawer, found a business card. Punched in the numbers, waited impatiently for the greeting on the answering machine, then the beep. He tried to force a smile into his voice.

"Danika, this is Sergeant Ed Cronin, Alexandria Police Department. Remember me? I'm the detective with the Vigilante Task Force who visited your office some months ago. When you get this message, please contact Dylan Hunter and tell him I need to see him right away."

TWENTY-FIVE

Hunter rose at dawn. He fed Luna, got in a fast, hard workout in the building's exercise room, showered, shaved, then put together a light breakfast. Just before seven-thirty he went downstairs to "Wayne's" apartment. He drank his second coffee as he sorted through more of the files and papers he'd carried off in big plastic trash bags from the Capital Resources office before he tore it down. In the background, the scanner monitored the three bug frequencies.

He was jotting notes from one of the files when he heard something and glanced up. The scanner display hovered on the frequency set for Nature Legal Advocacy. Noises of movement in Lockwood's office. A door closing. Another *thump*, much closer…two clicks…papers rustling…

A briefcase being opened?

He noted the time: seven forty-five.

The scanner resumed its rapid cycling through the three channels, then paused again on Lockwood's office. More noise…Then:

"Hello?…Thanks for taking my call so early…"

Hunter hit the start button on the digital recorder on his desk.

"…Yes, I know…Well, I'm sorry to be the bearer of more bad news. Our senior associate phoned me late last night. He spoke to the insurance company. He doesn't know how it happened, but somebody—probably the same people who did that to the office—also canceled the property insurance on it last week…That's right. A total loss. And without insurance coverage, the company has to eat it…Well, how the hell do you think *I* feel? I have a big stake in this, too…He's beside himself. After all, he's the one who put it together and brought us in…No idea at all. Face it: A *lot* of those people up there would be motivated to do something like this…Sure, but there's not much we can do yet. That's his opinion, too. Now, we just have to get past the hearing and wait until they decide on the moratorium…Okay, I said 'decide,' but we both know that's just a formality, barring the unforeseen…Fair point: Who could have foreseen something like *this?* But he assures me it's a done deal. So, after the moratorium, I'm confident we can bounce back…Yes, he thinks so, too…Sorry to interrupt, but I hear some people showing up outside my office. I'd better run…Sure, I'll keep you posted."

Silence.

The scanning resumed.

He shut off the recorder. Got up and paced the room while sipping his coffee.

They were playing it safe on the phone. No names—he had no idea who had been on the other end of the call. Nor the identity of the "senior associate." Not a peep about Silva's murder. Nothing legally incriminating at all.

Not that he could use his tape in court, or even in the newspaper, anyway. But the call did confirm his broad suspicions, and tell him a few new things, too.

He would have to put in a long day sifting through the pile of the files stacked on the floor and waiting for something more to happen on the scanner.

Just after eight his new burner chirped. He saw that the call was from Danika, forwarded through the usual circuitous relays. She told him that Cronin wanted to see him this morning.

"Call him back and tell him that I'll be in at eleven," he said.

Well. That didn't take long.

"Hell-o, Mr. Hunter!"

Danika Cheyenne Brown sang out from a visitor's chair in the reception area of the office suite. Seated beside her a little boy, feet dangling and kicking restlessly, gripped a children's picture book in his lap.

"Good afternoon, Danika." He approached and bent over the child. "And this must be Tyrone."

"My one and only." She slid her arm around the child's shoulders and gave a squeeze. He looked up at her and smiled; he had inherited his mother's dimples. "Tyrone's grandma had to go to the doctor today, so he's been here keeping me company. Tyrone, this is Mr. Hunter."

"Hi, mister!" He grinned and raised a tiny brown fist.

Hunter chuckled and gave it a light fist-bump. "Hi, Tyrone. Your mama told me you're *four years old* now. What a big boy you are!"

"I'm gonna be *real* big, like Daddy!"

"I bet you're going to be even *bigger*." He asked her, "And how is Melvin doing?"

Her smile melted into a cute little pout, making the dimples stand out even more on her smooth coffee skin. "He's working nights. But he's in line to get promoted to supervisor at the security company, so he doesn't have to work those scary night shifts." She patted the boy's tight black curls. "Maybe we can afford to get married then."

"Well, he'd better not wait forever, or somebody else is going to come along and scoop you up."

"I'm not so sure." She looked at him impishly through half-closed eyes and crossed her long dark legs under a tight beige skirt that rode to mid-thigh. "All the *good* men have been scooped up by gorgeous ladies."

"Any man would be lucky to have you, Danika. I hope Melvin realizes that."

"Any man, huh?"

"So, is Detective Cronin here yet?"

"I see how you just changed the subject. But yes. Office D."

"Now, now, I know that look. Sorry to break the news, but the detective is happily married."

The little pout again. "Aw, that's too bad." She closed her eyes. "He's certainly another *fine*-looking gentleman."

"Um…Danika: Remember Melvin? You know—Tyrone's daddy?"

She rolled her eyes, but planted a kiss on the little boy's forehead.

"Yeah," she sighed, "I remember."

Before Hunter entered the office, he saw the trim figure of the man framed at the window, looking out at Connecticut Avenue.

He came in and Ed Cronin turned to face him. The detective looked exactly as he had the first time they'd met on these premises months before: a lean, strikingly handsome middle-aged man with a square jaw, intense blue eyes, and a fringe of close-cropped blond hair on his balding head. This time, though, his expression lacked any of the warmth of that first occasion.

"Sergeant Cronin," Hunter said, approaching and extending his hand.

Cronin just looked at it. Then back at his face. Unblinking.

Hunter dropped his hand to his side. "Yikes. Is my deodorant failing?"

"Something smells, all right," the cop said. He nodded his head toward the coffee table and nearby chairs. "Why don't we have a little chat?"

Cronin took a chair where he'd already draped his overcoat, while Hunter settled into the one opposite him. The cop crossed his arms over his brown tweed jacket. Then continued to stare at him.

"So, detective, how do we score this? Does the first guy to blink lose?"

"You know why I'm here."

"Oh, I get it, now. You're here to test my psychic powers."

"Quit horsing around. Capital Resources Development."

"Aw, you read my article. I'm flattered."

"Not the article."

He frowned. "Then what?"

"So you still want to play games. Pretend you don't know anything. We've been to this rodeo before, Hunter. Last year you write articles about killers getting turned loose—and days later, they turn up dead, with your articles left at the crime scenes. Now, you write an article about some crooked 'green energy' outfit stealing land in Pennsylvania. And just days later, their headquarters is ripped down. And—guess what?"

Hunter blinked. "Capital Resources—was *torn down?*"

Cronin stared at him.

"Cronin, are you telling me that somebody—" He stopped. "Somebody did that, and *left my article there?*"

Cronin just stared.

Hunter rose to his feet. "Oh, come on, Cronin! Use your common sense. Do you think I could be that stupid? Even if I wanted to do something that bizarre, do you think for one minute that I'd leave my own name at the crime scene? Put my *signature* on the act?" He glared down at the cop, hands on his hips. "You're damned right. We've been to this rodeo before. And I'm getting more than a little pissed about it."

Cronin stood, too. "No, you're just trying to be very clever, in your own twisted way. You figure that by making yourself too obvious a suspect, I'd think exactly that: that there's no way a smart guy like you would possibly be that obvious. But this latest crime is the same M.O. as the vigilante killings. And you are the only common denominator tying them all together."

"No. From what you're saying, *newspaper clippings* are the only things tying them together. Do you have any idea just how many people buy the *Inquirer* every day? It could be anybody doing this."

"But why *your* articles? You attack the legal system in the paper, all of a sudden a bunch of criminals you mention wind up dead; the legal shysters who turned them loose are targeted with all kinds of embarrassing publicity stunts; and your articles are left behind. Now you write about some environmental scam, and the same thing happens. So, *you* 'come on'! Do you really expect me to believe that the same person or persons who are ripped about the legal system also have their panties in a bunch about 'green energy'? Enough to do crazy shit like this?"

"I don't know. Maybe whoever did this latest thing are just copycats. Besides, I don't expect you to believe anything. You're a cop—so I expect you to stick to the facts. And the fact is that, except for some newspaper clippings with my name on them, absolutely nothing links me to any of this."

"It's not just the clippings. That's just one set of facts. Here are some others." He held up his fingers, ticking them off. "Fact number two: You're a man without a past, living under an alias. Three: You have a girlfriend in the CIA—an interesting coincidence for a guy with an alias. Four: Her CIA boss interferes with my investigation last month. Five: You are able to take down a guy almost twice your size—a serial killer with advanced martial arts skills—in a knife fight."

"I've explained every single one of those things."

"No, you only explained them away. But that's not all. I was going to hold this back from you, but what the hell is the use? *Six*: In some of the vigilante crimes, the perp or perps used symbolic names. That fact was never reported in the media. Names like *Lex Talionis* and *Edmond Dantes*. So we find a sign posted at this new crime scene, with your clip nailed on it. Then we find out the excavator used to tear down the place is rented, and the renter signed the agreement *Rob N. O'Locksley.* It took a while for me and my partner to figure it out. But I suppose I don't have to explain any of those names to you, do I?"

Hunter tossed his hands skyward. "How am I supposed to answer? Either yes or no, and I'm guilty. Right?"

Cronin went on. "No 'copycats' could possibly know about those names. Yet they link all the vigilante crimes with this new one. So, it has to be the same perps." He paused. "Or perp."

"It seems you've already decided that I'm guilty. Guilty, until proved innocent. So, are you here to inform me that the legal system has suddenly flipped the burden of proof?"

Cronin glowered at him a moment more. Then he shook his head and sat down again. Hunter remained standing for a few seconds, then returned to his own seat.

"Look," Cronin said, his voice lower. "Whatever it is you think you're trying to do, this can't go on." He raised a hand. "No, don't bother denying anything. Just let me talk. Maybe this is the last time I can say this to you, in private.

"Hunter, I've been on the job a long time. I'm good at what I do. Maybe you can fool lots of people. But you can't play *me* for a fool. I'm on to you. And I'm going to stay on you, like a flea on a dog. That has nothing to do with what I think about your goals, incidentally. Hell, I agree with them. Those criminals that you—that *were* iced last year? Glad to see them gone, every goddamned one of them. Makes my job easier. And this energy company? If what you write is true, they deserve what happened to them this weekend."

He paused, scratched his scalp, dropped his hand on his lap. Slumped forward.

"But we have a system of laws in this country. Nobody gets to decide which ones they obey, and which ones they don't. You start taking the law into your own hands, where does it stop? You do it—and maybe the right people get the justice they deserve. But then other people do it, too. And maybe they aren't like you. Maybe they don't have your morals. They start using violence, but against the wrong people. Or they go to extremes—shooting somebody just for looking at them the wrong way. Pretty soon, it's like Mexico. Blood vendettas. Bodies in the streets everywhere. Total anarchy."

Hunter watched him, remaining silent.

"You're a real smart guy, Hunter—or whoever you are. Smart enough to know that this has to end badly. So use your head, dammit. You've got a great job where you do lots of good exposing bad shit. I gather you've got a lot of money. You certainly got yourself a gorgeous girlfriend. You've got it all, my friend. But the way things are going, you are about to blow it all."

Hunter had to work to keep his face blank.

"You don't need to make private war on all the world's bad guys. That's why they hire schmucks like me. Why they give us a badge and a gun. Making war on the bad guys—that's *our* job. Not yours. But meanwhile, we all have to obey the laws. I do, you do. The laws are for everybody."

Hunter couldn't resist.

"Including the people I've been writing about?"

Cronin lowered his gaze. "If we don't like the system, we've got to change it. But at the ballot box. Not in the streets. We can't let that happen." He looked up, his blue eyes intense again. "*I* can't let that happen, Dylan."

Hunter nodded slowly.

"I know. You're a good cop, Ed."

The desk phone beeped.

"Excuse me a second," Hunter said, rising. He went to the desk and poked the speaker button. "Yes, Danika?"

"It's Mr. Bronowski on line two."

"Thanks." He turned to Cronin, who was getting up and putting on his coat. "No, wait—I'll be just a minute." He hit the button. "Hey, Bill. What's up?"

"Glad I caught you. Maybe at last we'll get to meet."

"What are you talking about?"

"I have a package for you. It just arrived by messenger. He said you're supposed to pick it up in person, but I signed for it. Now you'll have to come in, at long last."

"What package? From whom?"

"I can't make it out…They used some kind of green ink, and the return address is all smeared, and—"

Hunter sagged forward, his arms propping himself on the desk over the phone.

"Bill! Shut up and listen to me! Do exactly what I say…Very gently, put that package down. Very gently, on your desk, Bill. Do it *right now*. Don't touch it anymore. Get out of the building. Get everybody else out of there, too. *Do it now, Bill!*"

TWENTY-SIX

Cronin got patched through to the bomb squad dispatched to the Inquirer Building. The team sent in a remote-controlled robot that confirmed the package did contain some kind of explosive, and they used the device to transport the bomb away from the scene.

The cop put his phone away and faced Hunter.

"So how did you know the package was a bomb?" he demanded.

"Just a hunch. I'd already gotten a threatening email a few days ago. And I'd been thinking a lot about that scientist I met up in the Allegheny Forest, the one who was killed by a bomber. Besides, nobody has ever sent me a package before. It all set off my warning bells."

Cronin watched him, stone-faced. "Why do I think there's a lot more to the story?"

"As I said: What does it matter what I tell you? You're going to believe what you want to believe."

They went back and forth for a while. Hunter had no desire to fill him in about Boggs. He didn't want the cops to go after him.

This was personal.

He finally escaped Cronin's grilling and got back to his Bethesda apartment after noon. He flopped onto his sofa, stuck a battery in his burner, and found a waiting text message from Wonk asking for a call-back. He hit the speed-dial button to the researcher's own secure phone.

"I got your text. What's up?"

"I have acquired more of the information that you requested. I have deposited it in the Option Two location. Do you wish a quick summary?"

"Yes. I'm pressed for time. Shoot."

"According to the filings I accessed, Capital Resources Development is a privately held company with a small number of investors. One of them is a Ms. Selena Stanton of Annapolis, Maryland. My initial background check indicates that she is the long-time domestic partner of Gavin Lockwood. Mr. Lockwood is—"

"I know who he is. Very interesting…Go on."

"Yet another significant investor is one E. Conn. It took a little digging, but I determined that this individual is none other than Emmalee Conn, wife of Senator Ashton Conn."

"Hold on. Let me absorb that." He recalled the image of the politician strutting on the platform outside the EPA. His mind began to race.

"I should add," Wonk continued after a moment, "that the office manager at Capital Resources, Arnold Kaplan, is the brother of Stuart Kaplan, the senator's chief of staff."

"You don't say. What about our friends Trammel and Sloan?"

"I found no direct involvement with Capital Resources. However, CarboNot is another matter. Trammel holds a substantial amount of CarboNot stock."

Luna hopped up onto the sofa and climbed into his lap.

"All right. What else did you learn?"

"While digging into the financials for CarboNot, I determined that a large number of its shares are held in a trust that is managed by GreenSmart Investments. Their website states that they—and I am quoting—'channel venture capital into environmentally friendly projects and serve as a catalyst for public-private partnerships effecting sustainable development.'"

"Translation: They help politicians and their cronies fleece the taxpayers. But please continue."

"Robin Manes, a vice-president of GreenSmart Investments, appears to be the account manager. It is a special blind trust into which a number of prominent public officials have sequestered substantial personal assets."

"A *supposedly* blind trust, Wonk. After all, this is Washington."

"That may be. But you would never guess who some of those officials are." Wonk's voice sounded smug. He loved knowing what no one else knew.

"Oh, let me see…Ashton Conn. And Kaplan, his flunky."

"You guessed!"

"Don't sound disappointed," he said, stroking the cat. "These people are entirely predictable."

"However, there are many more. It reads like a 'Who's Who' of Washington. Senator Conn appears to have most of his investments held in that GreenSmart trust. It also includes officials from the Department of Interior, the EPA, the Bureau of Land Man—"

His hand paused on Luna's head. "Wait a minute. You said EPA. Could you check and see if the names 'Weaver' or 'Crane' are in that trust?"

"Let me see." He heard papers rustling. "Here it is…Yes, indeed. A Charles Crane, and…Well, what do you know? In my haste, I skimmed right over the name 'J. Weaver.' Would that be the administrator?"

"Almost certainly. And Charles Crane would likely be Chip Crane, his deputy." Luna was purring under his hand, eyes closed. "Were you able to identify the various brokers and financial advisers for the individuals I mentioned?"

"That required special efforts. I was up most of last night. But yes."

"Great. You've done well again, my friend. I'll review your material and get back to you with any further questions."

"That," Wonk said, "is what I am here for."

He lifted the cat off his lap, stood, and deposited her back onto the sofa. She blinked at him, peeved, then sniffed the warm spot and decided to curl up there and stay put.

After a few minutes, he went downstairs to the other apartment, again changing into his Grayson disguise in the stairwell.

His first order of business was to rewind the long-play recorder he'd left running to monitor the scanner, then fast-forward through many minutes of dead spots. He was about to give up on it when he heard a squeal sound. He rewound a bit and hit play. Silence, then the sound of a door opening and closing.

"What's up, Chip?" Weaver's voice, loud. The EPA boss must have put the Muir bust nearby on his desk.

"I just spoke with Kaplan." Crane's voice, low and secretive. "He told me that the senator is not a happy camper."

"He's not the only one." Weaver lowered his own voice. "My personal email account was filled this morning after Hunter's latest hit piece. Messages from the usual pests. I checked the markets, and CarboNot is trading even lower. It's nose-dived almost thirty percent this month. So, what did you tell him?"

"I reassured him that without the report from Adair Energy to challenge the NLA study, the SAB was certain to back the fracking moratorium. He sounded cheery. He said in that case, the stock price was sure to rebound. I got the impression that's what his call was really all about."

Weaver laughed. "I'm way ahead of them. I told Robin things were looking good about the moratorium. I didn't have to say anything more. She knew what I meant, and what to do about it."

"So do I," Hunter said aloud.

The week started busy for Danika. This morning her district manager at Crown Office Suites emailed her a list of new virtual-office clients, along with their specific instructions. Between visitors and calls, she spent several hours going over the information, organizing and filing it, and rehearsing the various scripts for answering their respective phone calls and taking messages.

The stock market must be booming, she thought. Four of the five new clients were brokerages and investment firms. In each case she was to say, "Mr. X is not available at the moment. May I please take a message, and his office will get right back to you?" Then she was to call the number for the specific broker or investment adviser and forward the message, leaving it on an answering machine.

It struck her as odd that they were all deciding to outsource their client phone calls to a message service, rather than answering them in-house. She figured it had to be because rich investors were likely to be harried and bossy about their money, and the brokers needed somebody to run interference. Or maybe the investment advisers were too busy watching the markets and would answer their clients in their own sweet time. Although why the clients couldn't just call those answering machines directly to leave messages...

Well, it wasn't her business. But she had to smile to herself: She could only dream of having problems like where to invest extra money.

She looked at the wall clock. Two forty-five. The phone was quiet, and no one was in the reception area at the moment. She decided to go over the scripts one more time. She picked the first sheet and recited from it, in a low whisper:

"Good morning! GreenSmart Investments. This is Ms. Manes's office..."

Becky Hill, the receptionist at Nature Legal Advocacy, felt her stomach growling. It was only mid-afternoon, and the soup she'd had at lunch was a distant memory. She was about to dig into her desk for a granola bar when the phone rang. The button for Lockwood's line lit up.

She glanced at the Caller ID as she picked up the phone. *GreenSmart Investments.*

"Good afternoon, Nature Legal Advocacy, Mr. Lockwood's office. May I help you?"

"Hello. This is Mr. Grayson from GreenSmart Investments. Our vice-president, Robin Manes, handles some investments for Mr. Lockwood. Please don't disturb him; this is only a routine clerical matter. We've just changed our office phones, and we wanted him to be aware of Ms. Manes's new number. Would you take it down, please, and pass it along to him?"

Becky was already scribbling. "Why certainly, sir. I'll see that he gets it right away. Go ahead, I'm ready."

"Thanks. The new number is 202…"

It was three-thirty when Hunter finished phoning his targets' various secretaries and receptionists. He had routed his calls through a "spoof" website, to make it seem on their Caller ID screens that he was indeed calling from their bosses' brokerages and investment firms.

Now, the "new" phone numbers that he had just given to them would ring at Danika's desk.

He spun his swivel chair. On the table behind him, next to the radio receiver, lay four untraceable burner phones. Each was labeled to represent one of those investment firms. Each label also bore the names of that firm's respective clients…his targets.

Danika would intercept their calls, then unwittingly forward their messages to these four phones.

He had one more series of calls to finish up today. He picked up his burner and dialed again into the spoof site…

Fred Cohen heard the beeping, glanced at the Caller ID. He snatched up the phone quickly with one hand, pulling the paperwork toward him with the other.

"Selleck Insurance, Fred Cohen speaking."

"This is Mr. Lockwood's office again. Just following up to see if you received his signed fax."

"Yes, I did. Have it right here. The cancellation of Mr. Lockwood's policy will go into effect at midnight."

"Thank you. He appreciates your speedy service. He needed to cancel on this short notice only because of today's sale. He said that he'd be in touch with you again shortly about writing up a new policy."

"I'm glad to hear that," Cohen said, relieved. "I hope he got a good price for it."

He heard laughter. "Mr. Cohen, you wouldn't believe it if I told you."

TWENTY-SEVEN

The Georgetown Pike begins just outside of the CIA headquarters near McLean, Virginia. Then it runs northwest, paralleling the Potomac River for six or seven miles to Great Falls, where it breaks west. During the evening rush hour, the Pike becomes a major artery pumping government workers home from the heart of Washington. Along the way, tree-lined capillaries twist and curl off the highway, channeling the flow of high-ranking federal officials to gracious homes in some of the District's toniest Virginia suburbs.

More than one United States senator maintains a local residence in these sequestered neighborhoods. Ashton Conn was among them.

Just after five, he turned off the Pike onto one of those narrow lanes. After a moment, he poked a button on the dash of his Bentley Continental GT. Just ahead on the left, beyond the white rail fence that lined the front of his property, a gate of black metal spikes opened inward. The twelve-cylinder engine smoothly, automatically purred down through the gears as he braked. He made the turn between the two gray stone pillars, each topped by a glowing brass lantern, one bearing a small wooden sign labeled "STONEHAVEN."

Then he tapped the gas and the sedan easily powered up the long sloping driveway to the oval parking circle in front of his house.

The sight of his home, rising among the bare oaks like a mini-fortress, gave his unsteady nerves a small measure of comfort. The two-story gray stone Colonial graced the manicured hilltop with arched first-floor windows, second-floor dormers, a towering stone chimney, and a half-round white portico entrance with fluted Doric columns. Unlike his other, more contemporary residence outside of Philadelphia, this one evoked for him Virginia's landed-gentry heritage. Two centuries ago, the drive leading up to a place like this would have been paved in cobblestones, which would have resounded with the clopping and squeaking of horse-drawn carriages bearing visiting aristocrats and beauties in hoop skirts.

Conn looped the oval and parked the Bentley near the front door. Tonight's visitors would have to walk past it to enter. He got out, then paused to flick an errant speck of road dirt off its gleaming black hood. And to regain a bit of self-control before facing the evening ahead.

For all of the trappings of wealth and position, Ashton Conn was not a happy man this evening. Despite the assurances that Stu had received from Crane at EPA, Conn still worried whether the fracking moratorium was truly a done deal. Then there was the deliberate destruction of the Capital Resources offices, which gave him the jitters. That, on the heels of those *Inquirer* articles by that son-of-a-bitch reporter. At least he hadn't revealed the names of investors in CarboNot or Capital Resources. Nor had his stories been picked up by the rest of the media, which sympathize with environmental causes. At least, not yet. But the unwanted media spotlight was shining too close…

Conn took a deep breath to calm himself. His eyes rested on the imposing crystal chandelier blazing brightly through the big foyer window. He listened to the faint, rhythmic *ticking* of the Bentley's cooling engine, and to the sound of the American flag rustling softly on its tall steel pole in the nearby lawn…

You've spent a great deal of money to live like this, Ash—too much, really. What you haven't spent, you've leveraged in green energy ventures. Which only makes sense. They are the wave of the future: not only the *right* things to invest in, but the *smart* things to invest in, too. And up until the past few weeks, those investments have paid off handsomely…

He thought of his many friends throughout the federal bureaucracy who had helped, fast-tracking the Energy Department loan guarantees for CarboNot, and putting the screws to those predatory fracking companies and greedy landowners back in Pennsylvania…

It's poetic justice that you are building Capital Resources on the rotting carcasses of the dying fossil fuel industry. That's your legacy, your investment in the future—one that is going to pay off big for you.

And for the planet, too—that's the important thing, of course. It's never been about yourself, not really. As anyone reviewing your career can see. Your articles, speeches, books, legislation—all of it has been devoted to creating a more sustainable world. Nobody could possibly imagine how much you've sacrificed for that, how much you've been willing to do and to give.

Still…crusading for a sustainable future doesn't mean you have to live like a monk. That's silly. There isn't anything wrong with civilized living, not as long as it's sustainable. And no one can say that you aren't doing your part to reduce your own carbon footprint. Didn't you also purchase carbon credits to offset your energy consumption—from a company that you yourself launched? So, no one can question your commitments and principles.

Naturally, though, a U.S. senator has to maintain a certain lifestyle. You really don't have a choice about that, not in this town. Especially if you are about to take the next big step up the ladder. It's like they say: You must look, talk, and act as if you already have the job, before anyone is going to hire you for it.

But in every way, you've *earned* this lifestyle. Why shouldn't virtue be rewarded? You don't have to pay attention to the critics. Just answer them as you always do: *"Yes, I do well—by doing good."*

If only you can get through the coming week and that SAB hearing. And past that prick reporter. Sloan and Trammel promised to take the lead on doing something about the guy. What are they waiting for? Maybe tonight you can pull them aside and find out. Well, at the very least, *they'll* be here, and they'll open their checkbooks for you…

He jumped at the sound of approaching footsteps.

"Oh! Barry!" He took in the lean, well-dressed figure of the head of the security team, who was walking up the driveway.

"Sorry, Senator. I didn't mean to startle you. I was just checking in with the men on the grounds and saw you drive up."

"I understand. I gather they are all present and prepared?"

"Yes, sir. Two will be positioned at the gate to check IDs against the guest list. Three at the rear and sides of the house, providing perimeter security. I'll be here, at the entrance."

"That sounds fine." He checked his watch. "You won't have to worry for at least another half-hour, though. The caterers will arrive first. Just send them around to park near the kitchen entrance. I expect the jazz trio around six to set up. The guests won't begin to show until closer to seven for the reception."

"We're all set, sir. I hope you and your guests have a wonderful evening."

Conn flashed him a grin and slapped him on the back, then turned to enter his home. Normally he hired only one or two security people for social occasions with prominent guests, and mostly for show. But the destruction of the Capital Resources offices made him nervous. Better safe than sorry.

Inside the foyer, Joseph—a tall, distinguished-looking black butler—greeted him. Juanita, the frisky Hispanic maid, smiled coyly as she darted past with a tray bearing folded white napkins. He watched her ass, remembering, as she disappeared into the dining room. Both were part-time employees he hired from a local agency whenever he had to impress visitors.

"Is Emmalee home, Joseph?" he asked as the butler helped him out of his overcoat.

"Yes, Senator. Mrs. Conn arrived home just a few minutes ago. She said she was going upstairs to get ready."

He felt a wave of relief. "Good. I am going to do the same."

But the feeling didn't last. Conn felt his earlier mood returning and growing even darker as he climbed the broad walnut staircase. He entered their bedroom and found her seated before her vanity.

Emmalee Conn wore a pale blue silk bathrobe. Her hair, tousled and dirty blonde, fell to just below her shoulders. A highball glass, half-empty, sat within reach. She glanced at him in the mirror and, without a word, continued removing her makeup.

"So. You decided to attend after all," he said. A flat statement of fact.

"So it appears."

He couldn't resist. "What's the matter? Did this month's boyfriend get tired of you?"

Her hand, wiping her cheek with a small towelette, paused in mid-stroke. She met his eyes in the mirror and a slow leer formed on her face. Then she rose, pirouetted in her bare feet to face him, and untied the belt of her silk robe. With a little shrug, she let it slide off her shoulders to the floor. She stood there, tanned and insolently naked. And laughed at him. Her breasts, taut and high, jiggled a bit with each laugh, but nothing else on her did—the result of long hours with personal trainers and tennis instructors, half of whom he was certain she was screwing. He noticed a small new bruise low on her belly. She spun again, a half-turn, and he saw two more on her ass. She ran her hands down her hips and, turning her head only, looked at him over her shoulder coquettishly.

"Do you really think any man would get tired of me?" she said, her voice low. "Have *you*, Senator?"

He felt himself stirring, in spite of himself. He was used to wielding power over others. He hated himself for her power over him.

"You goddamned slut," he said, his voice tight.

She turned again to face him. Ran the tip of her tongue around her lips. "You love the fact that I'm a goddamned slut."

It was true, dammit. Images from their vacations floated up from memory, occasions when they experimented with threesomes and foursomes, in delicious anonymity…obscene images of her with other men, other women…

He swallowed and said, "Knock it off. We've got to talk."

She pouted, then bent over slowly to pick up the robe, making a show of it.

He sat on the edge of the bed. "Have you read the papers this weekend? Heard the news?"

She laughed. "I've been busy." She resumed her primping at the vanity.

"Well, while you were screwing your brains out, *we* were getting screwed in other ways." He told her about the vandalism at Capital Resources Development and the insurance cancellation. Her mocking expression vanished and grew solemn. "As a partner with Gavin's wife, Emmalee, you two are on the hook for the loss."

She whipped around on the stool. "*I* am?"

"All right. We are. You, legally, but me financially. Yes, we had to put the investment in your name, but it's my money at risk. And that's on top of the hits our CarboNot stock has taken this month. The bottom line is that we're stretched really tight right now."

"How tight?"

"Tight enough that we have to start watching our spending around here. At least until that EPA hearing is behind us and the moratorium finally issued. Once fracking is finished, our CarboNot stock will soar again."

"But what happens now with Capital Resources?"

"For the moment, we'll have to eat the loss of the facility and operate out of rented offices. But after the moratorium, the company will be able to buy up property deeds at fire-sale prices from all the holdout owners in the Allegheny. Then, within the next six months, CarboNot will announce its surprise plans to build its new alternative energy project up there. All sorts of workers and service businesses will have to move into the area. At that point, the property values will shoot sky high. And whatever land we don't sell to CarboNot directly, for its windmills and solar panel field, we can sell off at a big profit to developers. We'll make a killing."

She swallowed more of her drink. "It all sounds good…Speaking of killing: that poor scientist you told me about, the one who got himself blown up a couple weeks ago. Is there any more news about that?"

"Horrible, isn't it?" Conn stared at his shoes and shook his head. "My sources say the cops have questioned some local fracking protesters. But they aren't sure those people are involved. From a message sent to the media, it seems that it was some 'animal rights' group that targeted him—not for his work on fracking, but for past product testing he did using lab animals."

She paused while applying eyeliner. "Well, I don't like how they test cosmetics in the eyes of rabbits, either; but *murder?* Goddamned mental cases."

"You can say that again."

"Well…how is his death going to affect all this?"

"Ironically, out of that tragedy at least *some* good will come. Now, the fracking company that hired him can't challenge the scientific grounds for the moratorium. And without any challenge, the EPA moratorium is as good as granted." He looked up at her. "So, from the perspective of the greater good, that finally will open the market to give alternative energy a chance. Which will mean a brighter future for the planet."

"And for us." She saluted him with her glass.

"Always thinking of yourself, aren't you, Emmalee? Well, okay, yes—you can relax. From the personal perspective, a year from now we should be in great shape, both financially and politically."

She drew the robe open a bit and giggled. "Physically, I am already in great shape."

He got up, strode over, and grabbed the glass from her hand.

"You don't need any more booze this evening, Emmalee. And please—wear some underwear tonight, for a change. At least pretend to act like a future First Lady, will you? Try to remember that these initial contributions are the seed money for the presidential run. The last thing I need is for my core donors to wonder if there will be any future personal scandals."

"Then you'd better keep it in your pants, too, Ash. Like when you're around that Robin Manes bitch. And I've seen how you look at Juanita, too."

He turned on his heel and stalked out.

"But I don't understand! Why are you shutting me out?"

Dawn sat on the bed in tears as Boggs stomped back and forth across the threadbare carpet of the dingy motel room, trying not to snap at her, trying to tamp down a raging mixture of exasperation and fury.

The exasperation was directed at her. Two mornings after the Silva bombing, they had been spooked by the surprise visit to their camp by several cars filled with Pennsylvania State Police detectives. The cops corralled the whole group inside the big tent, then singled them out for individual interviews that took most of the day. He and Rusty had feigned shock; they were used to lying to authorities. But like the rest of WildJustice's members, Dawn's shock had been authentic, and they all persuasively pleaded complete ignorance to the investigators.

But in the days since, she began to look at him strangely, and to ask him more questions about where he was going, what he was doing. She also insisted on coming along with him whenever he and Rusty left the camp.

Assured by his friend that the EPA moratorium was imminent, Boggs was also told that there was no further need for him to continue their direct action campaign. The man congratulated him: He had fulfilled an indispensable role. Now, they could break camp and go home. Boggs also knew that it made sense not to stick around, with the cops crawling all over the area asking questions.

Still, he knew from experience that deals in Washington had a way of coming undone. So rather than head back to North Carolina, he told Rusty to drive to D.C. Until the EPA ruled, they would lie low in this New York Avenue dump and await the outcome.

Which meant that Dawn was now glued to his hip, probing him for more information.

Which, like the failed *Inquirer* bombing, left him exasperated.

But what he had just learned, after going online to the *Inquirer* website tonight, left him furious. And the fury was directed at his…should he still even think of him as his *friend?* After tonight's revelations, he was almost certain that he was being played, perhaps for years.

Almost certain.

He had to be sure. It was time they had it out, face to face. And he was just about to send him a text message, demanding a meeting, tonight. But he had made the mistake of telling Dawn that he had to meet with somebody privately.

"Why do you want me to stay here? Why can't I go along with you? You keep acting so secretly, Zak."

He spun to face her. "Look. The meeting is private, just between me and one other important contact. Rusty will drive me there and drop me off; not even he will be involved."

"What do you mean—*even* he? Don't I matter to you as much as he does?"

Damn. "I'm sorry. I didn't mean it that way. If I could drive myself, I'd leave you both here."

"Give me one good reason why I can't come with you, then, and Rusty and I *both* stay in the car?"

He looked at her, feeling helpless at the question.

"You've been acting so damned secretly, for so long! And then after the cops came and…" She stopped. Her red hair fell in tangled strands across her face; her tear-filled eyes looked desperate. "Zak. I *love* you. I want so much to believe in you, to trust you. But trust is a two-way street. I've trusted you all these years. Now you are going to have to trust *me.*"

It was unanswerable.

"All right! All right…Look. I have to meet with this individual alone. You can come along. But you and Rusty have to drop me off, then drive away. I'll call you when the meeting is done."

Her head fell, and she continued to sob, quietly now. He went to her, sat beside her, put his arm around her.

"Okay. Take it easy. I'm not trying to shut you out. My contact insists on security, and I'm just trying to protect that. Can you understand my position?"

She nodded. Looked up at him with eyes trying to believe.

"Good. Now that that's settled, I have to go outside and send my contact a text message to arrange the meeting. I'll be right outside the room, and as soon as I'm done, I'll be right back." He gave her a squeeze and a little kiss. Her cheek was warm, wet, and salty. Then he got up and headed outside.

Avery Trammel excused himself from the elderly couple who had been chatting with him and approached Damon Sloan, who towered over the crowd. Sloan was thumbing his cell phone with a sullen expression.

"Good evening, Damon."

The CarboNot CEO turned to him, startled. "Oh, Avery! Hello. Just give me a sec." He thumbed a bit more, made a final tap, then pocketed his phone. "There we go."

"You looked concerned. Problem?"

"Oh. No. No more than usual." He smiled, half-heartedly. "Just texting my broker. While I'm here, I want him to monitor the Asian markets and give me a head's-up about anything else that might affect our stock price tomorrow. With all that's happened, I may have to issue some kind of statement first thing tomorrow, to reassure the shareholders."

"Of course." Trammel gestured with his glass of Chardonnay at the well-dressed guests jamming the conservatory and hallways of Conn's spacious home. "Ash certainly managed to pack them in tonight."

"Oh, I don't think it's him. I give most of the credit to your wife."

Sloan nodded to where Julia Haight was posing for cell-phone photos amid a mob of bedazzled guests. Next to her, doing the same, were two others from Hollywood's A-list: a distinguished African-American actor and a famous writer-director of blockbuster spectacles. Both were known for doing films with progressive messages. A thin, middle-aged socialite preened nearby, in animated conversation with Emmalee Conn. Trammel had encountered the socialite many times; she ran a Beverly Hills group that enlisted people in the industry to slip environmental themes into movies and TV shows. Emmalee wore a low-cut cocktail dress; she kept running long red nails through her just-got-out-of-bed blonde hair. He wondered if the rumors about her were true. For the sake of Ash's campaign, he hoped they weren't.

"Julia recruited them on short notice to show up here for the photo op with donors," Trammel answered. "She is helping to line up others to attend his formal announcement fundraiser in Los Angeles next month." He sampled the Chardonnay; it wasn't bad. He moved in closer. "Have you been able to take another run at our reporter friend?"

Sloan's features tightened. "No. My contacts don't want to risk anything further after what happened last time…What about you?"

"I have someone on it. But since your effort, the reporter in question appears to be lying low. So far, the only things that we have learned are, first, that he never actually goes to the newspaper office. Second, his business address is one of those virtual offices downtown; to contact him, you must leave a message there. That is about it. We have not yet been able to discover where he lives, or to learn anything about his past." He watched Julia hugging a smiling couple while a camera flashed. "It is most curious."

"Well, it will be just a few more days till the hearing. If he causes no further trouble, we should be fine." Sloan craned his long neck even higher to scan the room. "I wonder where Ash has run off to?…Oh, there he is out in the hallway, playing with his phone. Let me see if I can chase him down."

Trammel nodded and watched him head off. He wandered toward the corner of the room where the jazz trio played, figuring it would be a good time to check his own messages. He set his glass on a tray next to the gleaming Steinway and pulled out his cell.

"…As many of you know, I've known Ash since he was fresh out of Harvard Law School, and came to us looking for a job." Gavin Lockwood turned to smile at his old friend, standing beside him. "In those days, he didn't have much money, and he was loaded down with college loans. But still, he was willing to take a low-paying job in Nature Legal Advocacy. That's because to Ashton Conn, convictions mattered. His principles always came first."

Lockwood let the applause go on as his eyes roved across one hundred twenty smiling faces, many of them familiar to him, all of them high rollers. For his part, Conn looked uncharacteristically serious, his head down. Clearly, this was an emotional moment for him.

"I don't have to repeat what others here have already said about his many accomplishments in the years since." He paused to look pointedly around the conservatory. "I *am* delighted that he has since found ways not only to pay off those college loans, but to acquire a few well-earned toys. In fact, he promised to give me a ride in the one sitting outside the front door."

Everyone laughed heartily and clapped. A brief, uneasy smile passed over Conn's lips.

"So it gives me great pleasure to introduce the man of the hour: the environmental movement's greatest champion in Washington—and our next President of the United States: *Ashton Conn!*"

The applause echoed off the marble floor and the walnut wainscoting. Lockwood moved to the side of the room to watch Ash, with Emmalee holding his arm, step to the center of the room. The jazz trio struck up a rendition of "It's Not Easy Being Green," which prompted gales of laughter. Conn grinned and pointed at them, making a shooting gesture with his forefinger and thumb.

Lockwood watched as his old friend and colleague began his speech. It was clear that the weight of the occasion was upon him. He seemed subdued, his voice soft enough that Lockwood had to cock his head to hear.

But almost immediately he heard the *pinging* of an incoming text message on his phone. A couple of people nearby frowned at him. He mouthed *"Sorry,"* then hustled to a nearby doorway and out into the hall. He pulled out the cell and saw who it was from. He would have saved it for later, but the subject line said *Urgent.*

He tapped the message. Read it.

Felt his blood run cold.

TWENTY-EIGHT

Rock Creek Park cuts an elongated swath of nearly three square miles in northwestern Washington, separating the upscale suburbs of Chevy Chase from those in Silver Spring. From the National Zoo to its south, the popular wooded camping and recreational area runs north along the creek from which it takes its name. Beach Drive, a paved two-lane road, parallels the stream through most of the park.

At two a.m., Rusty drove them into the park from the east, on Military Road. He then turned north onto Beach Drive. In about half a mile they passed a small stone structure on the right, a public restroom facility. A few hundred feet further they crossed the creek over a little bridge at a place called Milkhouse Ford. Just beyond that, a narrow paved road on the left, like a long driveway, angled back toward the creek. It dead-ended in a thick tangle of trees near the water, a spot virtually invisible from the main road.

"Stop here," Boggs snapped. Rusty pulled into the end of the driveway, up to a metal barrier that prevented further entrance. "I'll walk in from here and wait for my contact to show. Turn around and go wait back at that outdoor restroom we passed, just on the other side of the bridge. I'll call you on my cell when we're finished. Don't come back before then."

"Man, you've been awfully touchy tonight, Zak," Rusty complained. "What's going on?"

Boggs spoke through clenched teeth as he opened the door. "I need to find out tonight if somebody has been playing us all for suckers." He slammed it shut behind him.

Dawn watched him stalk off down the path into the distant trees. Weeks of gnawing anxiety, the sense that something was terribly wrong, had only intensified in the hours since Zak sent the text message. He had come back into the room and flopped onto the bed. He lay there with his arms crossed, his dark eyes fixed unblinking on the ceiling, his dark expression forbidding any questions. From time to time, he would mutter something to himself.

She had never seen him like that. It scared her.

Especially in combination with everything else that had been happening this past month. His eager violence at the fracking office and the diner. His secret absences and whispered conversations with Rusty. That mysterious bag that he sometimes carried off—but which he never brought back to their tent or motel rooms.

Where did he keep it hidden? Why? What was in it?

She didn't want to think about the bombing death of that scientist. Or the cops showing up and questioning them all. But mainly about Zak insisting that she lie to them, assure them that they'd all been together in the camp that night…the same night that he told her that he and Rusty had gone to meet with a cell in Warren.

"How could I explain *that* to the cops, honey?" he laughed easily, persuasively. He shook his head. "Just my dumb luck that some guy gets himself killed the same night."

It had seemed like such a strange way to put it. But she had gone along. Gone along, because she believed him. No—because she believed *in* him. She always had, since they first met, since his passion and unshakable confidence in his convictions had won her heart.

But now...She sat in the truck, staring into the impenetrable shadows where he had disappeared to meet some secret Washington contact...sat there in the dark, trying vainly to suppress the unstated doubts, the unmentionable fears...

Rusty backed out of the entrance and drove to the parking area outside the little restroom building. He turned off the headlights, then cracked open his window for fresh air while he let the truck rumble and the heater run. He eased back into the bench seat and closed his eyes.

She couldn't stand being alone with her fears.

"Rusty?"

"Mmmm."

"Did he tell you...I mean, do you know who this 'contact' is? A man or a woman, even?"

"No idea." He opened his eyes, gave her a brief look. "Me and Zak, we go back a long ways, and he never keeps secrets from me. But that one, he always has...So, he hasn't even told you, either?"

She shook her head. "Do you have any clue what this is about?"

"Wish to hell I knew. Like he always says, he'll tell us if and when we have a need to know." He pulled down the brim of his baseball cap and closed his eyes again.

They sat like that for a couple of minutes in silence. Even though the heater was blasting, she felt cold, cold that cut deep, and she found herself starting to tremble.

A pair of headlights appeared in the distance ahead of them, growing slowly as they got nearer.

Rusty blinked and pushed up his cap. "Hope that's the contact and not the Park police."

Her mouth went dry. The car drew abreast of them, its lights dazzling them, then swept past. Blinded, she couldn't make out what it looked like.

She twisted around to watch. It crossed the bridge behind them; then its tail lights flashed a brighter red.

"It's stopping. That must be the dude," Rusty said.

She watched the vehicle slowly turn left, rolling off the roadway right onto the grass. It proceeded across the frozen lawn, going around the metal barrier, then up onto the paved path behind it. In a few seconds, only the flickering of its lights could be seen as it moved behind the trees. Then nothing.

She was shaking now. This was too much.

She had to know. She had to be sure of him.

"I…I think I'm going to be sick," she said.

"Oh hell! Not in my truck!"

She got out and, bent forward, stumbled to the far side of the building, where the women's entrance was.

But she did not go inside. Unseen now, she straightened, pulled the laces of her jacket hood tighter around her face, then continued around the back of the building, and into the woods.

She had to know…

Zachariah Boggs raised a hand to shade his eyes from the glaring headlights. When the car got close, the driver killed the beams, leaving orange afterimages on his retinas. The vehicle rolled forward a few more feet. Stopped. The engine died.

Boggs took a step forward out of the trees, revealing himself to the occupant.

The driver's door opened. A dark shape in a dark overcoat stepped out. Closed the door with a solid thump. Then approached, shoes crunching across unseen patches of ice. Stopped about ten feet away, hands in his coat pockets.

"I can't believe you!" the man said. He turned around, scanning the surroundings. "Insisting on this cloak-and-dagger nonsense out here, in the middle of the night! And on *this* night! My God, Zak, are you trying to destroy everything we've been working for?"

Boggs was recovering his night vision. Even though he had seen him on TV, he hadn't met with him in person for several years. Now, up close, he was shocked at the changes. The puffiness that almost hid his eyes. The fleshiness around his chin and cheeks. The twin vertical gashes at the corners of his mouth. And the additional bulk under an expensive dark cloth overcoat.

"Are *you*, Ash?" Boggs shouted back.

Ashton Conn stepped closer.

"Do you believe everything you read in the papers? Especially in that fascist rag—and by *that* reporter?"

"Are you telling me it isn't true? That you are *not* investing in CarboNot?"

"I am not! Not knowingly, anyway. I'm a public official, and all my investments are managed by a blind trust, you know. I'm not permitted to know where—"

"Come on, Ash! That 'blind trust' is run by GreenSmart. When you hired them, you *knew* that you would be investing in solar panels and windmills, because that's all they do. Yet all the while, you were assuring *me* that you hated those things, too, and wanted to ban them. So now I see that GreenSmart is really just a money-laundering operation for you and your Washington pals. Or a 'greenwashing' operation, if you prefer."

"I tell you, Zak, I had no idea—"

"Bullshit! And I suppose you're going to tell me that your wife is *not* a big investor in that other company—the one that's gobbling up all that land in the Allegheny Forest. Land that is supposed to be held for the public interest—not for private greed. Land that really *should* be returned to its natural state—not sold off to money-grubbing developers!"

"Look, that's Emmalee's money. She doesn't necessarily share my values, and I stay completely out of her business."

"Oh really? I went online and read a bit tonight about your dear wife, Ash. She was a club dancer when you met her, not some rich bitch. She didn't have two nickels to rub together. So where did she get all the money to invest in that company, if not from you?"

"She inherited money a couple of years ago. From her...family." Conn's eyes darted around, as if he were trying to think of what to say next. "As I say, it's her business. I don't tell her what to do, and she stays out of my business, too."

Dawn stumbled through the woods, barely able to see where she was going, but staying parallel to the roadway. When she neared the creek, she held her breath, then darted out of the tree line to the bridge. She ran across it as fast as she could, praying that Rusty wasn't looking in the mirror at that moment. Reaching the other side, she whipped around the railing and down into the trees and bushes lining the stream bank.

She made her way through the tangle of branches toward the sound of angry voices.

Rusty was worried. About Zak, and what might be going down. Now, about Dawn.

He wasn't sure what to do. He was great at following instructions. You could always count on him to do that. But he was never good at making decisions. Which was one reason he looked up to Zak so much. Zak always knew what to do.

Well, Zak had left Dawn with him here. That meant she was his responsibility. Maybe he should check on her. See if she was okay.

Before he got out, he took an automatic peep into the rearview mirror. Then did a double take. He could have sworn he saw something moving along the edge of the bridge in the dark. Now it was gone.

He got an uneasy feeling. He jumped out of the truck and trotted along the length of the restroom structure to the women's side. He stood outside the door and listened for a few seconds. Heard nothing.

"Dawn?"

No answer.

He went up to the door and knocked. Louder: "Dawn? Are you okay?"

No response.

"Are you in there?" he shouted.

Nothing.

He grabbed the door handle and went inside.

Then knew what he had seen on the bridge.

Shit! He rushed outside, back to the truck.

She tiptoed through the trees. The voices grew loud enough to be understood.

"…and she stays out of my business, too."

A man's voice, not Zak's.

"You're lying, Ash! You've been lying to me for years."

Zak's voice…She stepped closer, cringing at every rustle and crunch underfoot, listening to Zak yelling…

"What happened to you? Where is the man I knew back in Cambridge? Where is the Harvard Law student I met on the speakers' platform at that Earth Day rally? You were a poor kid on a scholarship, then, just like me. And you had ideals, then, too. That man really was dedicated to saving the planet."

"I still am! Zak, I am the same man that I was then—the same man that I was when I hired you for your first job, at Nature Legal Advocacy. And everything I have done since—"

"Oh, spare me! I remember you then. You were lean and hungry and dedicated. But just look at you now, after all these years bathing in the Washington cesspool: fat, wearing fancy clothes, driving some extravagant gas-guzzler. What the hell is that thing, a Rolls?"

"No, it's—"

"I don't give a damn what it is! The point is: Look what's happened to you. You've become exactly what we were fighting against."

"Zak, let me speak, damn it! Can you shut up for a minute and just listen?…You're dead wrong about me. I haven't given up my ideals—our ideals—at all. Or our strategy. The long-term strategy that we devised way back then: You work the outside, I work the inside. You and your people take radical actions to push the envelope farther and farther; in response, I call what you're doing 'too extreme,' and then I propose something more 'moderate.' But farther down the road. With each step, we move the country closer and closer toward our ideal…Wait, don't interrupt; let me finish. Remember how we launched the plan, when I first got into Congress?"

Congress? The word shocked her.

"That year you organized WildJustice and began your direct actions, just as we planned. You started trashing logging companies and sawmills—destroying their equipment, to save wildlife habitats. Everyone condemned those actions as too extreme. But then I proposed tough new environmental restrictions on logging, which by then sounded moderate. And those bills passed! It worked, Zak! That was our strategy—good cop, bad cop. Together, we've implemented it beautifully over the years. Look what we achieved: I was able to ride the wave we generated right into the Senate…"

Her brain felt numb, now, unable to process what she was hearing. She inched forward toward the clearing ahead.

"Just listen to yourself, Ash! 'I was able to ride the wave.' I, I, I. It's all about you, now, isn't it?"

She moved behind a thick tree at the edge of the clearing. She could make out a car, a dark sedan gleaming in the pale moonlight.

In front of it, two figures, face to face.

"How can you say that?" the stranger shouted. "After all the things I've contributed to this cause in my career! And…look, I haven't mentioned this very often. But I *will* say it again, now: After all the things I've done for you *personally*, Zak. Have you forgotten? Ten years ago, I saved your ass from a prison cell, by inventing an alibi for you, and helping you pin your Technobomber killings on that other kid."

Dawn's knees gave way. She grabbed the tree trunk to remain upright.

"I just *knew* you were going to bring that up again," Zak sneered. "You've counted on my gratitude for that. And for years, you've exploited it to manipulate me—to do your dirty work against your enemies, things you didn't have the balls to do yourself. But that old debt has been more than paid, Ash. You just said it yourself: I helped to generate the wave that carried you into the Senate." His lips twisted in contempt. "But for what? You've proved yourself to be a fake! So don't expect me to help install Senator Ashton Conn in the White House."

Senator Ashton Conn…Zak—the Technobomber… Their images swam in her tears as she listened to the alien words of a man she thought she had known…

"It's not just that I don't know you anymore," Zak continued. "It's that you don't even know yourself! You equate yourself with the cause: What's good for Ashton Conn is good for the environment. I can only imagine how you rationalize your giant carbon footprint. Well, here's a footprint for you!"

He stomped past Conn, raised his foot, and kicked the fender of the car.

"Stop it!" Conn shoved his shoulder. Zak stumbled back, then put his hands on his hips, threw back his head, and laughed scornfully.

"You *like* pushing people around, don't you, Ash? It's all a power trip to you, isn't it? All these material trappings…just to impress and dazzle and lord it over people. Power is all you really want, now; environmentalism is just your rationalization."

Through the fog in her brain, she was vaguely aware of another sound…the noise of an engine on the road, somewhere behind her…

"Shut up, you pathetic loser!" Conn shouted. He was breathing hard. "Sure, of course I want power! I want it for all the *good* I can do with it. All the good I *have* done with it. But I figured out something about you a long time ago, Zak. Back on that night ten years ago, when you crawled into my home, begging me to save you from the cops. You told me a lot about yourself that night—much more than you knew. Between the lines, you told me that you felt impotent in the world, and that you wanted power, too. Except that unlike me, you don't feel empowered by doing anything constructive—anything productive or positive. Oh no, you get it the easy way: from destruction. By being a bomb-thrower. By destroying people and what they create!"

Even through the smear of tears Dawn could see the anger building in Zak. He clenched his fists at his sides; his skinny neck craned up, beard jutting out; his slight frame straightened inside the field jacket.

"You're nothing but a nihilistic punk, Zak! A nobody who feels like somebody only when he's playing God—only when he's blowing things up and taking lives, like that Adair scientist!"

A hot, searing pain burned from her throat to her stomach. She clenched her teeth...and felt the pain begin to turn into a towering rage...

Conn wasn't done. "Yes, I could see it, even then. But rather than stop you, which I could have done easily, I decided to *use* you, instead. To channel your warped impulses toward positive ends. You were a loose cannon; I turned you into a guided missile. I aimed you at the right targets. And it worked. Look what I've built from your sick obsession with destruction!"

"Destruction?" Zak yelled. "Well, I'll destroy *you*, you bastard! I'll let the whole world know about your part in all of this—even if I have to go down with you!"

It was Conn's turn to put his hands on his hips and laugh.

"*You?* Who would believe you? You have no evidence. It's just the word of a violent fanatic against the word of a United States senator. Everyone will see you for exactly what you are: a little man trying to build himself up by tearing down a greater one."

Zak's balled fists shook.

"Well, then, I'd better stick to my old methods. It might not be tomorrow, or next month, or even next year. But it *will* happen, Ash, that's a promise—and you'll never know when, and you'll never see it coming!"

Conn didn't speak for a moment. Then he nodded.

"I had hoped to come here tonight and settle you down. But sadly, I see that's going to be impossible."

He reached into his coat pocket. Dawn gasped when she saw his hand emerge with a gun in it.

"Frankly, Zak, I expected this, and came prepared. You've picked the perfect place to end your insanity, once and for all: out here in the middle of the woods."

Zak took a step back and raised his hands. "Now, wait a minute!"

"I'm truly sorry for you, Zak. We've accomplished a great deal together, you and I. But I still have much more to achieve." He raised the gun. "As for you—well, what do they say? 'Live by the sword—'"

"Noooo!" she screamed, rushing out of the trees.

It had happened without thought, a simple reflex. A moment before, she hated Zak for his unspeakable crimes, for his cold manipulation and utter betrayal of her. But then he stepped back and raised his hands—and in the next instant she reacted as if he were still the man she had loved.

Both their heads snapped around to look in her direction. In the two seconds that Conn was distracted, Zak spun and began to run. Conn turned back and snapped off a shot to where he had been. Then he began shooting wildly at Boggs, who vanished into the thicket of trees.

Dawn skidded to a halt in the open. She remained frozen in place, staring at the man with the gun. He spun to her, eyes wild, mouth wide. They stood there like that, separated by a distance of about thirty feet, just looking at each other. He aimed the gun in her direction.

She was going to die. She felt nothing. She felt empty.

She held his eyes.

"Ahhhhhhhh!"

Senator Ashton Conn snarled, turning away from her and stomping his feet like a child. Bent forward, he half-walked, half-staggered to his car, pawed at the door handle twice before his hand connected, and jerked it open. He collapsed into the seat, then slumped forward, his forehead falling against the steering wheel.

After a few seconds, he raised his head to look at her once again, the snarl still on his lips. Then slammed the door. Seconds later the engine roared to life, and the big sedan leaped into reverse. The car swept into a turn, then spun out across the lawn again, fishtailing on the frosty soil till it reached the road.

"Zak! Where are you?"

Rusty's voice. Not far behind her in the trees.

"I'm over here!...Dawn!...Dawn—are you all right?"

I'll never be all right...you son of a bitch...

She began to run—away from them, across the paved path, into the deeper woods on the other side.

Bursting from the trees, Rusty caught sight of the tail lights of the car speeding up the road—then spotted Dawn's figure disappearing into the trees in the distance.

He heard thrashing sounds in the brush behind him.

"Zak! Here!"

He emerged from the shadows and limped up. His eyes were wild; his beard, knees, and jacket were covered with dirt and leaves. He'd obviously taken a tumble.

"You okay?" Rusty asked, grabbing him by the shoulders.

"Yeah," he panted. "Just twisted my...ankle... Dawn...where is she?"

"She ran off. That way, Zak."

"Have…to find her." He began to hobble away, but Rusty seized his arm.

"No! Zak—listen to me. She wasn't running away from the guy who was shooting; I watched him drive off. She ran away *after* he left."

Zak looked at him, eyes dull and uncomprehending.

"Zak…She was running away from us…from *you.*"

He blinked, trying to process it. Then his eyes widened.

"Oh God…she…must have heard…"

The sound of a siren rose in the distance.

"Zak! We gotta get the hell outta here, buddy. *Now!* Can you walk over there to the truck?"

Boggs looked dazed, but nodded.

"Then let's haul ass, man!"

TWENTY-NINE

Hunter stayed up into the wee hours of Tuesday morning. He sat at the computer downstairs, drinking cold coffee, flexing his knees now and then, poring through emails, making notes.

The fake email that he'd sent in Sloan's name to Weaver, Crane, and Lockwood over the weekend had contained an innocuous-looking email attachment. But embedded in that attachment was a bit of hacking code, courtesy of Wonk. When opened by the recipients, the attachment embedded server routing modification software into their computers. That software secretly added Hunter as a recipient of any future emails that they sent from their private accounts.

The software already had harvested dozens of emails sent by the four men. Most were to other parties about irrelevant topics. But a few were exchanged among them, and they used only surname initials when referring to each other.

The first email was from Weaver, apparently sent out yesterday afternoon, right after the office conversation with Crane that Hunter had monitored. Weaver had blind-copied the recipients, so Hunter couldn't tell who they were. The message read:

"Want to reassure all about moratorium. C, I know you have special concerns. But I'm so confident I think M shd buy more shares for us before mkt close today, bec. current depressed price fantastic bargain. After moratorium Carb stock will rebound big for us. Do all agree?"

"—W"

A message from Lockwood, just moments later, said:

"Just got off the phone with C and T. They agree w/ you. We're all in. Will tell M to buy 1K more shares for me. C & T will email M with their own buy instructions within the half hour."

"M" would be Robin Manes, who ran the GreenSmart trust for the government employees. "T" most likely would be Trammel, who held substantial CarboNot shares independently. "C" would be Crane.

He drummed his fingers on the desktop. No, that made no sense. Weaver had just spoken to Crane in his own office about this, moments earlier; he didn't need to send him a reassuring message. Crane, in fact, had been the one reassuring…

Of course. Crane had just talked to Kaplan, to reassure Ashton Conn.

"C" could be Conn, then.

Something was nagging at him. Something said in an earlier phone conversation he'd overheard. He shuffled through his sheets of notes for a few minutes.

There. In the call Lockwood made to someone unknown early yesterday morning. The mention of a "senior associate" who had reassured them that the fracking moratorium was a mere "formality." That had bothered him, and now he knew why.

He'd been focused on Trammel, thinking that he had to be the ringleader of all this. But Wonk said Trammel wasn't invested in Capital Resources. The "senior associate" was deeply invested, though—and was upset about the uninsured loss of the building.

Conn was invested in Capital Resources, through his wife.

His chief of staff's brother ran the office.

Conn also was invested in CarboNot, through the GreenSmart trust.

Maybe he had it all wrong.

He scrolled through a fresh flurry of emails, sent late Monday night. Sudden panicked exchanges over the revelations he published in last night's *Inquirer*. He grinned as he read through them. That Hunter s.o.b. had raised questions about NLA's study possibly resting on faked data— then tied it to the "mysterious murder" of the very scientist who was preparing to challenge it. It looked bad. "W" admitted that the article might very well affect the SAB decision about the moratorium after all. He, "C," and "CC"—who had to be Crane—all agreed that, at the opening bell, "M" had to dump the trust's CarboNot stock, to avoid far deeper, perhaps irretrievable losses. "T," "S," and "L" said they, too, would notify their brokers first thing in the morning, and do the same with their own CarboNot stock.

A final email had arrived around midnight to Sloan's inbox:

*"If only you or T had followed through with our action
plan re that guy, we wouldn't be here."*
"—C"

Well, well, well…

His eyes were dry and burning from the long hours at the
screen and poring over all the paperwork. He desperately
needed a couple of hours of sleep.

Then he would have to take a closer look at Ashton Conn.

Dawn heard Zak's voice calling for her. She ran faster,
staggering on through the dark, through the scratching tangle
of branches that whipped by her.

After a few minutes, out of breath, she slowed her steps.
She felt dazed and drained. She had no idea where she was
going, what she would do whenever she got there. Wherever
there was…

She pressed on, stumbling often, getting her clothes caught
on bushes. She fell once, her knee striking something hard
and sharp. She sucked in her breath, suppressing a cry of pain.
She didn't know if Zak was behind her, or how close. She got
up, staggered forward. Felt a wet warmth spreading down her
shin.

After a time, she didn't know how long, she saw light
flickering far ahead. She weaved through the trees, heading for
it. The light became several. Bright and high in the treetops,
like street lights.

The knee was beginning to ache. She limped toward the
lights.

She finally emerged in a clearing. It was an area of bare,
frozen earth. The lights were to her right. She continued,

feeling dizzy, weaving toward them. She passed a small paved parking lot on her left, continuing down its driveway toward a building. Some kind of barn-like thing, with what looked like a corral beside it.

A car sat in front of the building. She limped closer, then saw what it was.

And halted in her tracks.

At that instant, the front door opened and a man emerged, holding a cup of coffee. He spotted her and stopped, a shocked look on his face.

Terrified, she turned to run, but her knee gave out and she fell face-down. She heard running steps behind her and tried to get up, but heard breathing and a rustle of cloth, and then felt a strong hand grip her upper arm. Then yank her over onto her back.

Hovering over her, the astonished face of a young officer of the National Park Police.

She began to shake again.

Then cry softly.

Hunter's watch beeped him awake at four-thirty. Less than three hours' sleep, and he felt it. But he had a lot to do. In the bathroom, he splashed cold water on his face, scrubbed it hard with a face cloth to get the blood flowing. In the kitchen, he put on some coffee. Then he went back to the computer.

He navigated to Ashton Conn's official website. Topping the home page, a photo of the smiling senator in his office, seated behind a big desk next to an American flag. The sight sickened him. He mouse-clicked the "Biography" tab. A photo popped up of Conn with his plastic-pretty trophy wife.

Name "Emmalee." Plastic name, too. Her eyes looked at the camera the way a snake looks at a mouse.

He scrolled down the page to read about Conn's background. The bio was topped by an overview paragraph touting his role as "Washington's most passionate champion of the environment," followed by bullet points about his multitude of achievements. His *New York Times* bestseller. A list of major pieces of legislation he had sponsored. His major charities. His church. His educational background—first in a Philadelphia prep school, then Harvard, where he eventually received his J.D.

Then his internship at Nature Legal Advocacy…

He took a moment to digest that.

Then reread the previous bullet point about Harvard.

Contemplated the span of years that Conn had been a student there. In Cambridge, Massachusetts.

He felt the familiar tingle on the back of his scalp. Like the feeling he'd had out in Woodrow Wilson Plaza that day.

The first forwarded call from Danika came through at 7:50 a.m. It was for the burner phone labeled for Robin Manes. He waited for her to leave her message, then he accessed it and listened:

"Hello, Ms. Manes. This is your answering service. I have just found three waiting messages—all urgent—from a Mr. Weaver, a Mr. Crane, and a Mr. Kaplan. Let me read you the one from Mr. Kaplan, who called twice: 'Urgent that you sell CarboNot at the opening bell.' The other two gentlemen said essentially the same thing, about selling CarboNot stock. They left phone numbers and asked that you call them back to confirm as soon as you make the sales."

She read off the numbers, repeating them; Hunter jotted them down.

"That's about it. Thank you for using Crown, Ms. Manes, and please have a nice day."

"Not likely," Hunter said to himself, swiveling back and forth in his chair before the burner phones.

The one marked "Trammel" rang a minute later. He picked it up, disguising his voice.

"Marcus and Reilly Financial Services. This is Robin Locksley. May I help you?"

"This is Avery Trammel. I need to speak to Mr. Marcus immediately."

"He's not here yet, but he's due in at any moment. May I take a message for him, Mr. Trammel?"

"Yes. This is urgent. He is to place a sell order right at the opening bell for my CarboNot stock. All of it. At whatever price he can get. Right at the opening. Is that understood?"

"Yes, sir. Let me write that down…All CarboNot shares for Avery, that's A-V-E-R-Y, Trammel, that's T-R-A…Is that one 'm' or two, sir?"

Trammel's voice sounded like cracking ice as he spelled it out.

"Very good, sir. I'll give him this message as soon as he enters the office, marked 'urgent,' and also tell him in person what you said. Would you care to leave your phone number, sir?"

"He has it. Tell him to call me as soon as he has done what I told him to do."

Ten minutes later the burner labeled "Lockwood" rang, and he went through the same routine.

At 8:25, he repeated it again with Sloan. He hung up, amused at the thought of the CEO dumping shares of his own company stock. Or believing that he was.

At 9:00, he turned on the Fox Business Channel and, as he chewed a toasted English muffin, enjoyed their reporting about his article and its anticipated devastating impact on CarboNot stock today.

At 9:30, he watched the opening bell ceremony. A group of Boy Scouts from Kansas did the honors, while people around them applauded and the bell clanged. Appropriately, it sounded like an old-fashioned firehouse alarm.

Immediately, the anchor went to the business reporter on the floor. As the dire numbers crawled across the bottom of the screen they discussed the CarboNot selloff. "Frankly, I don't know where it's going to find its bottom," the reporter said, shrugging. "We'll soon see," the anchor said, sighing.

At 9:31, within seconds of each other, all four burners began to ring.

Six powerful men, desperately seeking reassurance from their brokers that their stocks had indeed been dumped.

Dylan Hunter rocked back and forth in his office chair, enjoying the sight of the flashing red lights on the phones. Letting them ring, and ring, and ring…

He was back upstairs napping in the early afternoon when his burner beeped—the one only Wonk and Annie could reach. He rolled over in bed, snagged it, looked at the screen.

Annie.

"Hi, you," he said.

"Hello, Dylan." Voice flat. Hesitation. Then: "I need to see you tonight. We need to talk."

He closed his eyes. "Yes. We probably do."

She said nothing.

"I won't be at the apartment tonight, though," he said. "I'll be out at the house. Probably from about five until about eight or nine. Will that be a problem for you?"

"No. I'll be there…See you then."

Automatically he wanted to say, "Love you." But her coolness warned him not to.

"See you tonight," he said.

He clicked off. He lay there with his eyes closed.

He knew what this meant.

He beat most of the rush hour traffic out of D.C. to the Bay Bridge, then waited behind a line of cars for a couple of minutes so that he would pay the toll-taker in cash. Waiting in line was always a drag, but an EZ-Pass that logged his travels was out of the question.

He crossed the bridge behind a sluggish, fuming eighteen-wheeler. As he approached the Kent Island side he watched a small plane taking off from the Bay Bridge Airport over the gray water, into the gray sky.

It made him think of her eyes.

He went across the island to its east side, then over the arc of the Narrows Bridge. Another few miles and he turned off onto the road that led out to Connor's Point. He left the CR-V in the driveway and went inside.

The place felt quiet and still. Like him.

He took the inside entrance into the garage, then went out its back door. The pine trees there blocked anyone's view of him as he opened the padlock and entered the nearby shed. He closed and latched the door behind him. Yanked on the drawstring for the overhead bulb. Went through the pre-mission ritual of moving aside the stack of boxes filled with meaningless papers, which covered the trap door. Levered it up and open with a screwdriver.

Descended the wooden ladder into the small cinderblock room, where he stored his guns and gear.

He had what he needed spread out on the floor of the den when he heard her unlock the front door.

No more lies he had promised her. He wouldn't hide anything from her, now. She had to see who he was. Then decide.

He sat on a recliner near the unlit fireplace, waiting. She emerged from the hallway. She wore a long, light brown cashmere coat and dark brown boots. She had pulled off one dark brown glove, and her fingers were tugging at the other when she saw him.

Then her eyes took in the gear on the floor. She stopped all motion. Her eyes rose to his.

"Going out, I see." Her voice was tight.

He got to his feet. Nodded—just once.

"That's right."

She nodded, too—more than once.

"Like some coffee? Wine?" he asked.

She shook her head. "I won't be here long."

He came over to help her with her coat. He didn't touch her. Didn't try to kiss her. He went to hang the coat on the rack near the front door, then returned.

She was seated at the end of the sofa closest to his recliner. He returned to it. Then waited.

"I got a call today from Cronin," she began.

He hadn't seen that one coming.

"I can only imagine what he had to say."

"I'm sure. He's certain that you destroyed the Capital Resources offices."

"Ed Cronin is a very good detective."

She shut her eyes an instant. Then opened them and gestured at the items on the floor.

"So, what else are you planning to do?"

"I'm going to bring them down. All of them. In fact, it's already started."

She lowered her gaze. Nodded slowly. Then looked up at him again.

"What about Boggs?"

"I'm going to hunt him down. And kill him."

She swallowed, visibly. "I see."

He waited for her to continue.

"You know what this means, Dylan."

"Yes, Annie. I know what this means."

She gestured at the gear. "But you're going to go ahead and do it, anyway."

"You know why I can't let this go. First were their attacks on all those innocent people up in Pennsylvania. Then the bomb that almost killed you. Then the murder of Adam Silva—which is entirely on me. Then the attack on me by their goons. Then the bomb at the *Inquirer* office. This won't stop. They won't stop. The government won't stop them—because they *are* the government." He paused a few seconds. "Annie, I'm doing this because somebody has to stop them. But there is nobody else to stop them. There is nobody but me."

"You promised…" she began, then hesitated.

"I promised to try, Annie. And I truly did. I tried to let it go. But *they* won't."

"I know you did. But I didn't mean that. I meant that you made a promise at Adam Silva's funeral. To his widow and children."

He didn't see that coming, either.

"Yes," he said softly. "I did."

She closed her eyes. "If only I could deal with this. With the constant nightmares. If only I could get past it."

"But you can't. And it was cruel of me to expect you to stay with someone like me. Annie, I don't know exactly why I'm this way. Why simple justice matters so much to me. But it always has. And it always will. That part of me will never change."

When she opened her eyes, they held tears.

"I know, Dylan. And I don't *want* you to change. Because if you weren't as you are, I wouldn't love you as I do."

It felt like another stab wound, this one to his throat. It was all he could do to continue looking at her, steadily. At the stunning face, twisted with grief; at the wide gray slanting eyes, spilling tears.

"I would give anything..." he began, then stopped.

"Except what makes you who you are. And it was wrong for *me* to expect you to do that."

She rose to her feet. Walked to him, head down. He stood to meet her.

She slipped the diamond off her finger. Just as he had known all afternoon that she would.

"I'm sorry, Dylan," she said.

"No, I'm the one who owes you the apology." He extended his hand. "I'll regret this moment forever. Because I'll love you forever, Annie Woods."

She reached out, placed the ring on his hand. Then, with both of hers, she closed his fingers around it. She raised his hand to her lips and kissed it, then pressed it to her breast.

He leaned down and kissed her forehead. Straightening, he stared into those incredible eyes. No doubt for the last time.

Then she released his hand, and his eyes, and turned away.

He knew it would be unendurable for both of them if he followed her to the door and helped her on with her coat. So he just stood there in the middle of the room. He watched her leave the room. He heard the soft rustle as she put on her coat. Then the sound of the door opening.

And closing.

Lying back in the recliner, eyes closed, he tried to process what had just occurred.

He tried to convince himself that this had to happen—that it was for the best, for both of them.

Annie, I don't know exactly why I'm this way...

His mind searched back, back to the time before he had become "Dylan Hunter"—back to the years when he was still Matt Malone.

...Why simple justice matters so much to me. But it always has...

Always?

Then he thought of his dad.

Mike Malone.

"Big Mike"...

THIRTY

PITTSBURGH, PENNSYLVANIA
July 12, 1983, 6:40 p.m.

Tucked deep in the shadowed canyons of buildings in downtown Pittsburgh, the expansive construction site was the latest part of the city's revitalization effort. A sign on the metal security fence surrounding the perimeter described the new bank building to be erected there, along with an artist's rendition of a gleaming glass tower. At the bottom of the sign were the words:

Construction by
Malone Commercial Development

The crew had knocked off for the night. Only Matt and his dad, Big Mike, remained behind, in the glass-enclosed cab of a Caterpillar D9L bulldozer.

Matt sat in the operator's seat; his father stood, squeezed against the left-hand door of the closed, cramped cab. The interior was coated in dust and grime, and the smell of oil hung in the air. Here and there the mustard-colored finish of the walls and control levers was scratched and worn down to bare metal.

The beast idled in neutral, its throaty growl making Matt feel as if he were trapped in the belly of a huge yellow lion. The gas pedal, he had to remind himself, worked opposite from the one in a car: It was more like a clutch. When you took your foot *off* it, the dozer began to move. So he pressed his feet down hard on both the gas pedal and the brake to keep the thirteen-foot-high, 100,000-pound monster leashed. Its vibration shook him through the seat and the pedals.

He was sweating profusely, and not just from the heat and humidity of the July evening. He'd been at this for ten minutes under Big Mike's patient gaze, and he still couldn't manage to coordinate the various controls.

"Okay. Let's get her moving again," his father said.

He tried to remember the steps. The throttle lever was already pulled back. He raised his left foot off the brake, then his right off the gas pedal. The engine growled louder—but the dozer didn't move.

Then he remembered: *You have to put it in gear, stupid.*

His left hand reached for the gear shift lever at his side, but Dad bent down and grabbed his forearm.

"Remember, now," he said mildly, "you have to keep the gas pedal pressed in when you shift gears."

He felt his face grow warm. *Stupid.*

"Right," he said.

He took a breath; licked his dry lips. Pressed in the gas pedal, then pulled the gear shift lever back, into first gear. Black smoke puffed from the top of the vertical exhaust pipe that rose just outside the dirty windshield. He released the gas pedal, gingerly…and the beast began to crawl forward on its giant tracks across the expanse of dirt. His heart hammered with excitement.

"Good job. Now, remember how I showed you to turn. Try a left turn."

He raised his hand to two side-by-side levers next to the seat; pulled back on the left-hand one. The dozer obediently started a slow turn to the left.

"Great. Now, let's stop here and lower the blade."

He hit the brake with his left foot. The huge machine began to lurch in spasms. Dad had to seize a grab bar to keep from falling.

A jolt of panic surged through him.

"Push in the gas pedal, too," Dad said mildly.

He jammed both pedals to the floor. The dozer stopped rolling forward.

"Sorry," he said, for what seemed like the hundredth time.

Dad chuckled good-naturedly.

"Stop apologizing, Matt. You'll get the hang of it. It takes a while. My first time in the seat of a dozer, I was sixteen— already a couple years older than you are now. And I backed it right into an old pickup truck. Squashed it like a bug up against a cement retaining wall." He chuckled again, pale blue eyes distant, remembering. "Fortunately, nobody was inside the truck."

"Wow! That's awful…So, did they fire you?"

"No. Why should they? After all, it was *my* truck."

Matt burst out laughing. Dad laughed, too. Matt felt his jitters melt away.

"Well," he said, "at least I can't wreck anything out here in an empty dirt lot."

"That was the idea…Well, I wonder what *he* wants."

He pointed off to the right, toward the site's parking lot. A black-and-white police car sat in the lot, the blue-and-red light bar on its roof flashing. A uniformed officer stood outside the vehicle, motioning in their direction.

"Okay, shift into neutral; push forward the throttle lever; then set the brake…Good. Now let me take the controls, and we'll go see what he wants."

His father expertly steered the dozer over toward the prowl car, then shut it down at the edge of the lot. They climbed down from the high cab onto its track, then hopped down to the muddy ground.

The officer was young and brown-haired. His dark navy uniform was crisply creased; his hat bore the department's distinctive black-and-yellow checkerboard band; and his short-sleeved shirt revealed bulging biceps. He wasn't short, but at six-three Dad towered over him, as he did most people.

"Problem, officer?"

"Is that your vehicle over there, sir?" The cop pointed toward the Lincoln sitting at the far end of the lot.

"That's mine."

"Well, I was just driving by, and I spotted a guy stabbing at your tires with something. I pulled in and caught him. I'm sorry to tell you that he punctured two of your tires before I could stop him. He's sitting in the back of my car now.

"Oh, great."

The cop asked for his name and identification.

"Mike Malone," he said, handing over his driver's license. "I own Malone Commercial Development. We're the construction outfit here."

The officer jotted down a few notes onto a pad.

"Do you know who the guy is, officer?"

"His name is Louis Marino. Know him?"

"Name doesn't ring a bell."

"I haven't gotten much out of him yet. But he's an older guy, which surprises me. Vandalism is usually a young person's crime. So I wondered if this might be something personal between you two. Maybe if you saw him, you might recognize him."

Dad went over to the car and looked inside the rear-door window. The guy inside yelled something that Matt couldn't make out. Dad came back to the officer, shaking his head.

"Never saw the guy in my life. But for some reason he's really pissed at me. I'd like to know what this is all about, too. Would you mind bringing him out here, so I can ask him a few things?"

The cop thought about it. "Okay. He's cuffed, but still, keep your distance."

He hauled the man out of the back and took him by the arm to where they stood. Marino was middle-aged with a hooked nose and salt-and-pepper hair. He reminded Matt of Tony Bennett.

"You son-of-a-bitch!" he shouted.

The cop got in his face. "Hey! You calm down, okay? We want to know why you're out here trashing this gentleman's car."

"*Gentleman?* You call some prick who steals your house and business a 'gentleman'?"

"What the hell are you talking about—me stealing your house and business?"

"Not just me. The whole neighborhood! Ten blocks of the Bloomfield district—dozens of row houses, dry cleaners, barber shops, my neighborhood grocery, everything. Don't pretend you don't know about it. We got a notice about the city council hearing. The universities want to expand, and the council wants more high-tech firms to feed off them, by building another 'business incubator.' So they plan to vote to just *take* our houses and businesses, under 'eminent domain.' And your goddamned company is going to do the development—it says so in the *Post-Gazette*, don't say it isn't true. So tell me, Malone: Does a bastard like you enjoy making your millions by stealing other people's land? Or don't you even stop and think about it?"

"Hold on!" Dad was frowning. "Sure, we've been negotiating a development deal with the city and the university. But nobody told me they were going to get the land by eminent domain."

Marino snorted. "Well, how else do you think they'll get all that property?"

"They aren't buying you out? Offering you a fair price?"

"They're making offers, sure. 'Offers we can't refuse'—like in *The Godfather*...Why are you looking at me like that? I know you don't give a rat's ass about it, but a lot of us have lived in Bloomfield for years—generations. My parents came over on the boat and settled there. My brothers and sisters and our relatives and friends were all born and raised there. We've built our businesses, homes, *lives* there. So we don't *want* to sell, not at any price. But they're just going to force us out, then demolish everything we spent decades building— and then just turn our land over to the universities, or to some rich, connected company. And of course, they pay *you* millions to do it."

Matt had never seen his father look rattled by anything. It was a shock to see him standing with a stunned look on his face.

"My wife Marie and me, we sweat blood to build the grocery," Marino said, his voice growing thick. "It took years to finally turn a profit. We invested everything in it, including our hearts and souls. We hired our family members and friends to work there. Everybody in the neighborhood shops there. Now, Marie's crying her eyes out. We don't have the dough to hire fancy lawyers to fight you rich guys. We just have to sit there and take it—then figure out where the hell we're supposed to go, and what the hell we're supposed to do with the rest of our lives, after your goddamned wrecking balls move in."

He nodded toward the Lincoln.

"So, I'm driving by and I see your company's name on the fence. And I see the gate open, with that big Linc sitting here. I didn't know it was yours; but I figured it had to belong to one of your company big shots. So yeah—it was stupid what I did. But I lost it. If I had a crowbar, I would have smashed in the windows and doors. But all I had was a screwdriver, so I started on the tires."

"All right, Mr. Marino," the cop said. "I saw you do it, and now you admit you did it. So, you're under arrest for trespassing, for malicious destruction of—"

"Wait a minute," Dad said quietly. "Let him go."

The cop blinked. "What do you mean? He—"

"I said: *Let him go.* I won't be pressing charges." His voice softened again. "Please, officer—take Mr. Marino's handcuffs off."

The cop stood there a moment, then shrugged. He freed Marino, who rubbed his wrists as he glared at Dad.

"Feeling guilty, huh? Well, if you think you can make up for this by not pressing—"

"Mr. Marino, before you go on, let me say something." Marino opened his mouth, but Dad raised his hand. "Please, sir. Just give me a chance."

Marino stopped, breathing hard.

"Whether you believe me or not, Mr. Marino, I didn't know about the eminent domain takings. The city council and I have had it out about that stuff in the past. They know damned well that I don't get involved in that sort of thing. So I think they're trying to pull a fast one on me—get me to sign contracts for this project before I find out what they're up to."

His lips pressed thin, and his jaw muscles worked. He went on:

"I want you to know that this is *not* going to happen."

Marino blinked. "You mean, you're not going to be involved?"

"More than that. I mean this whole 'takings' thing—it just isn't going to happen. I'll make sure of that."

"Oh yeah? So, just how are you going to stop them?"

His father sent a quick look at the cop, who was watching him intently. His lips curled into that crooked little grin that Matt loved.

"You leave that to me."

Matt could tell that Marino was debating with himself whether to believe it. Finally he cleared his throat.

"Sorry about the car," he said.

"You've got nothing to be sorry about. I don't blame you one bit. I'm just glad you weren't carrying a gun."

"Yeah," Marino said, swallowing hard. "Still…" He dropped his eyes, then looked up. "Look. Can I give you a lift somewhere?"

Dad's grin broadened. "I know this Irish bar. You like Guinness? Or do you drink that wop *chianti* shit?"

Marino grinned back at him. "A bottle of Iron City will do fine."

As they walked toward Marino's car, Dad dropped back and said, "Sorry you didn't get your lesson tonight, Matt."

Matt looked up at him. "But I did."

The next day, Dad invited him to take a seat in his cluttered office at the company headquarters.

"One of life's most important lessons," he said, "is to own up to it and make amends whenever you make a mistake."

"Like you did last night."

"Like that. But I want you to learn another lesson, too. Don't ever be afraid to stand up to people who everybody else thinks are important. Politicians, celebrities—people with money, degrees, fancy titles. They're no better than you are, Matt. Most times they're a lot worse. So never let them intimidate you. You can't be a doormat and let them walk all over you. You got to stand up to them. Today I want to show you what that looks like."

He picked up his office phone, poked the buttons, and waited.

"Jerry. Mike here." He covered the mouthpiece of the phone and whispered to Matt, "Jerry's my lawyer."

Over the next ten minutes, Dad explained to the lawyer about the eminent domain plan. They discussed options.

"Far as I'm concerned, I'm out of the project, and they'll know why later this afternoon. But I want to go farther. I don't want them to proceed with another developer. I want to fight this whole thing...I know, I get that I don't have legal standing to sue them myself. But those property owners do. They just don't have the money to do it, which I do. That's where you come in, Jerry. I want to pay you to take on their case. Represent them in court. You're the best I can think of to handle this kind of thing...Uh huh...Well, I'm sure you're busy. So, how much would it take to persuade you to *make* time for it?...Yes, right away...Come on, that's ridiculous. Your time is more valuable than that. I'll double that, to one-fifty...Sure, I'm serious. And if you find that you need more, it'll be no problem. Okay?"

They continued the discussion for a few more minutes, and Dad gave the lawyer Marino's phone number. After they hung up, he dialed another number, winking at Matt as he did so.

"Now to get the media involved."

He drummed his fingers on the desk, waiting, then said: "Yes, could I have Dick Ryker in the city room?...Tell him Mike Malone's calling."

He gave the reporter a shorter version of the story.

"Dick, you've been covering urban renewal mostly from the politicos' point of view. But there's this whole other side: the human-interest angle. All these people are about to be run out of their homes and shops. It's outrageous. They'll wreck Bloomfield the same way they wrecked East Liberty and the Lower Hill District in the Fifties and Sixties. All that federal urban renewal money tore down thriving neighborhoods. They pushed 5,000 families out of their homes. Then they replaced it all with—what? Scores of parking lots. And empty, abandoned lots. And crime-infested high-rise public housing. Everybody admits it was a disaster. But now they want to do it all over again."

He explained that he was hiring an attorney to represent the neighborhood. "I aim to stop this bullshit, Dick. And you can print that." He chuckled. "Okay, maybe you change the word 'bullshit.' Anyway, I'm planning to hold a news conference with representatives from the district: families, mom-and-pop store owners..." He listened, then laughed. "Do I sound like somebody who gives a shit about 'repercussions'?...Yeah, you can quote that, too."

When he hung up, he looked over at Matt and said, "I don't think we'll have to wait long before this phone starts ringing. So why don't we go get some lunch before everything hits the fan?"

That afternoon, they were ushered into the office of the president of the city council. Perry Nickson was a thin little man with quick darting movements and tiny teeth. He reminded Matt of a weasel.

"What's with bringing the kid here, Mike? We have to talk serious business."

"The 'kid' is my son, Perry, and someday he'll be *running* my business. So I think this meeting will be a valuable civics lesson for him."

"Suit yourself. But don't expect me to pull any punches just because he's with you. I invited you here right after I got a call from Dick Ryker at the paper. He told me what you're up to. Mike, what the hell are you trying to pull here?"

"That's exactly what I came here to ask *you*. You know damned well I don't do projects built on eminent domain takings. But you guys on the council tried to hide that fact from me about the Bloomfield project."

Matt sat back, listening and watching as the argument unfolded and grew more heated by the minute. Nickson finally exploded in a torrent of profanity when Dad said he was hiring a lawyer to represent the property owners.

"Understand this, Malone: We won't put up with that kind of shit. Not from you, not from anybody. I don't give a shit how much work you have done for the city before, or what your reputation is, or what other contracts we have pending with you. I'm telling you right now: You pursue this, we'll ruin you. *I'll* ruin you. I'll make sure that your company never works again in this entire city. Hell, in this entire *state*. I have a lot of friends in Harrisburg. I can see—"

"Matt," Dad interrupted, turning to him. "I've changed my mind. I need a private moment with Mr. Nickson. Would you excuse us for a few minutes, and go wait in the outer office?"

Matt got up and left, closing the door behind him. Nickson's secretary was away from her desk. He stood there, not quite knowing what to do. He took a visitor's chair in the waiting area.

Then he heard noises from the office he had just left. Then a sharp squeal. Then more noise, and a heavy *thump* against the wall next to the office door. A scuffling sound, as if something were scraping against the wall.

Then the sound of a low voice that he thought was Dad's.

He waited anxiously for several minutes.

Finally, the door to the office opened.

Dad walked out, looking serene.

Behind him in the room he caught a glimpse of Nickson—tie askew, straightening his glasses and his suit jacket, a terrified look on his face.

"Come," Dad said, motioning him.

Matt got to his feet and walked beside him down the hall, toward the elevators. His father's face was always hard to read, but it had what seemed to be a look of amusement.

"So Dad…what happened?"

"It's all settled," Dad said simply.

Matt ventured, "What did you say to change his mind?"

Big Mike looked down at him, a twinkle in his pale blue eyes.

"I spoke the only kind of language people like him understand."

THIRTY-ONE

The first one was tricky.

His target, Gavin Lockwood, lived at the end of a peninsula that jutted out into the Severn River. Planning the op, he studied the site online, using satellite maps. Big problem: only one main access road in and out, branching off into a lot of curling cul-de-sacs. If he drove in, he couldn't park on those roads without some risk of being noticed by patrolling cops. Even if his car was overlooked, his only escape route might be blocked off once the 911 calls began.

Another option was to come in by water, using his boat. But that was tricky, too. A boat on the river would be conspicuous, particularly fleeing the scene. It also would be in a narrow channel of water that could be blocked in either direction, again cutting off escape. Very risky.

The satellite imagery revealed a third option. The peninsula where Lockwood lived was one of several that ran parallel to each other out into the river. They were separated by creeks a couple of hundred feet wide. Easy to swim from one peninsula to the other.

Just after midnight on Wednesday morning, he left the house in the CR-V and drove to the commuter bus stop on

Kent Island, right across from the K-Mart. He pulled in next to his BMW High Security 7, which he had driven out of D.C. two days earlier and left there among the other commuter cars. He got out, checked both directions. No approaching headlights. He went around to the back of the CR-V, pulled out a large Army-type duffle bag, then transferred it quickly to the back seat of his BMW. Seconds later, he had swapped out vehicles and was on his way.

Twenty minutes later, he turned off the Generals Highway in Annapolis onto a road leading to one of those peninsulas. He drove out slowly through a spider web of little streets with big houses, to the very end. He pulled into the lot at the community marina, backed the car in close to a stand of trees that marched right out to the water. Nobody would think that the luxury Beemer was out of place here.

He went around to the back seat, tugged out the duffle bag, and hauled it into the trees. Then he shrugged off his long overcoat. Underneath he wore a black, two-layer dry suit—neoprene over a polyester liner—with neoprene dive boots. The gear would make the swim possible in the frigid water. He opened the duffle, pulled out the integrated hood, gloves, mask, and flippers. And a lightweight waterproof backpack.

He shoved his overcoat inside the duffle and hid it in some bushes. After zipping and sealing the hood and gloves, he crept carefully through the trees toward the water, carrying the mask, flippers, and backpack.

At the edge of the dock he paused to scan the area. Not a soul. The tethered boats rocked almost imperceptibly in the river current, making soft squeaks, and the water lapped and gurgled against the wooden pylons. Above, the overcast sky hid the moon, but glowed faintly from the lights of the nearby city.

He moved cautiously out onto the pier, careful not to make sudden movements that might attract attention. Kneeling between a couple of bigger cruisers, he prepared and slipped on the mask, checking the seal against his skin. Then donned the flippers and backpack. Gripping the dock line of one of the boats, he eased himself down into the water.

Before moving out, he submerged his face and blew some bubbles, to alleviate stress on his lungs from the shock of the cold. Then he kicked off into a slow, deliberate swim across the creek, careful not to splash.

The neighboring peninsula lay barely two hundred yards ahead. Approaching, he veered right along its shoreline, skirting around the eastern end. A crumbling, abandoned pier jutted out before him. Rounding it, he saw another—and his target.

He had read about Lockwood's love of sailing, and the first sight of the boat almost caused him to change his mind. *Sundancer* was indeed a beauty, its graceful, stiletto-sharp lines silhouetted against water and sky.

As he came within eyeshot of the mansion on the hill above, he drew a deep breath and lowered his head beneath the surface. He powered forward underwater, mostly on the strength of his legs, just as he used to do in his old college meets. The drag from the backpack fought him, and his exposed mouth and chin stung from the cold. But he did not want to risk being seen by someone's chance glance from a window.

His lungs were aching when he finally surfaced. He had estimated pretty well; he was within ten feet of the pier. Eyes on the darkened house looming at the top of the slope, he moved around to the far side, where the craft was tied.

It was moored bow outward. He paused there, treading water. No lights on in the house; no indication that anyone had spotted him.

Grabbing the end of the pier with his left hand and giving a hard kick with the flippers, Hunter launched his body upward from the water and seized the gunwale with his right. He chinned up and hauled himself out of the water with his forearms. Rolling smoothly onto the deck, he scrambled immediately behind the low wall of the cabin. There he lay still, catching his breath in the frosty air.

After a moment, he pulled up his mask. The icy breeze bit at his hot cheeks and forehead and made his eyes water. He blinked to clear them, then crabbed along the deck toward the stern. Reaching that end of the cabin, he slipped off the backpack, opened a pouch on the side, drew out a screwdriver, then attacked the locked cabin door. He was inside in five seconds.

He checked his diver's watch. 0053 hours. Then he unzipped the backpack and went to work.

A rippling *flash* against his closed eyelids, then two loud *bangs*, jolted Gavin Lockwood awake. He felt Selena jerk beside him.

"Jesus!" she croaked. "What was *that?*"

"Damned if I know! It sounded like an explosion!" He glanced at the bedside clock. 1:25 a.m.

What the hell?

Then saw light dancing on the curtains.

He tore off the covers and rolled out of bed. Stumbled across the room to the window.

He had to grab the frame to steady himself.

"Oh dear *God!*"

Beneath him flames and smoke were pouring from the cabin of *Sundancer*, sparking and flickering off the ripples of the river.

"Gavin! What?"

He felt-heard her rush to his side. Then gasp.

"Ohhhh…Oh no!"

He turned to her, heart pounding. She was biting her fist.

"Call 911!" He shouted. "Get the fire department out here!"

He ran to the wall, clawed for the light switch. Then looked around wildly for something to put on. She was naked, too, scrambling for the bedside phone.

Lockwood dashed into the walk-in closet, yanked a pair of trousers off a hanger, then onto himself. He jammed his bare feet into a pair of loafers, then snatched a suit jacket, sending its wooden hanger and matching trousers flopping to the floor. He emerged to hear Selena whimpering *"Come on…come ON!"* into the phone. He pushed his naked arms into the sleeves while he rushed down the stairs to the kitchen, where a fire extinguisher rested somewhere in the pantry.

Back across the water, Hunter stood in the trees near the marina, wrapped again in the overcoat. His gear was back in the duffle at his feet. He pressed a compact pair of binoculars to his eyes with one hand; in the other hand was the cell phone he'd just used to set off the charge.

He watched orange flames spread across the deck of the cutter, then lick up the masts. Slowly, inexorably, the boat began to sink forward, where the hull had been breached.

He shifted the binoculars toward the house. Saw a figure slip-sliding down the slope, landing on his ass, then bouncing up and continuing a frantic zig-zag course to the wooden stairs that led down to the pier. As the figure ran toward the flaming boat, he could see that it was a man carrying something. Then he was at the stern, and even from this distance the flames revealed the horrified face of Gavin Lockwood, a fire extinguisher in his hands. He stopped. Dropped the extinguisher. Then bent forward at the waist, seizing his head in his hands.

Hunter moved the binoculars back to the cutter. Watched, emotions torn, as its graceful bow slowly settled beneath the inky surface of the river.

He raised the binoculars up the main mast. In the last flickers of flame before the river extinguished them, he could make out the little black flag he'd hoisted—the one with the skull and crossbones.

The second one was even trickier.

Due east of Dulles International Airport in Herndon, Virginia, lies a business park known as Dulles Corner. Incongruously, a well-maintained baseball field lies on its western edge.

He had found it online, again through satellite imagery. Given its placement, Hunter had no idea who used the field. Or cared. But it was sited just a few thousand feet from his next target.

At 0310 hours he reached the business park by means of the Dulles Toll Road, found his way onto Sunrise Valley Drive, then continued to where it intersected Dulles View Drive. Deceptive name: a short, quiet residential street whose view of Dulles Airport was blocked by a line of trees. The street led him past an apartment complex directly across from the ball field. Okay, that explained the ball field.

He hung a right into the driveway that led to a small parking lot on the third-base side. It was empty. He killed the lights and rolled on to the western end of the lot. Backed in right next to the trees. Killed the engine.

Nobody around. Even if they were, it would be almost impossible to spot him back here.

He got out and stretched. The dark overcoat now covered jeans and a sweatshirt. He'd changed out of the diving suit in the restroom of a Denny's, where he'd sucked down hot coffee.

He was dog-tired from the events of the day.

He had to push thoughts of her from his mind.

He went around to the trunk and unlocked it. Reaching into the well, he hoisted out several items, one at a time. He quickly assembled them on the ground. Then carefully lifted the ungainly contraption and carried it out into a grassy area alongside the ball field. No lights out here, as he'd hoped. He set it down, flipped several switches on it, stood back, and watched it shiver and buzz to life.

It was almost as noisy as a lawnmower. That wouldn't leave him much time before someone looked out a window, wondering what the hell was going on. He ran back to the car, to the laptop that he'd left running on the passenger seat.

With the door still open, he bent over and keyed in the first command.

Out in the field, the small helicopter drone rose straight up into the air, hoisted by three propellers. He watched it wobble a little in the invisible wind eddies before he turned back to the laptop. The computer was connected to a powerful radio transmitter, and the receiver on the drone was highly sensitive. The setup had cost a small fortune, and consisted of state-of-the-art parts from widely scattered manufacturers. From his CIA days, he knew which ones did contract work for the Agency. With his credentials, money, and a good pretext, it wasn't hard to get what he needed.

Last week he had flown his Cessna into Dulles in order to get the precise GPS coordinates of his target. Those were programmed into the drone's GPS. All he had to do now was get it up to the proper altitude and turn it loose. But he had a joystick attached to the laptop, too, for when he needed to intervene manually.

He tapped in a new elevation of three hundred feet, to clear any possible obstacles, followed by the program code. His eyes followed his machine as it soared west, right over the treetops.

One of the switches he'd flipped had activated the tiny ball-shaped video camera on the underside of the drone. He could make it swivel around with his touch pad, and did so now. He followed the flight path on the screen. It zipped quickly over Sully Road, which paralleled the east side of the airport, then crested another line of trees. As it emerged over the airfield, he immediately brought it down to an altitude of seventy-five feet.

The radio scanner on his dash was tuned to the tower, and it stayed quiet. No air traffic coming or going, so no risk that the drone would hit any plane. He let it continue on its way. He tilted up the camera lens so that he could see exactly where it was headed. The drone crossed a couple of hundred meters of open field, then a runway, then a tarmac. Then approached a group of planes parked on the tarmac and the grass in front of a general aviation hangar.

He had to make sure the area was clear of people, so he took over with the joystick and made the drone do a quick loop. No one in front of the general aviation hangar. No one anywhere near his target, which sat off by itself.

He swung the little aircraft around again, zooming the lens to confirm the number on the plane. That was it, all right. He swerved the drone around to the jet's nose, slowed its speed, and keyed another command. The camera, now tilting downward, revealed the object that he had just released, plunging to the tarmac in front of the plane.

Perfect.

Pulling back on the joystick, he gained altitude again. What happened next would require a lot of acceleration and momentum. At three hundred feet, he disengaged the joystick and let the program do its thing.

He watched as the camera dived straight down toward the rapidly growing image of Avery Trammel's Gulfstream 200.

Then the screen went dark.

He straightened, took a step back from the car.

Heard a sharp distant crack.

"Did you see that?" came a shout over the scanner.

He shut down the laptop. Went back and closed the trunk. Heard a louder, secondary explosion. Glanced up, saw billowing coils of orange-glowing smoke churning above the trees to the west. Sliding into the cushioning comfort of the heated driver's seat, he heard a siren begin to wail in the distance.

He closed the door against the outside noise. Pressed his skull back into the soft headrest. Shut his eyes for a few seconds.

Two tricky ops in one night. Not bad. The next wouldn't be tricky at all. Because it was already in motion and didn't need his further involvement.

He was yawning as he emerged from the business park onto the Dulles Toll Road, heading back toward D.C. He would return to the Bethesda apartment tonight, feed Luna, catch a little sleep.

It would be fun later today to check in on their recorded calls and emails.

Especially after they found out that their properties were no longer insured.

To Joe Moretti, it made no goddamn sense how rich people could blow through their cash like this.

As his demo crew moved in the heavy equipment, he stood smoking at the edge of the lake, looking back at the summer cottage. It was gorgeous, not a goddamn thing wrong with it. Cedar shingle siding, slate roof, big enclosed sun porch. Hell, he would give his right ball for a house like this. And this was only the dude's *summer* home.

And now the asshole wanted it demolished. To make space for some cold "contemporary" piece of crap, instead.

He cleared his throat and spat. Took another drag, shaking his head. Some people just had way too much money. But no values. They couldn't appreciate nothing.

He caught motion out of the corner of his eye and turned.

Smoky Scanlon walked up. It was his second day back on the job after he went out with a concussion. That fight a couple weeks back, where several of Joe's guys got the shit kicked out of them. Everybody was closed-mouthed about it when he asked. When he pushed it, Lou Russo called and told him to butt out.

Okay. Not his business. But he was glad the boss's nephew got his ass kicked. Joe had known for a long time the prick wanted his steward job. But apparently Smoky had screwed up something royally and was now on Uncle Lou's shit list.

"Yeah?" Joe demanded before Smoky could speak.

"Uh...I was just inside the place." The big blond jerk hooked a thumb in the direction of the cottage. "There's, like, all kinds of valuables in there. Furniture and TVs and clothes. It doesn't make sense. You sure about this?"

"*Yes*, I'm sure about this. The guy first hired Ambrose's outfit to do this job; but they got hung up somewhere else this week. So we got lucky and inherited it. The guy came out here himself yesterday, in his fancy Beemer, and he showed me *exactly* what we were supposed to do." He tapped a wad of papers sticking out of his coat pocket. "Here's the signed work order, and all the demo permits and paperwork that Ambrose already arranged with the city."

"But—"

Joe cut him off.

"Listen: This is about a divorce. All that shit in there belongs to his ex. She moved out on him and his kids for some other dude, and she abandoned it all. Now the sight of the house and her stuff makes him sick. He can't stand the idea of sorting through it. So he's paying us time-and-a-half to bring it all down before noon...Hey, I see what you're thinking—and *no*, you *can't* take away any of that stuff. I asked him, and he made that clear. He said he'd be out here checking on our progress this morning. So he could show up any time, and I don't want him finding that crap in your car. Got that? Now stop second-guessing me, and get your ass to work."

He watched Smoky skulk off toward the dozer. Worthless piece of shit. Only here because of his uncle.

He flipped the spent butt into the lake. Well, he'd be damned if he'd let the punk take *his* job. He just needed to impress Russo more. He'd start this morning, by making sure he did everything out here exactly the way the guy's work order said.

The excavator began to rumble toward the cottage, its arm rising.

Then afterward, he'd ask the owner to put in a good word for him with Russo. That would carry a *lot* of weight. After all, the owner was the boss of the goddamn EPA.

Diane Baer signed for the overnight package, then looked up and smiled at the delivery man.

"Thanks, Tom. It's nice to see you again. I see you got a nice tan. I hope you and your wife enjoyed the cruise."

"Sure did," Tom answered. "Thanks for recommending that line. The food and service was everything you said it would be. We liked St. John's especially...Well, gotta run. Probably see you again tomorrow."

"I hope so. Take care."

The brown-paper-wrapped package, bearing the words "URGENT/PERSONAL," was addressed to Mr. Sloan. The return address said "A. CONN," with the address of the Senate Office Building. It was all handwritten in green ink.

She was surprised at the informality; no official stamps and labels. But she knew the senator was a friend of Mr. Sloan. She remembered him from his recent visit here, with all those other people. It had been such a big deal, and everyone was so excited when he walked in. He even took time to shake hands with her, then all the rest of the staff. Such a friendly man. You could see why he was so successful in politics. It had been an exciting day for them all.

The mood in the office today was anything but. It had been bad the past few weeks, but yesterday it had gotten much worse. She didn't understand much about markets or follow the news much, but everybody in the office was whispering about how the stock price had collapsed in one day to just a quarter of its value—how the company was now in danger.

That scared her. She had enjoyed her job as Mr. Sloan's executive assistant for over a year. Sure, he could be tough and grouchy, but he had given her a big Christmas bonus. She was fifty-two now and divorced. Still a long way from retirement, and the recession made the job market terrible. She'd worried all night about what she would do if she lost this job.

Her usual routine was to open all of Mr. Sloan's mail and packages for him. She picked up a letter opener and pried it under the tape at the end of the box. Then stopped.

The label said "URGENT/PERSONAL." And it was from a senator. Maybe nobody else except Mr. Sloan was supposed to see this, whatever it was.

She had not seen him come in this morning; he had arrived before anyone else and had remained in his office with the door closed. He left a sticky note on her desk to intercept all incoming calls and take messages.

She put down the letter opener and picked up the package. It felt fairly heavy in her hands. She felt torn. On the one hand, he seemed to want privacy; but maybe he was expecting this. It was clearly private and important.

She walked it over to Mr. Sloan's office and rapped lightly at his door.

"Yes?" The voice, an impatient growl.

She entered. His swivel chair was turned away from her; he was looking out at the Washington skyline under a bleak sky.

"Excuse me, Mr. Sloan. A package from Senator Conn just arrived. It's marked urgent and personal, so I didn't want to open it."

He swung around. She was shocked at his appearance. His gray tie was askew, his thinning gray hair mussed, his long face gray, too. It was drawn and he looked as if he hadn't slept.

"What? From Conn?" He blinked a couple of times. "What the hell could *he* be sending me?...All right. Just put it on the desk."

She did so, straightened, and ventured: "Is everything all right, sir?"

His head was down, staring at the package. Only his eyes moved up to look at her. They were bloodshot.

"No. Everything is *not* all right…I need to be by myself today, Diane. Just close the door on the way out."

"Yes sir."

She retreated, closing the door softly behind her.

Oh God. It was as bad as she had feared.

The desks around hers were empty now, and she heard laughter from the lunchroom down the hall. She glanced at the wall clock. Just after noon. Then she remembered: It was Shirley's birthday. Morrie had brought in a small cake. Maybe this was the last time anyone would celebrate anything around here.

She entered the room and everyone looked up from the table and the candlelit cake. She forced a smile at Shirley.

"Sorry I'm late to the par—"

The blast behind her rocked the building and knocked her to the floor.

"I can't believe this!" Emmalee shrieked at him. "Goddammit, Ash! You're telling me we've lost *everything?*"

Conn sat on the sofa of the living room, bent over his knees, his throbbing skull braced in his hands as she hovered above him, howling like a goddamned banshee.

"Not everything!" he snapped. "The investments, all right, yes. Robin says they're pretty much gone. Even if EPA goes ahead and imposes the moratorium now, she says she can't see how CarboNot can recover. Sloan's not even taking our calls right now." He looked up. "But we still have my salary. This place, and the place in Florida, they're worth a lot. And the parcels we scooped up in the Allegheny Forest—those can be resold."

"But we've lost, what? Like, five million or something?"

He looked up at her and shouted, "Yes! About five million or something! Sorry, but you'll just have to cut back on your facelifts and New York shopping safaris until we bounce back from this!"

"How are we supposed to bounce back from *this?*" She grabbed the copy of the *Inquirer* off the coffee table and threw it at him. It hit his chest and scattered onto the floor. He jumped to his feet, stormed up to her. She took a step back.

"Listen to me! That bastard has nothing on me! Not a goddamned thing! It's all innuendo and speculation! Our Capital Resources money was in *your* name, and the CarboNot stock is in the blind trust. Those investments made perfect sense, and Robin is going to cover for us. That's why it's all going to blow over."

She blinked at him. Wanting to believe, he could tell.

He began pacing the Oriental carpet, trying to calm down.

"Look. Take it easy. As long as I keep Trammel happy, he'll keep the other campaign donors on board. I talked to him last night. He's *not* happy, of course, but he told me we're still fine. Stu and I are going to issue a statement late this afternoon. We'll probably hold a presser in a few—"

He felt his cell buzzing in his pants pocket, where he'd dumped it after he'd come home from the morning floor vote. He pawed for it, then saw the name.

"Yeah, Gavin..." He listened. Then felt everything drain from his body.

"Ash...what's wrong?" Her voice, anxious, somewhere in the distance behind him.

He shuddered. He spun around, looking for the TV remote. Spotted it on an end table. Rushed there, grabbed it, hit the power button for the big screen in the corner. The image came on.

Smoke pouring from the top of the familiar glass building in Arlington...tilted spikes of fire ladders rising around it, directing arcs of water into the windows...the news chyron at the bottom of the screen...

SUSPECTED BOMB BLAST AT CARBONOT HEADQUARTERS

He stood there, staring numbly, faintly aware of the voice of some offscreen reporter babbling...faintly aware of Emmalee making noises somewhere nearby...faintly aware of another voice repeating "Excuse me, sir...excuse me, Senator..."

He turned. Barry, the security guy. Peeking in through the half-open front door. Holding a brown box.

"Excuse me, sorry to disturb you, sir," he said. "But I just intercepted the mailman down at the end of the drive. He had this special delivery package. I signed for it for you." He glanced down at it. "It says it's from 'D. Sloan' at CarboNot, and it's marked urgent. So I—"

Conn's legs went soft. He stumbled backward, hands raised before him, waving him back.

"*No!* For God's sake, don't bring that damned thing in here! Take it outside, far away from the house! Then call 911!"

THIRTY-TWO

He heard the burner chirp outside the shower, where he'd left it on the sink. He debated whether to let it go. It had to be Wonk. She wouldn't call him now, of course.

At the third chirp he opened the shower door and, dripping, stepped out onto the mat. Just to make sure.

Her.

He scooped up the phone, almost dropping it from his wet fingers.

"Annie…"

"Please tell me that wasn't you!" Her voice was shaky.

He sighed. "So my little adventure last night has made the news."

"Little adventure! Dylan! Do you call cold-blooded murder an adventure?"

He saw his reflection, naked and ghostly through the steam-covered surface of the bathroom mirror…and the shock on his face.

"*Murder?* What in hell are you talking about?"

"I know how much you hate those people," she continued. "But to send a bomb to an office filled with innocent people—"

"Slow down! What bomb?"

There was silence for a moment.

"Dylan…Please be honest with me, now. No lies. You were going out last night. On an op. You told me you were going to bring them all down. And today it's all over the news. All your acts of sabotage. Lockwood's boat and Trammel's plane blown up. Weaver's house torn down. But now—my God, Dylan! CarboNot bombed, Sloan killed, a bomb mailed to Conn's house—"

"Hold on! CarboNot was bombed? And Conn, too?"

"Are…you saying you had nothing to do with that?"

He sat down on the edge of the bathtub. He gripped the phone tightly. His kept his voice tight, too.

"Annie, please listen to me. I promised I would never again lie to you. I'm not lying to you now. Here is exactly what I've done so far. Yes, I tore down Capital Resources myself, last Saturday night. I did some online hacking and planted some bugs in their various offices, to find out information about them all. I used some of that intel in my newspaper articles, to cause CarboNot's stock to crash. I also cancelled insurance policies on Lockwood's boat, Trammel's plane, and Weaver's summer home. I hired a demolition crew to go tear down Weaver's house this morning. And yes—I did go out last night, to destroy Lockwood's boat and Trammel's plane. But after that, I came right back here to the apartment and went to bed. I've been here sleeping until fifteen minutes ago…And that's *it.*" He paused. "Annie that is *all.* I am not lying to you."

She was quiet a moment. Her voice was quaking when she spoke again.

"I couldn't really bring myself to believe it. I couldn't believe you could do anything like bombing an office. Grant says you have a 'code' about this sort of thing. You've killed killers. But not—"

"And he's right. I have *never* harmed or risked innocent lives. I would never kill common thieves or politicians, either—only if they were directly involved in murder themselves."

Another moment passed.

"Dylan…I'm so sorry for doubting—"

"No! No, Annie, what else could *you* think, after what you saw laid out on my floor last night?…So a bomb went off at CarboNot. And Sloan is dead?"

"Yes. It happened just within the past hour."

"Was anyone else hurt?"

"No. Only him. He'd just received a package in the mail, and apparently it went off inside his office. But Cronin says the bomb sent to Conn's home was intercepted in time."

He straightened. "Cronin?"

"He just called me. He's really upset. He demanded to know where you were. I said I didn't know. But when he told me what happened, I was shocked. I said I'd try to find you. He said to tell you that he wants to see you right away. Are you at the house?"

"No, the apartment. But I'll be at the house later tonight. Did you tell him about it?"

"I didn't. I just said I would call you."

He nodded to himself. "Okay…Annie, those other bombs, to CarboNot and Conn. You know who that had to be."

"Boggs?"

"Who else? I don't know why, though. But Cronin undoubtedly thinks I'm responsible." He sighed. "I didn't expect things to get this messy."

"Violence usually does, Dylan. That's what I was trying to tell you. You start down that path, and you can't control where it will lead you."

He had no answer to that.

"Would you call Cronin for me? I don't want to do it from my burner. Let him know I'm at the apartment. He knows where it is; he spent enough time out here on stakeouts last fall. Tell him I'll be expecting him."

"Dylan...I—"

"Shhhh. You don't have to say anything more. I'm glad you called. And..."

"Yes?"

"I'm glad that, deep down, you knew that I could never do such a thing."

"I'm glad, too. Dylan...be careful."

He couldn't resist. "You aren't worrying about me, are you?"

"Not anymore."

She ended the call.

He stood. Caught himself in the mirror again.

Smiling again.

They were rolling up Route 270, well past Gaithersburg, Maryland, and well ahead of the evening rush traffic. Beside him in the cab, Zak leaned forward to catch every word of the latest reports from WTOP, the D.C. news station. He was smiling.

It was nice to see him happy again, after what happened with Dawn.

"We're doing it, Rusty," he said at a commercial break. "CarboNot is finished, now. And we stopped Silva—which probably means we've stopped fracking."

"It's not 'us.' It's *you*, Zak. You did this."

"No, my friend. I couldn't have done it alone." His voice fell. "You're the only person I've been able to trust, all these years."

Rusty tried to cheer him up. "Who woulda thought that just the two of us could pull off something like stopping fracking?"

That teased a small smile on Zak's face. "We may have. But we can't be quite certain of that yet. We have to make sure that Adair can't continue, not even if the sell-outs at the EPA give him the green light. And we must not only stop him; we have to make an *example* of him—so that no other company will want to proceed. Not if they know they'll be subject to environmental justice."

"Man, Zak! This is so cool. We're beating them all."

"Not 'all.' And not quite yet." Zak was brooding again. His mood was like he was on a rollercoaster. "There's still that reporter. Hunter. There's no telling how much he knows about us; he only hinted about it in his latest article. He could point the cops in our direction. He's a loose end."

He fell silent. After a minute, Rusty probed.

"So, what are we gonna do about him?"

Zak cocked his head around. A yellow smile broke through his bushy brown beard. Again, just like that, he looked almost back to his old self.

"Reading his articles gave me an idea, Rusty. So I started putting together something special at the camp. It's in my bag in the back. It needs just a few finishing touches."

"Yeah? I can't wait to see it."

Zak got serious all of a sudden.

"This may be our last battle, Rusty, at least until things cool off. I still don't think that they know this is our doing. But just to be safe, we'll go to ground again. I have some old friends outside Vegas. After tonight, I think we should head out there. We'll take back roads. It's safer that way and we'll see more of the country."

"That'll be great, Zak. Nothing's holding us here, now."

Zak's smile vanished.

Shit. Wrong thing to say.

"No. Nothing at all," Zak said, his lips pressed thin. A few seconds later his expression brightened again. "If I can finish putting together that item when we get to Adair's, I'll try to contact Hunter. Perhaps invite him to the party."

Rusty laughed. "Get us a 'two-fer,' huh?"

Zak laughed, too. "That's the idea. A 'two-fer.'"

"Come on in," Hunter said, opening the door wide and stepping back.

Cronin entered, followed by a portly middle-aged man with graying brown hair.

"This is my partner, Detective Sergeant Paul Erskine," Cronin said.

Hunter offered a handshake; Erskine ignored it.

"And I was hoping this was a social call," Hunter said. "Oh well. Let's go have a seat."

Their eyes roamed the apartment as he led them over to the sofa. He took the armchair across the coffee table from them. They glanced at the manila file folder he had placed on it.

Cronin dived right in. "The bombs, Hunter."

"What bombs are we talking about, Detective Cronin? The one up in the Allegheny Forest? The one over at the *Inquirer* office?"

"The ones last night and today. Dulles. Annapolis. The senator's house. CarboNot. Those bombs."

"I just heard. From Annie, when she called half an hour ago. You told her you thought I had something to do with all that. You know, you really upset her, Detective Cronin."

"A bit testy, are we?"

"Well, gosh darn, Detective Cronin. How would you feel if somebody tried to turn your girlfriend against you?"

Cronin's blue eyes were cold. "I do what I have to do."

Hunter stared right back. "So do I."

The cops traded a look, poker-faced.

"Which is the point," Erskine said. "What exactly is it that you do, Mr. Hunter?"

"You haven't heard? I write newspaper articles, Detective Erskine. But let me tell you what I don't do. I don't do anything to risk innocent lives. And I never would."

"So you say."

"So it is."

"You didn't send bombs to CarboNot, or Senator Conn, or—"

"Absolutely not."

"What about sinking that boat in Annapolis?" Cronin interjected. "And that private jet at Dulles—the one that belongs—"

"Hey, I'm forgetting my manners. Would you guys like some coffee? How about some doughnuts? Detective Erskine, you look like you enjoy doughnuts."

Erskine glared at him. Cronin went on.

"You have anything to say about those other things?"

"Detective Cronin, why don't you tell me more about those 'other things.'"

Cronin leaned forward.

"Okay, let's plod. Gavin Lockwood. Heads that green group you've been writing about. Lives near Annapolis, on the water. In the wee hours this morning, somebody set off a charge inside his yacht and sank it."

"Ah. So this is a water pollution investigation, then."

"And the asshole who did it stuck one of those Jolly Roger flags up on the mast. And also left a sign on the pier: 'Piracy No More.'"

"Well, then you have clues, Detective. Have you issued a BOLO for a guy with an eye patch and a peg-leg?...Oh—I'm sorry. Please continue."

"Then a couple hours later, this other guy, the billionaire...what's his name?"

"Trammel," Erskine prompted.

"Right. Trammel. You mentioned him in your latest article, too. So, a couple hours later, some kind of drone comes flying in over restricted space out at Dulles, drops a sign in front of his private jet, then crashes into it and blows it up."

"Wow. I see why you're concerned. Now the bastards have escalated from water pollution to littering."

"Hunter, do I have to tell you what the sign says?"

He spread his hands. "Do tell."

"'Reduce Your Carbon Footprint.'"

Hunter lowered his head and shook it slowly. "A yacht. A jet. What a waste." He glanced up at them. "You know—it sounds to me as if this could be the work of an ecoterrorist." He snapped his fingers. "Hey! I have an idea about just who it might be." He reached forward, slid the file folder toward them. "By sheer, wild coincidence, I've been doing a bit of research on *this* guy."

Cronin kept his eyes on Hunter's face as he picked it up and opened it. He scanned the contents as Erskine leaned in to have a look. Erskine picked up a magazine clipping. He and Cronin swapped yet another look; this one lasted several seconds.

"Dr. Zachariah Boggs," Cronin said. "You mentioned him in your last piece."

"'Latest' piece, not 'last'—at least I hope not. And from your reaction, you guys appear to be familiar with the name."

Erskine said to Cronin, "Maybe that girl wasn't so crazy after all."

"Maybe not."

"What girl?" Hunter asked.

The cops continued to look at each other for a few seconds. Then Cronin shrugged and turned back to him.

"A few nights ago, the park police found this young woman wandering in Rock Creek Park. She was a mess, like she was strung out. She had this crazy story about overhearing her boyfriend with some Washington big shot arguing out there in the middle of the woods. Said they were talking about bombing people. Then the other guy supposedly started shooting at her boyfriend, and they all scattered. I think they still have her at St. Elizabeth's. The story made the rounds with the local departments. It gave us all a good laugh."

"I don't see you laughing now. So what's her name? And her boyfriend's?"

He tapped the folder with his forefinger. "She said he was this Boggs guy. But I don't remember her name. Something weird."

"'Dawn' something," Erskine said.

Hunter kept his own poker face. "Did she say who the 'big shot' was?"

"The way I heard it, she was so hysterical she wasn't saying anything that made sense," Cronin said.

Hunter nodded toward the folder. "You can keep that. I have copies. You'll see why I think Boggs is your bomber. He was the FBI's first suspect in the 'Technobomber' cases years back. I still think he's good for those, and that they convicted the wrong guy. The M.O. was similar to the bomb that killed the scientist in Pennsylvania this month. The Technobomber also addressed his mail bombs using green ink—just like the one sent to the *Inquirer*. I wouldn't be surprised if you find the same thing on the bombs today."

Erskine crossed his arms. "You know, Ed told me you're a great bullshitter. Okay, so if you're not involved, you won't mind if we take a quick look around this place, right?"

"Not at all. I managed to flush my marijuana plants down the toilet just before you arrived."

Erskine rolled his eyes.

"You can even look through my computer files," Hunter added. "Take whatever time you'd like."

Erskine jerked, then looked down.

Luna was rubbing his trouser cuff with the side of her face. "What's this?"

"That? Oh, that's called a 'cat,' Detective Erskine. C-A-T. Luna, say hello to the nice detectives."

"Guy's a real riot, Ed."

"I know. Thinks he's Robin Williams."

They all rose and he led them toward the bedroom. He stopped at the bathroom and entered. They paused behind him in the doorway. He bent for something, then straightened and turned back to them.

He held out the scoop for Luna's litter box.

"Here you go, Detective Erskine. I know you'll want to dig around in the sand. Who knows what a devious guy like me might have hidden in there?"

THIRTY-THREE

"Come on in." Grant's voice, behind his closed office door.

She walked in carrying a small stack of memos and found him standing at his window. He was in white shirt sleeves and gray slacks, his back to her. A haze of smoke hung around his head, and the little boxy air-filter gadget on his desk was humming.

"So, what's the day's bad news?" he asked, not turning.

"Your air filter isn't working. I'm about to choke in here."

He turned. "I didn't notice."

"How could you? Your nose and lungs are used to it."

"I'll have to get my buddy in S&T to fix it. Just put those over there."

She felt his eyes on her as she walked to the desk and dropped the reports on it. She turned to leave.

"What's wrong?"

She stopped at the door. "Nothing."

She heard him exhale. "Come on, Annie."

No point in trying to hide anything from him. She faced him.

"All right. You'll know soon enough, anyway. The wedding's off."

He crushed out his cigarette butt in a bronze ashtray on the desk.

"I noticed earlier today that you weren't wearing the ring. I was afraid that might happen." He gestured to the chairs near his coffee table. "Let's talk."

"No. I don't—"

"I insist. Boss's prerogative."

"All right...But can we go somewhere with a breathable atmosphere?"

He smiled—almost. "Let me grab my jacket and we'll take a walk."

They went down in the elevator, then moved through the hallways in silence, acknowledging deferential hellos from people along the way. He led her to a familiar corridor; above its entranceway, in raised letters, were the words:

CIA MUSEUM
INFORM * INSTRUCT * INSPIRE

Pale-green display panels and tall glass-enclosed cases filled with exhibits, photos, and trophies ran down both walls of the corridor and off into the distance. They entered, strolling past a spotlight-illuminated panel on the left labeled "On the Front Lines: CIA IN AFGHANISTAN." It displayed a flag and photographs, including one of a helicopter filled with Agency officers during the post-9/11 invasion. The opposite wall bore a large map of Iran and Afghanistan, also bedecked with photos of various missions.

Grant strolled on without speaking. It was mid-afternoon and no one else happened to be around at the moment. They moved past panels of blown-up photos depicting various

Agency operations with explanatory signs. Inside the glass cases lay a host of exotic spy devices, disguises, and weapons.

He paused about halfway down the corridor, before a case containing memorabilia from a clandestine mission inside Iran. He nodded toward a photo showing a group of eight men posing in some rural field, heavily armed and wearing rough clothes. Their faces were deliberately blurred out in the image.

"See that?"

"What about it?"

"The dark-haired guy, upper left. I know you can't make out the face. But does he seem somehow…familiar?"

"Grant! That's not—"

"Hush. I haven't said a thing, now, have I? I merely thought you might like to see a typical NOC during a typical op."

She shot him a look. "Typical?"

"Okay. Maybe not so typical. That's what I wanted to chat with you about."

"What do you mean?"

"The wedding being called off—I'm guessing that was your idea, not his. Right?"

She looked back at the photo. At the dark hair, the lean body, the big hands cradling the AK. She thought of those hands. She swallowed and nodded.

"I thought so. I gather that your early counseling sessions haven't been helping with the nightmares yet."

"If anything, they've gotten worse…Grant—I have enough trouble with the memories. About what I went through. About what I saw *him* go through, back then. But he won't give it up. The violence. A few days ago I came to realize…I realized that somehow, he *can't.*"

"Because he's a sheepdog."

"You used that word before. What do you mean?"

"I went to a conference last year and got to chatting with a remarkable guy. A retired Airborne Ranger with a Ph.D. in psychology, who used to teach at West Point. He had been lecturing about how various people respond to violence. He said that an old Vietnam-era colonel once told him there are three kinds of people: sheep, wolves, and sheepdogs.

"Most people are sheep, Annie. They are peaceful, productive, and benevolent—the bedrock of any civilized society. Normally, they recoil against violence; it's just not in them. But that very squeamishness renders them helpless before the wolves. The wolves are society's predators. They exist to feed on the sheep. They enjoy it, and they're merciless about it."

She looked at the photo again. "I see where you are going with this."

"That's right. The third type is the sheepdog. You know, the sheep don't much like the sheepdog. To them, he looks and acts scary, a lot like the wolves. He has sharp teeth, and when aroused to violence, he will attack relentlessly and without mercy. But he's really no threat to the sheep. His only enemies are the wolves. In fact, he exists to protect the sheep from the wolves. That's his mission. He's the only thing that stands between the sheep and the wolves."

"Dylan."

"Yes, Dylan is a sheepdog. A warrior at heart. It's in his wiring. In his DNA. That's why we were able to recruit him in the first place, right after the first World Trade Center bombing. That was 1993, and he was still a kid, but he was ready to go."

Studying the photo, his eyes acquired a somewhat distant look, as if he were looking past it, recalling other things.

"You're a sheepdog, too, Grant."

"Me? Oh, sure. But Dylan is different from me in some respects. Which is why he had so much trouble fitting in here, over the years."

"How so?"

"I'm more of a pragmatist, Annie. I take the long view about our missions here, so I'm willing to make moral compromises in the short term. Such as dealing with unsavory people out in the field—cutting deals with scumbags and low-level terrorists and dictators, for the greater good. I don't like it, but I don't hesitate to do it if I have to."

He coughed for a few seconds before continuing.

"But Dylan often balked at that sort of thing. He's more of a pure idealist. He took the term 'mission' almost literally. To him, ops were like crusades. So he sometimes had problems working alongside bad guys. Or following orders when they clashed with his principles. Oh sure, he could and did lie, cheat, steal, and kill. That's what we do here, and he knew that going in. And it's not as if we don't have our own moral boundary lines."

"It's just that Dylan draws his moral lines in different places," she said.

"Which is why he went off the reservation so often. And why I had to intervene to save his ass so often. He also had problems working for fools, and keeping his opinions to himself when he despised some boss or co-worker. I've never met anyone so opinionated—or so willing to say bluntly exactly what he thought, consequences be damned. He never gave an inch. That made him plenty of enemies—not just here, but also in foreign stations and embassies."

"So the same ideals that first attracted him to the Agency are why he finally left it." She lowered her voice and looked away. "And they're also why he began doing…those other things last year."

They were quiet for a while, cocooned in private thoughts. She resumed moving down the corridor, into and out of the spotlights, as he followed. She halted at one exhibit, finding herself riveted by the sight of a long combat knife.

She felt him stop behind her.

"I understand what you're telling me," she said softly. "But it doesn't make it any easier for me to accept. Since Dylan is, as you say, a sheepdog by nature—"

"—yes. He'll always run toward the howling of the wolves," he finished. "No matter where he is in the future, no matter how peaceful the setting, a part of him is always going to be out there, patrolling the perimeter fences, ready to launch himself against threats to the flock."

She couldn't take her eyes off the knife. "Then how is a sheep like me supposed to live with someone like him?"

She felt his hand on her shoulder. "You're wrong about that."

She turned around and looked up into the weary, cast-iron-gray depths of his eyes. They and the rest of his features, always so flinty, revealed an unexpected hint of softness—not unlike what she often saw in the face of her own father.

"You're not a sheep, Annie. I don't hire sheep. You love him because you are a sheepdog, too."

That made her laugh.

"Me? God, look at me, Grant. I'm a mess. I'm not like him—or you. I can't depersonalize violence. I just can't detach myself. It stays with me. And I can't stop worrying about him whenever he goes off to do—what?—'patrol the perimeter,' as you put it. What he's gotten himself involved in right now scares me to death. In just the past month, we've both been in fights and almost gotten blown up. I've tried to imagine years of that sort of thing. And I know I just couldn't take it."

"I don't have any easy answers for you. I can only say that living with somebody like Dylan would be a lot like what thousands of wives of soldiers, cops, firemen, and our own officers have to face every day. Like those guys, Dylan is by nature a 'first responder.' Yet somehow, their women learn to live with it. They understand the nature of their men—which is exactly why they love them. They also know that what those men do is dangerous, but necessary—that it protects them and their kids and their country from harm…Look, I'm not saying that I approve of him operating outside the law. But really, would it be any different for you if society gave him a uniform, a badge, a gun, and its official benediction to do what he does?" A touch of amusement sparkled in his eyes. "Besides, can you really see yourself settling down with some guy who paints landscapes or sells used cars?"

She lowered her head. "To be honest, I'm not sure I can see myself with anyone."

He clasped both her shoulders.

"Please don't do anything hasty. You haven't really given the counseling long enough to help you. Give yourself some time. Trust me, I've been—" He stopped. Then went on. "I've been exactly where he is right now. On the edge of losing someone important to me. For similar reasons...He needs you, Annie. But you also need him. More than either of you realize, I think."

He released her shoulders. Looked at his watch.

"It's after three, now. Why don't you head home early. Maybe go see him tonight. Talk things over."

He walked her back toward the entrance, then stopped, coughing some more.

"I'm going to go grab a smoke outside. I'll leave you here to think over what I said."

A hint of a smile—then he walked away, a gray wintry figure heading out into a gray wintry day.

Leaving her beside a glass case—beside the photo of a man without a face.

The rest of the drive to the Allegheny took them five hours, because they had to obey the speed limits, to avoid any possibility of getting pulled over. That, and he'd had to take a few breaks to stretch his legs and get coffee.

Rusty's eyelids felt gritty and heavy as he drove up Route 62 past Tionesta, wishing that Zak could spell him behind the wheel. He asked him years ago why he'd never learned to drive. Zak said he didn't like to talk about his past. But that evening, after a few beers, he opened up more than usual. Zak confided that he'd been too scared to take lessons when he was a teen, mainly because his parents always made him feel so inadequate. He said that his old man, a carpenter, would often sneer at him and say, "You might be smart with books, Zachariah, but you don't know nothing practical." He could tell from the look on Zak's face that it still bothered him, after all these years.

Rusty told him that he could relate to what he was saying, because his own old man had been a drunk, a mean drunk who would smack him around a lot and laugh at him and call him a good-for-nothing. But Rusty got the last laugh one night when he was ten, and the old man, coming home loaded, fell asleep at the wheel and wrapped his Chevy pickup around a tree…

The lights of Tionesta vanished behind them, leaving them in the dark again. Rusty yawned and blinked, trying to get his blurry eyes to clear.

"Zak…mind if we talk a bit, so I can stay awake?"

"All right. What about?"

"I was just remembering stuff from when I was a kid. Like how things was after my old man died, and my old lady was trying to hold things together for me and my two sisters…Did I ever tell you about that?"

"I don't remember. I don't think so."

"Yeah. Well, she couldn't bring in much working as a K-Mart clerk there in Nashville. We didn't have a pot to piss in. So I had to drop out at sixteen and go to work. First job was in a body shop, working for my cousin. I hated it. Like I hated my whole dead-end life…This biker dude worked there, too, and he was a lot of fun. I started hanging with him and his buddies. Doing dope and shit." He hesitated. "That's when I got hooked on speed."

"You never mentioned that."

He nodded. "Never wanted to. I didn't know what you'd think about that. Because I'm not proud of them days. I don't even know why I'm telling you now…Well, anyway, I needed lots of bread to support my habit. That's when the burglaries started. The biker gang fenced the stuff I stole for them. Later, when I got more desperate, I started doing muggings and robberies, too."

"You did tell me once that you had a criminal record when you were young."

"Yeah, but not much of one. I still can't believe I managed not to get arrested for four years. But finally they busted me for assault and robbery. I beat the crap out of the guy. But because they said I was a first-time offender, at least for the record, the judge gave me probation. I had to show up at this drug program and do weekly urine tests for my P.O. And pay restitution for the guy's hospital bills. It was hell, but at least it got me off the uppers." He squinted at a road sign. "I still craved the shit, though. And I would of gone back on it, for sure...'Cept for Amy."

"She was the old girlfriend you mentioned a few times—right?"

"Yeah. I met her in the program. She was in there for alcohol. Booze wrecked her marriage. Right then, we was both at rock bottom. But she didn't act toward me like everybody else in my goddamned life up till then. Amy, she believed in me. She *believed* in me, Zak. And I believed in her, right back. So we managed to make it through the program together."

He paused to take a sip of cold coffee from a Styrofoam cup next to his seat.

"After that, my P.O., he helped me get work as a roofer. Amy, she got a job in a dry cleaners. We rented this cheap apartment and moved in together. We started to sock away money to get our own place." He moistened his lips. "We even talked about getting hitched."

He felt Zak's eyes on him in the dark. God, he hadn't meant to talk about this shit. But somehow, things felt funny tonight. Like everything was coming to a head, or something. He felt he had to say these things—explain to Zak how he got here.

Or maybe explain it to himself…

"After a few years, I fell off a roof on the job. It laid me up for three months. Me and Amy, we burned right through our savings. It was real bad, because we had to start all over again. It took us three more years just to get back to the same place, money-wise…And then…"

He put down the coffee cup. He couldn't go on.

"Then what, Rusty?" Zak's voice was soft.

He swallowed hard. "Amy got breast cancer."

He felt Zak's hand on his shoulder.

"We were together ten years before that happened. By then I was, what? Thirty-one, thirty-two. I forget. But it was bad. She had to have an operation. Lose the breast. That was awful for her. For me, too—for us both. The money was gone again. And things between us, they weren't ever the same. But I was loyal to her."

"You're the most loyal man I ever met, Rusty."

He swallowed again. "Me and Amy, we stuck it out another three years. Then…then the cancer came back. This time, it spread to her bones."

The grip on his shoulder tightened.

"We got her in this experimental chemo trial at Mass General in Boston. It worked for a while. But then it didn't…She…It was horrible…I watched her waste away. Another year and a half before she finally died."

"Rusty, I didn't know. I'm so sorry."

He wiped his eyes with his jacket sleeve.

"So here I was, in my late thirties, stuck in Boston, in this roach-filled Section 8 apartment, no job, living on food stamps. My whole life, back in the crapper again. I felt like it was all over."

He glanced toward Zak. Saw his beard and glittery eyes in the faint glow of the dashboard. He faced back to where the headlights probed the onrushing pavement.

"A month after she's gone, I'm going through all her stuff. And it's too much. I have to get out of the apartment. It's a nice day in May. So I start walking. Just walking. I find myself at Boston Common. And I hear this noise, loud voices and clapping. So I wander over and find this crowd there. And there you are, up in front of everybody, with this bullhorn. You're talking about cancer-causing chemicals. And then it hits me. I figure, that's what must of killed Amy: all them chemicals at the dry cleaners where she worked."

"No doubt about it."

"Yeah. And when the rally was breaking up, that's when I came up and introduced myself."

"I remember, Rusty. I remember because you looked really angry."

"I was. I asked if your group had any work, remember? And you said, 'Sure, there's always stuff to be done.'"

"I recall asking you why you wanted to join us, Rusty. But you never told me."

"I couldn't talk about it. Not then."

"Why not until now?"

He felt his jaw tighten. "My old man, he hated whiners. He slapped me hard whenever I complained about anything. So, I always figured, you know, I had to man up. Keep my problems to myself." He forced a chuckle. "That day was, when? Dozen years ago?"

"That's right. I was twenty-eight at the time. So you had to be thirty-seven."

"And I been with you ever since." He glanced toward Zak again. "Even though you didn't know it, you saved my life that day, Zak. After Amy, you gave me something to live for again. You showed me how I could get back at all the corporations and rich bastards who took her from me."

"So we have, my friend. So we have. Together, you and I have already executed nine corporate criminals. Tonight, we're going to eliminate number ten. And with any luck, we'll also take out one of his big media cheerleaders, too."

Rusty felt his mood turn on a dime. The exhaustion vanished, replaced by a rush of eager anticipation. He let his right hand drop from the wheel. His fingers found the stock of the Remington 700 lying just across the floor behind them. It made him feel powerful again. Back in control.

"We'll kill them bastards for Amy."

THIRTY-FOUR

Not far north from where 62 crossed Route 666, Rusty turned right, onto Higgins Hill Road. It began as a narrow lane hugged by dense trees. He had to drop into second gear as the slope grew steeper. About a half-mile in, at the crest, it opened up into a plateau. Half a dozen large homes and spacious yards pushed back the forest on either side of the road.

The first place on the left was Adair's. It stood alone and proud on its own bluff up on the ridge, about a hundred feet above the road. Adair had cleared the nearest trees to give himself a grand view of the forested slope they'd just climbed. His long driveway rose in a switchback up the steep incline. A couple of cars sat in front of his garage.

Rusty didn't like the sight of the cars. "Looks like he might have company."

"It doesn't matter. Any friend of his has to be an enemy of ours. Besides, with visitors here, he will have his alarm system off. That should make things easier for us."

Zak told him a month ago that he figured things might come to this. Which is why they'd been out here a couple of weeks earlier, to scope out the place. The road ran along the southern edge of Adair's land. To the west and north, forested slopes rolled right up to his yard. Out there in the trees they'd found all-terrain-vehicle tracks crisscrossing the area. "Toys for rich boys," Zak smirked. "Look at these ruts! The ATVs are ruining whatever the frackers haven't."

To the east, another uncut stand of trees separated Adair's property from his neighbor's. A dirt track led back into that thicket—an access point for ATVs. Rusty turned in there, killed the lights, and moved the pickup in far enough to make it invisible from the road.

They sat in darkness and silence for a minute. The clock on the dash said eight thirty.

"Let's do this," Zak said.

For the time being, they left in the truck most of what they'd need later. Rusty took a shotgun; Zak carried a .38 Smith & Wesson revolver, plus a shoulder bag. They moved through the trees to the edge of the yard, then hugged the tree line and headed to the back of the property, where they wouldn't be seen from the road. They found a secluded spot, and Zak swept the house with a pair of binoculars.

"People are moving around in that big room over to the right," he said. "That must be their living room, or maybe a den...See that rear door over there, to the left? Remember from last time, we figured that it probably goes into his garage. It's a good distance from that room where they are sitting, so I think we can get inside that door without being heard."

They crept among the bushes and trees in the yard and approached the door. Zak tried the handle; locked. He pulled a short crowbar from the tote bag and levered it between the frame and door while Rusty pulled steadily on the knob. The door popped open without much noise. Zak took out a small flashlight.

It turned out that they were in a workshop area at the rear of the garage. They closed the outside door behind them. Following the beam, they moved to the interior door leading into the house itself. They found it unlocked. Zak cracked it open a few inches; a hallway stretched ahead of them. They heard distant laughter.

"Ready?" Zak whispered, drawing the .38.

"Party time," Rusty whispered back, raising the shotgun cross-body.

Zak in the lead, they moved out into the brightly lit, carpeted hallway. Tiptoed past a bathroom on the left...past an office opposite it, on the right...then past a formal living room on the left...The chatter grew louder, coming from the next room ahead, on the right.

They were ten feet from its entranceway when they heard footsteps. They stopped.

A thin, pale-haired young man emerged, turned toward them—then also stopped dead in his tracks. His mouth and eyes widened in shock.

"Zak!" Will Whelan gasped.

Zak moved forward, raising the revolver to Will's face. Then gave him a shove, causing him to stumble backward. Another push propelled him back into the room.

Zak entered behind him and moved to the left while Rusty followed, moving right and pointing the shotgun in a back-and-forth arc that covered the whole room.

"Don't anybody move or say a goddamned word!" Zak shouted.

Dan Adair occupied a recliner across the room. A young, curly-haired blonde woman sat on the sofa next to an older brunette, whose coffee cup fell from her hand and splashed dark blotches onto the beige carpet at her feet.

"What the hell!" Adair roared and started to rise.

"You heard what he said!" Rusty yelled, training the shotgun on him. "Move and you're dead!"

Adair froze in position for a few seconds, then slowly sank back into his chair.

"Zak! What the hell!" Will's hands waved helplessly before him, like he was trying to erase a blackboard. "What's gotten into you, man? What—"

"You *know* these men?" Adair said.

Will looked at him; his Adam's apple bobbed; his mouth opened and closed. But he didn't answer.

"I asked you a *question*, Will!"

Zak motioned Will toward an empty chair. "Sit down, Will." Will obeyed meekly.

Adair stared at them both, his mouth half-open. Then understanding dawned in his eyes. His hands seized the arms of his chair and he leaned forward.

"So…it was *you*—wasn't it, Will? Look at me. I can see it on your face! *You* planted those samples. You've been working with these assholes all along!"

"Will!" the older woman gasped. "You didn't!"

Zak moved toward the women on the sofa. "Adair, I presume this one is your wife," he said, pointing to the brunette. "The next time you open your mouth without my permission, I'll shoot her. Do you understand me?"

Adair glared at him, saying nothing.

"I asked *you* a question, Adair."

"I understand."

"Good." He shoved the revolver into his field jacket pocket, then dropped the tote bag at his feet. "Rusty, come over here and put the shotgun to his wife's head while I tie them up. If anybody moves or says anything—pull the trigger."

Rusty nodded, then moved behind the sofa and did as he was told. Zak opened the bag and pulled out a handful of plastic cable ties and lengths of rope. He went to Adair first.

"Stand up and put your hands behind your back."

Adair did as he was told.

His wife's shoulders slumped and she cried softly.

She was looking at Will.

He was at the kitchen counter stirring half-and-half into his coffee when the doorbell rang.

He checked; the clock on the stove said eight forty-three.

He set down his mug. Opened an overhead cabinet door and grabbed an easily accessible Glock 26. He carried it to the door, stood to the side, and peeked through a crack in the little opaque curtain that covered the sidelight window.

Then he jammed the Baby Glock into his trouser pocket, unbolted the door, and stood aside.

"After last night, you were the last person I expected," he said.

She walked in and just stood there, looking uncomfortable.

"Let me take your coat."

He helped her slip it off and he hung it on the coat tree.

"I just made some coffee," he said, ushering her into the den.

"I'm good."

She went to the same place on the sofa that she had occupied the previous night. He fetched his mug from the kitchen, using the opportunity to put away the Glock, then returned to the recliner. Also just like last night.

"*Deja vu*," she said with a weak smile.

"God, I hope not."

That generated a bigger smile. Then she became serious again.

"Grant talked to me this afternoon. He gave me some things to think about."

"Such as?"

"Sheepdogs."

"Good. Now you can explain that reference to me."

She did.

He found himself studying the floorboards as she finished. He raised his eyes.

"Grant Garrett is a smart guy," he said. They looked at each other for a moment before he added: "But I assume you didn't drive all the way out here just to tell me that I'm a sheepdog."

"No. It's about us. About last night...Grant thinks I am being too hasty. He says I'm a 'sheepdog,' too. And that I should give the counseling more time."

"Grant Garrett is a *very* smart guy."

"He said that wives of soldiers and cops have to face this sort of thing every day, and somehow they learn to cope."

"But the analogy doesn't hold. They haven't been through what you have, Annie. They haven't experienced a direct violent trauma and suffered PTSD."

"My shrink says he isn't even sure I have full-blown PTSD. Because I'm still able to function in the world, and I'm not paralyzed by depression or anxiety. He says my reactions to a traumatic situation are pretty normal, and those are usually short-lived. He wants to try 'exposure therapy'—get me to face the past trauma in a relaxed setting, so that I can learn how to control my feelings about it."

"Makes sense. But for now—where does that leave us?"

"I'm not sure. I just don't know, Dylan. I don't know how long it might take for me to get the feelings under control. And it seems wrong to expect you to wait patiently while I am—"

The burner on the counter chirped.

"Go ahead, continue," he prompted. "I'm listening."

It chirped again.

"You should probably get that."

"Whoever it is can wait."

Another chirp.

"Dylan, after all that's been happening, it could be some emergency. You should check."

He sighed, got up, and went to the phone as it chirped a fourth time, then a fifth. This line was secure enough; any calls other than those from Annie and Wonk were forwarded through a spoof site and another burner. He glanced at the screen and frowned at the name and number.

"It's Adair," he said to her, clicking the *talk* button. "Yes, Dan?"

"Good evening, Mr. Hunter."

He'd heard the voice just once before, at the diner, so it took him a couple of seconds to place it. Only a second more to adjust to the surprise. No way that Boggs could have gotten this phone number—unless…

He had to put him off-balance while he tried to sort things out.

"Have you found it yet, Boggs?"

"Found what?"

"Your head. You should look for it in its usual hiding place—up your ass."

He heard two hard breaths, like snorts. Then: "You wanted to speak to Adair, right?"

"Actually, you should be flattered to know that you are my second choice for a phone chat. Of course, my first choice is anyone else. So, yes—why don't you put him on?"

Annie rushed to his side; her hand gripped his arm. He poked the speaker button so that she could listen in.

"Dylan?" Adair's voice, strained.

"Are you all right, Dan?"

"So far. But they've got us. Me, Nan, Kaitlin, and…Will." He almost spat out the last name. "We're tied up here in the den. He's rigged some kind of bomb to a gas cylinder they rolled in."

"How many of them, Dan?"

"Just two. They—" He heard a noise, then a grunt. In the background, women's voices cried out. A different male voice, not Boggs's, cursed and told them to shut up.

"Adair just broke one of the rules," Boggs broke in. "He added something to the script. So he'll have a serious headache in the morning—assuming that he lives that long." He chuckled. "Don't even think about it, Hunter. Calling the cops, the FBI, buying time—forget about it. If you try, I'll kill them all before anyone can lift a finger. In fact, I'm quite willing to die tonight to make that happen."

"In fact, I'm quite willing to assist you."

"Shut up! I'm not going to waste time fencing with you. I called you for a reason."

"I wouldn't assign the word 'reason' to any of your motives, Boggs. But I'll humor you. Other than send in the army of shrinks that you desperately need, what exactly do you want from me?"

"Your newspaper calls you 'a heroic journalist.' Well, let's see about that. I want you to conduct an interview with me, Hunter. To be published, in full and verbatim, in the *Inquirer*. You are to show up here alone, tonight, and conduct the interview. After that, we'll get out of here and call the cops, telling them to come and set you all free."

"Wow, what a deal. I'm supposed to trust someone who already sent a bomb to my newspaper to try to kill me. What could possibly go wrong?"

"You may trust me or not. Regardless, if you don't arrive by midnight, the Adairs all die. And if you don't show up alone—or if you try to send in cops or snipers or SWAT teams—the Adairs will die. I have people watching this house from a distance. As you know, it's perched up on a hill, exposed. So they will see any cops coming from a long way off, and alert me. Then I'll detonate the bomb remotely. Even if we're caught—which won't happen—the Adairs will die in the process. And their deaths will be on your conscience, Mr. Heroic Journalist."

"By midnight? That's ridiculous, Boggs. It's already after nine, and I'm in the D.C. area, over three hundred miles away."

He heard a *tsk-tsk*. "That's too bad. I won't allow you to stall and give the FBI's H.R.T. goons time to put a hostage rescue plan in place. So you have until midnight, on the dot. One second after that, Adair and his family will be scattered in tiny toasted pieces all over his showy, chemically-poisoned lawn...Or are you telling me that I should just go ahead and blow them up right now?"

"No. Wait...I can fly in. I have a private plane not far from here. It'll take a little time to get ready, but I can be at the house in about three hours, give or take."

"Give or take *nothing!* I said *midnight.* Not a second later. Also, know that when you get here, you *will* be thoroughly searched—and I know exactly what to look for. So don't even dream about bringing weapons or bugging devices. Bring only your notepad."

"I don't take shorthand, Boggs. If you want a full, accurate interview transcript to run in the paper, I'll need to use my microcassette recorder. It's the usual hand-held type."

Boggs hesitated. "All right. Just the recorder. But again: no weapons, wires, or cops."

"I'll be there."

Boggs hung up on him.

"It's a trap!"

He turned to her. "Of course it is."

"Dylan, you can't!"

"It's as he says. If I don't show up, alone, they're dead. If the cops show, they're dead. He'll spot them coming, and he said it's rigged to be set off remotely."

"But once you're inside, he'll blow you up with the rest of them, anyway!"

"I know. I'll have to play it by ear and think of something." He looked at her. "Annie, you were right. It's best that you stay clear of me, so you won't get involved in—"

"But I *am* involved."

He thought about that. Began to pace.

His watch said it was now nine eleven. Ironic.

All right. First, you need intel. Then you can figure out the right kit and resources.

He continued to pace, thinking. Feeling her watching him.

Back in the day, you could just call on the Pentagon or the Agency for all that. But now, it's just you—and there's no time for intel-gathering. So, how can you—

He stopped pacing.

She stood in the center of the den, a stricken, helpless look on her face.

He went over. Looked down into her eyes.

"You're right. You *are* involved."

"What do you mean?"

"I'm having a brainstorm. I just remembered a black op I was on with a team in Afghanistan. Something similar might work here. But I'm going to need your help."

"You want me to be involved in this?"

"Hell, no. You won't play any operational role. We both know you can't. But I think you *can* get me some things I'll need."

He took her by the arm, steered her to the interior door leading into the three-bay garage. He opened it and switched on the light. His blue Honda CR-V sat next to a black Ford panel truck and a motorcycle.

"Where are we going?"

He squeezed her arm, guiding her past the vehicles, toward the rear door.

"First, I want to show you where Vic Rostand keeps his toys."

THIRTY-FIVE

They reached Bay Bridge Airport just before ten o'clock. The back seat of the Honda CR-V held the gear he had selected from the small storage room under his shed.

Seeing the hidden cache for the first time had astounded her. "This is all 'state of the art,'" she said as she looked around at the racks of weapons and shelves of electronics. "Where did you manage to get all this stuff?"

"Oh, a little bit here, a little bit there. It helps to know the right sources."

"And to have millions of dollars to spend."

"That, too."

He parked the car, grabbed a small bag from the back, and walked with her to his Cessna 400. He had changed into jeans, boots, a dark pullover sweater, a lined leather jacket, gloves, and a black wool watch cap. She'd changed, too, into outdoor clothes that she'd left at the house after their recent weeks in the forest.

She stayed close beside him as he made a circuit of the plane, checking it out. His eyes were intense and his hot breath puffed little clouds into the cold air. It made her think of that cold morning when they had left for the diner—when he had paused outside the cabin to set his tell-tales, and she could see his breath. How long ago had that been? She was startled to realize that it had been barely a month.

"Do you think this can really work? It's so complicated."

"Are you kidding? Remember who's running this op." He bent to examine the landing gear.

"Am I allowed to be scared?" she said.

He stood. She looked up at his reassuring smile as he embraced her.

"I'm used to walking into traps involving bombs, you know. And surviving."

"Oh, Dylan!"

"Don't worry. The only one who's going to die tonight is Zachariah Boggs." He softened his voice. "I love you, Annie Woods."

"I love you, Dylan Hunter."

He hugged her tight. "I needed to hear that."

"I needed to say that."

He pulled back a little. Lifted a brow.

"Does this mean we're going steady again?"

She laughed, in spite of herself.

He bent and kissed her.

Then he climbed up into the cockpit. He gave her a little wave and wink, then pulled down the gull-wing door. It thumped shut with the sound of finality.

She stood at the car as the Cessna's wheels left the runway. Its flashing wing lights rose over the Chesapeake. She watched the space between the lights narrow as the plane receded from her into the distance, gaining altitude. It banked right, heading north over the Bay Bridge. Then its engine noise faded into the background of distant traffic noise. Then the blinking wing lights became one.

Then it vanished, too.

A gust of icy wind hit her in the face.

She turned to the side and checked her watch: ten twelve.

She took off a glove, took out her cell, and poked in the familiar series of numbers.

"Yes, Annie."

"Grant, please tell me you were able to do what he asked."

"Almost."

"What do you mean *almost*?"

"Let me explain. First, I'm using the pretext of an impromptu night-training mission, to test our emergency rapid-response capabilities to a sudden terrorist act. So far, everyone has bought it. On that basis I managed to commandeer one of our MQ-1 Predators out of Quantico."

"So we have a drone, then."

"Don't let their pilots hear you call them that. The official term is UAS, Unmanned Aircraft System."

"*Whatever.* The point is: Can it get there in time and do what Dylan needs?"

"Absolutely. I borrowed a UAS pilot and two sensor operators from the al Qaeda targeting team. They're in their command center next door, running it under my direction. The bird is already well on its way, and it should be on site in…let me see…another seventy minutes. Or 2330 hours. This one is unarmed—not that we could lob a Hellfire against a domestic target in any case. But its infrared cameras can track a person on the ground, at night, from ten thousand feet. And it also carries the experimental ASIP-IC package."

"English translation, Grant."

"Sorry. ASIP can monitor cell calls, radio transmissions, and a lot more. So we'll be able to watch everything on the big screens here while we monitor the commo, too. That takes care of Dylan's intel."

"Great. Now, what about getting a SOG operator out here, to pick up—"

"That's where the *almost* comes in," Grant cut in, his voice suddenly grim. "I'm afraid all our SOG guys are either deployed or unable to get here in time. So that means—"

"I *know* what that means, damn it! It means you'll be watching him with your fancy drone cameras while he walks into a trap and gets blown up!"

"Annie, hold on. There is another option."

She took a breath. "All right. I'm listening."

"Using the same pretext, I called the commander of the 12th Aviation Battalion at Fort Belvoir. An old light colonel buddy of mine. He's sending a Bell 429 chopper out to you. That's a brand-new model, not even in production yet. We've been testing it for possible addition to the Agency's fleet, because it's small, fast, and quiet. He told me the pilot is former 160th SOAR—a Night Stalker guy, combat-experienced and extremely capable. He should be there in another five minutes."

"So he'll pick up the gear from me and do this, then."

Grant was silent a moment.

"No. He will pick up the gear *and* you. *You* are going to do this."

She couldn't speak.

"Annie, listen to me. This pilot hasn't been briefed on what's really going on, and he can't be. Besides, he has to stay with the bird. But you've been through all the tough training at the Farm, including night insertions. You also had extra training when you worked in the Security Office."

"But—"

"No 'buts.' You can handle this as well as anyone. All we have to do is fly you there, and all you have to do then is get close to the house. That's it. No big deal."

She found herself trembling.

"But if I can't—"

"Annie, you can. There's nothing to it. I've looked at the satellite imagery of the site. The 'copter will drop you just a little more than a mile from the place. You'll hike in unseen, under cover of the forest. You'll sneak in close to the house. Then, once the immediate threat is neutralized, we'll call in a hostage rescue team."

"But what if Boggs and his people return to the house? They're armed. They can just shoot everyone."

He was quiet for a few seconds. "Do you have a weapon with you?"

"No, not here." Then she remembered. "Oh, wait a minute."

She opened the driver's side door, reached under the seat, and found it. She came up with his Beretta.

"Okay. I do have a pistol. A Beretta."

"Good. Listen, the chopper pilot is bringing night-vision goggles for you. And Dylan told me he already gave you an earpiece and mic. So when you get on site, you and I will be in constant contact through the Predator's satellite uplink. It will give us eyes and ears on the bad guys, and on you, too. I'll be able to tell you exactly where they are positioned and what they're doing. The details, we'll improvise. But please understand: You'll have every advantage over them."

She stared at the Beretta in her hand, feeling surreal, disembodied. The sudden image floated into her consciousness: Dylan on her kitchen floor, crawling toward her...bleeding...

"Annie—you can do this." Grant's voice, strong and firm.

She pushed the ugly image out of her mind and looked off, over the bay. Flashing lights, low in the sky, approached rapidly.

"I think I see the chopper," she said. Her voice sounded alien to her.

"Great. Just make sure you take along all your gear."

She opened the rear door of the car, pulled out the bulky backpack, and shrugged it onto her back.

"Grant...just how fast can this chopper get me there?"

"It can do 150 knots. From your current position to the site, and considering wind, it will take around ninety minutes. So, ETA will be about 2350."

"But that's almost *midnight!* And Grant, I've been to Adair's place. From the LZ, I'll have to hike over a mile through those woods, uphill and in the dark. It could take me fifteen or twenty minutes to get to the house."

"I know. Look, I'll call him right now and tell him to arrive at the house as close to midnight as possible—and then stall them for as long as possible after that."

"Have you told him yet that I'll be the one going in?"

"No."

"Then don't. I don't want him to be distracted by worrying about me."

"Of course...Annie—I *know* you can do this."

She slammed shut the rear door of the car. Then faced into the icy wind blasting in from the west, ahead of the rapidly oncoming chopper. Her eyes watered. But only from the cold.

"I'll have to," she said.

Once again he maintained a northeast heading after takeoff. To avoid having to file a flight plan or talk to air traffic controllers, he flew under 3,500 feet and along the eastern shore of the Bay, parallel to the restricted airspace stretching from Essex to Aberdeen. South of Elkton, he turned northwest and climbed. He crossed into Pennsylvania and dropped the Cessna low over the high ridges northwest of Harrisburg, then descended into some of the valleys, below radar visibility. He turned off his transponder and popped up again miles away—just another anonymous, untraceable blip on ATC screens.

Meanwhile, he pondered his just-ended radio conversation. Grant told him that the Predator would be in position before he arrived. The Bell 429 and its team of operators also were en route to Adair's, after picking up his gear from Annie.

It annoyed him that the Agency—the *CIA*, for God's sake—didn't have ready access to the same kit that he possessed. But Grant said they didn't, not on site, anyway, and there was no time to look anywhere else. So, the chopper had to fly all the way to Kent Island to pick up *his*. A waste of precious time.

He did some fast calculations. He didn't like them one bit.

At a cruising speed of 235 knots, his Cessna would make the 250 nautical mile run to Tidioute in just over an hour. ETA 2325 hours. He'd then drive from the airstrip to

Adair's—about ten more minutes, or 2335. That meant he would have to waste at least twenty minutes before showing up at the house, in order to give the helicopter team maximum time to get on site.

And they'd need every minute of it. The chopper had taken off from Bay Bridge Airport ten minutes after he did. Grant said he'd clear the red tape to let it cut across the restricted Aberdeen airspace, so it could make a beeline to Adair's. That would save a lot of miles and minutes. Still, at its much slower airspeed, it wouldn't arrive till almost midnight. Then the operators would have to traverse the rugged, wooded terrain between their LZ and the house.

Hunter had to be at the house by midnight. But he couldn't see any way for the team to get in position until ten or fifteen minutes after midnight.

And he had no doubt that Boggs planned to kill him and the hostages almost as soon as he entered the house.

He would have to do something to buy time.

Using the plane's customized commo system, he tapped in Adair's cell number, knowing who would pick up.

"Are you en route, Hunter?" Boggs demanded.

"I am. I'm fighting some nasty headwinds, though. I called ahead and, just by luck, found a car rental company up in Warren whose manager was still in the office late, doing paperwork. He's willing to bring a car down to Tidioute for me to drive to Adair's. I don't know how much time the rental paperwork will take, but I'm bringing a big cash deposit for him, and—"

"Listen, I don't want to hear about your petty problems. You're either here on time, or you'll be visiting a smoking crater."

Okay, you can't buy more time. But it's time for some pushback.

"Now, *you* listen, Boggs. I need assurances that Adair and his family are still okay. So if you expect to see me tonight at all, put him on the line right now, and let me talk to him for a few minutes."

"A few minutes? You need only seconds to make sure he's alive. I don't intend—"

"That's *not* a request, Boggs. Besides, you hold all the cards, anyway. You can kill him on the spot if you don't like our conversation. So let me talk to the man—*now.*"

Boggs was quiet for a moment.

"All right. But my pistol is pointing right at his head, and a shotgun is trained on his wife's. Got that?"

A pistol and a shotgun. Nice to know.

"Got it."

He waited a few seconds.

"Dylan?" Adair's voice, raspy.

"How are you holding up, Dan? Are you and everyone else okay?"

"We're all right. I'm still a bit punchy, but I'm okay…Dylan, I can't believe you're doing this! Taking this sort of risk to set us free. Why? What are we to you?"

"I told you before, Dan. You remind me of somebody."

"Who would that be?"

Hunter watched a cloud sailing by several thousand feet below the plane, a dark gray blob swallowing points of light scattered across an even-darker landscape.

"My dad."

The engine droned on, filling several seconds.

"I take that as a great compliment," Adair said softly.

"It is."

"Is your father still alive?"

"No. He died a long time ago."

"What was his name?"

"Mike."

"Well, Dylan, Mike Hunter would have been very proud of you."

Mike Hunter. He smiled to himself at that.

"Everybody called my dad 'Big Mike.'"

PART III

"When strength is yoked with justice, where is a mightier pair than they?"

— Aeschylus

THIRTY-SIX

The Cessna touched down on the airstrip at 2323 hours. Three minutes later Hunter was inside his car. He spent a moment to set up the item from his bag and hide it under the passenger seat. Then he headed out of the access road and onto the route that would take him to Adair's place.

At 2336 he pulled off Route 62, a mile north of the turnoff to Higgins Hill Road. He didn't want to announce his position to any lookouts. Instead, he waited another five minutes, then pulled out his cell and called Adair's number again.

"Where are you now?" Boggs asked, his tone harsh and impatient.

"I just landed. I see the car and the rental guy in the parking lot. I'll be on my way as soon as I finish up the paperwork with him. Please don't do anything crazy before I can get there."

"You'd better pick it up, Hunter. You have just nineteen minutes."

"Come on! I can't risk getting caught speeding."

"That's *your* problem."

He hung up.

Hunter waited, his car idling, watching the dashboard clock. He knew he could make the rest of the distance in two to three minutes. He had to let the time run out as close to midnight as he dared.

He waited easily, because he was trained and much practiced in the art of waiting. And he felt relaxed, because he had once again entered that cold, high place.

Almost no traffic went past. No cops, fortunately. He had a local map out on the passenger seat, just in case; his cover story would be that he was trying to figure out how much further he had to go to reach Franklin, Pennsylvania.

He also kept scanning the sky—at least the narrow tunnel of it that was visible overhead, between the trees on either side of the road. He saw no lights, heard no sound from an approaching chopper. Probably a good thing: If he couldn't, neither could Boggs and his people…

She felt the vibration of the chopper through her entire body. She tried to ignore it, tried to steady her nerves.

She glanced at the back of the pilot's head. "Ken"—which probably was a cover name, like her own, "Karen"—manned the controls calmly, with effortless precision. She knew that as a SOAR vet, he was among the best. Nobody could get her there faster or more reliably.

He was a handsome guy—blond crew cut, chiseled features, trim physique, cocky smile. Handsome…and randy. When he helped her board, he had put his hands on her hips quite unnecessarily. While handing over the night vision goggles he'd fetched for her, he invited her to ride beside him in the empty co-pilot seat.

She declined politely, taking a seat behind him and setting her backpack on the floor. She put on the headset so she could talk to him and to Grant.

"So Karen, tell me: Is this your first night mission?" Ken asked through the headset as he revved the rotors back up to speed.

"Not hardly."

"Your people must really put you officers through your paces. I mean, you're in really great shape, Karen. I can tell."

She didn't answer.

"Just wondering…Are you married?"

She closed her eyes and let out a long, slow breath.

"Listen, loverboy: Let's get something straight. I'm being graded on this training mission. And frankly, I'm also supposed to grade *you*. Your job is to get me to our LZ in one piece, and in record time—before 2400 hours. And to do anything else I ask of you. Got that?"

"Sorry. Got it."

From that point on, he was all business, though she wondered at times if some of his sudden maneuvers weren't just a wee bit too abrupt—including their stomach-churning takeoff and sudden veer northwest. Some guys just can't take rejection…

After Garrett shepherded them through the restricted airspace, Ken canceled instrument flight rules and squawked VFR, so they were no longer identified by radar. The air below 4,000 feet stayed choppy, so he popped up to 5,500 and held the course steady as an arrow.

Forty-five minutes into the flight she asked, "How's our time?"

"With the wind and drag, we're running a few minutes behind. I'm going to try to juice the RPMs to 105 percent and see if I can coax another knot or two out of her."

"Thanks. Anything you can do."

At 2347 hours Hunter called Boggs again.

"Yes?"

"I'm just about five minutes away."

"You believe in cutting it close, don't you?"

"I'll be there. You'll see my lights in just a few minutes."

He clicked off. Then tugged off his boots. He reached into the back seat, grabbed a pair of loafers, and slipped them on.

At 2351 he put the Forester into motion. Driving slowly, he made the left onto Higgins Hill Road. He kept his high beams on and took his time mounting the hill. He figured they'd be able to see him coming.

Cresting the hill, he scanned the area around him, looking for possible hiding places for a sniper. He noticed a ridge line rising sharply behind the houses to his right, opposite Adair's. That's where *he* would set up.

It was 2353 when he turned into Adair's driveway. He drove deliberately up the long switchback pavement to the top, then pulled up in front of the house.

To avoid being spotted or heard, they had to make the approach from the west. So the chopper raced up the far shore of the Allegheny River. Annie's stomach lurched again as Ken made the sharp banking turn, then dived toward the river surface.

"Two minutes out," he called back to her over his shoulder.

"Roger that."

She had ditched the chopper's headset and replaced it with an earpiece receiver and clip-on mic from Dylan's cache. She'd pulled on the NVGs, keeping the goggles up for the moment; the chin strap held the rig firmly in place. She'd jammed the compact Beretta from Dylan's car into the deep zipper pocket of her leather jacket; its weight rested on her thigh.

The all-important backpack sat on the floor between her knees.

Once more, she visualized what lay ahead. She'd hit the ground at 2355. Then cross the highway. Then start up that long hill. Through the woods. In the dark. But she'd have night vision, and Grant would be guiding her, using the Predator's cameras and sensors.

She only hoped that Dylan could buy her enough time…

"One minute out. Get ready."

"Ready," she called back.

Hunter checked the time again. 2354 hours.

Adair's front door was wide open. A guy he didn't recognize stood in the bright rectangle, holding a shotgun.

He lowered the driver's window. Cold air gushed in. With it, he caught a faint, familiar thumping noise in the distance, somewhere back down the hill.

He left the car idling to mask the sound. He opened his door. Got out cautiously. Raised his hands overhead.

"All right!" he called out. "You see? I'm here."

He needed to keep talking, keep them distracted. And waste time. He started walking toward the front door.

"You want to search me?"

"Stay right there!" the guy shouted, shouldering and aiming the gun. He looked middle-aged and wiry. He glanced behind him and said something. Probably asking his boss what to do.

"Hey, take it easy! Watch where you're pointing that thing. Where the hell is Boggs?" He raised his voice. "Boggs—I'm here! I kept my word, didn't I?"

Boggs appeared in the doorway, nudging the guy aside and pressing the barrel of his shotgun toward the floor. He had a revolver in his own hand, but held it down along the side of his thigh.

"Lower your hands!" he said in a harsh whisper. "We don't want the neighbors to see this."

Hunter obeyed slowly, killing another few seconds. He still heard faint thumping fading in and out.

"Okay, Boggs. I'll do whatever you say. Just don't hurt anyone. I've kept my end of the deal, and now—"

"Shut up! Go shut off your car. Then get back here."

"Okay, okay!" he said, trying to look scared. Still facing them, he walked backward toward the Forester. "Calm down. No need to—" He deliberately bumped into the open door, slamming it shut. "You're making me nervous with those guns." Never taking his eyes off Boggs, he groped blindly for the door handle. "All I can say is, the family had better be all right." His hand finally found the door handle. He opened it, but remained standing outside while bent over and reached in for the ignition key. He made a show of not being able to stretch far enough. He stood again.

"Would you please *hurry up?*"

He no longer heard the chopper. He slid inside and turned off the ignition. The dashboard clock now said 11:56.

He got out. Closed the door. Gripped the keys in his hand and walked toward the pair in the doorway. He moved warily, as if he was scared. Warily, so that he could walk slowly and keep most of his weight on the balls of his feet, rather than his heels.

"I'm coming."

Following instructions radioed by Garett, Ken had swooped the Bell 429 into the landing zone "blacked out"; he used night vision goggles, forward-looking infrared radar, and 3-D mapping systems to see the site in the dark. He set down the small copter fast but smoothly in the LZ: a field surrounded by trees, just across Route 62 from its intersection with Higgins Hill Road.

"Good luck, Karen," he shouted back at her.

She unbuckled her seatbelt and grabbed the door handle next to her.

"Thanks. You did great, Ken."

He flashed a thumb's up and a grin, barely visible in the darkened cabin.

She opened the door into a blast of rotor wash and noise. Though the rotor tips had been swept back for noise reduction, she winced, knowing that even the somewhat muted sound would carry a long way at night.

She grabbed the camouflaged backpack and cradled it in her arms. Bent low, she stepped out onto the landing skid, then slammed the door behind her. She flipped the goggles down over her eyes. The inky landscape around her instantly became visible, glowing phosphorescent green.

She hopped down into tall grass whipped violently by the rotors. Hugging the backpack to her body, she plunged through the weeds toward the highway. Behind her, the engine pitch rose, and as she ran she heard the chopper lift over the trees, to head back west across the river and away from the house.

She halted on the pavement of the deserted highway and shouldered the twenty-five-pound backpack. Glancing up into the weirdly lit night sky, she tried in vain to spot the circling Predator.

"Nightstalker to base," she whispered into her lapel mic. "Leaving LZ. Repeat, leaving LZ. Do you copy?"

After a few seconds, Grant's voice:

"Loud and clear. We're watching you from the bird. Remember, the sat uplink will add a few seconds' delay to our commo."

"Copy that," she said, trotting the rest of the way across the road, into the trees on the other side.

Immediately she confronted an almost impenetrable thicket.

"Damn it! This stuff is so dense I can barely move!"

"We'll guide you," Grant replied. "Head left about ten yards. You should pick up a path heading up the hill."

She pushed her way through the tangle of branches, trying to shield her goggles.

"Roger that," she said.

She was already breathing hard.

Hunter followed them into the foyer. They raised their weapons immediately after he entered, and Boggs slammed the door shut behind him and locked it.

"Now get your hands back up," he said, motioning with his handgun.

Smith & Wesson .38 snub revolver, six-shot...

He obeyed.

"All right. Toss me those keys."

He did as he was told. Boggs dropped them onto a small table just inside the entrance.

Well, there goes Plan A: the radio packet transmitter in the key fob...

Boggs nodded to his partner. "Search him for weapons, anything suspicious."

"I only have my cell and the recorder. And my wallet."

"Shut up."

The partner handed the shotgun to Boggs. It was a Stoeger Condor Outback, over/under. No way to tell whether it held slugs or shot. He hoped he wouldn't have to find out.

The guy approached him and patted him down, retrieving the items he'd mentioned. As the man squatted, the leather sheath of a hunting knife protruded from under his flannel jacket, hanging from his belt. Hunter thought about it for a few seconds. But it was mostly covered by the jacket—and Hunter was covered by the shotgun. Even if Boggs was a lousy shot, it would be hard for him to miss at this range, especially if it was carrying buckshot loads.

"This is everything." The partner fetched the items to Boggs, who swapped the shotgun for them. He pocketed the wallet, then dropped the cell to the floor and crushed it underfoot. He bent to examine the pieces for hidden bugs, also pulling out the battery and SIM card. Predictable.

Then he repeated the process with the recorder. Also predictable.

While Boggs pawed through the fragments, Hunter said, "I must say, I am deeply disappointed in you, Zachariah. I am so shocked to discover that the 'interview' was just a ploy, a cynical ruse to get me here."

Boggs glanced up from his kneeling position, smirking. "And like the moron you are, you fell for it."

"Tell me, Zachariah: Don't you ever brush your teeth? Or is that just another unnatural practice of our corrupt civilization?"

Boggs lost the smirk and stood. Hunter hoped that he would come over to slap him—and give him a chance to take him out. Instead, the man reached into his field jacket pocket and came out with a small squarish device with an antenna. He flipped a switch on its top and handed it to his partner.

Bug detector. Good thing I didn't activate that key fob after all...

"I'll take the shotgun again and watch him, while you scan him for any hidden transmitters."

The partner didn't seem very bright. Still, he did a thorough job, head to toe. The bug detector didn't beep. Boggs relaxed visibly.

"All right. Follow me into the den...Rusty, you stay behind him and blast him if he tries anything funny. Don't let him get too close to you."

"Hi there, Rusty. Say, do you have any idea what you're doing with that weapon?"

The man scowled and patted the barrel. "I been hunting game since I was a kid. You keep being a smart-ass, you'll be chewing a mouthful of double-o."

Buckshot, then. Not good. But good to know...

As they marched down the hall in single file, Hunter almost had to laugh at their amateur stupidity. If Rusty fired the shotgun in this narrow space, chances were that Boggs, in the line of fire, would get hit, too. He weighed the odds of making a move now. But behind him, Rusty kept his distance.

He entered the room after Boggs, and took it all in at a sweeping glance.

They had dragged in five chairs from the dining room. Four were occupied by the Adair family, arranged in a semicircle around the coffee table. Their wrists and ankles were bound to the chair arms and legs. They stared at him, eyes wide with terror.

The coffee table before them held the bomb: a gray metal rectangular affair, like an oversized briefcase. It was pushed right to the edge of the table, pressed against a tall red cylindrical gas tank that stood upright on the floor.

"Dylan, I'm sorry," Adair began. "I just—"

"No need to apologize, Dan. I'm a big boy. This was my call."

"How noble," Boggs sneered. "Now go join your friends, in that empty seat."

Hunter took the chair. Once again Boggs stood back, training the shotgun on him while Rusty moved toward him with short lengths of rope.

He raised his feet a few inches from the floor, then pressed his heels down—hard—first right, then left. Felt the two little clicks.

Plan B...

"Nightstalker, we have audio from inside the room," Grant said. "I'm going to patch you into the feed so you can listen in."

Annie was trotting up the steep slope on some narrow path made by dirt bikes or all-terrain vehicles. She had to zig-zag around low bushes, jump fallen limbs, and watch out for holes and ruts underfoot. At least the path was easier to navigate than the woods.

"Copy that," she panted.

The twenty-five pounds on her back were starting to feel like twice that, and the straps of the backpack stabbed into her aching shoulders with every step.

"How much...farther?" she gasped between strides.

"You're only a third of the way. You've got to pick it up."

She pushed down the panic. Tried to force the trot into a run. Raised her eyes.

The slope above her, glowing ghostly green, rose even steeper.

THIRTY-SEVEN

For the first time, Hunter noticed what sat propped on an end table next to the sofa. He nodded in the direction of the small black device, which stood mounted on a tiny tripod.

"So, what's that thing, Zachariah?"

He knew exactly what it was. But he also knew Boggs would love to show off and brag about it.

Boggs half-closed his eyes, and a little smile played at his lips.

"That's a 3G camera. Video and audio." He patted his pocket. "I can control it remotely, right from my smartphone."

Hunter tensed his muscles, raising his right wrist a fraction of an inch off the chair arm to give it a little play while Rusty bound it. Maybe he could work himself loose.

"Let me guess: You're going into the movie business, and this is going to be your pyrotechnic demo tape."

"Oh, it will be a 'demo tape,' all right. I'll release it in a day or two to all the media. I've already filmed my statement of introduction for it. But in a couple of more minutes, *you* will get to be the stars of the production."

A couple more minutes... You need to keep him talking.

"I'm truly flattered, Zachariah. All this trouble, just for us. So, why not just shoot us?"

"Because you need to be taught a final lesson in humility. You—and the world. You *all* do. It's human arrogance that brought you to this. I want your last moments to be spent contemplating your crimes against the natural order. Your punishment will be recorded so that I can release it to the world."

"Zak!" Will screamed. "Don't do this!"

Nan, Adair's wife, was sobbing uncontrollably. Beside her, Adair's daughter Kaitlin sat mute and motionless; her lips were parted, and she stared blankly into space.

"You're a monster, Boggs!" Adair shouted. "It's me you want—not my family. For God's sake, let them go! Then you can just shoot me and be done with it."

"Be serious. We can't have them running off and calling for help, now, can we? Anyway, I think their deaths will serve an educational purpose. What happens to them will be an object lesson for every other corporate predator out there. They'll learn that those they love won't be spared the consequences of their actions."

Hunter kept the heels of his loafers an inch off the floor while Rusty tied his ankles to the chair. By pressing down on his right heel, he had activated the miniature audio packet transmitter hidden inside. Before he'd turned it on, it couldn't be picked up by the bug detector. Now it was transmitting their conversations in brief UHF bursts, only milliseconds in length and on shifting frequencies. Even if Boggs used his bug detector again, it couldn't pick up those signals.

But the tiny transmitter's signal wasn't powerful enough to reach the Predator. The solution for that was the other transmitter, in his left heel. That one sent out a single burst signal that activated the UHF repeater under the passenger seat of the Forester in the driveway. The repeater amplified the transmission from the heel mic and—he hoped—was even now sending audio from the room up to the Predator. If everything was working properly, Garrett should be hearing every word in here now.

Boggs looked on with a strange look.

"Tie down his left forearm, Rusty—but not his wrist. I want his hand free to move."

Rusty finished up, then checked the bonds. Boggs picked up a small metal box resting atop the bomb. Four long wires trailing from one end of it ran back inside the bomb casing. He handed it to Rusty and fished a roll of duct tape from his jacket pocket.

"Now, tape this box to the arm of his chair, near his free hand, so that his fingers can reach those buttons."

Hunter examined the flat little box as Rusty taped it in place. It was featureless except for two plastic buttons on top—one black, one white. He sensed that this was some kind of sadistic game. So he wouldn't give Boggs the satisfaction of asking about it.

"Okay, Rusty," Boggs said, "I can handle the rest in here, now. Leave the shotgun with me and take the pistol. Drive the truck over to that little dirt access road we found the other day. Remember? The one that leads onto that ridge across the road. Park up there where you'll have a good vantage point. Then warn me on the walkie-talkie if you see any cops or visitors. Don't hesitate to shoot anyone who approaches this place."

"Sure thing, Zak."

"Rusty, I'm impressed," Dylan said. "You may be the first man in history who's sniper-qualified on a Smith & Wesson .38 revolver."

"Screw you, funny man. I got a Remington 700 in thirty-ought-six out in my pickup. I can put down anybody who tries to get in here."

"...I can put down anybody who tries to get in here," said the voice in her earpiece.

Her boots pounded up the slope, feeling as if anchors were attached. The pack on her back flopped back and forth with each stride, sometimes pulling her off balance and causing her to stumble.

Grant's voice crackled in the earpiece.

"Did you hear that, Nightstalker? We have two tangos; one inside with a shotgun; one outside with a rifle and .38 revolver. The man with the rifle will be in a pickup on the ridge south of the house. You'll have to stay out of his line of sight."

Her mouth and lips felt like paper. She could only manage to croak:

"Copy."

Hunter watched the older red-haired guy leave the room. He turned to Boggs.

"Zachariah, it looks as if all that's left of your organization are you and Rusty. Of course, it's got to be easier to lead a movement with just one follower—right, Zachariah?"

Boggs's expression grew dark. "Don't call me that."

"Call you what, *Zachariah?*"

Boggs strode over and swept the butt of the shotgun up and around. Hunter saw it coming, timed it, jerked his head to roll with it. The glancing blow only grazed his forehead.

"Shut up!"

Hunter straightened in the chair. He had to try to get Boggs ensnared in a time-killing debate. *Play on his narcissism…He loves to think he's smarter than anyone else.*

"Wow. Is violence your substitute for intellectual argument, *Doctor* Boggs?"

"I don't have time to argue with you."

"You mean you can't."

"Oh, I only wish I *did* have the time. Much as I loathe *him*"—Boggs nodded toward Adair—"*you* are far more despicable. You defend predators like Adair here."

Hunter shook his head. "You're confusing production with predation."

"What the modern world calls 'production' *is* predation. Adair and corporate jackals like him make their millions by preying on nature. By devouring limited resources for their own selfish gain."

"No, *Doctor.* They don't *devour* resources; they *develop* resources. They take untapped resources and transform them into things that are useful to us. What they do is creative, and it's for the betterment of us all."

"You mean: for the betterment of the most destructive creature in all of nature!" Boggs began to turn away.

Hunter's eyes went to the clock on the mantelpiece. Twelve-thirteen. *Come on, people—where are you?*

He had to keep this going.

"You know your problem, *Zachariah?* You want to live in a fantasy world. In an imaginary Garden of Eden—a place where fruit just drops from the trees into your lap, and crops magically transform themselves into food, which then magically materializes on your kitchen table."

Boggs turned back to him. "You're talking about the hunter-gatherer era. That's the only period when humans actually *did* live in harmony with nature."

"And when average life expectancies were about twenty years, due to starvation, diseases, and exposure. But we eventually solved those problems by *developing* natural resources. Oh, and tell me, Zachariah: How does that 'hunter-gatherer' thing work out for your own little tribe? Do you practice it? Hell, no. You go play Noble Savage in the woods while you enjoy all the benefits of modern civilization: food, tents, and clothes produced by industries you despise. Hell, you misfits wouldn't even have *gotten* here, except for the automobile and fossil fuel industries. So, you want to kill Adair? Every day, you should thank people like Dan Adair— thank them for using their brains to develop natural resources, and keep you alive."

"'Develop' natural resources? You mean *destroy* resources! You mean turning the *natural* into the *unnatural!*"

"Gee, *Doctor.* Since you're a genius, could you please explain to me why 'nature' consists of everything in the universe—animal, vegetable, or mineral—everything, except for *human* nature?"

"I don't have any more time to listen to your bullshit rationalizations for destruction!"

"Really?" Hunter nodded toward the bomb. "Look at that thing. Now, who is *really* offering bullshit rationalizations for destruction?"

Boggs spun on his heel, went over to the camera, and flipped a switch. Then he returned to the coffee table. He pulled two cell phones from his jacket pocket and placed one on the table beside the bomb. Then he used the second to dial the first. When the one on the table chirped, he clicked on its speakerphone.

"Test...test..." His voice came through the cell's speaker on the table. "There. I'll keep these two phones connected, so that when I leave, we can continue to chat."

He pocketed the second cell and rested his hand atop the bomb. His eyes gleamed.

"I'm especially proud of this one, you know. Nothing I've ever built before comes close. I customized it, just for you and Adair. Actually, Hunter, *you* gave me the idea for it, with your newspaper columns."

"They *are* inspiring, aren't they?"

"Let me explain. This thin casing"—he tapped the large metal box—"contains *ten* pipe bombs. Remember the bomb that destroyed the CarboNot office? That consisted of only two. Those contained ammonium nitrate and magnesium, among other things. Very potent. But these new ones are bigger and much better—far more powerful. Do you know what I did?"

"I'm sure you're going to tell me"—he nodded toward the camera—"along with the rest of your worldwide viewing audience, of course."

"I've developed a reliable way to stabilize acetone peroxide!" He sounded like a man boasting about landing on

Mars. "Those crystals pack a tremendous wallop; their power almost rivals some military-grade high explosives. But the chemical is terribly unstable. A lot of people have died handling it. Well, *I* figured out a solution to that problem!"

"I would applaud, but my hands are tied."

"Go ahead, mock me. But you're about to experience the results. As you see, I've also placed the bomb against this tank. It's holding natural gas. It's not really necessary, of course, given the power of the pipe bombs themselves; but I thought *natural gas* would add a nice symbolic touch." He looked at Adair, his twisted grin like a yellow scar parting his long dark beard. "Don't you think?"

"You sick son of a bitch!"

"Now, now, Adair. No need to get all upset. Especially since I'm going to give Hunter here a chance to save all of you."

Hunter stared into the glittering eyes of madness. Took in the dark, unkempt hair and beard. The sadistic little smile...A name from history floated into his mind. *Rasputin.*

"Here's how the game works, Hunter. Pay attention. See this switch on top of the bomb? When I flip it, it will start a four-minute timer that will detonate the bomb. That's plenty of time for me to get clear. Now, those two buttons near your hand: Observe that one is black, and one is white. One of them can deactivate the timer on the detonator. The other actually will set off the bomb.

"So, when I start the timer and leave, you'll have four minutes to figure out which of the two buttons to press in order to shut off the timer. If you choose the right one, you'll all live. But if you choose the wrong one—well, you'll hear a buzzer for about five seconds, just long enough to let you that know that you *blew* it…Hey, that was funny, wasn't it: 'blew it'…Anyway, you'll have those five seconds to contemplate the crimes that brought you here. Then there will be a big, blinding flash. Don't worry, I don't think you'll feel or hear anything, because you and most of this house will instantly be blown to bits."

She heard it all.

"Grant!" Her lungs and throat were on fire. "How far?"

"You're still about a third of a mile out. But you have time. You can make it."

His voice—calm…reassuring.

Her legs felt like rubber. She staggered, almost fell…recovered.

A third of a mile…uphill. It might as well be a hundred miles.

Dylan…

She thought of his face…his cocky grin.

She sucked in deep breaths, put her head down, and drove sheer will into her aching legs, forcing them to continue.

"You know, I don't get it, *Zachariah.*"

"Get what?"

"Why give us any chance at all to live?"

"Because if you do, you will write about it—and my story will spread to millions. In that case, I doubt that Adair or many of his kind will dare continue their current destructive careers. But if you don't live—" He shrugged. "No loss."

It was lame, an obvious lie. Boggs had already said he rigged the bomb to be set off remotely, too. If the timed detonator didn't explode, he would just trigger it with a phone call. But he played along, buying more time.

"So, you're giving us planet-rapers a fifty/fifty chance to live."

Boggs chuckled. "Oh, I'd say the odds are far less than that. You see, I've read your articles, Hunter. And I understand you. Like me, you see the world in black and white. Of course, your notions of what is black and what is white are opposite mine. But knowing that, I can predict exactly what you're going to do." He pointed at the twin-button device. "So that's why I've given you a black-or-white choice—and wired it accordingly."

He smirked again; his sharp yellow teeth reminded Hunter of a rodent.

"Well, it's time I leave you to ponder your symbolic choice. Will you identify your moral values with white, or with black? Normally, you would choose white. But knowing that's the *predictable* choice, maybe you'll choose black, instead. Then again—have I *anticipated* that you'll try to fool me, and pick black? Maddening, isn't it?"

"No—just mad." Hunter shook his head and laughed at him. "You know, you sound remarkably like the character Vizzini in *The Princess Bride.*"

"I'm not familiar with the reference."

"He invented a similar game of wits. It didn't work out very well for him, though. And there's a good reason why this one won't work out any better for you."

Boggs couldn't resist. "And what's that?"

"You both think you're much smarter than others—and much smarter than you are. You share the psychological affliction of terminal arrogance. And that's why *you* are so predictable, *Zachariah.*"

Boggs was irritated and it showed.

"Well, then, Hunter—let's see if you are smart enough to predict how *my* mind works." He reached toward the bomb switch.

"What 'mind'? You're a narcissistic lunatic. A nihilistic sociopath."

The words stopped the man's hand.

"Look at you standing there, Boggs," he went on. "You're *enjoying* this. Which proves my point. All your environmentalist blather is just a rationalization—a narrative that you recite to yourself, so that you don't have to face your *real* motive. Which is that you *like* to kill. Gives you a sense of *power*, doesn't it? Face it: You're nothing but a skinny little misanthropic loser who loves destruction."

Hunter didn't know why his words affected the man so much. Boggs stormed over to him and slapped his face. Then twice. And again.

The killer stood over him, shaking; his eyes seemed to be focused somewhere else. Then he blinked and returned to the here and now.

"Zak...*pleeeease!*" Will's voice was a pig-like squeal. "Don't leave me here!"

Boggs looked at Whelan blankly. "You said you were willing to sacrifice for our cause."

"But I did everything you asked! I don't deserve this!"

"You worthless piece of shit!" Adair snapped. "You're the only one here who *does* deserve this!"

Boggs moved to Adair. He smiled down at him—then spat in his face.

He turned and clicked the switch atop the bomb. A small plastic window on the casing lit up, displaying a digital countdown.

4:00…3:59…3:58…

"The clock is now ticking, Hunter. You now have less than four minutes to guess and second-guess yourself—to death."

THIRTY-EIGHT

"Nightstalker, did you hear that? You've got about…three and a half minutes, now."

A tangle of tall brush had overgrown the path, slowing her progress. As she forced her way through, thin branches whipped at her face, knocking the NVGs askew and snagging her backpack. Enraged, she lowered her head and with a low growling noise powered forward. She broke through to the other side suddenly, momentum and the unexpected loss of resistance pitching her forward to the ground.

She pushed herself to her feet. Her heart was pounding, her breathing labored, and she was soaked with sweat beneath her leather jacket and jeans. Her thighs and calves were on fire, and through the goggles the green world around her seemed to darken and brighten.

"Nightstalker, do you copy? Why did you stop? Are you all right?"

She stumbled forward on unsteady legs, weaving up the slope.

"Copy…proceeding," she panted.

"Tango Two is in position on the ridge near his vehicle. Tango One has just left the residence and moved east, a few feet into the treeline."

"Roger...that..."

She couldn't catch her breath. Her heart felt as if it were going to burst. She began to feel faint...disembodied. Her field of vision narrowed to a tunnel. She saw only the faint outline of the track ahead, a path leading toward the top of the hill.

She had to make it to the top of the hill...

"Three minutes, Hunter."

Boggs's voice, taunting him from the cell phone on the coffee table.

"What's the matter, Mr. Heroic Journalist? Can't you make up your mind? I see four frightened people around you. They are depending on you, you know."

Hunter glanced at the camera across the room. Then at the Adairs.

Nan, trembling violently, had twisted away from the sight of the bomb. Will slumped forward, his body wracked with sobs and loud moans. Kaitlin's eyes were fixed into the distance. "My babies," she was whispering. "My babies..." Hunter followed her gaze to a photo on the wall—a family shot of her on a beach with her husband and two children.

Adair sat in silence. His haunted eyes moved back and forth between Hunter's face and the digital clock on the bomb. His eyes were telling Hunter that they all were at the mercy of whatever decision he made...

"Two-and-a-half minutes, now." He heard a faint chuckle. "You're running out of time, Hunter."

Don't let him distract you. Think...

He thought about the Technobomber cases, about the M.O. in the various bombings. Most were letter or package bombs, triggered by release of pressure on a switch when they were opened. But two had been set off remotely, by cell phone.

He thought of the more recent bombings. CarboNot: another mail bomb, set off by release of a pressure switch. The bomb in the cabin: a trigger-switch device. The one that killed Silva: cell-phone activated...

He looked at the cell phone on the coffee table.

At the cell-phone-operated videocamera across the room.

At the twin-button electrical switch at his hand.

Then back at the digital clock on the side of the time bomb, three feet away.

2:15...2:14...2:13...

Time bomb?

His eyes returned to the two buttons. His index finger hovered above them...

"Only two more minutes, Hunter!"

Boggs's voice in her ear sounded distant now. She had pushed so hard she knew she was in danger of passing out. She tried to concentrate, to focus on following that faint green path into the glowing green tunnel ahead of her. Her throat and lungs ached. She pushed one foot after the other, her legs leaden.

"Nightstalker—you're still too far away. Why are you walking? You've got to move faster!"

That's not Boggs, she thought...that's Grant...

"The tangos are positioned on the east and south sides of the house. You'll be coming in behind its northwest corner. They shouldn't spot you. But you have to move a lot faster. Do you read? You have to run, now."

Run now, she thought.

Her heavy legs continued to walk.

He stared at the timer, only vaguely aware of commotion around him.

And it hit him.

Boggs had never used a timer in his previous bombings. Only cell phones or electrical switches.

He had a cell-activated detonator inside this bomb, as a backup.

But—a backup to *what?* To a time bomb?

He considered the black and white buttons beneath his fingertips. Pondered the psychology of the fanatic who devised this "game"...

"Ninety seconds, Hunter. I see that the ladies are praying. Will you be the answer to their prayers?"

A sociopath. A sadist who enjoys inflicting physical *and* psychological suffering...

"Eighty seconds. I'm sorry, ladies. It seems that Hunter doesn't want to even try to save you."

...a narcissist who needs to believe he's smarter than everyone else...who enjoys *symbolically* outsmarting everyone...

"Seventy seconds. What are you waiting for, Hunter?"

...goading him to press one of the buttons, black or white...

Black or white. Suddenly, he remembered Boggs's email to the *Inquirer.*

"You believe in a black-and-white morality...you and I both make binary moral choices...That makes you predictable—and that is your Achilles's heel..."

Black or white...a binary choice...a *predictable* binary choice...

Hunter sat back. Looked up into the camera. Grinned.

Moved his hand away from the buttons.

"What are you smiling about? Just one minute more and you'll die and kill all your friends, Dylan Hunter."

She heard the name in her earpiece...then immediately saw him, saw him crawling across the floor to her, crawling to her covered in his own blood, never stopping, refusing to stop because he was coming to save her...

"...Nightstalker, I said: Do you copy? You have to run! Annie—*run!*"

Suddenly there was only one all-consuming thought:

You have to run to Dylan...

She found herself stumbling forward, then trotting, then running again, running up the path. The green tunnel before her began to widen and the pain in her lungs faded and the weight of her legs lightened. The path began to level out and she saw bright light ahead through the trees and an opening at the end of the path, an opening that grew with every stride...

"Copy!" she heard herself whisper.

"Thirty seconds, Hunter! Why are you just sitting there, laughing? Are you crazy?"

She saw a yard at the end of the trail before her, fifty meters ahead.

"Fifteen seconds! Aren't you going to do anything?"

She pushed ahead with everything she had. Her lungs felt like they were tearing.

"Ten...nine...just eight seconds, Hunter!...seven..."

She burst from the tree line into the yard.

Then saw that the house was another hundred meters distant.

"Grant," she gasped, "I won't make it in time!"

But she continued to run, run as fast as she could, knowing that she had failed him, knowing that he was about to die, her only hope now that the blast that killed him would take her, too...

The whole family was screaming at him.

"It will be okay," he said quietly, his eyes never straying from the camera lens.

"...five...four..."

"Pick one! Just pick one!" Adair shouted, straining at his bonds. *"Do something!"*

Dylan continued to grin. "I am."

"...two...one..."

Their shrieking stopped and they closed their eyes.

"...zero!"

Nothing happened.

Five more seconds passed.

He turned to them, still smiling as they opened their eyes in disbelief.

"I told you it would be okay."

"I told you it would be okay."

Dylan's voice—instead of the blast.

She slowed and stopped. Stood paralyzed, fifty meters from the house, gasping for air, not understanding.

"Annie! Keep moving!" Grant shouted in her ear.

Then she realized that he was still in danger. She started to run again.

Adair's face was white and his eyes were riveted on the bomb, uncomprehending.

"It's all right, Dan," Hunter said softly. He turned back to the camera and raised his voice. "Well, *Zachariah:* Didn't I say you're really not as smart as you think you are?"

"You think you outsmarted me? Well, let me disabuse you of—"

Hunter cut him off. "Do you want to know how I figured it out?"

"Not rea—"

"It was very simple." He chuckled. "Because your mind isn't particularly subtle. In fact, you're stupidly predictable. It goes back to that letter you sent to me at the newspaper. You stupidly revealed the clue to your psychology, right there. Care to know what the stupid clue was?"

"You haven't won! Right now—"

"You were boasting that you had me all figured out, that *I* was predictable. You said, 'You're like me. You'll always make a binary choice.' Well, that was your stupid blunder. 'You'll always make a binary choice.' So, what did you do? You designed a trap that depended on me acting *predictably:* predictably making *some* binary choice. *Any* choice. Because *either* choice, black or white, would have set off the bomb— right, *Doctor* Boggs?"

He paused to waste a few more precious seconds. He heard Boggs take a breath, but before he could speak, Hunter pressed on.

"I've seen a few bombs in my time, *Doctor* Boggs. You wouldn't know that, of course. But I had reason to believe that this one isn't a time bomb at all. You see, I've studied your M.O., *Doctor*, and you always used either cell phone or electrical switch detonation. This button gadget is a just a simple electrical switch. It's rigged to set off the bomb at the press of a button—*either* button. Isn't that right, *Doctor?*"

With a last burst of energy she raced across the yard, listening to Dylan banter with Boggs, knowing he was trying to buy time, knowing he could salvage less than a minute more— perhaps only seconds.

She reached the corner of the house, then clawed at the straps of the backpack, frantic to get it off...

"You're still going to die! *Right now!*" Boggs shouted, so long that the cell phone speaker crackled.

"Sure, sure, because you have a back-up detonator inside the bomb—right, *Doctor?* A cell-phone activated one—right, *Doctor?* You plan to use your smartphone, right from out there in the trees where you're hiding—right, *Doctor?*"

Silence.

Then:

"You think you're very clever, don't you? But you've given yourself only a very brief Pyrrhic victory. There's not a thing you can do now. We're going to play the game again, Hunter, and in ten seconds you won't think you're so smart. You won't be thinking anything at all. So now, as I count down from ten, you may all say your goodbyes."

Adair looked at his wife. "I love you, Nan." His voice was hoarse.

"I love you," she whispered back, holding his eyes.

"Oh, Daddy!" Kaitlin cried out to Adair.

His features were tortured. "I'm so sorry, baby!"

Hunter had to grit his teeth to keep the smile fixed on his face.

She finally shrugged off the backpack and swung it in front of her. Now her fingers fumbled to undo the snaps at the top.

"Ten...nine...eight..."

She yanked it open, shoved her hand inside among the four spiky black antennas protruding from its top...found and flipped a switch.

"...seven...six..."

She hoisted the bag into her arms again and staggered along the back wall of the house, moving toward the den...

Smartphone in hand, Zachariah Boggs watched the house from his hiding place in the trees. When his countdown reached *five*, he ducked behind a thick tree trunk for protection and pressed the speed-dial button that rang the cell inside the bomb.

"...three...two...one...Bye-bye, all!"

He braced himself for the blast.

Five more seconds passed.

Nothing happened.

He frowned and pressed the speed-dial number a second time.

Waited…

Nothing.

He smacked his phone a few times, thinking the batteries may have been jostled loose—only to realize that the screen was lit, but the videocam feed from inside the house was gone.

What the hell?

He quickly thumbed in the entire nine-digit number of the cell phone inside the bomb.

Still nothing.

Desperate, he pulled out and keyed his walkie-talkie.

"Rusty, something's wrong with my phone!"

He released the key.

And heard nothing. Not static. Not anything.

"Rusty!"

Dead air.

Hunter wondered why Boggs halted the countdown at *six.* Dead silence gripped the room as they all held their breath, waiting for him to resume.

But no more sound came from the cell phone on the table.

"Boggs?" Hunter ventured.

Silence.

Some new twisted game?

"I'm talking to you, you pompous little prick."

No response.

Then he knew…

He began to laugh. Then he turned to the Adairs.

"We're okay, now, folks. The Marines have landed."

He took a long, deep breath and released it.

Grant Garrett, I owe you yet another box of cigars.

Eyes closed, back against the wall, Annie cradled the jammer and waited for the world to shatter.

Thirty seconds passed.

Then her lips began to tremble and her legs grew wobbly and gave way and she slid slowly to the ground. She sat there, shaking, staring into blurry green space, trying to stifle her little sobs. She flipped up the NVGs and wiped her eyes on her sleeve.

I did it, love…I did it…

It all caught up with her in an instant. She felt beyond exhaustion, physically and emotionally drained. She wanted to collapse right here, right now, on the cold earth.

Then she remembered that Boggs and his partner were somewhere close by. With a rifle, shotgun, and handgun.

She carefully placed the Man Pack Jammer on the ground next to her and slid it out of sight behind a shrub. It would continue to block any transmissions within a sixty-meter radius for hours. But of course that included her own commo with Garrett and the Predator. Until she got out of its range, she would be on her own.

Against two armed killers.

She drew the Beretta from her jacket pocket. Struggling to her feet, she teetered dizzily and leaned against the wall. After a few seconds she felt a little steadier. Weapon in hand, she lowered her NVGs once more and began to creep slowly along the back wall, toward the eastern side of the house.

Behind the tree, Boggs was eyeing the house, trying to figure out what had happened, when he thought he saw faint movement. He stared intently, wondering if it was only his imagination.

No—there.

A dark, spectral figure was sliding slowly along the lighter-colored wall.

FBI hostage rescue?

Now he knew why his communications weren't working.

And suddenly, Zachariah Boggs was scared.

Moving cautiously to avoid being spotted, he pocketed his smartphone and placed the cell phone and walkie-talkie on the ground. He picked up the shotgun lying there, then began to move, one careful step at a time, back into the trees. After a moment, he started to run toward the road, stumbling and crashing heedlessly through the branches.

Annie heard noise out in the trees. She recalled what Grant had reported.

That would have to be Boggs.

She was torn: Go inside and free Dylan—or go in hot pursuit and take out the threats?

He won't be safe as long as they are out there.

She knew the guy on the ridge had not just the rifle, but their vehicle. She had to prevent Boggs from reaching it and escaping. But to do that, she needed to re-establish commo with Grant.

Taking a breath and hoping her taxed legs wouldn't fail her, she dashed out from the house across the lawn, and into the trees at the eastern edge of the property. Nobody shot at her.

She immediately encountered an ATV trail heading through the woods back toward the road. And heard crashing noise in that direction. She hustled off after Boggs. And as she left the range of the jammer, her earpiece crackled to life.

"—stalker, do you copy?"

"Nightstalker copies. The bomb is neutralized. Repeat: bomb neutralized…I'm now in foot pursuit of Tango One."

"Thank God!…The UAS has eyes on you and both tangos. Tango One is heading east, away from the vehicle."

She made a snap decision. "Direct me toward the vehicle and Tango Two. That's their only escape. The Predator can track Tango One."

"Roger that."

She reached the roadway a moment later. When Grant reported that the man on the ridge appeared to be moving around the truck, she took the opportunity to run across the road and into the trees over there.

Grant directed her to a relatively easy path up the slope of the ridge, then guided her to circle behind the man's position. She crept toward him through the trees from the rear.

Soon she spotted his pickup truck on a narrow dirt road. He stood beside it, on the driver's side. Despite the cold, he wore only a flannel shirt. He held a pair of binoculars to his eyes, aimed toward the house; in his other hand he held a walkie-talkie. A rifle and handgun rested on the passenger side of the truck's hood, lying on what looked like the man's jacket.

She moved behind a tree about fifty meters away.

"Base," she whispered. "Tango Two in sight. His back is to me. Getting within range to take him out."

"Negative, Nightstalker! You can't do that. No shooting. Repeat: *No gunfire.*"

It astounded her. "Sir—why not?"

"You are within two hundred yards of homes. The last thing we need is shots fired, and neighbors alerting the cops.

Think it through. If either you or our mutual friend is caught up there, then much more than this one op is blown. You know how much flak the Agency takes for our black ops. So what happens to us if we're caught doing this sort of shit on American soil? We can't risk that."

"But sir—" she hissed into the mic.

"No 'buts.' This is not just about you, or him, or me. It's about the *Agency*—our very survival. That's why this op must remain black. Inky black. So, here is how you play it. You capture, subdue, and leave the tangos for the locals. You shoot *only* as a last resort, in direct self-defense. And if you *must* use deadly force, then you clean up the mess afterward, to make sure there is no blowback to us. That's an *order*. Do you copy?"

The Beretta's sights were trained on the back of the man in the distance. She wanted to scream in frustration. But Grant had already gone way out on a limb for them tonight. She owed him at least this much.

"Yes, sir. Copy."

She slipped from behind the tree and moved toward the man, pistol at the ready.

He stood beside the truck yelling into the walkie-talkie, his back still to her.

"Zak! Come on, man! Can you hear me?...What the hell's happening?"

She was within fifteen feet of him when he must have heard her or spotted her in the truck's outside mirror. Without warning, he spun and hurled the walkie-talkie at her.

It struck her hard, in her upper right arm. She gasped at the pain and barely managed to keep her grip on the Beretta.

He spun back to the truck and clawed for the rifle, just out of reach across the hood. Flipping up her NVGs, she rushed him. She slammed into his back, knocking him hard against the truck. He grunted and turned. She started a jiu-jitsu takedown—only to find that her right arm had gone numb.

He grabbed her useless gun hand and started to pry her fingers from it. She seized the gun's barrel in her left hand and tried to twist it from him. But he knocked her hand aside, grasped the barrel himself, and stepped back to wrench it from her grip. His momentum caused him to trip and half-fall against the truck.

He now held her handgun by the barrel in his right hand. Rather than try to run, she rushed him again, this time aiming a kick toward his midsection. It only grazed his hip, but he was off-balance and it sent him to his knees. As he struggled to rise, she kicked again, and this time luck was with her: It caught his right forearm and knocked the weapon several feet away into the darkness.

She went after it, but her legs felt like mush and couldn't move fast enough. He caught her from behind and wrapped his cable-like arms around hers in a bear hug. She tried to stomp his instep but, roaring like an animal, he lifted her right off the ground.

She felt helpless as a rag doll. Her energy was spent. Her flailing kicks against his shins had little power or effect. The hideous pressure on her ribs crushed the breath from her lungs. Trapped down along her sides, her hands could only scratch weakly against his thighs, trying in vain to get at his groin.

But then her left hand closed on something else. And she knew instantly what it was.

With a desperate twist of her body she yanked the hunting knife free of its sheath. Then plunged it upward, into the meat of his forearm.

"Ahhhhhhh!"

His scream pierced the air and his arms fell from her body, and before she could think or he could react she whipped around and jammed the blade forward into his stomach, as hard as she could.

It cut off his scream. The tall red-haired guy folded over, clutching his middle. His face bobbed inches from hers, his eyes and mouth gaping oval wounds filled with shock and pain.

Then another face drifted in from memory...the face of Adam Silva.

The blade, warm and sticky, shook in her fist.

"You son of a bitch!" she snarled.

Then drove it in again.

THIRTY-NINE

Within a minute after running across the street in front of Adair's house, Boggs had found an ATV path in the woods. But it was heading east, parallel to the ridge—away from Rusty and the pickup.

He paused to make a fast decision.

If those *were* FBI hostage-rescue thugs outside the house, then there was a strong chance that they already spotted Rusty and his truck. Or would, the minute he tried to flee. It was now too risky for *him* to head over there, too, where they could both be trapped on that little dead-end road.

He no longer had the walkie-talkie to warn Rusty. He hated to abandon him like this, to leave him behind to fend for himself. But Rusty was a good, loyal soldier. He knew the risks. Rusty wouldn't hesitate to sacrifice himself for the greater good, if he had to—

—unlike so many others. Unlike that *Judas,* Conn. Or that *coward,* Dawn. No, Rusty wouldn't blame him for leaving him behind. And if he were captured, he wouldn't betray him, either.

As for *her*—well, she had made her choice, hadn't she. When push came to shove, she revealed her *true* commitments. The rest had been nothing but talk, all pretense. Years of bullshit that he should have seen through, long ago. It was a good thing that he found out the truth about her *now,* instead of at some critical moment when it might have really mattered.

Good riddance to the bitch…

So he headed east, down the dark, almost invisible trail, pushing deeper into the forest. He knew that eventually this path would intersect some forest road. From there he would get his bearings and find his way out of the area…

After fifteen interminable minutes, Hunter heard the front door open.

"Dylan?"

The voice was faint. It took a couple of seconds for it to register.

"Annie?" he shouted, incredulous.

He heard steps coming down the hall.

Then she was framed in the entranceway, pistol in hand.

Her face, hands, jeans, and leather jacket—all smeared with blood.

"Annie!" he gasped. "You're bleeding!"

A faint smile touched her lips.

"It's not mine."

She paused there, just an instant, her smoky gray eyes holding his, telling him everything.

Then she rushed over, knelt, and wrapped her arms tightly around him. He felt her body trembling.

"You're all right," she whispered. "You're all right…"

"Are *you* all right?"

She looked up at him, eyes tired but relieved. "I am now."

"The blood," he said. "Boggs?"

"No. The guy working with him."

"So where is Boggs?"

"In the woods. Don't worry, the UAS is tracking him."

"I would hug you back," he said, "but I'm a bit tied up at the moment."

She laughed, squeezing him even tighter. She let go, then reached into her jacket pocket. Her hand emerged with a hunting knife.

Covered with blood.

"Let me cut you loose." She glanced at the others. They stared at her, wordless and open-mouthed. "I'll free all of you in another minute." She bent to work on the bonds at his feet.

He, too, was speechless as he watched her work. He had heard no gunshots. And he knew whose knife that was.

So he knew what all that blood had to mean.

"Grant sent you, then. *You* brought in the jammer."

"Don't blame him. There was no one else."

A rope on his ankle parted. She paused, not looking at him.

"I didn't think I'd make it in time."

"But you did," he said, gently. "You did it, Annie."

She looked up at him, the blood-coated knife steady in her grip.

"I did what I had to."

Hunter sent them all outside to wait in his car at a safe distance while he worked on the bomb.

He didn't think it would be booby-trapped, and it wasn't. Boggs had meant to set it off here himself, not plant it for later accidental detonation by some unwary victim. The top of the outer case, which was little more than a carrier, was open; he could see inside. With tools from Adair's garage workshop he dismantled it inside of fifteen minutes. He carefully wrapped the pipe bombs, the cell-phone and button switches, and the detonator in separate rags, then in individual plastic bags. After placing the items in a large cardboard box he found in the garage, he carried it out to his car.

Will wasn't inside the Forester with the rest of them. He sat by himself on the short brick wall along the driveway, hunched over, head in hands.

They got out and went back into the house. He placed the box gently in the rear cargo area, cushioned it so that it wouldn't move around, then locked the car. Turning, he saw Adair standing outside the front door, waiting for him. Hunter walked over.

"You're a man of many talents, Dylan Hunter," he said, gesturing toward the car.

"Oh, that? I had some EOD training in the service. During the Iraq War."

Adair made a face. "Bullshit. I watched you tonight. The way you look around, never missing anything. The way you took command of the situation. How you dealt with Boggs and his punk. Now you dismantle a bomb without breaking a sweat...And then there's your girlfriend. Annie comes waltzing in here, toting a gun; she takes out an armed man, apparently in hand-to-hand combat; and she brings along some kind of James Bond gadget that keeps the bomb from exploding. I also notice that she's wearing some kind of body wire, and she's constantly whispering to somebody. Dylan, I feel like I'm in some kind of spy movie. So, level with me. What gives?"

"Dan, look. I—"

"Listen, you don't have to explain anything, if you don't want to. I figure you two are probably from some government counterterrorism agency, so whatever you tell me is going to be some cooked-up story, anyway. It also dawned on me tonight that you and Annie must be the same pair that my people ran into at the diner about a month ago. Those two called themselves 'Brad and Annie.'" Adair chuckled. "Coincidence? I don't think so. And please don't insult my intelligence by telling me any different."

"I would never insult your intelligence, Dan."

"So, then. I'm right about all this spy shit, huh?"

Hunter had to laugh. He just shrugged.

"You don't want to talk about it."

"I don't want to talk about it."

"Fair enough. But can you at least tell me why Annie had to bring in that bomb-jamming gizmo at the very last minute? My God, Dylan, why didn't *you* fetch it here in the first place, and spare all of us the scare of our lives?"

"That wouldn't have worked, Dan. The people helping us tonight were electronically monitoring everything that was being said inside the house. But the jammer would have blocked their communications and monitoring. They would have had no way of knowing what was happening, or what they were up against. Besides, if Boggs discovered too soon that his walkie-talkies, video monitoring, and cell transmissions were being blocked, he would have just shot us before anyone could have gotten here."

"Oh. I see that, now."

Dylan turned to go.

"Before you run off, do you mind if I ask you a quick personal question?"

"Go ahead."

"The thing I can't figure about you is: If you're government, why do you write what you do in the newspaper? Taking on all these politicians and government agencies? Dylan, I think I'm a good judge of character. You seem completely sincere about what you write, and what you've been doing to help us."

"I am, Dan. That part—being a newspaper reporter, writing what I write—it's all real. All true."

Adair stepped forward, hesitantly—then reached out and gripped Hunter by the shoulders.

"I *want* to believe that. We need somebody like you, Dylan. God, the world needs somebody like you. I can't tell you how much." He lowered his eyes. "I can't put into words...just how grateful—"

"It's not necessary, Dan."

"No, it *is*." He blinked rapidly, cleared his throat. "You saved our lives tonight. You and Annie. You saved my wife and daughter and..." He stopped; his eyes moved to his stepson across the driveway, then back to Hunter. "And me. And my business, too. How can I ever—"

"Dan, do you know the greatest thing you can do for Annie and me, right now?"

"Name it."

"Tonight never happened."

They stood looking at each other a long moment.

Adair nodded again. "Okay."

"I'd appreciate it if you and your family don't breathe a word about this. To anyone. Ever."

"I'll make sure they all understand." He looked again toward Will. "Especially *him*. Did you know he was working with Boggs all along? *He* was the one who planted those fake samples, for God's sake. My own *stepson!*"

Hunter squeezed Adair's arm. "I'm really sorry, Dan."

"He almost got all of us *killed.*"

"It looks as if he realizes that now…Maybe he can make some amends."

"*Amends?* Are you kidding? How could he possibly—"

"He can start by telling the police everything he knows. Not about tonight, of course, but about WildJustice. What they've done. Who they're working with. Who finances them. That could bring a lot of bad people to justice. And also, he needs to tell the media about planting those fake chemical samples. Believe me, that will cause a sensation—enough to save your business, I think."

"I'll damned well see to it that he *does*. More than that: I'll make sure *you* get his story first, for your paper."

Hunter grinned. "My editor will love that…There's one more favor I'd like to ask of you, Dan. I saw some items in your garage that I'd like to borrow for the next few hours."

"Sure. Go ahead, take anything you need." Adair's brows furrowed. "Do you mind my asking what for?"

He looked off to the east, into the forest.

"I'm going hunting."

In a bay of the three-car garage, Hunter secured various items from the workshop and placed them into the rear bed of Adair's Kawasaki Mule ATV. The last thing to go in, on a blanket for cushioning, was the Remington 700 that Annie had fetched from Rusty's pickup. Then he set Annie's night-vision goggles on the seat.

The Beretta was in his jacket pocket. He had ditched the bugged loafers and put on his boots again, tucking Rusty's sheathed hunting knife into the right one, along his calf.

Annie stood nearby, watching him. The butt of Boggs's S&W .38 protruded from her jacket pocket. She still wore the earpiece and lapel mic.

He went over to her. "I'll need to borrow those."

She unclipped them and handed them over. He took her hand and drew her close.

"You know why I have to do this."

"I know." She held up her bloodstained hands, gave him a little smile. "Who am I to argue?"

He laughed. Ran his thumb across her smudged cheek.

"I love you, Annie Woods."

"I love you, Dylan Hunter."

Then he kissed her.

He put on the NVGs and turned over the engine. Then took the ATV down the driveway, across the road, and into the forest on the other side.

He had already tested the earpiece to establish contact with Garrett. Using the Predator's sensors, the spy boss directed him onto the same ATV trail that Boggs had taken forty minutes earlier. The bird still tracked him; Grant told Hunter that Boggs had traveled barely a mile through the rough terrain.

"I must say how nice it is to hear your voice again, Grant," he shouted above the growl of the engine.

"You, too. I was sweating bullets until Annie told me she had neutralized the bomb."

"Speaking of Annie: I don't know whether to hug you for all you've done tonight, or kill you for sending her in."

"Frankly, I don't know which threat frightens me more. But there really was no one else available to do it on such short notice. And you must admit: She performed magnificently."

He thought of her in the den's entranceway, holding the Beretta.

"That she did."

The Mule's powerful headlamps revealed a large boulder in his path; he navigated around it, bouncing over a bone-jarring rough patch next to the trail.

"So how much trouble have I gotten you into tonight?" he asked.

Garrett actually *laughed*. It turned into a coughing fit. He cleared his throat.

"Nada. The people here know better. Besides, everybody's buying the cover story. The two sensor guys and the UAS pilot think this is just a cool training mission, and that they're being graded for extra brownie points. I told them to butt out of the audio monitoring, and to send the feeds directly to my headset. So they don't know squat about what's been happening. I did hate to lie to my colonel buddy at Belvoir; but in my position, he would have done the same thing. And the chopper pilot is none the wiser, either. So I'd say that all my bases are covered."

"You know that I owe you another box of cigars for this. What's your poison?"

Garrett told him.

"Ouch. Those are pricey. And hard to come by."

"Are you telling me that you don't have the money or resources to get them?"

"Of course I can. But you know how much I hate sending my hard-earned cash to Fidel."

"Tough shit."

Boggs stopped at the crest of a small hill to catch his breath and figure out what to do next. But he saw nothing in the dark—nothing but an endless black expanse of trees.

He had run and walked for what seemed like miles and hours, even though his smartphone told him it had been only forty-five minutes. But he was exhausted. The shotgun was a burden, but not one he could afford to discard; he might have to use it.

Well, he would just have to continue, looking for some—

The noise of a distant motor…

At first he couldn't tell from which direction the sound was coming. But within half a minute he knew it was behind him.

And getting louder.

His heart began to race. He gripped the shotgun tightly in both hands and began to run down the path.

Within another two minutes, he realized it was futile. He was too tired, and the noise was only getting closer. It sounded now like a lawnmower or small tractor—

An ATV…

He looked around desperately into the near-pitch black of the woods. The area to his left looked as if it might be easier to move through. He plunged off the path in that direction.

In a moment he found himself in obsidian darkness, barely able to see branches until they swept by, inches from his face, or scraped his exposed knuckles. His knees crashed through weeds and small bushes, the shotgun that he held protectively before him bumped small limbs, a branch slashed painfully along his ribs. He had to veer around several trees that materialized out of nowhere.

He found himself at the foot of what seemed to be another slope rising into the graphite sky, a sky almost obscured through the spiky branches overhead. He stomped and pushed his way forward, as the throbbing noise of the engine behind him grew ever louder, ever nearer…

…then died abruptly.

He staggered to a halt, tottering in place, trying to stifle his loud panting. He pivoted slowly in a complete circle, straining his ears for any sound from the ominous shadows.

And heard nothing.

That chill silence scared him more than the engine noise. The vehicle had stopped close by, near where he had left the path. As if they knew where he was. Maybe they had seen his footprints or some branches he'd broken.

He had to find a place to hide—fast.

He tried to keep quiet as he continued pushing forward. After another minute or two, he found just what he needed: a thicket so dark and dense that he would be invisible. He moved around it, searching for an access point. On the far side, he found an indentation in the vegetation and slipped inside. He faced inward, away from the opening, hoping to hide the glinting metal surface of the shotgun.

It was almost totally dark in there, and so quiet that he thought he could hear his own heart beating in his chest. He stood as still as he could, sweat soaking the inside of his clothes.

Stood there, listened, and waited…

Moments passed. At times he thought he heard something, and he tried to focus on the sound—only to conclude after a few seconds that his fevered imagination was playing tricks.

He was wondering how long he would have to remain still when something hard crashed into the back of his skull…

Hunter lowered the butt of the Remington. He stared at the glowing green heap lying in the glowing green brush, and released a long-held breath.

"All right, Grant. I have him. He never saw me coming. Thanks for being our eyes and ears tonight."

"Glad to be of help," came the voice through the earpiece. "Guess I can send our bird and its flight crew home, now."

"Roger that. I don't think either of us wants anyone to be looking over my shoulder from this point on."

"For sure…Well, I'll be heading home, now, too. Just make sure that the death of Boggs's partner looks like the result of some kind of falling-out between the two of them."

"Annie's already taking care of that," he said, then added: "Grant…thanks again."

His ex-boss didn't respond immediately. When he did, he said, "You and I need to have another chat when you get back."

Through the NVGs his eyes were fixed on the motionless figure at his feet.

"I know."

He gagged and trussed up the unconscious man, dragged him through the woods back to the ATV, and dumped him into the rear cargo bed. He emptied his pockets, picking up his smartphone carefully so as not to leave his own fingerprints on it, and sealed it in a small plastic bag. Then he consulted his own smartphone—the one he had left in his car, before he entered Adair's house—for a sat map of the forest.

As the crow flies, his destination was perhaps five miles away. But nothing ran in a straight line through the forest, and he couldn't risk using any paved roads, where he might encounter patrolling rangers. He had to follow meandering ATV trails and little-used dirt roads, then find shallow spots to ford creeks. After a while, he thought he heard Boggs moaning in the back, but the engine noise drowned him out.

It took well over an hour to reach the place where Forest Service Road 209 crossed Otter Creek. He followed the bank of the creek a fair distance, well out of sight and earshot of the road and the few isolated homes in the area.

He chugged along slowly, looking for a good spot. Found it. He stopped and shut down the engine.

Now he could hear Boggs groaning through the gag.

He went back and undid the ropes securing him inside the ATV, then pulled him out and dumped him onto the ground. Boggs gave out a muffled yelp through the gag.

Hunter grabbed him by the rope that bound his ankles and dragged him over the rough ground to the base of a large maple. He left him there, whimpering in the dark, and returned to the ATV to fetch what he needed. He stuffed the items inside a plastic garbage bag and brought it along.

He hauled Boggs to sit upright against the tree. Then he raised the goggles from his face. He took out a small flashlight, clicked it on, and set it on the ground, aiming it so that it would illuminate both of them.

Hunter leaned in.

"Look at my face, *Zachariah*. Look very closely. Remember me? I'm the guy that beat the crap out of you and your gang at the diner a few weeks ago."

Boggs eyes, glistening with tears, suddenly widened in shocked recognition.

Hunter grinned.

"Yep, that was me. I won't bother to explain it to you. I'll leave it for you to puzzle out. After all, you're a *genius*—right? So much smarter than the rest of the world. Besides, you'll have plenty of time to ponder the mystery."

He drew the blood-covered hunting knife from his boot.

"Recognize this? Ah, I see you do. Know whose blood that is?"

Boggs recoiled from the knife, horror in his eyes.

"That's right. That's Rusty's blood. Poor Rusty. It was a pretty nasty death, too. He was in a lot of pain, and it took a while for him to bleed out. So much blood in the human body…"

He tapped the blade against the Bogg's cheekbone, causing him to flinch.

"You know, all the way here, I've been debating with myself whether to use this knife on you. Carve you up, right here, and leave the pieces for the animals. And why shouldn't I? You hid a bomb in my cabin. It almost blew my girlfriend to pieces, except for the last-minute intervention of my cat. Oh yes, almost forgot: You left my cat outside to die, too."

Hunter placed the knife under Boggs's runny nose, giving him a metallic whiff of Rusty's blood. He cringed back against the tree trunk and whined.

"But I haven't made up my mind about that. Not yet. Since you played a game with *me*, offering me a fake chance to survive, I thought I might play one with *you*, now. The only difference is that, unlike you, I'm a man of my word. You called it my 'black and white' moral code—remember? So, if you tell me what I want to know, right now—the whole truth, and no bullshit—I promise you that I will *not* use this knife on you. You have my word of honor. Is that a deal? Nod if that's okay."

Boggs couldn't take his eyes off the knife. He nodded rapidly.

"Hey, that's great. I prefer it that way, frankly, because I like this jacket a lot and I don't want to get your blood all over it. So, here is what we're going to do. I'm going to take off the gag, now. Then I'll ask you some questions, which you will answer fully and completely. If you do, I promise that I will *not* carve you to pieces. Understand?"

Boggs nodded frantically.

Hunter reached around to the back of the man's head, grabbed the end of duct tape that held the gag in place, and gave it a hard yank, ripping it around the front of his mouth. Dark wads of hair and beard came along with it. Boggs shrieked and spat out the wad of cloth from his mouth. Then sat shaking and sobbing.

Hunter got inches from his face.

"Now, I need to know something. You are working with somebody. Somebody powerful, somebody connected." He waved the knife in front of the killer's face. "Remember our deal. If you don't want to feel even more pain, pain like you've never experienced in your life, you're going to tell me who that person is."

He pulled out a microcassette recorder and pressed the "record" button.

Eyes glued to the blade, Boggs began to talk.

And once he started to talk, he couldn't stop. Without further prompting, he just kept talking, sobbing and talking, a torrent of words, words filled with apologies and excuses and information. Boggs told him everything.

Hunter listened, absorbing it, saying nothing. When the flood of words finally slowed to a trickle, then dried up, he lowered the knife. Switched off the recorder.

"Well. That was extremely interesting, Zachariah. Your testimony in court would be devastating. Unfortunately, though, this taped confession out here has been coerced, and it would never stand up in court. You could and probably would deny everything you just told me. But even if you didn't, there's one thing that prevents me from exploring that option."

"What?" he whimpered.

"These days, even a guilty verdict to first-degree murder would leave you and Ashton Conn alive. And that is simply unacceptable. That is just *not* going to happen."

"Wait a minute! You can't do that! You *promised*—"

"I promised I wouldn't use the knife on you. And I won't. In fact, I'm not even going to kill you outright tonight."

He pulled a roll of duct tape from the plastic garbage bag. Used the knife to cut off a long strip. Boggs sensed something unpleasant was about to happen and began to yell; a quick punch in the solar plexus shut him up. Hunter retrieved the wet ball of cloth from the ground, yanked open Boggs's mouth by the beard, jammed it back inside, and immediately slapped the strip of tape across his lips, so that he couldn't spit it out. As Boggs gagged, Hunter cut off another, longer strip of tape and wrapped it across his mouth and around the back of his head.

Then he reached inside the garbage bag and pulled out two other items from Adair's workshop.

A thin, one-foot-square scrap of sheet metal.

A battery-powered nail gun.

He placed them on the ground. Boggs was so focused on them that he never saw the punch coming. It knocked him senseless—not entirely unconscious, but close enough.

The rest was a bit awkward. Standing over him, Hunter picked up the sheet metal piece and nail gun and tucked them under his right arm. With his left hand, he grabbed Boggs's bound wrists, raised them above the man's head, and pressed them against the tree trunk. Using his left knee to hold Boggs's forearms in place there, he took the metal sheet in his left hand and positioned it flat across the forearms.

Then, aiming carefully, he fired a large nail through the metal and into the man's right forearm, pinning both the sheet and the arm to the tree.

Boggs, still dazed, jerked with the impact, but only groaned.

He fired another nail through the sheet metal, this time into his left forearm.

Another into his right.

And another, into his left again.

The metal sheet now sandwiched Boggs's forearms to the tree, so that he couldn't work them off the bare nails. Hunter tugged at the metal; it didn't move.

He crouched in front of Boggs again. Held up the nail gun.

"You like symbolism, Zak. Well, this has a lot of symbolism. You and your gang used to spike trees. That's what gave me this idea. And it also symbolizes all the nails you used in the bomb that butchered Adam Silva. And in all the other bombs you've used over the years to maim and kill innocent people."

Boggs's eyes looked glassy; he was about to pass out. Hunter slapped him hard and brought him around.

"You know, Zachariah, in exchange for all that useful information, I do feel that I owe you at least one explanation. You've probably been wondering: 'Why did he drag me all way out here?' Well, on the day you and I first met, a guy back at the diner unknowingly gave me the idea. He told me that there are bears down here around Otter Creek. Lots and lots of bears."

Hunter paused to give him a little smile.

"Now, I don't know much about the habits of the local bears. If you're lucky, maybe they're all still hibernating. Then again, hunters tell me that they see a few wandering around even in the dead of winter. Well, if any of them *are* prowling around out here tonight, I suspect they must be mighty hungry."

Boggs was crying uncontrollably now.

"What's the matter, Zachariah? I read that you're always quoting John Muir saying, 'If there is a war between the wild beasts and Lord Man, I would be tempted to side with the bears.' Well, you picked your side. And now, you get to live with the bears."

Hunter gathered the various items and put them back inside the garbage bag. He got to his feet and looked down upon the killer, hanging grotesquely from the tree by his arms.

"Oh, one more thing. This is for Dan Adair."

He spat on Zachariah Boggs.

Then turned his back on him and walked back toward the ATV.

After about ten yards, he could no longer hear the weak, muffled moans.

FORTY

He took the roads back to the house, no longer worried about police stops. It was almost four in the morning when he arrived. Alerted by the noise, Adair came outside and greeted him at the front entrance.

"How did the hunting go?"

"Very well." He added: "I've almost filled my quota for the season."

Adair smiled slowly. Then extended his hand.

Hunter clasped it.

"Where is she?" he asked.

"In the guest bedroom. Nan made her a sandwich and some hot chocolate, then put her clothes in the wash while she showered. Leave your clothes outside the door and we'll do them, too."

"But I have—"

"Don't argue. Both of you are too wiped out to go anywhere tonight. Sleep in as late as you want."

"Thanks, Dan. Thank Nan for us, too."

In the bedroom he found her asleep, huddled in an armchair, wrapped in a white terrycloth bathrobe. He knelt quietly next to the chair, bent and softly kissed her hand.

Her eyes blinked open. Then she smiled and raised her arms to him.

He held her tightly, his cheek pressed against her damp hair, taking in the floral scent, feeling her warm breath against his neck.

"You found him," she murmured.

"No one else will."

She squeezed him tighter.

After a while, she pushed back and wrinkled her nose.

"You need a shower."

"I know. Get in bed, and give me five minutes."

He stood under the hot spray much longer than that. He felt as if he were washing much more than dirt and blood down the drain at his feet.

When he emerged, she was asleep again. He tiptoed over, clicked off the bedside lamp, and slipped under the thick comforter. He curled up against her warm curves. Wrapped his arm around her.

In the morning they found a breakfast tray outside their door. They sat in the bed, the comforter drawn up around their bodies, sipping hot coffee poured from the carafe and eating buttered croissants.

"Now to figure out the logistics of getting home," he said. "I need to be in downtown D.C. tonight. But I can't fly carrying that bomb into any city airports. So I guess I'll have to leave the Cessna here and drive the Forester."

"You take the car. I'll fly your plane back to Bay Bridge Airport."

He set down his cup. "You can fly? You never told me that."

"You never asked."

He laughed.

"Annie Woods, to paraphrase someone I spoke with recently: You are a woman of many hidden talents."

Her gray eyes twinkled. Holding his gaze, she let the comforter slide down her body, exposing her breasts. Then she lay back against the stacked pillows. Slowly slid the comforter down her thighs.

"Perhaps I should reveal a few more of my hidden talents."

His picked up the tray and set it aside on the night table.

"Perhaps you should."

He waved to her as she raced the Cessna past him, down the strip. He watched the wheels lift from the pavement, watched as she piloted it into the sunny blue sky, banked smoothly toward the south, then vanished over a forest-capped hill.

He had one more duty to perform before he drove back to Washington.

He arrived in the city of Warren twenty minutes later. He found the place east of town, in a wooded, residential neighborhood. He saw the hand-lettered name on the mailbox and turned into the driveway, then climbed a small incline to the house hidden back in the trees.

The acrid stench of burnt wood assaulted him from the pile of charred rubble not far from the house. The home itself stood largely intact, but he noticed that many of its windows still bore store stickers and looked newly installed. He parked in the gravel driveway. Walked across a yard still strewn with small scraps of debris. Mounted the steps to the front door. Took a breath. Rang the bell.

It was the boy who opened the door. He wore glasses and looked a lot like his dad. He also looked wary.

"It's Martin, right?"

He nodded. "Yeah."

"Martin, we met—" He began again. "You might remember me from some days ago. I'm Dylan Hunter, the reporter from the Washington newspaper."

"Oh, yeah. I remember. You...you were nice to my mom."

"Is she home right now?"

"Sure. I'll get her."

The boy led him into the living room, then left. He stood in the middle of the room, turning slowly, taking in the photos on the walls and the top of their piano. Family photos. Images of love and vacation fun. Ghosts from happy days, gone forever...

She entered the room so quietly he almost didn't hear her. He turned to face her.

Sharon Silva had lost even more weight. The pretty blonde from the photos around him had become almost unrecognizable. She wore no makeup and looked emaciated— cheeks sunken, eyes too prominent, stick-like limbs protruding from her blouse and skirt. He wondered how long it had been since she had eaten a full meal.

"You're the reporter."

"Yes. Dylan Hunter...I have some news for you, Mrs. Silva." He gestured to the sofa. "May we sit down?"

She followed him obediently and sat. Clasped her hands in her lap. Looked at him without curiosity, almost abstractly. Waiting for him to say something.

"Mrs. Silva...when I met you not long ago, I made you a promise. Do you remember? I promised to find out who did this to your husband. And to make them pay."

She blinked. Something seemed to stir in her.

He went on.

"Please don't ask me how I know what I'm about to tell you. Not even the police know—at least not yet. But I want *you* to know...Mrs. Silva, I did find the men who were responsible. Two men. Their names are Zachariah Boggs and Rusty Nash." He paused. "And I came here to tell you that they *have* paid, Mrs. Silva...The two men who killed your Adam are now dead."

She sat completely still, not blinking, her blue eyes frozen on his. For the second time, he watched those eyes fill. She began to tremble. He slid closer to her.

Let her collapse into his arms.

He heard something and looked up. Martin and Naomi stood in the entranceway of the living room, tears streaming down their faces. They had heard, too.

He tried to imagine the grief of these two kids losing their dad.

Then thought of Big Mike...

Hunter held out his hand toward them.

They hesitated. Naomi came forward first. She knelt at their feet and hugged her mother.

Then Martin joined them.

Hunter sat in their midst, embracing them all in the circle of his arms. Held them as they sobbed. He sat still, trying hard to remain in control, trying very hard to stay up there, in his cold, high place...Trying...

And failing.

The digital clock on the roll top desk in the corner read 11:14 p.m.

Ashton Conn took another swallow of bourbon as the disastrous images flickered on the big-screen TV in his den. All day he just hadn't been able to tear himself away from the cable news. He kept changing channels obsessively, flipping between Fox News and CNN, then over to CNBC, finding no solace anywhere.

Over the past twenty-four hours, things had only gone from bad to worse. The demolition of Capital Resources had been bad enough, but that was dwarfed by the hit on his CarboNot stock. Almost all his assets had been tied up between the two companies. The simultaneous attack on both had just about ruined him.

And it *was* a deliberate attack. That was obvious, now. A highly coordinated attack, very sophisticated, conducted in sequence. First, Capital Resources. Then the run on the CarboNot stock—with somebody giving out fake phone numbers, to make sure that none of them could reach Robin in time to sell and avoid crushing losses. Then the attacks on Gavin's boat, Avery's jet, Jon Weaver's summer home—with the attackers canceling the property insurance in advance.

Then the bomb at CarboNot. And the bomb sent to him…

It had been too much for Emmalee, especially the bomb sent here. They'd had a big fight after that, and she stormed out. She still hadn't returned…

Well, the bitch was the least of his worries.

Most immediately, there was the money. He had to tell Barry to send most of the security detail packing. Scary though it was with Boggs still out there somewhere, he could no longer afford full-time protection from a first-rate outfit like Public Security LLC. Now he was down to only two bodyguards: Barry at the driveway gate, and another guy patrolling the grounds. He could only hope they'd be enough.

Most importantly, though, there were the long-term political implications. Those were even more ominous. He sensed that Avery was getting cold feet about his candidacy, now. The articles had revealed nothing *criminal*, exactly, but things just didn't *smell* right—especially Conn's links to Capital Resources. Prior to the newspaper articles, nobody, Avery included, had known about his involvement with the company. Not that it was anyone else's business. Capital Resources was a side investment, a way for him to capitalize on the anti-fracking campaign. What was so wrong with that? Why shouldn't he benefit a little from all his hard work to stop that rapacious industry in its tracks?

He saw that his glass was nearly empty. He poured some more of the amber liquid from the bottle on the nearby tray, and tried once again to figure out who was out to get them all.

The bombs had to be from Boggs. They bore his stylistic signatures. And after their confrontation Monday night, Boggs had every reason to go after him and Sloan. But he couldn't have pulled off all the rest of this—not in a million years. Whoever put this complicated scheme together had to have high-tech resources and a team of specialists.

Conn pressed the remote button, switching from CNBC's stock futures report back to CNN. They were running a commercial. He got up and began to pace, glass in one hand, remote in the other.

Everything had been proceeding swimmingly until that Hunter prick started going after them, painting big fat targets on their backs. His articles instigated much of this; some of his columns were even turning up at the vandalism scenes…

He stopped pacing. *Just like during those vigilante killings last year.* Hunter articles had been found at those crime scenes, too…Well, copycats obviously loved that idea and had adopted it…though it did seem strange that it was always *Hunter's* columns…

His eyes drifted over to the CNN news crawl and spotted the words *Allegheny Forest.* He frowned and moved closer to read the rest of the words marching across the bottom of the screen. Saw that somebody had just gotten stabbed up there in the woods.

He raised the glass to his lips when the name of the victim drifted into view.

…Russell "Rusty" Nash, 49, of Nashville, Tennessee…

He lowered his glass, returned to the recliner, and sat down heavily.

He knew who Rusty Nash was. Boggs had mentioned him many times: his best friend, his right-hand man…

What in hell was going on here?

Dressed in black, Hunter slipped like a wraith through the trees and shadows of Conn's sprawling yard, heading back down the slope toward the street. Vaulting the rail fence again, he jogged back to where his van was parked on the side of the road. He unlocked and entered its rear, used a towel to wipe the grime from his hands, then quickly changed back into casual street clothes.

It was time now to end this.

He picked up a burner and dialed Conn's number.

No one answered. He tried again.

It took four tries before he heard Conn's voice.

"Who is calling this number, and at this hour?"

"It's Dylan Hunter, Senator. And I've just had a long, informative chat with your pal, Zachariah Boggs."

Ten seconds passed before Conn spoke again.

"Did you say Boggs? Isn't he that crazy ecoterrorist?"

"That's a strange way to describe a man who told me he's your bosom buddy."

"What? Is this some kind of joke? What in God's name are you talking about?"

"I'd love to tell you all about it, Senator—and especially hear what *you* have to say. Maybe Boggs was lying to me. Maybe you have a simple explanation that will prevent me from writing about this."

Ten more seconds of silence.

"If that criminal claimed to know me, you're damned right he's lying. But of course: I'll be happy to talk to you. The last thing I need is to have you spreading more ugly rumors about me. I'll have my assistant schedule an appointment with—"

"I'm afraid I'm on a very tight deadline, Senator. My editor needs my next piece late tomorrow morning. I happen to be just a minute or two from your home. Do you mind if I stop by now?"

"Right now?…Well, all right. I'll tell my security officer down at the gate to let you in."

Hunter smiled to himself and turned over the ignition.

Three minutes later he was seated across from Ashton Conn in his den. He pulled a recorder out of his sports jacket.

"Mind if we go on the record?"

"Yes, I *do* mind, until you tell me what this nonsense is all about. Then I shall be happy to give you a statement for the record."

Hunter shrugged and put it away. "Fair enough. Anyway, I got this phone call today. The caller identified himself as Boggs, and from the details he gave me, I believe him. He had quite a tale to tell, too. He told me everything about the two of you, Senator. Your whole history together, from back in college. How you were allies, from your earliest—"

"What?"

"How *he* actually was the Technobomber. How you helped him cover up his acts of terrorism by framing an innocent student for the crimes. How you conspired to commit other crimes ever since—including the recent murder of Dr. Adam Silva."

Conn leaped to his feet.

"That's outrageous! That's insane! *I* didn't kill Silva—or anyone else!"

"I have good reasons to believe otherwise."

"Bullshit! You can't prove that I had anything to do with Boggs, let alone—"

"What if I were to tell you he gave me a taped confession?"

"That's hearsay! From a criminal, a killer, no less. I suspect that he even tried to kill *me* with that bomb that was sent here."

"And with good reason. You betrayed him. Just as you betrayed your alleged cause. You're good at double-crossing people and betraying principles, Conn—but Boggs was too stupid to see it. He believed what he wanted to believe about you. Because you gave him a *narrative* he wanted to believe.

The same narrative that millions have bought into, for thousands of years. The myth of Eden. The myth of the lost Golden Age. The ancient fairy tale of evil humans corrupting a perfect, primitive past."

"What are you talking about? I don't have to listen to this! I can't believe you'd come here to—"

"Boggs used that narrative as his rationalization for killing and destruction. You've used it as a tool of manipulation— and as a rationalization for your ruthless climb to political power."

Conn stomped across the room and stood over him. His eyes were narrowed slits in his fleshy face.

"If you *dare* print such libelous accusations, I shall initiate a lawsuit that will shut down your goddamned newspaper and end your career!"

Hunter sat back, crossed his legs, and continued as if Conn had never spoken.

"You've paved your career path over anyone who got in your way. Over the property owners your company plundered in Pennsylvania. Over former allies, like Boggs. Over the dead bodies of good people—like Adam Silva."

"Get out of my house!"

"You conspired with Boggs to kill Silva. In fact, you used Boggs for years to do your dirty work for you. Mainly so that you could continue to pretend to yourself that your hands were clean."

Conn was sweating and breathing hard. "I said, *get out!*"

"But your hands aren't clean. He couldn't have done those things without your help. You were the sponsor of a killer. And that makes you a killer, too, Conn. A disgrace to your current office—and someone far too dangerous to allow to seek the presidency."

"My right to seek the presidency is not yours to decide!"

Hunter stood. Stepped in close, inches from Conn's face.

"Adam Silva's right to go on living is not *yours* to decide—you bastard."

Conn took an uneasy step back.

"You have nothing on me! Nothing but the word of a lunatic killer."

"Also his girlfriend, Dawn Ferine. She saw you two talking and heard what you said."

"Her? Another *mental case?*" He barked out a laugh. "You've got nothing. Not a thing that can stand up in a court of law. There's no independent evidence, is there? *Is* there?"

Hunter shrugged. "Alas, that is true."

"Of course there isn't! Because it doesn't exist."

"Oh, it exists. I just have to find it. Then write about it. Then perhaps leave my published articles at the scenes of your crimes…as I usually do."

Conn stared at him. His mouth hung open.

"My God," he said softly. "*You're* the one. The one they've been looking for. Aren't you." It wasn't a question.

Hunter smiled. "Whatever could you possibly be referring to?"

Conn shook his head slowly. "Well, well. Things make perfect sense, now."

"Things always do."

"Well, you won't get away with it!" he shouted. "Now that I know, I'll make it my personal *mission* to bring you down, you son of a bitch. To put you behind bars, where you belong. I'll hire detectives to follow you—no, better: I'll put federal agencies onto you. I am going to *bury* you, Hunter."

"Gee, I certainly wouldn't want any of that. But two can play at that game. For instance, there are the wiretap recordings I have from your phone calls. In fact, I have an interview scheduled tomorrow morning with Avery Trammel, who is on some of those recorded phone chats with you. It will be interesting to match his story against yours. You know, I think you should call him right away—get together with him tonight to get your stories straight...before I go to press tomorrow morning. Have a nice evening, *Senator*."

He turned on his heel and headed for the door, leaving Conn standing with his mouth open.

He walked to his van, which he'd parked behind Conn's Bentley. He rolled out past it, then coasted down the long drive to the gate. Waited while the security man opened it. Then exited, turned down the street...and parked again, about fifty yards away.

Hunter left the car. A pair of binoculars swung from a strap around his neck as he trotted back toward the gate in the darkness. He stopped about a hundred feet from it, hiding in the shadows of some trees. Then raised the binoculars to his eyes.

Conn was visible through the window of his den, a phone to his ear, gesturing wildly. He was on the call for less than a minute before rushing out of the room.

Hunter smiled to himself and lowered the binoculars, letting them hang on their strap.

Then he retrieved two burner phones from his jacket pockets, and held one in each hand.

After a moment, Conn emerged from the front door, struggling into an overcoat. He clambered down the steps and hurried to the Bentley.

Hunter heard the engine rev. Just as the car began to roll forward, he hit a speed-dial button on the cell in his left hand. It was spoofing Trammel's cell number.

"Yes, Avery?" Conn answered.

"Oh, I forgot to mention, Senator: Boggs is dead. I know, because I killed him. I killed him for leaving a bomb in my cabin, and a much bigger one in Dan Adair's house. It's only fitting that I return those bombs to his sponsor, now. In fact, they're inside and underneath your car."

He thumbed a speed-dial button on the cell in his right hand as he said:

"Senator—you're unsustainable."

He saw the brake lights flare in the dark at the top of the driveway. The Bentley had almost squealed to a halt when a dazzling blue flash lit its interior, blasting out its windows. An enormous detonation followed an instant later, this time from beneath the vehicle. It blew the sedan skyward, riding a blinding column of orange-white flame into the black sky, then flipped it in mid-air. As the thundering blast shook the ground and echoed throughout the neighborhood, the Bentley plunged back to earth and landed on its roof, sliding down the ice-slicked grass to rest against the flagpole in Ashton Conn's perfectly manicured front lawn.

The American flag waved brightly above the blazing vehicle.

Hunter trotted back to the van. He drove slowly back past the gate. Near the top of the hill, the two security men stood transfixed, dark silhouettes against the inferno.

He lowered the window as he rolled by. Opened the small plastic bag in his hand, and dumped Zachariah Boggs's smartphone next to the mailbox outside the gate.

Then Dylan Hunter headed home.

FORTY-ONE

He entered the reception area just before ten in the morning and approached her desk.

"Hi, Danika."

She looked up. A radiant smile blossomed.

"Hell-o, Mr. Hunter!" Then frowned. "My, you look as tired as you sounded when I called you this morning."

"I've been up late working on that CarboNot story. I have to submit a new article later today."

Danika rocked back in her chair. She wore a smile, plus a snug, cream-colored sheath dress in what looked like satin, cut low at the top and high at the bottom. The smile seemed bigger than the dress. Her dark, sculpted thighs were crossed, and she bounced the top leg rhythmically, from the knee. A beige shoe with a spiked heel dangled only from her toes, swinging hypnotically.

"I read your latest article," she said. "It made me so mad! I just can't *believe* the stuff that goes on in this town."

"Believe it," he said. "Are my two police guests here, yet?"

"In room 8. But just one," she said, her smile taking on a dreamy quality. "Detective Cronin."

He chuckled. "Danika…remember Melvin?"

She pouted. "Oh. Yeah."

Cronin surprised him. He was seated behind the office desk, leaning back in the swivel chair, his fingers steepled.

"Gee, I hope I'm not late for my job interview, sir," Hunter said, slipping into the guest chair in front of the desk.

"You're really not that funny."

"Your partner made that clear last time. By the way, where *is* Detective Erskine? Did you send him out for doughnuts?"

"You've heard the news, I assume."

"I'd better, given my job. But which news item are you referring to?"

"Senator Conn."

"*That* news. I haven't brushed up on my Constitution for a while; but does this mean he doesn't get to become President?"

Cronin sighed and rocked forward. He looked tired, too.

"The feebs found some interesting stuff at the crime scene."

"Please don't tell me they found another one of my clippings."

"Not this time. Are we off the record?"

"Sure."

"A smartphone, apparently dropped by accident right outside the property. They dusted it, and guess whose prints came back?"

"Damn. I *wondered* where I lost that thing."

"Hunter, can you be serious for just one minute? They belong to Boggs. His prints were on record from back when they investigated him as a Technobomber suspect. My feeb source says they still have lots of tests to run, but at first glance the pipe-bomb fragments look a lot like what they found in the CarboNot office."

"So they think Boggs is good for both of those, then."

"Looks that way. The forensics guys also found something else, though. A message, stuck on a bush out in the yard. It looked like it was planted there."

"A message. But not one of my columns."

"Not one of your columns. Just a typewritten note. It says: 'Returned to Sender.'"

"What's that supposed to mean?"

Cronin shrugged. "Not my case. That's for the dicks at the FBI to figure out."

"I'm curious. Why are you telling me all this?"

Cronin leaned forward, folded his hands on the desk. He looked like an executive.

"I picked this up from a D.C. cop on our task force. He says their people are investigating something connected to that CarboNot company you've been writing about. It looks like somebody was tapping phones and intercepting email of the biggest CarboNot investors. People you mentioned. Then they interfered with their stock transactions. It's complicated, but the bottom line is, their calls were routed here. To your office girl out there—Danika."

"Wait a minute. Are you saying that *Danika* is involved in some kind of scam?"

"No, no. Not at all. She doesn't even know about this, yet. Her boss got calls from the irate CarboNot investors, wondering what the hell was going on. So he pulled his records and shared them with the D.C. police. Seems that some scam operation established a bunch of accounts here to have Danika answer their phone calls. They represented themselves as brokers, insurance agents, and financial advisers. Then the scammers contacted the various CarboNot investors, pretending to be their brokers and insurers. They gave the investors what they claimed were new contact phone numbers. But those numbers would actually ring here, at Danika's desk. So, when the investors phoned what they thought was their brokers to buy or sell CarboNot stock, their calls were routed to Danika. She would forward the messages to other numbers, just as she was told. The bottom line is, the CarboNot investors' transactions never went through. These guys wound up losing millions."

Hunter whistled. "Slick." He frowned. "But how did the scammers make their money?"

Cronin was looking at him, hard. "Apparently they didn't. It looks like their whole setup was just meant to make these CarboNot stockholders *lose* a ton of money."

"You mean, it was just malicious? Somebody went to an awful lot of trouble just to hurt these stockholders."

"Exactly. And so I asked myself: Ed, who has it in for these guys?"

"Cronin, I don't like where you're going with this."

"And I asked myself: Ed, isn't it a coincidence that the phone numbers for this scam were routed right through the same office used by Dylan Hunter?"

Hunter rolled his eyes. "Ed, have you seen the musical *Les Misérables?* They should cast you as Javert."

"I haven't seen it, so I don't know what you're talking about."

"I'm talking about an obsessed cop who wastes a lot of time chasing innocent people."

"Innocent?"

"Give it a rest. You know I had nothing to do with the bomb that killed Sloan. That's on Boggs. And you admit he looks good for the senator's murder, too. It's obvious that he and his gang hated CarboNot. So it makes perfect sense that *they* would be the ones going after those investors."

"You think those losers, hiding in the woods, could pull off scams like these?"

"Why not? Isn't Boggs supposed to be some kind of genius?"

"Well, *whoever* did these schemes didn't know much about the insurance business."

"What do you mean?"

"I mean whoever knocked down that Capital Resources building and the EPA director's house. And blew up those other properties—the jet and the yacht. The persons"—he paused, eyes steady on Hunter's—"or *person* who did that stuff probably didn't know that in cases of provable fraud, insurance companies will honor the policies retroactively, and pay the claims, anyway. So, it doesn't look like the people who owned those properties will have to eat those losses after all."

Hunter kept his face impassive and nodded thoughtfully.

"Well, then, let me see where that leaves things—just so I have it all clear for my next article. Capital Resources's investors will be reimbursed for their building losses. But that won't make much difference for them, anyway, since it looks as if the company is likely to shut down, regardless."

Cronin shrugged. "That's what I read in your paper."

"If what you say is true, the EPA director, Weaver, will be compensated for the loss of his house. But I saw him on the news last night. He said that he had a lot of personal items in there that can't be replaced. The same with the owner of that yacht, Lockwood; I gather that he was really fond of it. So, both of them lost things that money can't buy."

"So it would seem."

"But as for that billionaire, Trammel—I doubt he had much sentimental attachment to his plane."

"Him? I doubt he has much of a sentimental attachment to anything."

"Still, by my estimate, he did lose the $13 million or so that he had sunk into CarboNot stock."

"Just a drop in the bucket for somebody like him." Cronin folded his arms, looking amused. "You disappointed about that one, Hunter? The fish that got away?"

Hunter smiled back. "You just won't let it alone, will you? Why should I care about that character? Besides, from what I've read about him, this past week represents a significant setback for his interests, which are mainly political and ideological, not financial. So I'd say that Trammel got hit where it hurts, too."

"You happy about that?"

"It certainly couldn't happen to anyone more deserving."

Hunter heard his phone chirp. He fished it out. Saw who it was.

"Cronin, why is it that every time I see you, my editor calls? Give me a minute, okay?"

He answered the call. Listened for a minute.

"You're kidding!" He looked steadily at Cronin. "Bill, that's incredible. It puts everything in a whole new light. Can you email the MP3 file to me? I'll want to listen and write about it, ASAP...Great. Thanks."

He clicked off. Sat back, folded his arms, and smiled serenely at Cronin.

"What?"

"Bronowski, my editor, just received a thumb drive in the mail. Anonymous, no return address. It contains a recorded confession by Zachariah Boggs, admitting everything. That *he* was really the Technobomber. Also, that he bombed CarboNot, and killed that scientist, Adam Silva. But that's not the big news. He also said—are you ready?—that he had been working for years with Ashton Conn."

Cronin blinked. "The *senator?*"

Hunter nodded. "Which confirms what his girlfriend, Dawn Ferine, has been saying, doesn't it."

It was Cronin's turn to whistle. "I'll be damned."

"Yes, well, if we're through here, I've got work to do," Hunter said, rising.

"Yeah." Cronin stood, too. "So do I."

They walked to the reception area. Hunter turned to the detective.

"So. Are we good?"

Cronin said, "We're good. For now." A hint of amusement touched his cool blue eyes. "I'm sure our paths will cross again."

Hunter shook his head and sighed.

Hunter strolled along the Tidal Basin pathway in the waning sunshine of late afternoon. The sky was clear and the temperature unusually warm for early March, a reprieve from the cold of recent weeks. Though the cherry trees along the water were still bare of blossoms, just the sight of them held the promise of spring.

He reached the Jefferson Memorial and spotted the still gray figure amid the flow of tourists. He stood at the edge of the water, hands buried in the pockets of his long coat, staring into the distance. Hunter followed his gaze to the Washington Monument rising like a bright lance into the sky. Its sunlit stone sent a shimmering golden reflection onto the slate surface of the water.

Grant Garrett's small security detail held positions around the plaza below the Memorial, and one stood beneath the Ionic columns of the portico. Hunter felt their eyes on him as he approached their boss. He stopped at the water's edge a few feet away, sharing the view.

Garrett didn't acknowledge his presence by looking at him. He took the cigarette from his lips, exhaled a stream of smoke through his nostrils, and began to speak.

"So. Are you done tilting at windmills, Mr. Quixote?"

Hunter forced himself not to smile. "'Windmills.' Nice. You must have stayed awake all night thinking up that one...Here. I brought you a present." He held out the plastic bag he'd been carrying.

Garrett raised a brow. "Bribe?"

"It can't be a bribe if I give it to you after the fact. A thank-you present."

Garrett took the bag and looked inside. "Wow. That was fast. Did you fly your speedy little plane all the way to Havana today to fetch these?"

"No. I just know people who know people."

"Thanks. I can't wait."

Hunter studied the ripples in the water. "You wanted to see me. About last night, I assume."

"You assume correctly." Garrett took a long drag on the short cigarette butt and started to pitch it into the water. Then thought better of it, ground it against the heel of his shoe, and dropped the crushed stub into the bag with the cigars. Then looked Hunter in the eye.

"I want you to know that I can't do things like this for you anymore."

"I know, Grant. I never expected you to."

Garrett resumed staring into the distance. "This time was for Annie as much as for you."

"I know that, too."

"I could rationalize what I did, as an emergency response to an imminent act of domestic terrorism. But you and I both know that would be complete bullshit. I probably broke a hundred laws."

"I shouldn't have put you in that position."

"I'm not trying to be sanctimonious. Breaking laws is nothing new for me, of course. I've broken thousands over the years. But what you did last night—that went too far...It *was* you who took out Conn—right?"

"Of course...Gee, I hope you're not wearing a body wire, or I'm in deep doo-doo."

Garrett snorted. "Only if I wanted to share the cell with you...Seriously—you *do* realize you went too far last night."

"I did?"

"You murdered a United States senator. A presidential candidate, no less."

"Now, now—be fair: He hadn't even announced, yet."

"That's not very funny, Dylan."

"People keep telling me that. I need to work on my comic timing."

Garrett sighed.

"You crossed a line, son. I can't be a party to that sort of thing. Okay, yes—I gather that he conspired with Boggs in several of his murders. So he deserved it. I get that. But he needed to be arrested and prosecuted for it. Not blown up in a residential neighborhood. This is Washington, not Baghdad or Kabul."

Hunter faced him.

"All right. Then tell me how he could have been successfully prosecuted, Grant. No, really—please tell me. There was no physical evidence against him. Only the word of a terrorist and his emotionally unstable girlfriend, against that of a popular U.S. senator. I have some emails and taped phone calls—all illegally obtained—that suggested he was a hypocritical slime ball. But not a killer. So, there is no evidence he participated in those murders. None. The same thing goes even for his lesser crimes.

"Grant, you say that I should have waited for him to be arrested or prosecuted, when we both know that would never have happened. Here's the bottom line: Ashton Conn was about to get away with multiple murders. He also was about to make millions by looting scores, maybe hundreds of people. And the scariest thing of all? That same man stood on the brink of becoming our next president. That means *your boss*, Grant. Prosecute him? How? The law was impotent to stop him. Nobody else was even trying to stop him. So, I did. Now, please explain to me why what I did was wrong."

Garrett looked down into the dark depths of the water.

"I have no good answer to that. I don't know what we're supposed to do when the political process becomes this corrupt. I just don't know what people like us are supposed to do anymore."

He put a hand on Hunter's shoulder.

"I can't pass judgment against you, Dylan. I don't know what to tell you to do, or not do, in these situations. The only thing I *can* tell you is: I can't be a part of it anymore. I won't try to stop you, or get anyone else to stop you. But I can't protect you, either. You're on your own, my friend."

Then Garrett smiled—actually smiled.

"But I guess you're used to that."

Hunter clasped his arm and grinned in return.

"Oh, I almost forgot," Garrett said. "I've got a present for you, too. Do you mind taking a little walk, over to where my car is waiting?"

They strolled past the Memorial and behind it, out to the Jersey barriers lining East Basin Drive. His black armored SUV sat nestled in a small pull-off area, with a security man standing beside it.

Garrett walked to the rear, pulled open the door, and motioned him over.

Hunter looked inside. His mouth fell open.

"Grant, you have got to be kidding."

"Why?" His steel-gray eyes danced impishly. "Don't you like the symbolism?"

FORTY-TWO

It was dark when he pulled the Ford van into his driveway on Connor's Point. He parked beside her Camry. Then fetched the box from the passenger side and carried it up the front steps. Setting it down at his feet, he unlocked and opened the door, then brought it inside. He hung up his coat, left the box in the foyer, and walked down the hall.

"Annie?"

"In here, Vic."

Chuckling, he went into the den. He found her curled up with a book in the recliner next to the fire. A glass of white wine perched on a tray table nearby. She wore a dark green sweater over black jeans; her bare feet were drawn up under her. She kept her nose in the book, pretending not to notice him.

"Already I am taken for granted," he said. "Aren't you supposed to greet me at the door, stark naked, and throw yourself into my arms?"

She frowned, not looking up. "Mmm…just give me one more minute. I'm almost finished with this chapter."

He stomped across the room, grabbed the book and tossed it onto the floor. Then picked her up and crushed her against him as she squealed and he laughed. Within seconds they were no longer laughing. Not breaking the kiss, he carried her to the sofa and held her on his lap.

"So you *did* miss me, then," he murmured into her ear.

She stroked his hair. "Little bit, I suppose."

He searched her face. "How did you sleep last night?"

The gray cat's eyes were calm.

"Like a baby."

He kissed her again.

She pushed away, alarmed. "What's that noise?"

"Come and see."

They got up and he led her by the hand into the foyer, over to the cardboard box, watching her eyes.

"Oh!"

She reached down and lifted the whimpering little puppy out of the box. It was a bundle of soft, fluffy, honey-colored fur, with a snow-white chest and legs.

"Oh, Dylan!" She pressed its face to her cheek. "Dylan, she's absolutely *adorable!*"

"It's a 'he,' not a 'she.' Between you and Luna, I have enough estrogen in my life."

"Where did you get him?"

"I didn't. Grant did. He thought it was an appropriate gift."

"Appropriate?"

"Sure. It's a Sheltie."

"What's that?"

"A sheepdog."

She began to giggle—then laugh. She laughed so hard and so long that tears came. Pressed to her face, the puppy turned and began to lick her wet cheeks. That made her laugh even more, and so did he.

They brought the pup into the den and put him down on the floor. He waddled around, sniffing things, his little claws making scratching noises on the bare hardwood.

"We have to give him a name," she said.

"Grant thinks we should call him 'Cyrano.'"

She laughed again. "I wonder why."

They held hands, enjoying the spectacle of the little dog clambering around the room. After a moment she asked, "So why is he giving *us* a present? Shouldn't it be the other way around?"

"He said to tell you that it was an early wedding present."

She looked at him. He could tell that she was trying to suppress a smile.

"Oh, he did, did he? Well, we'll just have to see about that."

Hours later, they lay in each other's arms in the darkness. His head was pressed against her breast. He heard the slowing of her heartbeat and breathing. He heard the sleeping puppy stir and squeak in his box across the bedroom floor. He heard the clock ticking on the dresser.

He turned to kiss the warm hollow between the soft curves of her breasts. Then traced his lips up her skin, to her neck, leaving light kisses that made her sigh and squirm a little. He rested his head on the pillow next to hers. Ran his fingers through the short, tangled curls of her hair. Inhaled the scent of her perfume and skin. Felt her fingers caressing his shoulder.

"I love you, Annie Woods," he said softly.

"I love you, Dylan Hunter," she whispered.

Gently, he disengaged from her and rolled away. His hand searched the nightstand. Then he moved back to her. He found her left hand.

Opened it, and pressed the ring into it.

He heard the sudden intake of her breath.

"Put it back on," he said gently. "Please."

She began to tremble. "Oh, Dylan…"

"Remember what I told you, months ago? The only word that is forbidden when we are in bed together is 'no.'"

She began to laugh softly. Then snuggled close, the full length of her naked body pressed to his.

The kiss lasted a long time. When it ended, she began to caress his face. He raised his hand and covered hers.

Felt the ring on her finger.

Dylan Hunter closed his eyes.

EPILOGUE

Finally.

Standing at the balcony of the street-level shopping arcade, he pretended to read the *Post* and sip coffee. Out of the corner of his eye he watched his target in the lower food court.

Dylan Hunter was buying a bagel and a cup of coffee from one of the little eateries down there.

He felt a surge of adrenaline.

Certainly his client would be elated. After losing Hunter outside the EPA, it had taken weeks to locate him again. His client hadn't been happy about the delay. Nor was *he* happy about getting chewed out constantly for his supposed lack of professionalism and skill.

But now, at last, he had eyes on the reporter again. And this time, he wasn't going to let him get away.

He still didn't know where the guy lived. Nor had he, or anyone else, been able to find out a damned thing about his background, nothing that went back more than three years. It was obvious now that "Dylan Hunter" was a fake name. A pen name, writers called it; but after all his inquiries, he wondered if it might be something more than that.

From a secretary at the *Inquirer*, he'd learned that Dylan Hunter had a monthly rental arrangement with the "virtual office" company on the tenth floor of this office building on Connecticut. It served as his mail drop and phone answering service. It also was the only place anyone *knew* the guy visited occasionally, for rare business appointments.

That was all he had learned, so he had to do this the hard way. He spent two long, boring weeks here, watching and waiting. It wasn't easy, because there were so many ways Hunter could enter and leave. Multiple entrances. An underground parking garage, where he could drive in, then take an elevator, unseen, right up to the offices. Several nearby entrances to the Farragut North Metro stop. You really needed a team for this kind of surveillance. But the client had said no—said that it would be too conspicuous.

Of course the goddamned client wasn't a pro, and he didn't realize that it was just as conspicuous for the same man to be seen hanging around an area for days on end. So, he had to change his routes and appearance constantly, often several times per day. He would hang out in the lower food court, hoping the guy would stop by for a snack or pass through the access door to the parking garage. After a while, to avoid suspicion, he would go to the men's room and change into a different look. Then go hang around the shops and boutiques in the street-level arcade. He spent plenty of cash there, buying crap he didn't need, just to maintain his cover.

But today, he finally got lucky.

He watched Hunter collect his change from the clerk and head toward the escalator. He immediately moved away from the balcony and walked over to a store window in the busy lobby. He pretended to study the suits on the mannequins while he watched the reflections in the glass. He saw his target reach the top of the escalator, then turn toward the revolving doors and head out to the street.

He gave Hunter a five-second lead, then followed.

Hunter picked up the tail the second he turned away from the clerk. Big blond guy, crew-cut, newspaper and paper cup, loitering near the escalator on the street-level balcony above him. Then moving away the instant that Hunter reached the escalator.

As he rode up, he considered how to handle this. Given what had been happening lately, he didn't want to take any chances. He decided to lose the guy.

So he walked out of the building nonchalantly, turned right, and strolled south on Connecticut toward K, munching his bagel and sipping his coffee. He knew the guy would be behind him, so he didn't bother looking back and tipping him off.

At K, he stood in the middle of a mob of rush-hour office workers, waiting for the light. He crossed east, reaching the bustling area in front of the Metro entrance. He paused there a few seconds, making a show of looking at the escalator, then his watch. Instead of going in, he dumped his empty coffee cup into a trash can, then continued down the sidewalk. He paused outside the nearby Starbucks, then went inside.

There was a line at the counter to his left. He squeezed between the people waiting there and the small tables to his right, heading toward the back of the place, where the restrooms were. Nothing suspicious about that.

But this was one of his favorite choke points when he ran surveillance detection routes. Across from the restrooms was the rear exit. He pushed out through it—and right into the lobby of the corner office building that housed all the stores. He immediately darted left and ducked down the stairway.

The stairs led into a large basement restaurant. Only a few tables were occupied. He had eaten here before, so he waved to the man behind the bar and said hi to the waitress as he walked the length of the restaurant.

At the far end he reached a flight of steps that led up and outside again. This brought him right back onto Connecticut, and just around the corner from where he had entered Starbucks.

He was grinning as he emerged back into the sunshine. The tail would be watching the Starbucks entrance, waiting for him to emerge. He would wait there a long time.

He walked back up Connecticut, heading north again. Instead of taking the Metro back to his apartment, he decided to return to the office, then fetch one of his cars from the underground garage. Nothing like sowing more confusion in whoever was tailing him.

In the middle of the block, he noticed a break in the traffic. He didn't want to stay visible on the sidewalk any longer than he had to, so he decided to cross right there. He stepped off the curb and trotted across the broad thoroughfare. As he approached the other side, a car pulled abruptly out of a parking spot next to him. The driver spotted him at the last instant and laid on his horn. Hunter had to do a little hop-skip around the vehicle to avoid getting tagged.

Back on the other side of the street, he continued on. He tried to puzzle it out along the way.

This was the second time in a few weeks that he'd spotted someone following him. This guy looked hard, a professional. Maybe an operator. Not good.

Who was following him—and why?

He watched Hunter duck into the Starbucks, and frowned. *Another coffee—that soon?* It didn't make a lot of sense.

He had good intuitions. As an operator, you always had to be sensitive to things that seemed off, out of place. Plus, he didn't like the fact that he no longer had eyes on his target.

So instead of waiting for him to emerge, as he normally would do, he followed him right in, just five seconds behind—

—only to spot him hustling out the back exit.

Shit!

He pushed past the people in his way and hit the exit door just as it was closing shut. He found himself in the lobby of the office building. In front of him stood a bank of elevator doors, all closed. To his right, the lobby exit back onto K. But there was no sign of Hunter over there—and he'd had no time to go outside this quickly.

Then he noticed stairs on his left, leading into the basement.

He rushed down there fast. Found himself in a small hallway. A men's room was nearby. He pushed his way inside. Saw that it was empty.

He spun back outside and moved down the hallway. It opened into the lobby of a restaurant. He looked around the spacious area—then spotted Hunter at its far end, trotting up stairs that led back outside.

Weaving through the tables, he hurried after him, feeling the stares of the bartender and waitress on his back. He now was about ten seconds behind the guy.

Coming out onto the street, he found himself right back at the Metro entrance. He rushed around to the escalator, looked down the long descending column of stairs…

He wasn't there.

Standing on the corner, he looked around wildly, feeling a rising sense of panic. Up and down Connecticut. Up and down K.

Nowhere to be seen.

Then he heard the sustained blare of a horn up the street. His eyes automatically veered there—

—and spotted him, on the street, dodging a car—making a funny little dance-skip around it, then trotting up onto the sidewalk.

Something crawled across his spine.

Why was that little hopping move so familiar?

He ran up the sidewalk on his side of the street, desperate to keep up, but knowing in his gut that it was pointless. The guy had made him. And he was deliberately trying to lose him.

When he reached the next intersection, he knew for sure that it was hopeless. The light was now against him, and an unbroken stream of rush-hour traffic roared down Connecticut, blocking him from crossing. He tried to keep Hunter in sight; but after a few seconds he vanished.

He couldn't believe it. How could he have blown it—again?

How could this guy know he was tailing him? How could a mere reporter—

He felt the tingle across his spine again.

A reporter with a fake name. With no background. Who knows how to run a surveillance detection route through a choke point to lose a tail...

And then that little move out there on the street, so familiar. Where had he seen that before?

He closed his eyes. Felt people moving around him on the sidewalk. Focused, trying to conjure that image again in his memory...

Then knew.

It stunned him.

He drifted up Connecticut, walking obliviously now. In a couple of minutes he found himself outside the Mayflower Hotel. Damn, he needed a drink. He entered the ornate vault of the lobby. Its gleaming marble floors and walls, glittering chandeliers, bronze fixtures, and gilded decor barely registered. He found his way to a bar, a more contemporary spot with high stools, mirrored pillars, globe light fixtures, and flat-screen TVs.

For the next hour, he sucked down martinis and pondered what he had learned.

This guy, this "Dylan Hunter," was no reporter. Or if he *was* a reporter, then that was only his cover. The dude was a lot more. He was an operator—like himself.

But more: Incredibly, this same dude had been *the shooter* out there in Linden, at the safe house, almost exactly one year ago. The shooter who took out Muller at an impossible range. And who then *waved at him* as he escaped...

His mind reeled at the realization and its implications. Through the haze of the martinis, he tried to sort through them.

The man who had hired him only wanted him to follow Hunter, find out where he lived, find out who he truly was. Find out something that could be used against him. Those were his marching orders.

But now there was a problem. Hunter had been the real sniper that day—not *him*. For what reason, he didn't have a clue: He had no idea who the guy was working for. But now he was more than a surveillance target. He was a danger. A personal danger to *him*. If it came out that Hunter, and not he, had whacked Muller, then his credibility was shot. And so was his career.

He stared at himself in the mirrored pillar before him.

You're losing your touch, you know. You were good, once. The best. But maybe you aren't what you used to be.

The client had made it clear that Hunter wasn't to be killed.

But he had other ideas about that.

The client. Now he had to explain to the guy why he had lost track of Hunter once again. Damn.

Well, like they say in court, truth is a defense. Why don't you tell him the truth about the guy—at least some of it. Maybe you can bring him around. Get the green light to take him out. Score another big payday, and get rid of a professional threat, all at once. Problem solved.

He drained the last of his current martini, threw a wad of cash on the bar, and left.

An hour later he was back in his hotel room across town, seated on the edge of the king bed, sipping coffee and mentally rehearsing his lines.

Finally, he raised the encrypted sat phone from his lap and punched in the sequence of numbers.

After half a minute, he heard the client's voice.

"Yes? Do you have news for me?"

"Oh, I have news for you, all right. Are you sitting down, sir?"

"Get to it."

"Mr. Hunter is not what he seems to be. I can confirm that his name is an alias. And now I can also tell you why. The guy is an operator. I mean, he is involved in special ops, probably as a merc, like me. Or maybe some intel agency. But his reporter gig is just a cover."

The client was silent for a few seconds.

"And just how would you know this?"

"This afternoon, I finally picked him up and started tailing him. I was discreet about it. But he made me—I mean, he detected me almost immediately. He then did a series of maneuvers to lose me—the kind of tactics that only a highly trained intelligence officer or spec ops guy would know how to do. He did it all brilliantly, if I must say so. Which now explains why I lost him at the EPA a month ago. Sir, I'm telling you that this guy is a real pro."

He let that bait dangle for a few seconds, then moved to set the hook.

"Since that day at the EPA, I've been studying his published articles, trying to learn more clues about him. I wondered how he managed to get all the information that he puts into those articles. Well, a trained intel officer would know to get it. He may have access to resources that you can't imagine...The bottom line is that this man who calls himself Dylan Hunter poses a much, much bigger threat to you than you've assumed. If you don't mind my saying so, sir, I think you ought to chew on that for a while, then decide whether you need to change your current strategy toward this individual."

The phone remained silent for almost a minute.

"What you have told me is fascinating," the client said slowly, his voice steady. "You have indeed given me much to 'chew on,' as you put it. And you are correct: Dylan Hunter apparently represents a much greater threat to my interests than I had imagined. It is clear that we shall have to do something about him. I shall be back in touch very soon. Thank you. You have restored my confidence in you, Mr. Lasher."

Lasher felt the grin spread across his face.

"Thank *you*, Mr. Trammel."

***

DISCOVER THE *ORIGINS* OF DYLAN HUNTER IN

HUNTER

#1 KINDLE BESTSELLING THRILLER
A *WALL STREET JOURNAL* "TOP 10 FICTION EBOOK"

Two people, passionately in love.
But each hides a deadly secret.
He is a crusading vigilante, on a violent quest for justice.
She is tracking this unknown assassin, sworn to stop him.
Neither realizes the truth about the other.
And neither knows that a terrifying predator is hunting them both…

"*HUNTER* delivers in a way few thrillers do…a fantastic debut thriller."
—Stephen England, author, *Pandora's Grave* and *Day of Reckoning*

"…a terrifically paced suspense novel with a killer premise. If you're a fan of
Lee Child's Jack Reacher series, I suspect you'll like *HUNTER*."
—Randy Ingermanson, author, *Writing Fiction for Dummies*

BUY IT NOW!
Kindle ebook:	http://amzn.to/1iZ241a
Trade paperback:	http://amzn.to/TiuTkt
Audible audiobook:	http://amzn.to/1sHnK7E
iTunes audiobook:	http://bit.ly/1jISteU

IF YOU ENJOYED THIS
DYLAN HUNTER ADVENTURE,
you won't want to miss his *next* one!

JOIN THE DYLAN HUNTER EMAIL LIST:
http://eepurl.com/xObUz

We will notify you whenever a
new Dylan Hunter thriller is released.
*Your email information will NOT be shared
with any person or company.*
It will be used *ONLY* to notify you about the latest
Dylan Hunter books, news, and
public appearances by author Robert Bidinotto.

To learn more about Dylan Hunter, author Robert Bidinotto,
and how to obtain personally inscribed copies of these books,

VISIT "THE VIGILANTE AUTHOR" BLOG:
http://www.bidinotto.com

Do you have questions or comments for the author?

CONTACT ROBERT BIDINOTTO:

Email:
RobertTheWriter@gmail.com
Facebook:
https://www.facebook.com/RobertBidinottoAuthor
Twitter:
@Robert Bidinotto

ACKNOWLEDGMENTS

This book relied so heavily on the assistance of others that it is really a team effort. That my name is alone on the cover is an injustice. In fairness, dozens of remarkable people played decisive roles in producing it. So while this list is long, I want their contributions to be on record.

When I published *HUNTER*, I said that my "beta readers"— the volunteers who generously read, critiqued, and corrected the manuscript before publication—"saved my butt." They caught innumerable errors, typos, and problems that my tired eyes missed.

   This time, though, they *really* saved my butt. In my haste to finish this long-delayed novel, I was even less cautious than last time. The goofs and glitches were legion. Worse were the plot holes, logical contradictions, and physical impossibilities scattered throughout the text. I utterly *cringe* when I contemplate what would have happened to my reputation— and to your enjoyment—without the extraordinary feedback and input provided by the following friends, listed in alphabetical order:

Larry Abrams, Charity Ayres, Jon Barnhart, Kathy Barnhart, Pramod Challa, William and Tamra Dale, Roger Donway, Anne Foss, Greg Gerig, Samantha Hallock, Abigail Hand, Donald Heath, Robert Jones, Claudia Leone, Steve Lord, Kevin Ormsby, Karen O'Shea, Eric Palfreyman, Alan Paul, Jeff and Aydé Perren, Kevin Pickell, Shawn Reynolds, Rose

Robbins Schild, Henry Scuoteguazza, Gabrielle Suglia, Jan Traeg, Francisco Villalobos, Gregory Wall, and Kyrel Zantonavitch.

Many of these beta readers sent me multiple emails and pages of notes and comments. Their generosity with their time (on my very tight deadline), their many insights, and their brilliant suggestions improved this novel immeasurably. I can never thank these amazing and talented friends enough.

In addition to the beta readers, I relied upon other people for their technical expertise on specific aspects of the story:

Barry Donadio, president of Public Security LLC (http://www.publicsecurity.us) provided insights about security measures. You'll find "Barry" and his company mentioned in several scenes at Senator Ashton Conn's home.

Sheila Stephens gave me pointers on covert cameras and other spy gadgets. Hans Schantz provided an education about electronic jamming devices.

In addition to being a beta reader, Jon Barnhart schooled me in the explosive properties of a variety of chemicals, which made Zak Boggs far more lethal.

Firearms experts Jack Patterson and Mark Gardner helped me maintain the public fraud that I actually know something about rifles and handguns. The credibility of the Prologue sniper scene owes much to their input.

Likewise, my good friend Francisco Villalobos—a martial arts expert and trainer, as well as a personal fitness instructor (http://www.isfny.com)—helped me choreograph Dylan's fight scene in the CarboNot garage, so that he would actually *win* rather than be pummeled senseless. (Francisco also served as a beta reader.)

Besides being my closest buddy, Alan Paul is a techie's techie—an expert in computer hardware, software, and all manner of electronic communications. Dylan's ambitious electronic warfare against the various conspirators owes everything to Alan's input and suggestions. If you find anything wrong in those scenes, it's only because I didn't understand him or take good notes. (Alan, too, served as a beta reader.)

When Dylan and Annie had to take wing, I needed first-rate experts in aviation, aircraft, and air traffic control procedures. I found the best:

Lieutenant Colonel Steven Todd, an Air Cavalry Ops Officer, is a peerless expert in all manner of aircraft—but especially helicopters, like the Blackhawk, which he has piloted in defense of our nation on many missions. He provided exhaustive information and suggestions that led to my choice of the helicopter that transported Annie to Adair's house, as well detailed aviation procedures.

Talented thriller author Allan Leverone has a day job as a veteran air traffic controller. Along with LTC Steve Todd, Allan was indispensable in explaining how Dylan could fly out of Bay Bridge Airport and avoid radar tracking records or tower communications. He also helped me to whittle down the options in selecting Dylan's Cessna 400 as his private plane, and the Bell 429 as Annie's chopper. From radar to transponders, cruising altitudes to aerial maneuvers, runway lengths to tower communications, Allan and Steve had my back. (By the way, I *urge* you to check out Allan's top-shelf thrillers here: http://www.allanleverone.com)

Another big requirement for the climax of the story was the selection and use of the right Unmanned Aircraft System to monitor communications and keep "eyes" on the heroes and villains outside of Dan Adair's house. Steve Todd put me in touch with CW4 Ricky Tackett. He's another expert on all kinds of aircraft, but his specialty is various unmanned aircraft, such as the MQ-1 Predator. Ricky explained all I needed to know about that remarkable bird, and persuaded Grant Garrett to deploy it on this sensitive mission.

If the climactic "aerial" scenes of BAD DEEDS ring with Clancy-like authenticity, you have these extraordinary gentlemen to thank. I certainly do.

Let me also acknowledge Lt. Col. Dave Grossman, U.S. Army (Ret.), and director, Warrior Science Group (www.killology.com). He and I have never corresponded or met. But his essay "On Sheep, Wolves and Sheepdogs" (from his book On Combat) has become a widely quoted classic. It was so applicable that I just had to allude to it within the story. I'm pleased to credit it here with a specific reference.

Among others whose contributions to the success of this book can't be adequately measured is my awesome cover designer, Allen Chiu (http://allenchiu.com) His cover for HUNTER was outstanding. This one is simply sensational, don't you think?

Jason & Marina Anderson at Polgarus Studio (www.Polgarusstudio.com) deserve the credit for the formatting and layout of both the ebook and print editions of BAD DEEDS.

Gratitude also goes to my web designer, Joshua Zader (www.atlaswebdev.com), for his superb work in designing and maintaining my blog, "The Vigilante Author" (www.bidinotto.com).

And to Rob Walton, designer of the fantastic novel-writing software I have now used on both novels: "WriteItNow" (www.ravensheadservices.com).

Thanks to entertainment attorney Kevin Koloff (http://www.kevinkoloff.com), for his ongoing efforts to bring Dylan Hunter to the silver screen.

Then there are the Dylan Hunter fans who—at my instigation, for a little online contest I ran—suggested names for some of the villains in *BAD DEEDS*. A host of folks participated, but here are those whose suggestions I accepted, in whole or in part:

Greg Gerig, Robert Jones, and Gabrielle Suglia (all three of whom are also beta readers), plus Jennifer Brooks Anderson, Shannon Farren, Richard Gleaves, Rob Hampton, Mary Harp, Terri Kiley, Angie Killian, Vinay Kolhatkar, Janet Landi, and Lisa Mize.

The intensity of fan loyalty to Dylan, Annie, and the rest of the cast of *HUNTER* is remarkable. Many, many readers have recommended the book to others. I can't possibly know, remember, or thank all those who have promoted it.

But here, I want to single out a handful of special friends that I *know* have gone far above and beyond the call of friendship or "fandom." These ladies have promoted *HUNTER* to countless others. I honestly don't know what I've done to deserve their enthusiasm and loyalty; but a huge *thank you* goes to Pam Timony, Samantha Hallock, Janice Sidun, my cousins Janet Landi and Mary Beth McManus, and—last but *certainly* not least—to Sandra "Peaches" Hubbard from the Island Athletic Club.

Special thanks to talented fellow authors who are never too busy to share tips, suggestions, and encouragement. Here are just a few:

Stephen England (www.stephenwrites.com), a masterful writer of military and special operations thrillers.

Rose Robbins Schild (www.roserobbinsonline.com), a prolific author of romantic suspense who writes under the name Rose Robbins.

Edd Voss (http://eddvoss.com), my truck-driving pal and author of Western and sci-fi tales.

Ian Graham (www.iangrahamthrillers.com), another author of gripping thrillers.

Neil Russell (www.neil-russell.com), a film and television producer who also has launched a series featuring another exciting vigilante named Rail Black.

Larry Abrams, whose debut mystery, *The Philosophical Practitioner*, is great fun.

Robert McDermott (http://www.remcdermott.com), who writes rip-roaring nautical thrillers featuring a "part-time spook" named Tom Dugan.

Steven Konkoly (www.stevenkonkoly.com), author of the popular "Black Flagged" thriller series.

J.Carson Black (http://jcarsonblack.com), bestselling author of over a dozen thrillers.

Michael J. Sullivan (http://riyria.blogspot.com), bestselling fantasy author and mentor to authors like me.

Martin Crosbie (http://martincrosbie.com), the bestselling author of *My Temporary Life* and other stories.

Kevin Pickell (http://kevinpickell.blogspot.com/), writer of "dark fiction."

Again, these are just a few of the many writer friends whom I could list. I'll have to add another batch in the next book.

My deep appreciation to some other folks who brighten my days in so many different ways:

To Kay and the whole gang at Holly's Restaurant—a place where everybody knows your name.

To the crew at the Kent Island Dunkin' Donuts, who have now kept me caffeinated and functional through two novels.

To John Murphy and the staff of Island Athletic Club, whose facilities have no doubt staved off weight gains and heart attacks.

To all of the many friends and fans at Kent Island United Methodist Church, CNB Bank, and Queen Anne's Chorale, whose support has been simply phenomenal.

To my friends Frank and Shelda Bond, Hank and Erika Holzer, Gene and Sally Holloway, Marty and Buena Silverman, the entire Slate clan, and the entire Bidinotto clan.

To my brother Ed Bidinotto and my daughter Katrina and her family, who bring joy into my life. And to Margaret, who brought *Kat* into my life.

And, finally, to my wife Cynthia. Cyn, you've endured great challenges over the past several years, not the least of which has been my woeful neglect during writing binges. Yet you have stood by me through it all, a source of constant encouragement and support. Sweetheart, now that this monkey is finally off my back, it's time that I repay you with the attention you deserve.

Let's go have some fun, shall we?